Rob Harlow's Adventures

George Manville Fenn

Illustrated by W. Burton

ESPRIOS DIGITAL PUBLISHING

Chapter One.

Two Travellers.

"Don't they bite, sir?"

"Bite?"

Smick! smack! flap!

"Oh, murder!"

"What's the matter, sir?"

"My hand."

"Hurt it, sir?"

"I should think I have."

"You should wait till they've sucked 'emselves full and then hit 'em; they're lazy then. Too quick for you now."

"The wretches! I shall be spotted all over, like a currant dumpling. I say, Shaddy, do they always bite like this?"

"Well, yes, sir," said the man addressed, about as ugly a specimen of humanity as could be met in a day's march, for he had only one eye, and beneath that a peculiar, puckered scar extending down to the corner of his mouth, shaggy short hair, neither black nor grey—a kind of pepper-and-salt colour—yellow teeth in a very large mouth, and a skin so dark and hairy that he looked like some kind of savage, dressed in a pair of canvas trousers and a shirt that had once been scarlet, but was now stained, faded, and rubbed into a neutral grub or warm earthy tint. He wore no braces, but a kind of belt of what seemed to be snake or lizard skin, fastened with either a silver or pewter buckle. Add to this the fact that his feet were bare, his sleeves rolled up over his mahogany-coloured arms, and that his shirt was open at the throat, showing his full neck and hairy chest; add also that he was about five feet, nine, very broad-shouldered and muscular, and you have Shadrach Naylor, about the last person any one would take to be an Englishman or select for a companion on a trip up one of the grandest rivers of South America.

But there he was that hot, sunny day, standing up in the stern of the broad, lightly built boat which swung by a long rope some fifty feet behind a large schooner, of shallow draught but of lofty rig, so that her tremendous tapering masts might carry their sails high above the trees which formed a verdant wall on each side of the great river, and so catch the breeze when all below was sheltered and calm.

The schooner was not anchored, but fast aground upon one of the shifting sand-banks that made navigation difficult. Here she was likely to lie until the water rose, or a fresh cool wind blew from the south and roughened the dull silvery gleaming surface into waves where she could roll and rock and work a channel for herself through the sand, and sail onward tugging the boat which swung behind.

It was hot, blistering hot! and all was very still save for the rippling murmur of the flowing river and the faint buzz of the insect plagues which had come hunting from the western shore, a couple of hundred yards away, while the eastern was fully two miles off, and the voices of the man and the boy he addressed sounded strange in the vast solitudes through which the mighty river ran.

Not that these two were alone, for there were five more occupants of the boat, one a white man—from his dress—a leg being visible beneath a kind of awning formed of canvas, the other four, Indians or half-breeds—from the absence of clothing and the colour of their skins as they lay forward—fast asleep, like the occupant of the covered-in portion.

The great schooner was broad and Dutch-like in its capacious beam, and manned by a fair-sized crew, but not a soul was visible, for it was early in the afternoon; the vessel was immovable, and all on board were fast asleep.

Shadrach Naylor, too, had been having his nap, with his pipe in his mouth, but it had fallen out with a rap in the bottom of the boat, and this had awakened him with a start to pick it up. He valued that pipe highly as one of his very few possessions—a value not visible to any one else, for intrinsically, if it had been less black and not quite so much chipped, it might have been worth a farthing English current coin of the realm.

So Shadrach Naylor, familiarly known as "Shaddy," opened his one eye so as to find his pipe, picked it up, and was in the act of replacing it in his mouth prior to closing his eye again, when the sharp, piercing, dark orb rested upon Rob Harlow, seated in the stern, roasting in the sun, and holding a line that trailed away overboard into the deep water behind the sand-bank.

Perhaps it was from being so ugly a man and knowing it that Shaddy had a great liking for Rob Harlow, who was an English lad, sun-burnt, brown-haired, well built, fairly athletic, at most sixteen, very good-looking, and perfectly ignorant of the fact.

So Shaddy rose from forward, and, with his toes spreading out like an Indian's, stepped from thwart to thwart till he was alongside of Rob, of whom he asked the question respecting the biting, his inquiry relating to the fish, while Rob's reply applied to the insects which worried him in their search for juicy portions of his skin.

But they were not allowed to feed in peace, for Rob smacked and slapped sharply, viciously, but vainly, doing far more injury to himself than to the gnat-like flies, so, to repeat his words,—

"I say, Shaddy, do they always bite like this?"

"Well, yes, sir," said Shaddy, "mostlings. It's one down and t'other come on with them. It's these here in the morning, and when they've done the sand-flies take their turn till sun goes down, and then out comes the skeeters to make a night of it."

"Ugh!" ejaculated Rob, giving himself a vicious rub. "I'm beginning to wish I hadn't come. It's horrible."

"Not it, youngster. You'll soon get used to 'em. I don't mind; they don't hurt me. Wait a bit, and, pretty little creeturs, you'll like it."

"What! Like being bitten?"

"To be sure, sir. 'Livens you up a bit in this hot sleepy country; does your skin good; stimmylates, like, same as a rub with a good rough towel at home."

Rob gave vent to a surly grunt and jerked his line.

"I don't believe there are any fish here," he said.

"No fish! Ah! that's what we boys used to say o' half-holidays when we took our tackle to Clapham Common to fish the ponds there. We always used to say there was no fish beside the tiddlers, and them you could pull out as fast as you liked with a bit o' worm without a hook, but there was fish there then—big perch and whacking carp, and now and then one of us used to get hold of a good one, and then we used to sing quite another song.—I say, sir!"

"Well?"

"This here's rather different to Clapham Common, isn't it?"

"Yes," said Rob, "but it isn't what I expected."

"What did you 'spect, then? Ain't the river big enough for you?"

"Oh! it's big enough," said the lad, snatching his line in. "Didn't seem like a river down behind there."

"Right, my lad; like being at sea, ain't it?"

"Yes, and it's all so flat where you can see the shore. An ashy, dusty, dreary place, either too hot or too cold! Why, I wouldn't live at Monte Video or Buenos Ayres for all the money in the world."

"And right you'd be, my lad, says Shadrach Naylor. Ah! Why, look at that! Fish is fish all the world over. You don't expect they'll bite at a bare hook, do you?"

"Bother the bait! it's off again," said Rob, who had just pulled in the line. "It always seems to come off."

"Not it, lad. There, I'll put a bit o' meat on for you. It's them little beggars nibbles it off.—There you are; that's a good bait. Perhaps you may get a bite this time. As I says, fish is fish all the world over, and they're the most onaccountable things there is. One day they're savage after food; next day you may hold a bait close to their noses, and they won't look at it. But you're hot and tired, my lad. Why don't you do as others do, take to your sister?"

"My sister!" cried Rob, staring. "I haven't got one."

"I didn't say sister," said Shaddy, showing his yellow teeth; "I said sister—nap."

"I know you did," grumbled Rob; "why don't you say siesta?"

"'Cause I don't care about making mouthfuls of small words, my lad."

Splash! went the freshly thrown-in bait.

"I don't like sleeping in the middle of the day," said Rob as he took a fresh hold of his line.

"Wait a bit, my lad, and you'll like getting a snooze on there when you can get a chance. And so you're a bit disappynted in the country, are you?"

"Yes, but it's been getting better the last few days."

"Yes," said Shaddy, "ever so much; and as soon as you get used to it you'll say it's the beautifullest place in the world."

Rob turned to him quickly, his irritation passing away.

"Yes, it is getting beautiful," he said; "the trees all along that side are very grand."

"Ah," said Shaddy, replacing the great sheath-knife with which he had been cutting up his tobacco in his belt, "and it's bigger and wilder when we get higher up. I don't wonder at their calling it the Grand Chaco."

"The trees are wonderful," said Rob softly as he gazed at the great wall of verdure.

"And it's wonderfuller inside as you go on and up the little rivers or creeks. Just you wait a bit, my lad, and you'll see. I can show you things as'll open your eyes. You won't think the place dull."

"I suppose we are getting up toward quite the middle of South America, aren't we?"

"Getting that way, my lad, but not yet. Wasn't that a bite?"

"No," replied Rob confidently. "I say, Shaddy, are there really any good fish in this river? Isn't it too big?"

"Wants a big river to hold big fish in, millions of 'em, big as you are. Wait, and you'll see."

"But one gets so tired of waiting."

"But we has to wait all the same, and how those 'Talians get up and down as they do is always a wonder to me. I suppose they like waiting, and having their snoozes in the hot sun. 'Tis their nature to. Naples is hot enough, but not like this."

"Have you been to Italy?"

"'Ain't many places I haven't been to, my lad."

"But you've been here a long time."

"Nigh upon twenty year up and down; and when I go to a place I like to forage and ferret about, being fond of a bit o' sport. That's how it is I know so much of the country up here. Couldn't help larning it. No credit to a man then."

"What are you looking at?" said Rob.

"Nothing, but looking out for squalls."

"Change of weather?"

"Nay, not yet. I meant Indian squalls. I didn't know as there were to be no watch kept, or I wouldn't have slept. It ain't safe, my lad, to go to sleep close to the shore this side."

"Why! Wild beasts?"

"Nay, wild Indians, as hates the whites, and would come out from under the trees in their canoes and attack us if they knowed we were here. I told the skipper so, but he's like them 'talians: knows everything himself, so that he as good as told me to mind my own business, and so I did. But this side of the river's all savage and wild, my lad. The people had rough hard times with the old Spaniards, so that every white man's a Spaniard to them, and if they get a chance it's spear or club."

Rob looked rather nervously along the interlacing trees hung with the loveliest of vine and creeper, and then jerked his line.

"Ah, it's all right enough, sir, if you keep your eyes open. I can't, you see: only one."

"How did you lose your eye, Shaddy?"

"Tiger," said the man shortly.

"There are no tigers here," said Rob. "They are in India."

"I know that. Striped ones they are, and bigger than these here. I've known 'em swim off from Johore across to Singapore—though they're big cats—and then lie in wait for the poor Chinese coolie chaps and carry 'em off. They call these big spotted chaps tigers, though, out here; but they're jaggers: that's what they are. Call 'em painters up in Texas and Arizona and them parts north. Jaggered my eye out anyhow."

"How was it?"

"I was shooting, and after lying in wait for one of the beggars for nights, I saw my gentleman—coming after a calf he was—and I shot him. 'Dead!' I says, for he just gave one snarly cry, turned over on his back, clawed about a bit, and then lay down on his side, and I went up, knife in hand, meaning to have his spotted skin."

Shaddy stopped and laid his hand over the scar and empty eye cavity, as if they throbbed still.

"Well?" cried Rob eagerly.

"No; it wasn't well, my lad. All the worst's coming. He wasn't dead a bit, and before I knew where I was, he sent my rifle flying, and he had me. It was one leap and a wipe down the face with his right paw, and then his jaws were fixed in my right shoulder, and down I went on my back. If I hadn't twisted a bit he'd have torn me with his hind claws same as a cat does a great rat, and then I shouldn't have been here to be your guide. As it was, he kicked and tore up the earth, and then he left go of my shoulder and turned over on his side, and died in real earnest."

"The bullet had taken effect?"

"Nay, my lad; it was my knife. I thought it was my turn again, and, as I had it in my hand, I felt for his heart, and found it."

"How horrible!"

"Yes, it was, my lad, very; but I won that game. I didn't get the skin money, for I didn't care for it then. I couldn't see very well. Why, I was quite blind for a month after, and then all the strength of two eyes seemed to go into this one. Painters they call 'em nor'ard, as I said; and he painted me prettily, didn't he, right down this cheek? Never saw a girl who thought me handsome enough to want to marry me."

Shaddy laughed.

"What is it?" said Rob.

"I was thinking about Mr Brazier yonder when I came to you at Buenos Ayres."

"What, when he was waiting for the guide Captain Ossolo said he could recommend?"

Shaddy nodded.

"He looked quite scared at me. Most people do; and the captain had quite a job to persuade him that I should be the very man."

"Yes, and it was not till the captain said he would not get one half so good that he engaged you."

"That's so, my lad. But I am a rum 'un, ain't I?"

"You're not nice-looking, Shaddy," said Rob, gazing at him thoughtfully; "but I never notice it now, and—well, yes, you are always very kind to me. I like you," added the boy frankly.

Shaddy's one eye flashed, and he did not look half so ferocious.

"Thank ye, my lad," he cried, stretching out his great hand. "Would you mind laying your fist in there and saying that again?"

Rob laughed, looked full in the man's eye, and laid his hand in the broad palm, but wished the next moment that he had not, for the fingers closed over his with a tremendous grip.

"I say, you hurt!" he cried.

"Ay, I suppose so," said Shaddy, loosing his grip a little. "I forgot that. Never mind. It was meant honest, and Mr Brazier shan't repent bringing me."

"I don't think he does now," said Rob. "He told me yesterday that you were a staunch sort of fellow."

"Ah! thank ye," said Shaddy, smiling more broadly; and his ruffianly, piratical look was superseded by a frank aspect which transformed him. "You see, Mr Harlow, I'm a sort of a cocoa-nutty fellow, all shaggy husk outside. You find that pretty tough till you get through it, and then you ain't done, for there's the shell, and that's hard enough to make you chuck me away; but if you persevere with me, why, there inside that shell is something that ain't peach, nor orange, nor soft banana, but not such very bad stuff after all."

"I should think it isn't," cried Rob. "I say, it would make some of our boys at home stare who only know cocoa-nut all hard and woody, and the milk sickly enough to throw away, if they could have one of the delicious creamy nuts that we get here."

"Yes, my lad, they're not bad when you're thirsty, nor the oranges either."

"Delicious!" cried Rob.

"Ay. I've lived for weeks at a time on nothing but oranges and cocoanuts, and a bit of fish caught just now and then with my hands, when I've been exploring like and hunting for gold."

"For gold? Is there gold about here?"

"Lots, my lad, washed down the rivers. I've often found it."

"Then you ought to be rich."

The man chuckled.

"Gold sounds fine, sir, but it's a great cheat. My 'sperience of gold has always been that it takes two pounds' worth of trouble to get one pound's worth o' metal. So that don't pay. Seems to me from what I hear that it's the same next door with dymons."

"Next door?"

"Well, up yonder in Brazil. I should say your Mr Brazier will do better collecting vegetables, if so be he can find any one to buy 'em afterwards. What do you call 'em—orkards?"

"Orchids," said Rob.

"But who's going to buy 'em?"

"Oh, I don't know," said Rob, laughing. "There are plenty of people glad to get them in England for their hothouses. Besides, there are the botanists always very eager to see any new kinds."

"Better try and get some new kinds o' birds. There's lots here with colours that make your eyes ache. They'd be better than vegetables.

Why, right up north—I've never seen any down here—there's little humpy birds a bit bigger than a cuckoo, with tails a yard long and breasts ever so much ruddier than robins', and all the rest of a green that shines as if the feathers were made of copper and gold mixed."

"Mr Brazier hasn't come after birds."

"Well then, look here; I can put him up to a better way of making money. What do you say to getting lots of things to send to the 'Logical Gardens? Lions and tigers and monkeys—my word, there are some rum little beggars of monkeys out here."

"No lions in America, Shaddy."

"Oh, ain't there, my lad? I'll show you plenty, leastwise what we calls lions here. I'll tell you what—snakes and serpents. They'd give no end for one of our big water-snakes. My word, there are some whackers up these rivers."

"How big?" said Rob, hiding a smile—"two hundred feet long?"

"Gammon!" growled Shaddy; "I ain't one of your romancing sort. Truth's big enough for me. So's the snakes I've seen. I've had a skin of one fellow six-and-twenty foot long, and as opened out nearly nine foot laid flat. I dessay it stretched a bit in the skinning, but it shrunk a bit in the drying, so that was about its size, and I've seen more than one that must have been longer, though it's hard to measure a twisting, twirling thing with your eye when it's worming its way through mud and water and long grass."

"Water-snakes, eh?" said Rob, who was beginning to be impressed by the man's truth.

"Ay, water-snakes. They're anti-bilious sort of things, as some folks calls 'em—can't live out of the water and dies in."

He laughed merrily as he said this.

“That’s true enough, my lad, for they wants both land and water. I’ve seen ’em crawl into a pool and curl themselves up quite comfortable at the bottom and lie for hours together. You could see ’em with the water clear as cryschial. Other times they seem to like to be in the sun. But wait a bit, and I’ll show ’em to you, ugly beggars, although they’re not so very dangerous after all. Always seemed as scared of me as I was of—hist! don’t move. Just cast your eye round a bit to starboard and look along the shore.”

Rob turned his eye quickly, and saw a couple of almost naked Indians standing on an open patch beneath the trees, each holding a long, thin lance in his hand. They were watching the water beneath the bank very attentively, as if in search of something, just where quite a field of lilies covered the river, leaving only a narrow band clear, close to the bank.

“Don’t take no notice of ’em,” said Shaddy; “they’re going fishing.”

“Wish them better luck than I’ve had,” said Rob. “Fishing! Those are their rods, then; I thought they were spears.”

“So they are, my lad,” whispered Shaddy. “They’re off. No fish there.”

As he spoke the two living-bronze figures disappeared among the trees as silently as they had come.

“Of course there are no fish,” said Rob wearily as he drew in his baitless line, the strong gimp hook being quite bare. “Hullo, here comes Joe!”

Chapter Two.

Catching a Dorado.

For at that minute a slight sound from the schooner made him cast his eyes in that direction and see a lithe-looking lad of about his own age sliding down a rope into a little boat alongside, and then, casting off the painter, the boat drifted with the current to that in which Rob was seated.

"Had your nap?" said Rob.

"Yes," replied the lad in good English, but with a slight Italian accent, as he fastened the little dinghy and stepped on board. "How many have you caught?"

Rob winced, and Shaddy chuckled, while Giovanni Ossolo, son of the captain of the Italian river schooner *Tessa*, looked sharply from one to the other, as if annoyed that the rough fellow should laugh at him.

"Shall I show him all you've caught, sir?" said Shaddy.

"Haven't had a touch, Joe," said Rob, an intimacy of a month on the river having shortened the other's florid Italian name as above.

The Italian lad showed his teeth.

"You don't know how to fish," he said.

"You'd better try yourself," said Rob. "You people talk about the fish in the Parana, but I've seen more alligators than sprats."

"Shall I catch one?" said the new-comer.

"Yes; let's see you."

The lad nodded and showed his white teeth.

"Give me an orange," he said.

Rob rose and stepped softly to the awning, thrust his hand into a basket beneath the shelter, and took out three, returning to give one to the young Italian and one to Shaddy, reserving the last for himself and beginning to peel it at once.

Giovanni, alias Joe—who had passed nearly the whole of his life on his father's schooner, which formed one of the little fleet of Italian vessels trading between Monte Video and Assuncion, the traffic being largely carried on by the Italian colony settled in the neighbourhood of the former city—took his orange, peeled it cleverly with his thin brown fingers, tossed the skin overboard for it to be nosed about directly by a shoal of tiny fish, and then pulled it in half, picked up the gimp hook and shook his head, laid the hook back on the thwart, and pulled the orange apart once more, leaving two carpels, one side of which he skinned so as to bare the juicy pulp.

"The hook is too small," said the boy quietly.

"Why, it's a jack hook, such as we catch big pike with at home. But you're not going to bait with that?"

"Yes," said the lad, carefully thrusting the hook through the orange after passing it in by a piece of the skin which, for the first time, Rob saw he had left.

"I never heard of a bait like that."

"Oh, I dunno, my lad," said Shaddy. "I've caught carp with green peas and gooseberries at home."

"Orange the best bait for a dorado," said the Italian softly, as he placed the point of the hook to his satisfaction.

"Dorado? That ought to be Spanish for a golden carp," said Rob.

"That's it. You've about hit it, my lad," cried Shaddy, "for these here are as much like the gold-fish you see in the globes at home as one pea's like another."

"Then they're only little fish?" said Rob, with a contemptuous tone in his voice.

"Oh yes, only little ones, my lad," said Shaddy, exchanging glances with the new-comer, who lowered the baited hook softly over the side of the boat, and rapidly paid out the line as the orange was borne away by the current.

"There, Rob, you fish!" the Italian said. "Hold tight if one comes."

"No; go on," replied Rob. "I'm hot and tired. Bother the flies!"

The young Italian nodded, and sitting down, twisted the end of the stout line round a pin in the side of the boat, looking, in his loose flannel shirt and trousers and straw hat, just such a lad as might be seen any summer day on the river Thames, save that he was bare-footed instead of wearing brown leather or canvas shoes. Excepting the heavy breathing of the sleepers forward, there was perfect silence once again till Shaddy said,—

"Wind to-night, gentlemen, and the schooner will be off the bank."

"The pampero?" said Giovanni—or, to shorten it to Rob's familiar nickname, Joe—quietly.

"Looks like it, my lad. There you have him."

For all at once the line tightened, so that there was a heavy strain on the side of the boat.

"That's one of them little ones, Mr Rob, sir."

Joe frowned, and there was a very intense look in his eyes as the line cut the water to and fro, showing that some large fish had taken the bait and was struggling vigorously to escape.

Rob was all excitement now, and ready to bewail his luck at having given up the chance of holding so great a capture on the hook.

"To think o' me not recollecting the orange bait!" grumbled Shaddy. "Must have been half asleep!"

Those were intense moments, but moments they were; for after a few rushes here and there the taut line suddenly grew slack, and as Rob uttered an ejaculation expressive of his disappointment Joe laughed quietly and drew in the line.

"Look," he said, holding up the fragment of gimp attached by its loop to the line. "I knew it was not strong enough."

"Bit it in two," said Shaddy. "Ah, they have some teeth of their own, the fish here. Ought to call 'em dogfish, for most of 'em barks and bites."

While he was speaking Joe had moved to the side of the dinghy, reached over to a little locker in the stern, opened it, and returned directly with a big ugly-looking hook swinging on a piece of twisted wire by its eye.

"They will not bite through that," he said as he returned.

"Oh, but that's absurdly big," said Rob, laughing. "That would frighten a forty-pound pike."

"But it wouldn't frighten a sixty-pound dorado, my lad," said Shaddy quietly.

"What?" cried Rob. "Why, how big do you think that fish was that got away?"

"Thirty or forty pound, perhaps more."

By this time the young Italian was dividing the orange which Shaddy had laid upon the thwart beside him, and half of this, with the pulp well bare, he placed upon the hook, firmly securing this to the line.

"Now, Rob, your turn," said Joe; and the lad eagerly took hold, lowered the bait, and tossed over some twenty yards of line.

"Better twist it round the pin," said his companion.

"Oh no, sir; hold it."

"Well, then, let me secure the end fast."

Rob was ready to resent this, for he felt confidence in his own powers; but he held his tongue, and waited impatiently minute after minute, in expectation of the bite which did not come.

"No luck, eh?" said Shaddy. "I say, I hope you're not going to catch a water-snake. I'll get my knife out to cut him free; shall I? He might sink us."

"Do be quiet," said Rob excitedly. "Might have one of those John Doreys any moment."

But still the minutes went on, and there was no sign.

"How are you going to manage if you hook one?" said Joe quietly.

"Play him till he's tired."

"Mind the line doesn't cut your fingers. No, no, don't twist it round your hand; they pull very hard. Let him go slowly till all the line's out."

"When he bites," said Rob in disappointed tones. "Your one has frightened them all away, or else the bait's off."

"No; I fixed it too tightly."

Just then there was a yawn forward, and another from a second of the Indians.

"Waking," said Rob. "May as well give it up as a bad job."

"No, no, don't do that, sir. You never know when you're going to catch a big fish. Didn't you have a try coming across?"

"No; they said the steamer went too fast, and the screw frightened all the fish away."

"Ay, it would. But you'd better keep on. Strikes me it won't be fishing weather to-morrow."

Thung went the line, which tightened as if it had been screwed by a peg, and Rob felt a jerk up his arms anything but pleasant to his muscles; while, in spite of his efforts, the line began to run through his fingers as jerk succeeded jerk. But the excitement made him hold on and give out as slowly as he could. The friction, though, was such that to check it he wound his left hand in the stout cord, but only to feel it cut so powerfully into his flesh that during a momentary slackening he gladly got his left hand free, lowered both, so that the line rested on the gunwale of the boat, and, making this take part of the stress, let the fish go.

"Best way to catch them fellows is to have a canoe and a very strong line, so as he can tow you about till he's tired," said Shaddy.

"Is the end quite safe?" panted Rob, whose nerves were throbbing with excitement; and he was wondering that his new friend could be so impassive and cool.

"Yes, quite tight," was the reply, just as all the line had glided out; and as Rob held on he was glad to have the help afforded by the line being made fast to the pin.

"What do you say now, sir?" cried Shaddy.

"Oh, don't talk, pray."

"All right, sir, all right; but he's going it, ain't he? Taking a regular gallop over the bottom, eh?"

"I do hope this hook will hold."

"It will," said Giovanni; "you can't say it's too big now."

"No," said Rob in a husky whisper. "But what is it—a shark?"

"I never heard o' sharks up in these parts," said Shaddy, laughing.

"Or would it be an alligator? It is awfully strong. Look at that."

This was as the prisoner made a furious rush through the water right across the stern.

"Nay; it's no alligator, my lad. If it were I should expect to see him come up to the top and poke out his ugly snout, as if to ask us what game we called this. Precious cunning chaps they are, and as they live by fishing, they'd say it wasn't fair."

"Oh, Shaddy, do hold your tongue!" cried Rob. "I say, Joe, how long will it take to tire him?"

"Don't know," said the lad, laughing. "He's tiring you first."

"Yes; but how are we to get him on board?"

"Hullo, Rob, lad! caught a fish or a tartar?" said a fresh voice, and a bronzed, sturdy man of about seven-and-thirty stepped up behind them, putting on a pith helmet and suppressing a yawn, for he had just risen from his nap under the awning.

"Think it's a Tartar," said Rob between his set teeth.

"Or a whale," said the fresh comer, laughing. "Perhaps we had better cut adrift."

"No, no, sir," cried Rob excitedly. "I must catch him."

"I meant from the schooner, so as to let him tow us if he will take us up stream instead of down."

"No; don't move; don't do anything," cried Rob hoarsely. "I'm so afraid of his breaking away."

"Well, he is doing his best, my lad."

"Getting tired, Mr Brazier," said the Italian lad. "They are *very* strong."

"They? What is it, then—a fresh-water seal?"

"No; a dorado. I know it by the way it pulls."

"Oh, then, let's have him caught," said Martin Brazier, head of the little expedition up the great Southern river. "I am eager to see the gilded one. Steady, Rob, my lad! Give him time."

"He has had time enough," said Giovanni quickly. "Begin to pull in now, and he will soon be beaten."

Rob began to haul, and drew the fish a couple of yards nearer the boat, but he lost all he had gained directly, for the captive made a frantic dash for liberty, and careered wildly to and fro some minutes longer. Then, as fresh stress was brought to bear, it gradually yielded, stubbornly at first, then more and more, till the line was gathering fast in the bottom of the boat, and a sudden splash and tremendous eddy half a dozen yards away showed that the fish was close to the surface.

Just then the Italian captain's son came close up to Rob, and stood looking over, holding a large hook which he had fetched from the dinghy; but he drew back, and looked in Mr Brazier's face.

"Would you like to hook it in?" he said, "or shall we let him go? It is a very big one, and will splash about."

"Better let me, sir," said Shaddy, drawing his knife. "Keep clear of him, too, for he may bite."

Martin Brazier looked sharply at the man he had engaged for his guide, expecting to see a furtive smile, but Shaddy was perfectly serious, and read his meaning.

"It's all right, sir; they do bite, and bite sharply, too. Give us the hook, youngster."

He took the hook the young Italian handed, and as Rob dragged the fish, which still plunged fiercely, nearer the side, he leaned over, and after the line had been given twice and hauled in again, there was a gleam of orange and gold, then a flash as the captive turned upon its side, and before it could give another beat with its powerful caudal fin, Shaddy deftly thrust the big hook in one of its gills, and the next moment the dorado was dragged over the gunwale to lay for a moment in the bright sunshine a mass of dazzling orange and gold, apparently astonished or half stunned. The next it was beating the bottom heavily with its tail, leaping up from side to side and taking possession of the stern of the boat, till a sharp tug of the hook brought its head round, and a thrust from Shaddy's knife rendered the fierce creature partially helpless.

"THE NEXT MOMENT THE DORADO WAS DRAGGED OVER THE GUNWALE."

Rob's arms ached, and his hands were sore, but he forgot everything in the contemplation of the magnificent fish he had captured. For as it lay there now, feebly opening and closing its gills, it was wonderfully like an ordinary gold-fish of enormous size, the orange-and-gold scale armour in which it was clad being so gorgeous that, in spite of his triumph in the capture, Rob could not help exclaiming,—

"What a pity to have killed it!"

"There are plenty more," said Joe, smiling.

"Yes, but it is so beautiful," said Rob regretfully.

"Yet we should not have seen its beauty," said Brazier, "if we had not caught it." And he bent down to examine the fish more closely.

"Mind your eye, sir," shouted Shaddy.

"You mean my finger, I suppose," said Brazier, snatching back his hand.

"That's so, sir," replied Shaddy. "I'd a deal rather have mine in a rat-trap. Just you look here!"

He picked up the boat-hook and presented the end of the pole to the fish as its jaws gaped open, and touched the palate. In an instant the mouth closed with a snap, and the teeth were driven into the hard wood.

"There, sir," continued Shaddy, "that's when he's half dead. You can tell what he's like when he's all alive in the water. Pretty creetur, then," he continued, apostrophising the dying fish, "it was a pity to kill you. They'll be pretty glad down below, though, to get rid of you. Wonder how many other better-looking fish he ate every day, Mr Harlow, sir?"

"I didn't think of that," said Rob, feeling more comfortable, and his regret passing away.

"With teeth like that, he must have been a regular water tyrant," said Brazier, after a long examination of the fish, from whose jaws the pole was with difficulty extracted. "There, take it away," he continued. "Your cook will make something of it, eh, Giovanni?"

"Yes," said the lad; "we'll have some for dinner."

"But what do you suppose it weighs?" cried Rob.

"Good sixty-pound, sir," said Shaddy, raising the captive on the hook at arm's length. "Wo-ho!" he shouted as the fish made a struggle, quivering heavily from head to tail. "There you are!" he cried, dropping it into the dinghy. Then in the Guarani dialect he told two of the Indian boatmen to take it on board the schooner, over whose stern several dark faces had now appeared, and soon after the gorgeous-looking trophy was hauled up the vessel's side and disappeared.

Chapter Three.

An Italian Alliance.

"Now, sir, if you please," said Shaddy, "I think it's time to do something to this covering-in. We've had fine weather so far, but it's going to change. What do you say to spreading another canvas over the top?"

"If you think it's necessary, do it at once."

"It's going to rain soon," said the Italian lad, who was seated by Rob carefully winding up the line so that it might dry.

"And when it do rain out here, sir, it ain't one of your British mizzles, but regular cats and dogs. It comes down in bucketfuls. And, as you know, the best thing toward being healthy's keeping a dry skin, which you can't do in wet clothes."

Work was commenced at once after the boat had been swabbed clean, and a canvas sheet being unfolded, it was stretched over the ridge pole which covered in a portion of the boat, tightly tied down over the sides, and secured fore and aft.

"There," said Shaddy when he had finished, the boys and Mr Brazier helping willingly, "if we can keep the wind out we shall be all right now. Nothing like keeping your victuals and powder dry. Not much too soon, sir, eh?"

Martin Brazier and his companion had been too busy to notice the change that had come over the sky; but now they looked up to see that the sun was covered by a dull haze, which rapidly grew more dense. The heat that had prevailed for many days, during which they had fought their way slowly up the great river, passed rapidly away, and Rob suggested that rain would begin to fall soon.

"Not yet, my lad. These are not rain-clouds," said Shaddy; "that's only dust."

"Dust? Where are the roads for it to blow off?" said Rob incredulously.

"Roads? No roads, but off the thousands of miles of dry plains."

Just then a hail came from the schooner, the captain looking over, and in extremely bad English suggesting that the party should come on board; but directly after he lapsed into Italian, addressed to his son.

"Father says we shall have two or three days' rain and bad weather, and that you will be more comfortable on board till the storm has gone by."

"Yes," said Mr Brazier, "no doubt, but I don't like leaving the boat."

"She'll be all right, sir," said Shaddy. "I'll stop aboard with one of the Indians. Bit o' rain won't hurt us."

Mr Brazier hesitated.

"Better go, sir."

"To refuse would be showing want of confidence in him," said Brazier to Rob, and then aloud,—

"Very well. Take care of the guns, and see that nothing gets wet."

Just then there was a whirling rush of cool wind, which rippled the whole surface of the water.

"I shall take care of 'em, sir," said Shaddy. "Here comes the dinghy. Better get aboard whilst you can. She'll be off that sand-bank 'fore an hour's past. You can send us a bit of the fish, Mr Harlow. Haul us up close, and drop some in."

"Yes, I'll look after you, Shaddy," replied Rob.

"And if this wind holds we shall soon be in the Paraguay river, sir, and sailing into another climate, as you'll see."

They went on board the schooner, where they were warmly welcomed by the Italian skipper, and in less time than Shaddy had suggested there was a heavy sea on, which rocked the loftily masted vessel from side to side. Then a sail or two dropped down, a tremendous gust of moisture-laden air came from the south, the schooner rose, dipped her bowsprit, creaked loudly, and as quite a tidal wave rushed up the river before the storm she seemed to leap off the sand-bank on its crest right into deep water, and sailed swiftly away due north.

All whose duty did not keep them on deck were snugly housed in the cabin, listening to the deafening roar of the thunder and watching the lightning, which flashed incessantly, while the rain beat and thrashed the decks and poured out of the scuppers in cascades.

"They were right," said Brazier to Rob. "We're better here, but if this goes on our boat will be half full of water, and not a thing left dry."

"Shaddy will take care of them," said Rob quietly. "Besides, most of the things are packed in casks, and will not hurt."

Mr Brazier shook his head.

"I don't know," he said; "I'm afraid we shall have to renew our stock of provisions and powder at Assuncion, and they'll make us pay pretty dearly for it, too."

The storm lasted well through the night, but at daybreak the rain had ceased. When they went on deck, there, swinging behind them, was the drenched boat, with Shaddy seated astern, scooping out the last drops of water with a tin, and saving that the canvas tent was saturated and steamed slightly, nothing seemed wrong. The morning was comparatively cool, a gleam of orange light coming in the east, and a pleasant gale blowing from the south and sending the shallow-draughted schooner onward at a rapid pace.

A couple of hours later, with the sun well up, the temperature was delicious, the canvas of the boat tent drying rapidly, and Shaddy, after hauling close up astern for the fish he had not forgotten, had reported that not a drop of water had got inside to the stores.

Days followed of pleasant sailing, generally with the pampero blowing, but with a few changes round to the north, when, as they tacked up the river, it was like being in another climate.

One or two stoppages followed at the very few towns on the banks, and at last the junction of the two great rivers was reached, the Parana, up which they had sailed, winding off to the east and north, the Paraguay, up which their destination lay, running in a winding course due north.

As Shaddy had prophesied, the change was wonderful as soon as they had entered this river, and fresh scenes and novelties were constantly delighting Rob's eyes as they slowly sailed on against the current.

"Oh yes, this is all very well," said Shaddy; "but wait till we've got past the big city yonder and left the schooners and trade and houses behind: then I shall show you something. All this don't count."

Mr Brazier seemed to think that it did, and a dozen times over he was for bidding Captain Ossolo good-bye, thanking and paying him for towing him up the river, and turning off at once into one of the streams that ran in through the virgin land west. But Shaddy opposed him.

"I'm only your servant, Mr Brazier, sir," he said, "and I'll do what you say; but you told me you wanted to go into quite noo country. Well, it will be easier for me to take you up one of these creeks or rivers, and you'll be able to hunt and collect; only recollect that it isn't such very noo country—other folks have been up here and there. What I say is, give the skipper good-bye when we get to Assuncion, and then we'll sail and row and pole up a couple of hundred miles farther, and then turn off west'ard. Then I can take you up rivers where everything's noo to Englishmen, and in such a country as shall make you say that you couldn't ha' thought there was such a land on earth."

Similar conversations to this took place again and again, and all fired Martin Brazier's brain as much as they did Rob's.

They had an unexpected effect, too, for, on reaching Assuncion, where the schooner cast anchor to discharge her cargo and take in a fresh one for the downward journey, Captain Ossolo came over into the boat one evening with his son, just as Brazier and Rob were busy with Shaddy packing in stores which had been freshly purchased, as possibly this would be the last place where they could provide themselves with some of the necessaries of life.

"Ah, captain," cried Brazier, "I'm glad you've come. I want to have a settlement with you for all you've done."

The captain nodded, and rubbed one brown ear, making the gold ring therein glisten.

"What am I in your debt?" continued Brazier, "though no money can pay you for your kindness to us and excellent advice."

The captain was silent, and took to rubbing the other ear, his face wearing a puzzled expression.

"Don't be afraid to speak out, sir," continued Brazier; "I am sure you will find me generous."

"*Si*! yes," said the captain, holding out his hand, which was at once taken; "much please—good fellow—*amico*—*bono*—*altro*—*altro*!"

He broke down and looked confused.

"I understand you," said Brazier, speaking slowly; "and so are you a good fellow. I wish I could speak Italian. Do you understand me?"

"*Si! si*!" said the captain, nodding his head.

"We both hope to find you here again when we return, for you to help us down the river again with the collections we shall have made."

This last puzzled the captain a little; but his son, who was at his elbow, interpreted, and he nodded his head vehemently.

"*Si! si*!" he cried. "Take you back on *Tessa*. Get fever? No. Get hurt? No. Come back safe."

"My father means you are to take care of yourselves," said Joe, "both you and Rob. Shaddy has promised to help you all he can."

"Ah, to be sure I will; depend upon that," said the individual named.

"And father wants to say something else," said Joe.

"Yes, of course," said Brazier rather impatiently. "What am I in his debt?"

"Shall I tell him, father?" said the lad in Italian.

"*Si! si*!"

The lad cleared his voice, and fixed his eyes on Rob, but turned them directly after upon Brazier.

"My father says he will not take any money for what he has done."

"Oh, nonsense!" cried Brazier; "he must."

"No!" cried the skipper, frowning as he shook his head till his earrings glistened.

"He wants you to do him a favour."

"What does he so want—a gun, a watch, some powder?"

"No," said the lad, clearing his throat again; "he wants you to be a friend to me and take me with you in the boat."

"What?" cried Rob, with an eager look.

"Father—*il mio padre*—says it would do me good to go with you and travel, and learn to speak English better."

"Why, you speak it well now."

"But better," continued Joe. "He would like me to go with Rob, and help you, and shoot and fish and collect things. He would like it very much."

Captain Ossolo showed his teeth and laughed merrily as he clapped his son on the shoulder.

"Do you understand what your son says?" cried Brazier.

"*Si*! All he say. Giovanni want go bad, very much bad."

"I thought so," said Brazier. Then turning to the lad, "Do you know that we may be months away?"

"Yes, I know," said the lad eagerly. "Father says it would— Please take me, Signore Brazier. I will be so useful, and I can fish, and cook, and light fires."

"And lay the blame on your father, eh? He wants you to go?"

"He says I may, signore—I mean sir. He promised me that he would ask you."

"I understand," said Brazier; "but, my good lad, do you know that we shall have to rough it very much?"

"Bah!" exclaimed the boy. "You will have the boat, and Shaddy, and the four Indian rowers. The country is paradise. It will be a holiday, a delight."

"And the insects, the wild beasts, the dangers of disease?"

"What of them? We shall be on the rivers, and I have been on rivers half my life. Pray take me, signore."

Brazier shook his head, and a look of agony convulsed the boy's Southern features.

"Speak to him, my father," he cried excitedly, "and you, Rob. We were making friends. Beg, pray of him to say yes."

"*Si!*" said the captain, nodding his head. "Do boy *mio* good. Much, very good boy, Giovanni."

"Well, I hardly like to refuse you, my lad," said Brazier. "What do you say, Rob? Could we make room for him?"

A light seemed to flash from Giovanni's eyes, and his lips parted as he waited panting for Rob's reply.

"Oh yes; he would not take up much room."

"No, very little. I could sleep anywhere," cried the lad excitedly, "and I could help you so much. I know the country almost as well as Shaddy. Don't I, Shaddy?"

"Say ever so much more, boy, if you like. But he does know a lot about it. Me and he's been more than one trip together, eh, lad?"

"Yes. But beg him to take me, Rob," cried the boy. "I do so want to go."

"You will take him, will you not, Mr Brazier?"

"I shrink from the responsibility," said Brazier.

"I'll take the responsibility, then," cried Rob eagerly.

"Suppose I say 'no'?"

Giovanni's countenance changed at every speech, being one moment clouded, the next bright. And now as that word "No" rang out he clasped his hands together and raised them with a gesture full of despair. Then his eyes lit up again, for Rob said quickly,—

"Don't say it, then. He would be so horribly disappointed now."

"*Si*! Take Giovanni," said the skipper, and the boy gave him a grateful glance.

"But suppose anything happens to him?"

The Italian captain could not grasp the meaning of this last speech, and turned to his son, who rendered it into their own tongue.

"Oh," replied the captain in the same language, "it is fate. He must take care of himself. Suppose I fall overboard, and am drowned, or the fish eat me? Yes, he must take care."

"You would like him with us, then, Rob?" said Brazier.

"Yes, very much."

"That's enough, then. You shall come, my lad. Wait a moment; hear what I have to say. You must be obedient and follow out my instructions."

"Yes; I'll do everything you tell me," cried the boy.

"And you will have to do as we do—live hard and work hard."

"I'm not afraid of work," said the boy, smiling.

"And now interpret this to your father. I will do everything I can to protect you, and you shall be like one of us, but he must not expect me to be answerable for any mishaps that may come to us out in the wilds."

Giovanni turned eagerly to his father, but the skipper waved his hand.

"Understand," he said, nodding his head. "I you trust. Take *il mio* boy."

He held out his hand to Brazier, and shook his solemnly as if in sign manual of the compact, and then repeated the performance with Rob, whose hand he retained, and, taking his son's, placed them together.

"*Fratelli*! broders!" he said, smiling.

"Yes, I will be like a brother to you," cried Giovanni.

"All right," said Rob unpoetically; and then the skipper turned to Shadrach, and grumbled out something in Italian.

"Toe be sure," growled the man in English. "'Course I will. You know me, cap'en."

"*Si*!" replied the skipper laconically; and then, asking Rob to accompany him, the Italian lad made for his little cabin to begin the few preparations he had to make.

The result was that a canvas bag like a short bolster was handed down into the boat, and then the boy followed with a light, useful-looking rifle, belt and long keen sheath-knife, which he hung up under the canvas to be clear of the night dew or rain.

It was still grey the next morning when the boatmen sat ready with their oars, and Captain Ossolo stood in the dinghy beside Brazier's boat, which swung astern of the *Tessa*, down into whose hold scores of light-footed women were passing basketfuls of oranges.

They paused in their work for a few minutes as the captain shook hands with all in turn.

"*A revederla*!" he cried, taking off his Panama hat. "I see you when you come back, ole boy; goo'-bye; take yourself care of you."

The next minute he was waving his soft hat from the dinghy, while Brazier's boat was gliding up stream, and the two boys stood up and gave him a hearty cheer.

"Now, youngsters," said Shaddy, as he cleared the little mast lying under the thwarts, "we shall catch the wind as soon as we're round the next bend; so we may as well let Natur' do the work when she will."

"What's that, Shadrach?" said Brazier; "going to hoist the sail?"

"Ay, sir. No *Tessa* to tow us now."

"True. What do you mean to do first?"

"Ask you to resist all temptations to stop at what you calls likely bits, sir, and wait till we get up a hundred mile or so, when I'll take you into waters which will be exactly what you want."

"Very good; I leave myself then in your hands."

"Just to start you, sir. After that it's you as takes the helm."

As their guide said, the wind was fair as soon as they had rowed round a bend of the great, smooth river; the sail was hoisted, the oars laid in, and the Indian rowers too, for as soon as they had ceased pulling they lay down forward to sleep, and that night the boat was moored to a tree on the eastern side of the stream, far-away from the haunts of civilised man, while Rob lay sleepless, listening to the strange and weird sounds which rose from the apparently impenetrable forest on the far-away western shore.

Chapter Four.

Noises of the Night.

"Not asleep, my lad?" said a voice at his elbow as Rob crept out from under the awning to the extreme stern.

"You, Shaddy? No, I can't sleep. It all seems so strange."

"Ay, it do to you," said the man in a husky whisper. "You've got it just on you now strong. You couldn't go to sleep because you thought that them four Indian chaps forward might come with their knives and finish you and drop you overboard—all of us."

"How do you know I thought that?"

"Ah, I know!" said Shaddy, with a chuckle. "Everybody does. I did first time. Well, they won't, so you needn't be afeared o' that. Nex' thing as kept you awake was that you thought a great boa-constructor might be up in the tree and come crawling down into the boat."

"Shaddy, are you a witch?" cried Rob.

"Not as I knows on, my lad."

"Then how did you know that?"

"Human natur', lad. Every one thinks just like that. Next you began thinking that them pretty creeturs you can hear singing like great cats would swim across and attack us, or some great splashing fish shove his head over the side to take a bite at one of us. Didn't you?"

Rob was silent for a few moments, and then said,—

"Well, I did think something of the kind."

"Of course you did. It is your nature to think like that, but you may make your mind easy, for there's only one thing likely to attack you out here."

"What's that?" whispered Rob—"Indians who will swim out from the shore?"

"No, wild creeturs who will fly—skeeters, lad, skeeters."

"Oh," said Rob, with a little laugh, "they've been busy enough already, two or three of them. But what's that?"

He grasped Shaddy's arm, for at that moment there was a plunge in the river not very far-away in the darkness from where they were moored, and then silence.

"Dunno yet," said Shaddy in a whisper. "Listen."

Rob needed no telling, for his every nerve was on the strain. There came a peculiar grunting sound, very unlike any noise that might have been made by a swimming Indian, and Shaddy said quietly,—

"Water hog. Carpincho they calls 'em; big kind of porky, beavery, ottery, ratty sort of thing; and not bad eating."

Rob pressed his arm again as a sharp, piercing howl came from far-away over the river, here about four or five hundred yards across.

"That's a lion," said Shaddy quietly. "Strikes me they shout like that to scare the deer and things they live on into making a rush, and then they're down upon 'em like a cat upon a mouse."

"Lion? You mean a puma."

"Means a South American lion, my lad."

"There it is again," whispered Rob in an awe-stricken voice, "only it's a deeper tone, and sounds more savage."

"That's just what it is," said Shaddy, "ever so much more savage. That wasn't a lion; that was a tiger—well, jagger, as some calls 'em. Deal fiercer beasts than the lions."

The cries were repeated and answered from a distance, while many other strange noises arose, to which the man could give no name.

"One would want half a dozen lives to be able to get at all of it, my lad," said Shaddy quietly, "and there's such lots of things that cheat you so."

"Hist! There's another splash," whispered Rob.

"Ay; there's no mistake about that, my lad. There it goes again, double one. It's as plain as if you can see it, a big fish springing out of the water, turning over, and falling in again with a flop. You don't think there's no fish in the river now, do you?"

"Oh no. I don't doubt it now," whispered Rob, as he listened to fish after fish rising, and all apparently very large.

"Makes a man wonder what they are jumping after, unless it is the stars shining in the water. You hear that?"

"Yes."

"And that, too?"

"Yes, I hear them," replied Rob, unable to repress a shiver, so strange and weird were the cries which came mournfully floating across.

"Well, them two used to puzzle me no end—one of 'em a regular roar and the other quite a moan, as if somebody was a-dying."

"You know what it is now?"

"Yes, and you'd never guess, my lad, till you said one was made by a bird."

"A bird?"

"Yes, a long-legged heron kind of thing as trumpets it out with a roar like a strange, savage beast; and the other moaning, groaning sound is made by a frog. I don't mind owning it used to scare me at first."

Rob sat listening to the weird chorus going on in the forest and watching the stars above, and their slightly blurred reflections in the water which went whispering by the prow and side of the boat. It was all so solemn, and strange, and awe-inspiring that, in spite of a feeling of dread which he could not master, he was glad to be there, wakeful, trying to picture the different creatures prowling about in the darkness of the primeval forest. He had listened time after time on the voyage up, but then the schooner was close at hand, and they passed towns and villages on the east bank; but here they were farther away in the heart of the wild country, and on the very edge of a forest untrodden by the foot of man, and maybe teeming with animal life as new as it was strange. And in amongst this they were soon going to plunge!

It had been the dream of the boy's life to penetrate one of the untrodden fastnesses of nature, but now that he was on the threshold listening in the darkness of night, there was something terrible both in the silence and in the sounds which made him ask himself whether he had done wisely in accompanying Martin Brazier, an old friend of his father, who, partly for profit, but more for the advancement of science, had made his arrangements for this adventurous journey. But it was too late now to recede, even had he wished to do so. In fact, had any one talked of his return, he would have laughed at him as a proposer of something absurd.

"I suppose it comes natural to most boys to long for adventures and to see foreign countries," he thought to himself, and then he went mentally over the scene with Giovanni.

"Joe is as eager as I was," he muttered, and then he started, for something swept by his face.

"What's matter, my lad?" said Shaddy quietly.

"I—I don't know, something— There it goes again, some bird. An owl, I think, flew past my face. There, it skimmed just over our heads with a fluttering noise."

"I heard it, lad—bat, big 'un. Put your toes in your pockets if you haven't got on your shoes."

"What do you mean?"

"It's a blood-sucker—wampire, that's all."

"But that's all nonsense," said Rob, with a slight shudder, "a traveller's tale."

"Oh, is it, boy? You'll see one of these times when we wake in the morning. They come in the night and suck your blood."

"Oh, that can't be true?"

"Why not? Get out, will you?" said Shaddy gruffly, as he made a blow at the great leathern-winged creature that kept fluttering about their heads. "He smells his supper, and is trying for a chance. You don't believe it, then?"

"No."

"Humph! Well, you've a right to your own opinion, my lad," said Shaddy quietly, "but I suppose you believe that if you dabbled your legs in the water a leech might fix on you and suck your blood?"

"Oh yes; I've had many on me in England."

"And you've had skeeters on you and maybe sucked your blood here?"

"Yes."

"Then why can't you believe as a bat wouldn't do the same?"

Rob found the argument unanswerable.

"It's true enough, my lad. They'll lay hold on a fellow's toe or thumb, ay, and on horses too. I've known 'em quite weak with being sucked so much night after night."

"Horses? Can they get through a horse's thick skin?"

Shaddy chuckled.

"Why, dear lad," he said, "a horse has got a skin as tender as a man's, so just you 'member that next time you spurs or whips them."

Rob sat in silence, thinking, with the weird sounds increasing for a time; and, in spite of his efforts, it was impossible to keep down a shrinking sense of dread.

Everything was thrilling: the golden-spangled water looked so black, and the darkness around so deep, while from the Grand Chaco, the great, wild, untrodden forest across the river stretching away toward the mighty Andes in the west, the shouts, growls, and wails suggested endless horrors going on as the wild creatures roamed here and there in search of food.

Plash! right away—a curious sound of a heavy body plunging into the river, but with the noise carried across the water, so that it seemed to be only a few yards away.

"What's that?" whispered Rob.

"Can't tell for sartain, my lad, but I should say that something came along and disturbed a big fat 'gator on the bank, and he took a dive in out of the way. I say! Hear that?"

"Hear it?" said Rob, as a creeping sensation came amongst the roots of his hair, just as if the skin had twitched; "who could help hearing it?"

For the moment before Shaddy asked his question a blood-curdling, agonising yell, as of some being in mortal agony, rang out from across the river.

"Ay, 'tis lively. First time I heered that I says to myself, 'That's one Injun killing another,' and I cocked my rifle and said to myself again, 'well, he shan't do for me.'"

"And was it one Indian murdering another in his sleep?"

Shaddy chuckled.

"Not it, lad. Darkness is full of cheating and tricks. You hears noises in the night, and they sound horrid. If you heered 'em when the sun's shining you wouldn't take any notice of 'em."

"But there it is again," whispered Rob, as the horrible cry arose, and after an interval was repeated as from a distance. "Whatever is it?"

"Sort o' stork or crane thing calling its mate and saying, 'Here's lots o' nice, cool, juicy frogs out here. Come on.'"

"A bird?"

"Yes. Why not? Here, you wait a bit, and you'll open your eyes wide to hear 'em. Some sings as sweet as sweet, and some makes the most gashly noises you can 'magine. That's a jagger—that howl, and that's a lion again. Hear him! He calls out sharper like than the other. You'll soon get to know the difference. But I say, do go and have a sleep now, so as to get up fresh and ready for the day's work. I shall have lots to show you to-morrow."

"Yes, I'll go and lie down again soon. But listen to that! What's that booming, roaring sound that keeps rising and falling? There, it's quite loud now."

"Frogs!" said Shaddy promptly. "There's some rare fine ones out here. There, go and lie down, my lad."

"Why are you in such a hurry to get rid of me? You are watching. Can't I keep you company?"

"Glad to have you, my lad, but I was picked out by Skipper Ossolo because I know all about the country and the river ways, wasn't I?"

"Yes, of course."

"Very well, then. I give you good advice. You don't want to be ill and spoil your trip, so, to keep right, what you've got to do is to eat and drink reg'lar and sensible and take plenty of sleep."

"Oh, very well," said Rob, with a sigh. "I'll go directly."

"It means steady eyes and hands, my lad. I know: it all sounds very wild and strange up here, but you'll soon get used to it, and sleep as well as those Indian lads do. There, good-night."

"Good-night," said Rob reluctantly. "But isn't it nearly morning?"

"Not it, five hours before sunrise; so go and take it out ready for a big day—such a trip as you never dreamed of."

"Very well," replied Rob, and he crept quietly back to his place under the canvas covering, but sleep would not come, or so it seemed to him. But all at once the mingling of strange sounds grew muffled and dull, and then he opened his eyes, to find that the place where he lay was full of a soft, warm glow, and Joe was bending over him and shaking him gently.

Chapter Five.

A Watch in the Dark.

"You do sleep soundly," said the young Italian merrily.

"Why, it's morning, and I didn't know I had been sleeping! Where's Mr Brazier?"

"Forward yonder."

"Why, we're going on."

"Yes; there's a good wind, and we've been sailing away since before the sun rose."

Rob jumped up and hurried out of the tent-like arrangement, to find Shaddy seated in the stern steering, and after a greeting Rob looked about him, entranced by the scenery and the wondrous tints of the dewy morning. Great patches of mist hung about here and there close under the banks where the wind did not catch them, and these were turned by the early morning's sun to glorious opalescent masses, broken by brilliant patches of light.

The boat was gliding along over the sparkling water close in now to the western shore, whose banks were invisible, being covered by a dense growth of tree and climber, many of whose strands dipped into the river, while umbrageous trees spread and drooped their branches, so that it would have been possible to row or paddle in beneath them in one long, bowery tunnel close to the bank.

"Going to have a wash?" said Joe, breaking in upon Rob's contemplative fit of rapture as he gazed with hungry eyes at the lovely scene.

"Wash? Oh yes!" cried Rob, starting, and he fetched a rough towel out of the tent, went to the side, and hesitated.

"Hadn't we better have a swim?" he said. "You'll come?"

"Not him," growled Shaddy. "What yer talking about? Want to feed the fishes?"

"Rubbish! I can swim," said Rob warmly; and leaning over the side, he plunged his hands into the water, sweeping them about.

"Deliciously cool!" he cried. "Oh!"

He snatched out his right and then his left, and as he did so a little silvery object dropped into the water.

Joe looked on in silence, and a peculiar smile came over Shaddy's countenance as he saw Rob examine the back of his hand.

"Something's been biting me in the night," he said. "It bleeds."

Rob thrust in his hand again to wash away the blood, but snatched it out the next minute, for as the ruddy fluid tinged the water there was a rush of tiny fish at his hand, and he stared at half a dozen tiny bites which he had received.

"Why, they're little fish," he cried. "Are they the piranas you talked about, Joe?"

"Yes. What do you say to a swim now?"

"I'm willing. The splashing would drive them away."

Shaddy chuckled again.

"The splashing would bring them by thousands," said Joe quietly. "You can't bathe here. Those little fish would bite at you till in a few minutes you would be covered with blood, and that would bring thousands more up to where you were."

"And they'd eat me up," said Rob mockingly.

"If somebody did not drag you out. They swarm in millions, and the bigger fish, too, are always ready to attack anything swimming in the stream."

"Come and hold the tiller here, Joe, my lad," growled Shaddy, "while I dip him a bucket of water to wash. When he knows the Paraguay like we do, he won't want to bathe. Why, Mr Rob, there's all sorts o' things here ready for a nice juicy boy, from them little piranas right up to turtles and crocodiles and big snakes, so you must do your swimming with a sponge till we get on a side river and find safe pools."

He dipped the bucket, and Rob had his wash; by that time Brazier had joined him.

"Well, Rob," he cried, "is this good enough for you? Will the place do?"

"Do?" cried Rob. "Oh, I feel as if I do not want to talk, only to sit and look at the trees. There, ain't those orchids hanging down?"

Brazier raised a little double glass which he carried to his eyes, and examined a great cluster of lovely blossoms hanging from an old, half-decayed branch projecting over the river.

"Yes," he cried, "lovely. Well, Naylor, how soon are we to land or run up some creek?"

"Arter two or three days," said the guide.

"But hang it, man, the bank yonder is crowded with vegetable treasures."

"What! them?" said Shaddy, with a contemptuous snort. "I don't call them anything. You just wait, sir, and trust me. You shall see something worth coming after by-and-by."

"Well, run the boat in closer to the shore, so that I can examine the plants as we go along. The water looks deep, and the wind's right. You could get within a dozen yards of the trees."

"I could get so as you might touch 'em, sir. There's plenty of water, but I'm not going no closer than this."

"Why?"

"Because I know that part along there. We can't see nobody, but I dessay there's Injuns watching us all the time from among the leaves, and if we went closer they might have a shot at us."

"Then they have guns?"

"No, sir, bows and arrows some of 'em, but mostly blowpipes."

"With poisoned arrows?"

"That's so, sir, and, what's worse, they know how to use 'em. They hit a man I knew once with a tiny bit of an arrow thing, only a wood point as broke off in the wound—wound, it weren't worth calling a wound, but the little top was poisoned, and before night he was a dead man."

"From the poison?"

"That's it, sir. He laughed at it at first. The bit of an arrow, like a thin skewer with a tuft of cotton wool on the end, didn't look as if it could hurt a strong man as I picked it up and looked where the point had been nearly sawed off all round."

"What, to make it break off?" cried Rob.

"That's so, my lad. When they're going to use an arrow they put the point between the teeth of a little fish's jaw—sort o' pirana thing like them here in the river. Then they give the arrow a twiddle round, and the sharp teeth nearly eat it through, and when it hits and sticks in a wound the point breaks off, and I wouldn't give much for any one who ever got one of those bits of sharp wood in their skins."

"What a pleasant look-out!" said Brazier. "Oh, it's right enough, sir. The thing is to go up parts where there are no Indians, and that's where I'm going to take you. I say, look at that open patch yonder, where there's a bit o' green between the river and the trees."

"Yes, I see," said Joe quickly—"three Indians with spears."

"Right, lad!"

"I don't see them," said Brazier. "Yes," he added quickly, "I can see them now."

"Only one ain't got a spear. That's a blowpipe," said Shaddy quietly.

"What! that length?" cried Rob. "Ay, my lad, that length. The longer they are the smaller the darts, and the farther and stronger they sends 'em."

"But we don't know that they are enemies," said Brazier.

"Oh yes, you do, sir. That's the Injuns' country, and there's no doubt about it. White man's their enemy, they say, so they must be ours."

"But why?" said Rob. "We shouldn't interfere with the Indians."

"We've got a bad character with 'em, my lad. 'Tain't our fault. They tell me it's all along o' the Spaniards as come in this country first, and made slaves of 'em, and learnt 'em to make 'em good, and set 'em to work in the mines to get gold and silver for 'em till they dropped and died. Only savages they were, and so I s'pose the Spaniards thought they weren't o' no consequence. But somehow I s'pose, red as they are, they think and feel like white people, and didn't like to be robbed and beaten, and worn to death, and their children took away from 'em. Spaniards never seemed to think as they'd mind that. Might ha' known, too, for a cat goes miaowing about a house if she loses her kittens, and a dog kicks up a big howl about its pups; while my 'sperience about wild beasts is that if you want to meddle with their young ones, you'd better shoot the old ones first."

"Yes, I'm afraid that the old Spaniards thought of nothing out here but getting gold."

"That's so, sir; and the old Indians telled their children about how they'd been used, and their children told the next lot, and so it's gone on till it's grown into a sort of religion that the Spaniard is a sort o' savage wild beast, who ought to be killed; and that ain't the worst on it."

"Then what is?" said Rob, for Shaddy looked round at him and stopped short, evidently to be asked that question.

"Why, the worst of it is, sir, that they poor hungered, savage sort o' chaps don't know the difference between us and them Dons. English means an Englishman all the wide world over, says you; but you're wrong. He ain't out here. Englishman, or Italian, or Frenchman's a Spaniard; and they'll shoot us as soon as look at us."

"Why, you're making for the other shore, Naylor."

"Yes, sir. I'd ha' liked to land you yonder, but you see it ain't safe, so we'll light a fire on the other side, where it is, and get a bit o' breakfast, for I'm thinking as it's getting pretty nigh time."

"But is it safe to land there?" asked Brazier.

"Yes, sir; you may take that for granted. East's sit down and be comfortable; west side o' the river means eyes wide open and look out for squalls."

"But you meant to go up some river west."

"True, sir; but you leave that to me."

As they began to near the eastern shore, where the land was more park-like and open, the wind began to fail them, and the sail flapped, when the four boatmen, who had been lying about listlessly, leaped up, lowered it down, and then, seizing the oars, began to row with a long, steady stroke. Then Shaddy stood up, peering over the canvas awning, and looking eagerly for a suitable place for their morning halt, and ending by running the boat alongside of a green meadow-like patch, where the bank, only a couple of feet above the water level, was perpendicular, and the spot was surrounded by huge trees, from one of which flew a flock of parrots, screaming wildly, while sundry sounds and rustlings in that nearest the water's edge proved that it was inhabited.

"What's up there?" whispered Rob to Joe as he looked. "Think it's a great snake?"

"No," was the reply. "Look!" and the captain's son pointed up to where, half hidden by the leaves, a curious little black face peered wonderingly down at them; and directly after Rob made out one after another, till quite a dozen were visible, the last hanging from a bough like some curious animal fruit by its long stalk, which proved to be the little creature's prehensile tail, by which it swung with us arms and legs drawn up close.

"Monkeys!" cried Rob eagerly, for it was his first meeting with the odd little objects in their native wilds.

"Yes; they swarm in the forests," said Joe, who was amused at his companion's wondering looks.

Just then Shaddy leaped ashore with a rope, after carefully seeing to the fastening of the other end.

"May as well give you gents a hint," he said: "never to trust nobody about your painter. It's just as well to use two, for if so be as the boat does break loose, away she goes down-stream, and you're done, for there's no getting away from here. You can't tramp far through the forest."

He moored the boat to one of the trees, gave a few orders, and the Indian boatmen rapidly collected dead wood and started a fire, Shaddy filling the tin kettle and swinging it gipsy fashion.

"I'd start fair at once, gentlemen," he said. "One never knows what's going to happen, and I take it that you ought to carry your gun always just as you would an umbrella at home, and have it well loaded at your side, ready for any action. Plenty of smoke!" he continued, as the clouds began to roll up through the dense branches of the tree overhead.

The result was a tremendous chattering and screaming amongst the monkeys, which bounded excitedly from branch to branch, shaking the twigs and breaking off dead pieces to throw down.

"Hi! stop that, little 'uns!" roared Shaddy. "Two can play at that game. It ain't your tree; be off to another, or we'll make rabbit-pie o' some on you."

Whether the little creatures understood or no, they chattered loudly for a few moments more, and then, running to the end of a branch, which bent beneath their weight, they dropped to the ground, and galloped off to the next tree, each with his peculiar curling tail high in air.

The guide's advice was taken respecting the pieces, and, in addition to his cartridge-pouch, each mounted a strong hunting-knife, one that, while being handy for chopping wood or cutting a way through creepers and tangling vines, would prove a formidable weapon of offence or defence against the attack of any wild animal.

"That's your sort," said Shaddy, smiling as he saw Rob step out of the boat with his piece under his arm. "Puts me in mind of handling my first gun, when I was 'bout your age, sir, or a bit older. No, no, don't carry it that way, my lad; keep your muzzle either right up or right down."

"Well, that is down," said Rob pettishly, for he felt conscious, and wanted to appear quite at ease, and as if he were in the habit of carrying a rifle; consequently he looked as if he had never held one before in his life.

"Ay, it's down enough to put a bullet in anybody's knees."

"No, it isn't, Shaddy, for it's a shot-gun, and has no bullet in it."

"I know, lad, one o' them useful guns with a left-hand bore as'll carry a bullet if you like. More down. Wound close at hand from charge o' shot's worse than one from a bullet."

"Because it makes so many wounds?" said Rob.

"Nay, my lad; because at close quarters it only makes one, and a big, ragged one that's bad to heal. That's better. Now, if it goes off, it throws up the earth and shoots the worms, while if you hold it well up it only shoots the stars.—Water boils."

Breakfast followed—a delightful *alfresco* meal, with the silver river gliding by, birds twittering, piping, screaming, and cooing all around, and monkeys chattering and screeching excitedly at having their sanctuary invaded; but they were quite tame enough to drop down from the trees and pick up a piece of biscuit, banana, or orange when thrown far enough. But this was not till they felt satisfied that they were not being watched, when the coveted treasure was seized and borne off with a chattering cry of triumph, the actions of the odd little creatures taking up a good deal of Rob's time which might have been devoted to his breakfast.

The travellers had brought plenty of fruit and provisions with them, and an ample supply of *maté*—the leaves that take the place of tea amongst the South American tribes, whose example is largely followed by the half-breeds and those of Spanish descent; and after watching how the preparation was made Rob found himself quite ready to partake of that which proved on tasting to be both palatable and refreshing.

Then, somewhat unwillingly—for both Brazier and the lads were disposed to stay on shore to collect some of the natural objects so plentiful around them—they re-entered the boat; it was pulled into mid-stream, with the monkeys flocking down from the trees about the fire to pick up any scraps of food left, notably a couple of decayed bananas, and then running quite to the edge of the water to chatter menacingly at the departing boat.

The sail was soon after hoisted, and for the whole of that day and the next the little party ascended the river, making their halts on the right bank, but sleeping well out in the stream, held by a rope mooring the boat's head to a tree, and a little anchor dropped in the stream.

Progress was fairly swift, and there was so much to see along the banks that the time glided by rapidly; but at every cry of exultation on the discovery of some fresh bird, flower, or insect, Shaddy only smiled good-humouredly, and used the same expression:—

"Yes; but just you wait a bit."

The third day had passed, and the conversation in the boat threatened a revolution against the will of Shaddy, whose aim seemed to be to get them up higher, while they were passing endless opportunities for making collections of objects of natural history such as they had never had before, when all at once, as he stood in the boat looking up stream, after she had once more been carefully moored for the night, the guide turned and said quietly:—

"To-morrow, long before the sun's highest, I shall get you up to the place I mean, and, once there, you can begin business as soon as you like."

"A river on the left bank," said Brazier, as eagerly as a boy.

"Yes, sir, one as runs for far enough west, and then goes north."

"And you think there are no Indians there?"

"I don't say that, sir, because we shall see some, I daresay; but they'll perhaps be friendly."

"You are not sure?"

"Well, no, sir. There, the sun's dipping down; it will be heavy darkness directly in this fog, and what we want is a good night's rest, ready for a long, hard day's work to-morrow."

It was Brazier's turn to keep watch half the night, and at about twelve, as nearly as they could tell, Rob rose to take his place.

"Nothing to report," said Brazier. "The same noises from the forest, the same splashings from the river, the Indians sleeping as heavily as usual. There, keep your watch; I wish I had it, for you will see the day break that is to take us to the place which I have been longing to see for years."

Saying "good-night," Brazier went into the shelter, and Rob commenced his solitary watch, with his brain busily inventing all kinds of dangers arising from the darkness—some horrible wild creature dropping down from the tree, or a huge serpent, which had crawled down the branch, twining its way along the mooring rope and coming over the bows past the Indian boatmen. Then he began to think of them, and how helpless he would be if they planned to attack him, when, after mastering him, which he felt they could easily do, he mentally arranged that they would creep to the covered-in part of the boat and slay Brazier and Giovanni.

"Poor Joe!" he said to himself. "I was beginning to like him, though he was not English, and— Oh, Joe, how you startled me!"

For a hand had been laid upon his shoulder as he sat watching the dark part where the Indians lay, and he started round to find that Giovanni had joined him.

"I did not mean to frighten you," said the lad, in his quiet, subdued way. "Mr Brazier woke me coming in to sleep, and I thought you would be alone, and that I could come and talk to you about our journey to-morrow."

"I'm glad you've come, but it would be too bad to let you stop. There, stay a quarter of an hour, and then be off back to bed—such as it is," he added, with a laugh.

"Oh, I'm used to hard beds. I can sleep anywhere—on the deck or a bench, one as well as the other."

"I say, have you ever been up as high as this before?"

"No, never higher than the town. It's all as fresh to me as to you."

"Then we go up a river to-morrow?"

"I suppose so. Old Shaddy has it all his own way, and he keeps dropping hints about what he is going to take us to see."

"And I daresay it will all turn out nothing. What he likes may not suit us. But there, we shall see."

Then they sat in silence, listening to the rustlings and whistlings in the air as of birds and great moths flitting and gliding about; the shrieks, howls, and yells from across the river; and to the great plungings and splashings in the black water, whose star-gemmed bosom often showed waves with the bright reflections rising and falling, and whose surface looked as if the fire-flies had fallen in all up the river after their giddy evolutions earlier in the night, and were now floating down rapidly toward the sea.

Rob broke the silence at last.

"How is it this stream always runs so fast?" he said.

"Because the waters come from the mountains. There's a great waterfall, too, higher up, where the whole river comes plunging down hundreds of feet with a roar that can be heard for miles."

"Who says so? who has seen it?"

"Nobody ever has seen it. It is impossible to get to it. The water is so swift and full of rocks that no boat can row up, and the shores are all one dank, tangled mass that no one can cut through. Nobody can get there."

"Why not? I tell you what: we'll talk to Shaddy to-morrow."

"He wouldn't go. He told me once that he tried it, and couldn't get there. He nearly lost his life."

"I'll make him try again and take us."

"I tell you he wouldn't."

"Well, you'll see."

"What will you do?"

"Tell him—fair play, mind: you will not speak?"

"Of course not."

"Then look here, Joe; I'll say to him that I've heard of the place, and how difficult it is, and that I wish we had some guide who really knew the country and could take us there."

Joe shook his head.

"Beside, we could not attempt it without Mr Brazier wished to go."

"If you told him about that great fall, he would wish to go for the sake of being the discoverer. You'll see. What's that?"

A tremendous splash, so near to them that quite a wave rose and slightly rocked the boat as the boys sat there awe-stricken, listening and straining their eyes in the darkness which shut them in.

The noise occurred again—a great splash as of some mighty beast rearing itself out of the water and letting itself fall back, followed by a peculiar, wallowing noise.

This time it was lower and more as though it had passed the boat, and directly after there was another splash, followed by a heavy beating like something thrashing the water with its tail. Then came a smothered, bellowing grunt as if the great animal had begun to roar and then lowered its head half beneath the water, so that the noise was full of curious gurglings. The flapping of the water was repeated, and this time forty or fifty yards away, as near as they could guess, and once more there was silence.

"I didn't know there were such horrible beasts as that in the water," whispered Rob.

"Nor I. What can it be?"

"Must have been big enough to upset the boat if it had seen us, or to drag us out. Shall we wake Shaddy and ask him?"

"No," said Joe; "I don't suppose he would be able to tell us. It sounds so horrible in the darkness."

"Why, I thought you were too much used to the river to be frightened at anything."

"I did not say I was frightened," replied Joe quietly.

"No, but weren't you? I thought the thing was coming on right at the boat."

"So did I," said Joe, very softly. "Yes, I was frightened too. I don't think any one could help being startled at a thing like that."

"Because we could not see what it was," he continued thoughtfully. "I fancied I knew all the animals and fish about the river, but I never heard or saw anything that could be like that."

Just then they heard a soft, rustling sound behind, such, as might have been made by a huge serpent creeping on to the boat; and as they listened intently the sound continued, and the boat swayed slightly, going down on one side.

"It's coming on," whispered Rob, with his mouth feeling dry and a horrible dread assailing him, as in imagination he saw a huge scaly creature gliding along the side of the boat and passing the covered-in canvas cabin.

It was only a matter of moments, but it was like hours to the two boys. The feeling was upon Rob that he must run to the fore-part, leap overboard, and swim ashore, but he could not move. Every nerve and muscle was paralysed, and when he tried to speak to his fellow-watcher no words came; for, as Joe told his companion afterwards, he too tried to speak but was as helpless.

At last, in that long-drawn agony of dread, as he fully expected to be seized, Rob's presence of mind came back, and he recollected that his gun was lying shotted beneath the canvas of the sail at the side, and, seizing it with the energy of despair, he swung the piece round, cocking both barrels as he did so, and brought them into sharp contact with Joe's arm.

"Steady there with that gun," said a low familiar voice. "Don't shoot."

"Shaddy!" panted Rob.

"Me it is, lad. I crep' along so as not to disturb Mr Brazier. I say, did you hear that roar in the water?—but o' course you did. Know what it was?"

"No!" cried both boys in a breath. "Some great kind of amphibious thing," added Rob.

"'Phibious thing!—no. I couldn't see it, but there was no doubt about it: that threshing with the tail told me."

"Yes, we heard its tail beating," said Joe quickly. "What was it?"

"What was them, you mean! Well, I'll tell you. One of them tapir things must have been wading about in a shallow of mud, and a great 'gator got hold of him, and once he'd got hold he wouldn't let go, but hung on to the poor brute and kept on trying to drag him under water. Horrid things, 'gators. I should like to shoot the lot."

Rob drew a long breath very like a sigh. An alligator trying to drag down one of the ugly, old-world creatures that looks like a pig which has made up its mind to grow into an elephant, and failed—like the frog in the fable, only without going quite so far—after getting its upper lip sufficiently elongated to do some of the work performed by an elephant's trunk! One of these jungle swamp pachyderms and a reptile engaged in a struggle in the river, and not some terrible water-dragon with a serpentlike tail such as Rob's imagination had built up with the help of pictures of fossil animals and impossible objects from heraldry! It took all nervousness and mystery out of the affair, and made Rob feel annoyed that he had allowed his imagination to run riot and create such an alarming scene.

"Getting towards morning, isn't it?" said Joe hastily, and in a tone which told of his annoyance, too, that he also should have participated in the scare.

"Getting that way, lad, I s'pose. I ain't quite doo to relieve the watch, but I woke up and got thinking a deal about our job to-morrow, and that made me wakeful. And then there was that splashing and bellowing in the water, and I thought Mr Rob here would be a bit puzzled to know what it was. Course I knew he wouldn't be frightened."

"None of your sneering!" said Rob frankly. "I'm not ashamed to say that I was frightened, and very much frightened, too. It was enough to scare any one who did not know what it was."

"Right, my lad! enough to scare anybody!" said Shaddy, patting Rob on the shoulder. "It made me a bit squeery for a moment or two till I knew what it was. But, I say, when I came softly along to keep you company, you warn't going to shoot?"

"I'm afraid I was," said Rob. "It sounded just like some horrible great snake creeping along toward us out of the darkness."

"Then I'm glad I spoke," said Shaddy drily, "Spoiled your trip, lad, if you'd shot me, for I must have gone overboard, and if I'd come up again I don't bleeve as you'd have picked me up. Taken ever so long to get the boat free in the dark, and if you hadn't picked me up I don't see how you could have got on in the jungle. Look here, now you two gents have taken to gunning, I wouldn't shoot if I were you without asking a question or two first."

"But suppose it is a jaguar coming at us?" said Joe.

"Well, if it's a jagger he won't answer, and you had better shoot. Same with the lions or bears."

"Bears?" said Rob eagerly; "are there bears here?"

"Ay, lad! and plenty of 'em, not your big Uncle Ephrems, like there is in the Rocky Mountains—grizzlies, you know—but black bears, and pretty big, and plenty savage enough to satisfy any reasonable hunter, I mean one who don't expect too much. Wait a bit, and you'll get plenty of shooting to keep the pot going without reckoning them other things as Mr Brazier's come out to hunt. What d'yer call 'em, awk'ards or orchards—which was it?"

"Orchids," said Rob.

"Oh! ah! yes, orchids. What's best size shot for bringing o' them down?"

"Don't answer him, Rob; it's only his gammon, and he thinks it's witty," said Joe.

Shaddy chuckled, and it was evident that his joke amused him.

"There," he said, "it ain't worth while for three on us to be keeping watch. One's enough, and the others can sleep, so, as I'm here, you two may as well go and roost."

"No," said Rob promptly; "my time isn't up."

"No, my lad, not by two hours, I should say; but I'll let you off the rest, for it's a-many years since I was up this part, and I want to sit and think it out before we start as soon as it's light."

But Rob firmly refused to give up his task till the time set down by Mr Brazier for him to be relieved. Joe as stubbornly refused to return to his bed, and so it was that when the birds gave note of the coming of the day, after the weird chorus had gradually died away in the forest they were still seated upon one of the thwarts, watching for the first warm rays of the sun to tinge the dense river mist with rose.

Chapter Six.

Through the Green Curtain.

A fair breeze sprang up with the sun, and the boat glided up stream for many miles before a halt was called, in a bend where the wind railed them. Here, as on previous occasions, a fire was lit, and the breakfast prepared and eaten almost in silence, for Brazier's thoughts were far up the river and away among the secret recesses of nature, where he hoped to be soon gazing upon vegetation never yet seen by civilised man, while Rob and Joe were just as thoughtful, though their ideas ran more upon the wild beasts and lovely birds of this tropic land, into which as they penetrated mile after mile it was to see something ever fresh and attractive.

Shaddy, too, was very silent, and sat scanning the western shore more and more attentively as the hours passed, and they were once more gliding up stream, the wind serving again and again as they swept round some bend.

The sun grew higher, and the heat more intense, the slightest movement as they approached noon making a dew break out over Rob's brow; but the warmth was forgotten in the beauty of the shore and the abundance of life visible around.

But at last the heat produced such a sense of drowsiness that Rob turned to Joe.

"I say, wouldn't an hour or two be nice under the shade of a tree?"

"Yes," said Brazier, who had overheard him. "We must have a rest now; the sides of the boat are too hot to touch. Hullo! where are we going?" he continued. "Why, he's steering straight for the western shore."

Brazier involuntarily stooped and took his gun from where it hung in loops under the canvas awning, and then stood watching the dense wall of verdure they were approaching till, as they drew nearer, their way was through acres upon acres of lilies, whose wide-spreading leaves literally covered the calm river with their dark green discs, dotted here and there with great buds or dazzlingly white blossoms.

The boat cut its way through these, leaving a narrow canal of clear water at first, in which fish began to leap as if they had been disturbed; but before the boat had gone very far the leaves gradually closed in, and no sign of its passage was left.

"I don't see where we are to land," said Brazier, as he stood in front of the canvas cabin scanning the shore.

"No; there is no place," said Rob, as they glided out of the lily field into clear water, the great wall of trees tangled together with creepers being now about two hundred yards away.

"Go and ask. No; leave him alone," said Brazier, altering his mind. "He'll take us into a suitable place, I daresay."

Just then Shaddy, from where he was steering, shouted to the men, who lowered the sail at once; but the boat still glided on straight for the shore.

"Why, he's going to run her head right into the bank," cried Rob, though the said bank was rendered invisible by the curtain of pendent boughs and vines which hung right down to the water.

"How beautiful!" exclaimed Brazier, as he gazed at clusters of snowy blossoms draping one of the trees. "We must have some of those, Rob."

"I say," cried Joe, "what makes the boat keep on going?"

"Impetus given by the sail," replied Brazier. "But it couldn't have kept on all this time," cried the lad, "and we're going faster."

"We do seem to be," said Brazier; "but it is only that we are in an eddy. There always is one close in by the banks of a swift stream."

"But that goes upward while the stream goes down," cried Joe. "This is going straight in toward the trees."

"Better sit down, every one," shouted Shaddy. "Lower that spar, my lads," he added, in the *patois* the men used.

Down went the mast in a sloping position, so that it rested against the canvas cabin. But Rob hardly noticed this in the excitement of their position. For there was no doubt about it: some invisible force had apparently seized the boat, and was carrying it swiftly forward to dash it upon the shore.

But that was not Brazier's view of the question. "The river is flooded here and overrunning the bank," he cried. "Hi! Naylor! Do you see where you're going?"

"Right, sir. Sit down."

But Brazier, who had risen, did not sit down, for he was quite startled, expecting that the next moment the boat would be capsized, and that they would all be left to the mercy of the reptiles and fish which haunted the rapid waters.

"Hi!" he shouted again. "Naylor, are you mad?"

"No, sir, not yet," was the reply. "Better sit down. Mind your hat!"

For all through this the boat was gliding slowly but straight for the curtain of leaves and flowers which hid the bank of the western side of the river; and as the position seemed perilous to Rob, he saw with astonishment that the four Indian boatmen lay calmly back furling up the sail as if nothing was the matter, or else showing that they had perfect faith in their leader and steersman, who was not likely to lead them into danger.

What followed only took moments. They were out in the dazzling sunshine, were rapidly, as it seemed, approaching the bank, and directly after plunged right into the lovely curtain of leaves and flowers which swept over them as they glided on over the surface of the swiftly running clear black water, the sun entirely screened and all around them a delicious twilight, with densely planted, tall, columnar trees apparently rising out of the flood on either hand, while a rush and splash here and there told that they were disturbing some of the dwellers in these shades.

"What does this mean?" said Brazier, stooping to recover his hat which had been swept off on to the canvas awning, and which he only just recovered before it slipped into the stream.

There was no answer to the question as they watched, and then they saw light before them, which rapidly brightened till they glided into sunshine and found that they had passed through a second curtain of leaves, and were in a little river of some hundred yards wide, with lovely verdure on either side rising like some gigantic hedge to shut them in; in fact, a miniature reproduction of the grand stream they had so lately left.

"Why, Naylor," cried Brazier, "I thought you were going to run us ashore or capsize us."

"Yes, sir, I know you did," was the reply.

"But where are we? What place is this?"

"This here's the river I wanted to bring you to, sir."

"But it does not run into the Paraguay, it runs out."

"Yes, sir, it do. It's a way it has. It's a curious place, as you'll say before we've done."

"But it seems impossible. How can it run like this?"

"Dunno, sir. Natur' made it, not me. I've never been up it very far, but it strikes me it's something to do with the big waterworks higher up the big river."

"Waterworks! Why, surely—"

"Natur's waterworks, sir, not man's; the big falls many miles to the north."

Rob and Joe exchanged glances.

"Strikes me as the river being very full here the bank give way once upon a time, and this stream winds about till it gets close up to where the falls come down."

"But water can't go up hill, man."

"No, sir, course not; but I thought that if it goes along some valley up to the mountains where the falls come down, it would be an easy way of getting to the foot of the high ground and striking the big river again."

"Stop a moment: I have heard some talk of a great cascade up north."

"Yes, sir, where nobody's never been yet. Seemed to me as it was rather in your way, and you might find some orchids up there as well as here."

"Of course, of course!" cried Brazier; the idea of being first in the field with a great discovery making his pulses throb. "Tell me all about it."

"Right, sir, when we've had something to eat. It's 'bout twelve o'clock, and here's a shady place, so if you give the word we'll land and cook a bit. Place looks noo, don't it, sir?"

"New, Naylor! I can never thank you enough."

"Don't try then, sir," said Shaddy, steering the boat in, and with the help of the boatmen laying it ashore close to some huge trees. "Now we shall have to make her fast, for if our boat gets loose the stream will carry her where nobody will ever find her again."

"I can't understand it," said Brazier impatiently, as the Indians leaped ashore, one to make a rope fast, the others to light a fire; "this stream running out of the main river is contrary to nature, unless where it divides at its mouths."

"Not it, sir; it's right enough. Right down south in the Parana the river does it lots of times, for the waters there are like a big net all over the land, and— I say, Mr Rob, sir, where's your gun? There's a carpincho just yonder among them reeds. Try for it, sir; we can manage with it for a bit o' roast and boiled."

Rob seized the piece, and Shaddy pointed out the spot where he was to fire and hit the beast in the shoulder, but just then they were interrupted by a hideous yell.

Chapter Seven.

The First "Tiger."

The cry, which thrilled Rob and made Brazier and the young Italian seize their weapons, came from one of the Indians, who, axe in hand, had been about to cut up a dead bough he had seized for the fire, when something dark struck him in the chest, sending him backward amongst the low growth, and a magnificent cat-like animal bounded into the middle of the opening, driving the boatmen among the trees and taking up its position in the bright sunshine, with its coat glistening and the brown spots on its tawny hide shining with almost metallic lustre.

And there it stood, with its ears lowered and eyes blazing, looking from one to another of the occupants of the boat, and from them to Shaddy, who leaped ashore knife in hand, while the brute's tail writhed and twisted as if it were a serpent.

"Hadn't one of you better shoot?" said Shaddy calmly. "He's, too much for me with only a knife."

Just then the Indian who had been knocked down began to crawl cautiously toward the trees.

The movement was enough for the jaguar. It was the cat again that has stricken down a mouse standing perfectly careless till the unfortunate little animal begins to stir. The fierce beast turned, gathered itself together, and was about to launch itself upon the boatman in one tremendous bound, when simultaneously there was a sharp click from Brazier's gun, but with no further result, for he had drawn the trigger of his rifled barrel in which there was no cartridge, and a sharp stab on the loins as Shaddy hurled his knife with unerring aim at the savage beast.

The jaguar turned with a fierce snarl and struck the knife from where it stuck in its back. Then, seeing in Shaddy its assailant, it crouched again to bound upon the guide.

Once again its aim was spoiled; for with fingers trembling Rob had cocked his piece and taken aim, being about to fire when the knife was thrown; but the rapid movement of the animal checked him till it crouched and he saw it about to spring upon Shaddy.

This time he pressed the stock firmly to his shoulder, and, taking aim at the jaguar's head, fired twice, the first charge taking effect full in the creature's back, and, as it sprang up, the second in its flank.

With a fierce howl it twisted itself round and bit at the side, tearing out the glossy fur in its rage and pain. Then turning sharply it looked round for its assailant, when Joe's piece rang out, the bad powder with which it was heavily loaded making a cloud of dense smoke which prevented Rob from seeing for a few moments, and when it rose the jaguar had gone.

They all busied themselves reloading now, but there was no animal to shoot, and Shaddy picked up his knife, wiping its point carefully on his trousers as he straightened himself.

"Which way did it go?" cried Brazier.

"Yonder, sir, through the trees. But it's of no use for you to follow."

"It must be dangerously wounded."

"Not it, sir; only a bit tickled. That was only bird shot you fired, was it, my lads?"

"Number 5," said Rob promptly.

"Thought so. Best keep a bullet always in your guns, gentlemen, out here, for you never know what's going to turn up next."

The Indians were back now, going about picking wood for the fire as if nothing whatever had happened.

"But that man," whispered Rob; "isn't he hurt—clawed?"

"No, sir," replied Shaddy calmly; and he asked a question of the man in the mixed Indian tongue. Then turning to Brazier, "Only got the wind knocked, out of him a bit, sir. No clawing. He don't mind."

"But the brute may come back," said Rob.

"Well, Mr Rob, sir, if he do he's a bigger fool than I take him to be. No, there'll be no coming back about him. Just while he was up he was ready to fly at anything, but every one of them little shot will make a sore place which it will take him a fortnight to lick quite well again. I daresay they're all lying just under his skin."

"And what a skin!" cried Rob. "You could have got it off and cured it for me, couldn't you?"

"Oh yes, or these chaps here, sir; but if you wants tiger jackets you mustn't try to kill them as wears 'em with Number 5 shot.—Now, lads, more wood," and a good fire was soon burning, over which the kettle was hung.

A meal was quickly prepared, but Shaddy indulged in a bit of a growl over it.

"And me 'specting pork chops frizzled over that fire on the iron sheet," he said. "Why it wouldn't have been no good, my lad, going about with a pinch of lead snuff in your gun. You want something like small marbles out here, I can tell you, or good buck shot. You'll mind that next time."

"But I want to get some of the birds we see," said Rob, in tones of remonstrance.

"That's right, sir; but keep one barrel always for play and one for work. I don't want to make too much of it, but in a country like this it must be dangerous sometimes."

"He is quite right, Rob," said Brazier. "He is giving you a lesson, but he means some of it for me. Don't you, Naylor?"

"Well, sir," said Shaddy grimly, "I s'pose you'd like the honest truth?"

"Of course."

"Then I'll tell you what I said to myself. How a gentleman at his time o' life could leave his weepun, as ought to be ready for action, without a good bullet for wild beast or Indian, I can't think."

"I have learned my lesson, Naylor," said Brazier, "and you shall not have an opportunity for reproaching me again."

"And you ain't offended, sir? In course I'm only like your servant."

"Give me credit for more sense, my man.—You take it to heart, too, both of you, and keep a bullet in your left-hand barrel."

"For food or enemy," said Shaddy in his deep growl.

"But that's what I meant to do. I thought I had loaded that way," said Rob.

"Hah—hoo!" ejaculated one of the Indians who was standing with his arms full of wood close to the spot where the jaguar had disappeared.

"What's the matter, my lad?" said Shaddy, joining him with the others, when an eager burst of conversation ensued.

"They say as the tiger's lying wounded not far in among the trees. Bring your guns, gentlemen."

The pieces were eagerly raised and cartridges examined, so that there should be no further mistake, and then, with the Indian who was knocked down as a guide, Brazier next with Shaddy, who contented himself with his knife, and then Rob and Joe and the rest of the Indians, the party entered the forest, which was so dense that they soon had to take to Indian file.

But they had not far to go, and in spite of the danger that might be ahead the leading Indian proved that Shaddy's selection was a good one, for he went straight on, cutting right and left with his heavy knife to divide the growth that was in their way, and so on for about fifty yards, when he stopped short and said a few words to Shaddy.

"Yes. Get back," said the latter, after listening. "Now two guns forward; but I think he has had enough as it is?"

"Be careful, man!" said Brazier anxiously; "you are unarmed."

"Not quite, sir!" said Shaddy, showing his big knife. "If he jumps on me he'll jump right on to that point, and if he does, though he may claw me, it will be his last leap. Silence!"

They all listened, Rob hearing the shriek of some great parrot and the dull heavy throb of his heart, but from out of the dense growth a little way ahead he could make out a gurgling moan.

Shaddy gave him a look and a nod.

"No, my lad," he said, "that isn't a frog, nor anything else, but some animal as has got his death. It's either that tiger, or else it's a deer he has pulled down on his way. I'll go and see."

"Let me," said Brazier; "and if it is only wounded I can fire again."

"Powder and shot's valuable out here, sir," said Shaddy, "and we mustn't waste a single charge. Stand fast, and if I want help come and give it to me; but I shan't."

He parted the bushes and creepers with his left hand holding his knife well before him with the right; but before he had gone six yards with great caution there was a horrible cry, and a sound as of a struggle going on—a sound which made Rob press forward and thrust the barrel of his gun in front of Brazier.

"Has he got hold of Shaddy?" he panted, with a chill of horror running through him.

"No, my lad; I'm all right—it's all over," cried the guide, as the sound ceased. "Ah! I can see him plain now: quite dead."

"A deer?" said Brazier, eagerly.

"Deer don't make a noise like that, sir," said Joe from behind.

"Nay, it's no deer," said Shaddy; "I'll let you see what it is. Hi!" he called; and the Indians crowded past through the dense growth, went boldly right to the front, and Shaddy reappeared smiling.

"Back again," he said; "they'll bring him along."

Rob turned back unwillingly, for he was eager to see what the dead animal might be, Shaddy's mysterious manner suggesting the possibility of its being something extraordinary. But he followed the others out, the guide seeming to drive them all before him back into the open spot by the fire, while almost directly after the Indian boatmen appeared, half carrying, half dragging—each holding a paw—with his white under fur stained with blood—the great jaguar, perfectly dead.

"There," cried Shaddy, "now you can have your skin, sir; and you deserve it for those two shots."

"But I couldn't have—" began Rob.

"But you did, sir," said Shaddy, who was down on his knees by the beautiful animal. "Here you are: face and head all full of small shot, and down here right in the loins—yes: back regularly broken by a bullet. Your piece was loaded proper after all."

"A splendid shot, Rob," cried Brazier, and Joe patted his back.

"But it was quite an accident," said Rob, excitedly.

"Accident?" growled Shaddy. "If you shot at a man in England and killed him, do you think the judge would say it was an accident?"

"Well, no," said Rob, laughing.

"'Course not. Splendid shot, as the captain says. So now let's finish our bit of eating and have a nap while my chaps here takes off the skin."

Chapter Eight.

Hidden Dangers.

It did not take the lads long to finish the interrupted meal, seated in the shade of a magnificent tree, one side of which sent out branches and pensile boughs laden with leaf and flower from the summit almost to the ground, while the other side was comparatively bare, so closely was it placed to the dense crowd of its fellows whose limbs were matted together and enlaced with creepers of endless variety, out from which the sheltering tree stood like a huge, green, smoothly rounded buttress, formed by nature to support the green wall which surrounded her forest fastness.

As soon as they had eaten their meal the two lads hurried off to where the boatmen were deftly skinning the great cat-like creature,—rather a disgusting operation, but one full of interest, as limb after limb was cut down right to the toes and the skin stripped away, to show the tremendous muscles and sinews which enabled the animal to bound like lightning upon its prey.

"Seems a pity to waste so much good, fresh meat when a bit would be welcome, eh?" said Shaddy, with a grim smile.

"Would you like to eat some of it?" asked Joe.

Shaddy shook his head.

"No," he said, "I should as soon think of roasting a tom-cat at home and calling it hare. Rum thing it seems, though, that those creatures which live upon one another should be rank and nasty, while those which eat fruit and green-stuff should be good. Keep your guns ready, my lads. It's very quiet here, and you may get a shot at something good for the supper to-night: some big pigeons, or a turkey, or— I'll tell you, though; I can hear 'em rustling about in the trees now. They'll be easy, too, for a shot."

"What? Parrots?"

"Nay, better than them. A nice, plump young monkey or two."

"What?" roared Rob.

"A nice young monkey or two; and don't shout, my lad. If you make that noise, we shan't be able to hear anything coming."

"Bah!" cried Joe. "I should feel like a cannibal if I even thought of it. I say, look at Mr Brazier!"

Rob turned and smiled as he saw his leader eagerly making up for lost time, and, after climbing about twenty feet up a tree with a hatchet in his belt, holding on with one hand while he cut off a great bunch of flowers hanging from the bough upon which, like so much large mistletoe, it had taken root.

Shaddy saw him almost at the same moment, and turned to the tree, followed by the lads.

"I say, sir, don't do that!" he said, respectfully.

"Why not, my man? We are not trespassing, and damaging anybody's property here."

Shaddy laughed.

"No, sir, you won't do much trespassing here," he said.

"Then why do you interfere? This is a magnificent orchid, different from any that I have ever seen. I thought you understood that I have come on purpose to collect these."

"Oh yes, I understand, sir; but you're captain, and have got to order. We'll get 'em for you. My four chaps'll climb the trees better, and be handier with the axe; and as they'll have scarcely anything to do, we'll set 'em to work at that sort of thing."

"They will have the rowing to do."

"Precious little, sir, now. The rowing's done. All we've got to do is to float along the stream."

"Ah, well, I'll finish this time, and they shall do it another."

"Better come down now, sir," whispered Shaddy. "You see they're a dull, stupid lot, who look up to white people as their natural masters; and, without being a brute to 'em, the more you stands off and treats 'em as if they were servants the more they look up to you. If you don't, and they see you doing work that they're paid to do, they'll look down on you, think you're afraid of 'em, and grow saucy."

"Ah!" ejaculated Brazier, giving a start, and nearly losing his hold of the branch.

"What's the matter, sir?"

For answer Brazier cut frantically with his axe at something invisible to those below, but evidently without avail, till he struck a small bough so violently that they saw the object dropping down, and Rob had only time to leap aside to avoid a small snake, of a vivid green with red markings, which fell just where he had been standing, and then began to twine in and out rapidly, and quite unhurt, ending by making its escape into the dense forest, where it was impossible to follow.

"Did you kill it?" cried Brazier from up in the tree.

"No," said Rob; "it's gone!"

"Ah," said Shaddy, thoughtfully, "I never thought to warn you against them. That's a poisonous one, I think, and they climb up the trees and among the flowers to get the young birds and eggs and beetles and things. Better always rattle a stick in amongst the leaves, sir, before you get handling them. Try again, now, with the handle of the hatchet."

Brazier obeyed, and snatched his hand back directly, as he held on with his left, after violently striking the branch close to the plant he tried to secure.

"There's another here," he said.

"Better come away, sir!" cried Rob.

"No; I must have this bunch. I have nearly cut the boughs clear from it, and a stroke or two then will divide the stem, and it will drop clear on to those bushes."

"Shall I come, sir?"

"No; I'll keep away from where the thing lies. It is coiled-up, and I only saw its head."

"Better mind, sir: they're rum things. Only got one inch o' neck one moment, and the next they're holding on by their tails, and seem to have three foot."

"I'll take care," said Brazier. "Stand from below; I shall cut the stem at once."

There was the sharp sound of the hatchet, as he gave a well-directed cut, and then a rustling, and the gorgeous bunch of flowers dropped, with all its bulbous stems and curious fleshy elongated leaves, right on the top of the clump of bushes beneath the great bough.

"All right!" cried Rob: "not hurt a bit. Oh, how beautiful!"

"Mind, will you!" cried Shaddy, savagely: "do you hear?"

He whipped out his knife as he stepped forward, and made a rapid cut horizontally above the bunch of orchids. For as Rob approached, with outstretched hand, to lift off this, the first-fruits of their exploration, a little spade-shaped head suddenly shot up with two brilliant eyes sparkling in the sun, was drawn back to strike, and darted forward.

But not to strike Rob's defenceless hand, for Shaddy's keen knife-blade met it a couple of inches below the gaping jaws, cut clean through its scale-armed skin, and the head dropped among the lovely petals of the orchis, while the body, twisting and twining upon itself in a knot, went down through the bush and could be heard rustling and beating the leaves out of sight.

There was a peculiar grey look on Rob's face as he looked at Shaddy.

"Only just in time, master," said the latter. "It'll be a lesson to you both in taking care."

Rob shuddered; but, making an effort, he said, laughing dismally, "I don't suppose it was a venomous snake, after all."

"Praps not," said Shaddy drily. "There, lift the bunch down with the bar'l of your gun. Shove the muzzle right in."

"You do it, Joe," whispered Rob; "I feel a bit sick. It's the sun, I think."

Just then Mr Brazier, who had been scrambling down the trunk of the huge tree by means of the parasites, which gave endless places for hold, dropped to the ground, and stood beating and shaking himself, to get rid of the ants and other insects he had gathered in his trip up to the branch.

"Ah! that's right, Giovanni," he said; "no, I must call you Joe, as Rob does."

"Do, please, sir; it's ever so much shorter. Here it is," he continued, as he lifted the bunch of lovely blossoms off the bush on to the clear space where they stood.

"Oh, if I could only show that in London, just as it is!" cried Brazier. "Why, that bunch alone almost repays me for my journey: it is so beautiful and new."

"Give it a shake, Mr Joe, sir!" said Shaddy.

"Ah, yes, let's make sure."

"Can't be anything else in it," said Rob boisterously, in his desire to hide the fact that he had been terribly frightened.

"Never you mind whether there is or whether there ain't, sir," said Shaddy; "I want that there bunch shook."

Joe gave a few jerks, and at the last something fell with a light *plip* in amongst the leaves at their feet.

"Ah!" ejaculated their guide; and, bending down, he pressed the leaves aside with the point of his knife till he saw the object which had fallen, and carefully took it up with his left finger and thumb to hold out before the others the head and about an inch or so of the little snake—one much thinner, but otherwise about the size of an English adder.

"Horrid-looking little thing," said Rob carelessly; "but I don't think it's poisonous."

Shaddy gave a grunt, and holding the neck tightly, he thrust the point of his knife in between the reptile's jaws, opened them, and then shifting his fingers to the angle, he held the snake's head upside down, and with the point of the blade raised from where they lay back on the roof of the mouth, close to the nose, two tiny glass-like teeth, the creature's fangs, which could be held back or erected at its pleasure.

"Not much doubt about them, sir," said Shaddy.

"Not the slightest," replied Brazier, frowning. "We've both had narrow escapes, Rob."

"You have, sir, and all for want of knowing better, if you'll excuse me. What you've got to do is to look upon everything as dangerous till you've found out as it's safe. And that you must do, please, for I can't help you here. If it's a clawing from a lion or tiger, or a dig from a deer's horn, or a bite of 'gator, or a broken limb, or spear wound, or even a bullet-hole, I'm all there. I'll undertake to pull you through a bit of fever too, or any or'nary complaint, and all without pretending to be a doctor. But as to fighting against snake poison, I'm just like a baby. I couldn't help you a bit, so don't get running your hands among the things anywhere. They'll get out of your way fast enough if you give them a chance; so just help me by minding that."

One of the boatmen came up and said something in a sour way to the speaker, who added,—

"They've skinned the tiger, and want to know what to do with the carkidge, sir. Come along with me, and I'll show you something else."

"No, no: stop a moment. Look here!" cried Joe.

They all turned to where he stood holding the bunch on his gun-barrel, and saw his eyes fixed upon something playing about—a great humble-bee apparently—which paused before one of the orchid blossoms.

The little thing was dull-looking, and they saw directly after that it was probing the flowers with a long curved beak.

"Humming bird," cried Rob; "but I thought that they were bright-coloured."

In an instant, as if it had heard his words, the tiny creature changed its position to such an angle with the sun that for a few seconds its breast glowed with gorgeous green and flame-coloured scales, which looked as if they had been cut out of some wonderful metal to protect the bird's breast. Its wings moved so rapidly that they were invisible, and the beautiful little object seemed to be surrounded by a filmy haze of a little more than the diameter of a cricket-ball.

Again there was a sharp motion, such as is noted in one kind of fly in an English summer, when it can be seen poised for a few moments apparently immovable, but with its wings beating at lightning speed. And as the humming bird changed its position the breast feathers looked dark and dull, while its head displayed a crest of dazzling golden green.

It appeared to have no dread of the group of human beings close to it, but probed blossom after blossom as calmly as a bee would at home; and it was from no movement they made that it suddenly made a dart and was gone.

"Pretty creatures!" said Shaddy, smiling, and looking the last man in the world likely to admire a bird; "you've come to the right place for them, gentlemen. Those lads of mine would soon make blowpipes and arrows, and knock you a few down, or I could if you wanted 'em, with one of your guns."

"The shots would cut them to pieces," said Brazier.

"To be sure they would, sir, and I shouldn't use none. I've knocked one down with a charge of powder, shot off pretty close, and other times with half a teaspoonful of sand in the gun. But I tell you what acts best, only you can't do it with a breechloader. It must be an old muzzle gun, and after you've rammed down your powder very tight with a strong wad, you pour in a little water, and fire soon as you can. You get a shower then as brings 'em down without damaging your bird."

"Let's look at the jaguar skin," said Rob; and stepping aside to where the boatmen stood in the broad sunshine, instead of gazing upon the tawny fur, with its rich spots of dark brown along back and flanks, shading off into soft white, he found, stretched out tightly by pegs, a sheet of unpleasant-looking fleshy skin, hardening in the ardent sunshine, which drove out its moisture at a rapid rate.

"Do it no end of good to stop like that till to-morrow," said Shaddy. "It would be pretty nigh stiff and hard by then."

"But I don't want it stiff and hard," cried Rob. "I want it soft, like a leather rug."

"Yes, sir, I know," replied the guide. "Let's get it dry first; I can soon make it soft afterwards."

Brazier was looking round the open patch of slightly sloping ground, about half an acre in extent, forming quite a nook in the forest through which the river ran.

"There is plenty of work here for a day or two," he said; "and it is a suitable place for our halt."

"Couldn't be better, sir. We shan't find another so good."

"Then we'll stop for one day, certain."

"'Cording to that, then," said Shaddy thoughtfully, "we'd better take the carkidge somewhere else."

"Of course—get rid of it or bury it. Before long in this sun it will be offensive. Why not throw it in the river?"

"That's what I meant to do, sir; but I was a bit scared about drawing the 'gators about us. Don't want their company. If they see that came from here they'll be waiting about for more. I dunno, though; perhaps the stream'll carry it down half a mile before they pull it under or it sinks."

He made a sign to the boatmen, who seized the carcass of the jaguar, bore it just below where the boat was moored, and the two lads followed to see it consigned to the swift river.

Here the men stood close to the edge, and acting in concert under Shaddy's direction, they swung the carcass to and fro two or three times, gathering impetus at every sway, and then with one tremendous effort and a loud expiration of the breath they sent it flying several yards, for it to fall with a tremendous splash and sink slowly, the lighter-coloured portions being quite plain in the clear water as it settled down, sending great rings to each shore. Then the carcass rose slowly to the surface and began to float down-stream.

"Look," cried Rob the next instant, as the smooth water suddenly became agitated, and dark shadows appeared to be moving beneath the surface. Then the jaguar moved suddenly to one side, as if it were alive, then back, to alter its course directly straight away from them, and again to begin travelling up stream; while the water boiled all round about it, and several silvery fish flashed out of the water and fell back; then heads and tails appeared as the fierce occupants of the river fought for morsels which they bit out of the flanks and limbs of the dead animal.

"Makes 'em mad to get at it," said Shaddy, as the water grew more disturbed; "they're coming up the river in shoals. You see there's no skin to get through and fill their teeth with hair. Say, youngsters, talk about ground bait, don't you wish you'd got your tackle ready? Might catch some good ones for supper."

"And eat them after they've been feeding on that animal?"

"Better have them after feeding on that, Rob," said Brazier, "than after a feast of I don't know what. Why not try, Naylor?"

"No meat for a bait, sir. Let's wait till they've done, and then I'll fish for a dorado. We've got some oranges left."

He ceased speaking, and they stood watching the carcass, which still floated, from the simple fact that a shoal of fish were attacking it from below, while so many came swarming, up from lower down the stream, attracted by the odour of the pieces of the jaguar, and the many fragments which ascended and floated away, that the carcass not only could not sink but was driven higher and higher toward the main river.

"Hah!" ejaculated Shaddy suddenly, "I thought that was coming."

For suddenly there were dozens of silvery fish leaping in the air to fall back into the water, which ceased to boil, and a wave formed by the shoal swept down-stream.

"What's that mean?" cried Rob. "Why, they've left it."

"Yes, sir, *they* have," said Shaddy, emphasising the personal pronoun. "Look!"

A fresh splash about twenty yards from them had already taken Rob's attention, and then there was another caused by a peculiar dark-looking object, which rose above the surface.

"'Gator's tail," said Shaddy, grimly. "It's their turn now, and the hungry fishes have to make room."

Just then a long black, muddy-looking snout glided out of the water, followed by the head, shoulders and back of a hideous lizard-like creature, which glided over the carcass of the jaguar and disappeared, followed directly by a head twice as large, and as it rose clear of the water the jaws opened wide and closed with a loud snap. Directly after this head sank down out of sight there was a tremendous swirl in the water, and then it began to settle down, but only to be disturbed once more about opposite to where the party stood, and again some twenty yards lower down, after which the river ran swiftly and smoothly once more.

"That was an old bull 'gator," said Shaddy. "The small ones, three or four, came first and scared off all the fish that didn't want to be eaten, and then the old chap came and soon sent them to the right-about, and he has carried off the carkidge to enjoy all to himself down in some hole under the bank."

"Plenty of natural history for you here, boys," said Brazier, "eh?"

"Yes; but how horrid!" cried Rob. "And yet how beautiful it all is to compensate!" said Brazier, thoughtfully. "But what about something fresh to eat, Naylor? We must shoot something, or you must fish. There, Rob, you said how horrid just now; and yet we are as bad. The alligators and fish only sought for their daily food. We are going to do worse than they did with our guns and tackle. Well, Naylor, what are we to do?"

"I'm thinking, sir, that if the young gents here, or one of them, will try a fishing-line with an orange or half an orange bait, you might sit quiet at your corner and watch for something—bush turkey, or parrots even, for they're good eating."

"But suppose I shoot a bird, and it falls in the river, what then?"

"Why, we must go after it with the boat; but I expect that something or another would take it down before we could get to it. This river swarms, sir, with big fish and 'gators."

"Why not go a few hundred yards into the forest? We might put up a deer."

"Dessay you would, sir, if you could get in. Why, you couldn't get in a dozen yards without men to hack a way for you; and if you went in alone, even so far, it's a chance if you could find your way out again. You'll have to be careful about that."

"Why?" said Rob, eagerly. "The wild beasts?"

"They're the least trouble, sir," replied Shaddy. "It's the getting lost. A man who is lost in these forests may almost as well lie down and die at once out of his misery, for there's no chance of his getting back again."

"I'm afraid you try to make the worst of things, Naylor," said Brazier, smiling. "Well, I'll take my position at the corner yonder while you lads fish."

Rob felt as if he would far rather try his luck with a gun, for he wanted to practise shooting; and Shaddy read the disappointment in his face.

"It'll be all right, my lad," he said, as Brazier went to the boat to get some different cartridges; "you'll have plenty of chances of shooting for the pot by-and-by. Why, you haven't done so very bad to-day—bagging a whole tiger. Here, I'll help you rig up a line."

"And suppose I hook one of those alligators?"

"Hardly likely, my lad; but if you do it will be bad for the 'gator or bad for your line. One'll have to come, or the other'll have to go."

Just then Brazier returned from the boat with the cartridge-pouch and examining the breech of his gun, after which he walked slowly to the corner of the green opening and took his place close to the edge of the river, where he was partly hidden by some pendent boughs, while Rob, Joe, and Shaddy got on board the boat again, and were soon fitting up a line with an orange bait.

"May as well fish from the boat, my lads," said Shaddy; "it's peaceabler and comfortabler. What do you say?"

"No," said Joe, "but one from the boat, and one from the other corner there. If we fish together we shall get our lines tangled."

"Right, my Hightalian man o' wisdom," said Shaddy. "There you are, then," he continued, as he fixed the half of an orange as securely as he could; "you begin there, and Mr Rob will try up yonder, while I'll go to and fro with the gaff hook ready to help whichever of you wants a hand."

"Hi! you chaps," he shouted to the men in their own tongue, as they were settling themselves down for a long sleep, "make that fire up again; we're going to stop here to-night."

"I wish I could speak their language, Shaddy," said Rob, as the men deliberately began to pile some of the wood they had collected on the embers.

"You'll soon pick it up, my lad. It's soft and easy enough. Not as I speak it, you know, because I'm so rough and keep chopping in broken English. They're not bad fellows. But now look here," he continued, as they reached their corner where the stream flowed very deep and made quite an eddy; "it strikes me that the best thing we can do is to try a different bait, one as will tempt the fish that don't care so much for flesh. What do you say to a quarter of a biscuit?"

"Too hard, and will not stick on."

"Get soft in the water; and it will stick on, for I shall tie it with some thin string, making quite a net round it."

"That will do then," said Rob, who felt some compunction at trying for fish which had been lunching off a large cat; and in due time the bait was carefully bound on.

"This place will suit," said Shaddy, "because the water will carry the hook out softly right toward the middle in this eddy, and we shan't have to throw and knock off our bait. Ready?"

Bang!

Chapter Nine.

The Double Catch.

The sharp report was from Brazier's piece, and as all looked round it was to see a large turkey-like bird beating and flapping the ground with its strong pinions, evidently being badly wounded.

"Ah!" cried Shaddy, "that'll be better meat than our fish;" and dropping the line, he trotted towards the spot where the bird lay close to the edge of the forest, just as Brazier started on the same mission from his end of the opening; while quite a flock of small birds and a troop of monkeys came flying and bounding through the trees, as if to see what was the meaning of the strange noise, and filling the air with their chatterings and cries, but hardly displaying the slightest dread.

"I happened to look round," cried Brazier, "and saw it come out from among the trees."

This was just as he and Shaddy neared the bird, where it lay half a dozen yards from the dense mass of interwoven foliage, when, to the disgust of both, the bird suddenly rose to its feet, made a bound, and, with its wings whistling loudly, flew right in through an opening, while its would-be captors were brought up short by the to them impenetrable forest.

"How vexatious!" cried Brazier, stamping his foot.

"There goes our supper!" grumbled Shaddy; "and that's about the joociest bird I know."

"I wish I'd given it the other barrel," said Brazier.

"Better load, sir," said Shaddy. "Never mind. You'll get another chance soon. Eh? Oh, very well then, have a try."

This was to one of the boatmen, who, roused by the shot, came up smiling with his sword-like knife in his hand, evidently with the intention of cutting his way in and trying to retrieve the bird.

"I don't think it is of any use," said Brazier.

"Dunno, sir. Perhaps it is. The bird was hard hit, and maybe hasn't gone far. Let him try. He may just as well do that as lie and sleep."

They both stopped for a few minutes watching the man, who bent down, and going on all-fours, passed in between the interlacing growth. They saw his feet for a few moments, and then he disappeared altogether, while Brazier and Shaddy both returned to their stations.

"What a pity!" grumbled the latter. "'Bout the nicest birds I know—when you're hungry. There'll be another shot for him soon, though, for they go in flocks in open bits of land near water."

"What bird was it?" said Rob—"a turkey?"

"Nay, not so big as a turkey, lad; I dunno what they call 'em. I call 'em Argentine larks."

"What?" cried Rob, with a laugh.

"Ah, you may grin, my lad, but it ain't such a bad name; and if you'd seen 'em do what I have, you'd say so too."

"What do you mean?" said Rob; "do they make their nests on the ground?"

"I don't know nothing about their nests, but I'll tell you what they do: they rise off the ground and fly up in the air higher and higher, and sail round and round singing just like a lark does, only lots of times as loud."

Rob looked keenly in the man's face.

"Oh, I ain't a-stuffing of you with nonsense, my lad; that 'ere's a nat'ral history fact. They flies up singing away till they're out of sight, and the music comes down so soft and sweet then that it makes you want more and more, as you get thinking of when you was away in the country at home."

"But that bird was so big," cried Rob.

"All the better, my lad. Holds more music and sings all the longer."

"Caught anything?" asked Joe from the boat, for both lines had been cast now, and the lads were patiently holding the ends.

"No; haven't had a bite," replied Rob; and the words had hardly left his lips when Brazier's gun raised an echo across the river, which ran to and fro, reflected by the wall of trees in zigzag course till it died out.

But no one listened to the echo, for all attention was taken by a large duck, one of about a dozen which had come skimming along over the surface of the water till its course had been stopped by Brazier's accurate shot, when it fell flapping heavily and raising quite a spray around it as it began to float rapidly down-stream.

"Come, we mustn't lose that," cried Shaddy, running to unfasten the rope which moored the boat. "We'll go together. Mr Joe, sir, haul in your line."

But before the boy could obey there was a cry of annoyance from Brazier as, with a slight splash, something seized the duck and drew it under.

"'Nother supper gone!" growled Shaddy.

"What was it?" cried Brazier.

"Didn't see, sir. Either a 'gator or a big fish. Look sharp, Mr Joe, sir. Now, if you could catch that there fish with the duck in his jaws too, it would be something like."

But Joe did not have the chance to catch a fish with the duck or without, and Rob fervently hoped that he might not catch the captor of the duck, for he felt certain that he had seen the jaws of a small alligator close upon the unfortunate bird as he held the end of his line tightly and waited for the bite which would not come.

But in the midst of that lovely solitude there was no room for disappointment. Though they could not obtain exactly what they sought, Rob felt that nature was offering them endless treasures, and his eye was being constantly attracted by the flowers high up on the trees across the river and the still more beautiful butterflies and birds constantly passing here and there. Now it was some lovely object whose large flat wings flashed with steely or purply blue, according to the angle in which it was viewed, then butterflies of velvety black dashed with orange and vermilion. Parrots of vivid green with scarlet heads flew to and fro across the stream; and twice over a great *ara* or macaw, with its large, hooked beak and scarlet-and-blue feathering, a very soldier in uniform among birds, flew over them, watching them keenly as it uttered its harsh, discordant cry. Then, too, there were the humming-birds darting here and there with bee-like flight, emitting a flash every now and then as their metallic, scale-like feathers caught the sun on their burnished surface.

"No," said Rob to himself, "one can't feel disappointed here," and soon after, as he drew a long, deep breath full of satisfaction, "Oh, how gloriously beautiful it all is! What would they say at home?"

Now he gazed down into the deep, clear, swiftly flowing water, where, brilliantly illuminated by the sun, just beyond where he sat shaded by a tree, he could see fish of all sizes floating motionless, apparently at different depths, while farther out there were more and more, larger it seemed, and as the depth and density of the water increased looking more shadowy and strange.

"There are plenty of them, even if they don't bite," thought Rob; "and if it were not that we must have them to eat, I don't know that I want to catch them. Ugh!"

He involuntarily shrank away, but resumed his position at the edge of the river, gazing down at where, with its four legs outstretched and its tail waving softly, an alligator swam by some five feet below the surface. It was only a small one, between three and four feet in length, but showing all the ugly configuration of its kind; and it fascinated Rob as he gazed at it till it slowly grew more shadowy and shortened in length and disappeared.

"Wonder how Joe's getting on!" he thought; and then his mind dwelt again upon their surroundings, and as his eyes wandered from spot to spot he felt that they ought to go no farther, but make a temporary stay there.

Just then he looked to his right, to find that Mr Brazier had given up his task of watching for birds and was busy with Shaddy arranging the bunch of orchids on a branch in the full sunshine, to dry as much as was possible before being transferred to their destination—the bottom of one of the tubs.

"Slow work!" muttered Rob, drawing in his line now, to find the biscuit softened, but still held tightly enough to the hook. Then, dropping it in again, he watched it as it was carried out by the eddy, and ended by tying the line fast to one of the overhanging branches and walking to where the boat was moored.

"How are you getting on, Joe?" he said; but there was no answer. "Not here?" he muttered as he stepped on board, to find the young Italian lying back fast asleep, while the end of the line was secured to one of the thwarts.

"Oh, I say!" muttered Rob, "you lazy beggar!" Then stooping down, so that his lips were near the sleeper's ear, he said loudly, "Ready for supper?"

Joe leaped up in confusion.

"Have I been asleep?" he said hastily.

"Looks like it. Where's the dorado?"

"I—that is—I grew so drowsy, I—yes, I fastened the end of the line for fear it should go overboard, and—here, look out!" he cried sharply, "I have him!"

"Not you," said Rob; "the hook caught it."

For the line had been drawn tight while Joe slept, and as he took hold of it he found that it was fast in something heavy, which now sent a quiver along the line, as if it were shaking its head angrily at being disturbed.

"Why, it's a big one," said Rob excitedly.

"It's a monster," panted Joe. "Oh, I wish I had not been asleep."

"Caught anything?" came from behind them, and Brazier and Shaddy drew near.

"Yes; Joe has hooked a very big one," cried Rob eagerly. "Get your hook ready, Shaddy."

"All right, sir," said the guide grimly, "but you won't want it just yet. You'll have to play that chap before you get him up to the boat."

So it seemed, for the captive lay sulky for a few moments, resenting the strain on the line, till Joe gave it a jerk, when there was a rush away to the left, the line suddenly slackened, and Rob exclaimed in a tone of disappointment,—

"Gone!"

"No," growled Shaddy. "Pull in a bit, my lad. Steady!"

Joe began to haul in the line, drawing in yard after yard, which fell in rings to the bottom of the boat, till half the fishing cord must have been recovered.

"He has gone, Shaddy," said Joe.

"Beginning to think you're right, my lad. Fancied at first he'd swum up to the side, for there's no telling what a fish may do when— Look out; he's on still," roared Shaddy. "Hold the line, my lad. Don't let him haul it quite out, or he'll snap it when he gets to the end."

Joe seized the line and let it slip through his fingers, but the friction was so painful that he would have let go again had not Shaddy stepped to his help and taken hold behind him.

"Won't hurt my fingers," he growled; "they're a deal too hard," and he kept hold so that he did not interfere with Joe's work in playing the fish, but relieved him of the strain and friction as the line cut the water here and there.

Brazier looked on with plenty of interest in the proceedings, for the capture of a fish of goodly size was a matter of some consequence to the leader of an expedition with eight hungry people to cater for day after day.

"Think it's a dorado, Shaddy?" asked Rob.

"Ought to be, my lad, from its taking an orange, and if it is it's 'bout the heaviest one I've knowed. My word, but he does pull! Can't say as ever I felt one shake his head like that before. Shall I play him now, my lad?"

"No," cried Joe through his set teeth as he held on, "not yet. I will ask you if I want help. No: Rob will help me."

The struggle went on so fiercely that it increased Brazier's interest, and but for the clever way in which the two lads in turn played the fish, the cord, strong as it was, must have been broken. But they were fortunate enough to get a good deal of the long line in hand, and were thus enabled to let their captive run from time to time, merely keeping up a steady strain till the rush was over and then hauling in again.

"Why, boys," said Brazier at last as he stood on the bank resting upon his double gun, "it will be supper-time before you catch your prize, and in this climate fish will be bad to-morrow. Better let him go."

"What!" cried Rob, whose face was streaming with perspiration. "Let him go? Do you hear, Joe?"

Joe nodded and tightened his lips, his face seeming to say, —

"Let him go? Not while I can hold him."

So the fight went on till the fish grew less fierce in its rushes, but none the weaker, keeping on as it did a heavy, stubborn drag, and though frequently brought pretty near to the boat, keeping down close to the bottom, so that they never once obtained a glimpse of it.

"It ain't a dorado," said Shaddy at last. "I never see one fight like that."

"It must be a very grand one," said Joe, wiping his face, for he had resigned the line for a time.

"It pulls like a mule," said Rob, as the captive now made off toward the middle of the river.

"What sort of a hook have you got on, Mr Jovanni?" cried Shaddy.

"One of those big ones, with the wire bound round for about two feet above it."

"Then I tell you what, my lad: I don't believe that strong new cord'll break. S'pose both of you get hold after he's had this run, haul him right up, and let's have a look at him! Strikes me you've got hold of one of them big eely mud-fish by the way he hugs the bottom."

"Shall we try, Joe?"

"I—I'm afraid of losing it," was the reply. "It would be so dreadful now. Perhaps it will be tired soon."

"Don't seem like it, my lad!" said Brazier. "It is not worth so long and exhausting a fight."

"Right, sir, and they've been too easy with him. You get his head up, Mr Rob, as soon as he gives a bit, and then both of you show him you don't mean to stand any more nonsense. That'll make him give in."

"Very well," said Joe, with a sigh. "We have been a long time. Wait till he has had this run."

The line was running out more and more through Rob's fingers as he spoke, and the fish seemed bent on making for the farther shore; but the lad made it hard work for the prisoner, and about two-thirds of the way it began to slacken its pace, almost stopped, quite stopped, and sulked, like a salmon, at the bottom.

"Now both of you give a gentle, steady pull," said Brazier; and Joe took hold of the line and joined Rob in keeping up a continuous strain.

For a few minutes it was like pulling at a log of wood, and Rob declared the line must be caught. But almost as he spoke the fish gave a vicious shake at the hook, its head seemed to be pulled round, the strain was kept up, and the captive yielded, and was drawn nearer and nearer very slowly, but none the less surely, the line falling in rings to the bottom of the boat.

"Bravo!" cried Brazier.

"That's right, both of you!" shouted Shaddy excitedly. "He's dead beat, and I shall have the big hook in his gills before he knows where he is. Haul away!"

"Are these mud-fish you talk about good eating, Naylor?" asked Brazier.

"Oh yes, sir. Bit eely-like in their way; not half bad. Come, that's winning, gents. Well done. Give me a shout when you want me. I won't come yet so as to get in your way."

"Sha'n't be ready yet," panted Rob. "He is strong. I think you ought to have a harpoon.—I say."

"Yes, sir."

"Do these mud-fish bite?"

"Well, yes, sir," replied Shaddy; "pretty nigh all the fish hereabouts are handy with their teeth."

"Ah, he's off again!" cried Joe; and they had to let the prisoner run. But it was a much weaker effort, and a couple of minutes later they had hauled in all the line given, and got in so much more that the fish was at the bottom of the river only four or five yards from the boat.

"Now then, both together; that line will hold!" cried Shaddy excitedly; "get him right up and see what he is, and if he begins to fight fierce let him have one more run to finish his flurry, as the whalers call the last fight."

"Ready, Joe?"

"Yes."

"Both together, then."

There were a few short steady pulls, hand over hand, and the prisoner was drawn nearer and nearer, and raised from the bottom slowly and surely, while, as full of excitement now as the lads, Brazier and Shaddy stood close to the edge watching.

"Hurrah!" cried Rob, who was nearest to the gunwale. "I can see him now!"

"Well, what is it—a mud-fish?" asked Brazier.

"No," said Joe, straining his neck to get a glimpse through the clear water, the disturbed mud raised by the struggles of the fish being rapidly swept away. "It's a dorado: I can see his golden scales!"

"Then he's a regular whopper, my lads. Steady, don't lose him!" cried Shaddy. "Shall I come on board?"

"No, not yet," said Joe excitedly. "He may make another rush."

"Why, I say, it isn't a very big one," said Rob.

"No," cried Joe, in a disappointed tone; "but he's coming up backwards, which shows how strong he is."

"Ha, ha!" shouted Rob; "we've caught him by the tail."

"Got the line twisted round it, perhaps," said Brazier. "That's what makes the fish seem so strong."

"Ugh!" yelled Rob, letting go of the line, with the result that it was drawn back rapidly through Joe's fingers, till at a cry from his lips Rob took hold again as the fish ran off and nearly reached its former quarters.

"What's the matter?" said Brazier. "Did the line cut your fingers?"

"No. We've caught a horrid great thing. It isn't a dorado. I saw it well, and it's nearly as long as the boat."

"Gammon!" growled Shaddy. "Here, what's it like, Master Joe?"

"I don't know. I never saw a fish like it before: its tail was all golden scales, and then it was dark at the top and bottom, and went off dark right toward the head."

"Then it must be a mud-fish, I should say, though I never knowed of one with a tail like that. Haul him in again, and I'll get aboard now ready with the hook."

He stepped into the boat, and lay down in the bottom with his arms over the side and his landing-hook, securely bound to a short, stout piece of bamboo, held ready.

"Shan't be in your way, shall I?" he asked.

"No, not at all," replied Joe. "Now, Rob, are you ready?"

"Yes."

"I say, don't let go again."

"I'll try not," replied Rob, and the hauling began once more, with almost as much effort necessary. But at the end of a minute it began to be evident that the fish was tired, for it yielded more and more as the line was drawn in, but kept to its old tactics of hugging the bottom till it was close up to the boat, where, after pausing a moment or two, Rob cried,—

"Now then, both together! Don't miss him, Shaddy! Mind, he's a hideous great thing."

"All right, my lads; haul away!"

They hauled, but instead of the fish suffering itself to be dragged like a lump of lead close in to the boat, it now commenced different tactics, and rose till the gilded tail appeared above the surface quite clear of the line, and beat and churned up the water so that it was too much disturbed for them to see the head, the creature seeming to be fighting hard to dive down again straight to the bottom.

"That's right, my lads: he's coming. 'Nother fathom, and I'll get the hook into him. Haul steady. He's, done. He's— Well, I'm blessed!"

Shaddy roared out this last exclamation, for all at once, as the boys hauled persistently at the line, the tail half of a large dorado was thrust above the surface, agitated violently, and directly after there followed the hideous head of an alligator with its jaws tightly closed upon the fore half of the fish. It was shaking its head savagely to break the line, and began giving violent plunges while it made the water foam with its struggles, and in another moment would no doubt have broken away; but just at the crisis, on seeing what was the state of affairs, Brazier raised his gun, took a quick aim, and discharged rapidly one after the other both barrels of his piece.

The result was magical. As the smoke rose, and quite a cloud of brilliantly tinted birds flew here and there from side to side of the river, whose trees on both banks seemed to have grown alive with monkeys, the alligator made one leap half out of the water, fell back with a heavy splash, and then lay motionless save for a quivering of its tail as it was drawn nearer, when Shaddy managed to get his hook inside the jaws, which were distended by the dorado, and then, stepping ashore, he hauled the reptile right out on to the grass.

"Is he dead?" said Brazier, who was reloading.

"Not yet, sir; but you've shattered the back of his head, and he'll soon be quite. No wonder you didn't land him quicker, Master Joe."

"But what does it mean?" cried Rob. "Oh, I see! Joe hooked a dorado, and this fellow tried to swallow it head first, and couldn't get it right down."

"That's it, my lad," replied Shaddy. "He'd half managed it when Mr Jovanny here gave a pull, and has got the hook in him somewhere. I thought so. Here's the pynte sticking right through outside his neck, and he couldn't bite because of the fish stuck in his jaws just like a great gag."

"Well, what's to be done?" said Rob; "we can't eat the dorado now. Wonder whether I've got a bite yet."

He went slowly and wearily up to the tree where he had fastened the end of his line, and to his delight saw that the branch was rising and falling as a fish on the hook tugged to get away.

"Hi! Joe! Got one!" he shouted; but before the lad could reach him he had the line in his hand and was hauling, sore as his fingers were, a heavy fish toward the shore. Then with a cry of disappointment he pulled in the line easily enough, for the fish was gone.

They returned to the spot where Brazier and Shaddy stood, near the captured alligator.

"Good six feet long, Rob," said Brazier, who had measured it by taking two long paces. "Something like a catch, Giovanni. Can you get the fish out of its jaws, Naylor?"

"Oh yes, I think so, sir."

"Mind, for these creatures are very retentive of life."

"Oh yes, I know 'em, sir. I'll get the chopper and take his head off first."

"But we are not going to eat that fish now, Mr Brazier, are we?"

"Well, I don't know, Rob. If it is well washed and skinned, it cannot be any the worse, and we have nothing else in the way of fish or meat."

"Wrong, sir," said Shaddy, making a very wide smile; "look at that."

He pointed toward the top of the little clearing where the boatman had forced his way in amongst the tangled growth, and gone on hewing his way through bush, thorn, vine, and parasitical growth, to reappear just in the nick of time with the bustard-looking bird hanging from his left hand, dead.

"Says he had to go in a long way," said Shaddy, after a short conversation with the man, who, weary though he was with his exertions, immediately set to work by the fire picking the bird and burning its feathers, with the result that the Europeans of the little expedition confined themselves to the windward side of the fire till the man had done.

"Never had such a delicious supper before in my life," said Rob two hours later, as they sat in the boat eating oranges and watching the gorgeous colours of the sky.

"Think this place 'll do, sir?" said Shaddy, after washing down his repast with copious draughts of *maté* made by his men.

"Excellently, Naylor."

"And you ain't hardly begun yet," said Shaddy, smiling. "Wait till you get higher up, where it's wilder and wonderfler: this is nothing. Suit you, Master Rob? Never had such fishing as that before, did you?"

"Never, Shaddy; but what did you do with the alligator and the fish?"

"My lads cut all off as the 'gator hadn't had down his throat, and tumbled the other into the stream. Ain't much of him left by this time."

The night came on almost directly after, with the remarkable tropical absence of twilight; and, as if all had been waiting for the darkness, the chorus of the forest began. Then, well making up the fire with an abundance of wood, the boatmen came on board, and immediately settled themselves down to sleep.

Chapter Ten.

The Wonders of the Wilds.

It was a weird hour that next which was passed with the fire sending up volumes of smoke, followed by glittering sparks which rose rapidly and looked like specks of gold-leaf floating away over the river, red now as blood, now orange and gold, as the fire blazed higher and cast its reflections on the rapid stream.

The bright light had a singular attraction for the birds, which came skimming round and swooping through the dark smoke, small birds with bright wings, and large-headed owls with soft silent pinions; these latter every now and then adding their mournful cries to the harsh screeching, whirring, drumming, throbbing, and piping of bird, insect, and reptile which mingled with the fine, thin, humming *ping* of the mosquitoes and the mournful fluting of the frogs.

No one spoke for a time, the attention of three of the party being taken up by the novelty of their position and the noises of the forest, for though they had passed many nights on the river and listened to the cries on the farther shore, this was their first experience of being right in among these musicians of the night as they kept up their incessant din.

"Can you tell what every sound is that we hear, Shaddy?" whispered Rob at last.

"Nay, hardly; some on 'em of course," said their guide. "You know many of them too already, though they get so mixed up it's hard to pick out one from the other."

"But that?" whispered Rob, as if he dared not raise his voice, and he started violently, for there was a splash close at hand.

"Didn't mean that fish, did you, sir? That won't hurt you here so long as you don't walk overboard in your sleep."

"No, no, I didn't mean that; I meant that bellowing noise. You heard it, didn't you, Mr Brazier?"

There was no reply.

"Sleep," said Shaddy gruffly.

"Joe, you heard that bellowing down the river there?" whispered Rob.

Again there was no reply.

"Sleep too," growled Shaddy. "Well, don't you know what that was?"

"No."

"'Gator. Don't suppose he thinks it's bellowing. Dessay he'd call it a song. There it goes again. Comes along the river as if it was close to us. But there, don't you think you've done enough for one day, and had better do as the rest are doing? We're the only two awake."

"But what about keeping watch?" said Rob, rather excitedly.

"Oh, I don't know as there's any need to keep watch here, my lad," said Shaddy coolly.

"What, not with all kinds of wild and savage beasts about us, and monstrous reptiles and fishes in the very water where we float! Why, it seems madness to go to sleep among such dangers."

"Nay, not it, my lad. Why, if you come to that, the world's full of dangers wherever you are. No more danger here than on board a big ship sailing or steaming over water miles deep."

"But the wild beasts—lions and tigers, as you call them?"

“Lions won’t hurt you so long as you don’t meddle with them, and the tigers won’t pass that fire.”

“Then the Indians?”

“No Indians about here, my lad, or I should have that fire out pretty soon and be on the watch. You leave all that to me, and don’t you get worrying yourself about danger because you hear a noise in the forest! Noise is a noosance, but it don’t hurt. There was five thousand times as much danger in the fangs of that little sarpint I chopped to-day as in all the noise you’re listening to now.”

Rob was silent.

“So just you take my advice, my lad: when night comes you say your bit o’ prayers and tuck your head under your wing till it’s near daylight. That’s the way to get a good night’s rest and be ready for the morning.”

Rob started again, for a great, soft-winged thing swept silently by, so near that he felt the wind of its pinion as it glided on, its outline nearly invisible, but magnified by the darkness into a marvellous size.

“On’y a bat, my lad!” said Shaddy, yawning.

“Is that one of the blood-sucking ones?”

“Very likely.”

“And you talk about there being no danger out here!”

“Nay, not I. There’s plenty of dangers, my lad, but we’re not going to be afraid of a thing that you could knock down with one of your hands so that it would never fly again. It ought to feel scared, not you.”

"Is that a firefly?" said Rob, after a few minutes' silence, and he pointed to a soft, golden glow coming up the river five or six feet above the stream, and larger and more powerful than the twinkling lights appearing and disappearing among the foliage at the river's edge.

"Yes, that's a firefly; come to light you to bed, if you like. There, my lad, it's sleep-time. Get under shelter out of the night damp. You'll soon be used to all the buzzing and howling and—"

"That was a tiger, wasn't it?" said Rob excitedly, as a shrill cry rang out somewhere in the forest and sent a thrill through him.

"No. Once more, that's a lion, and he's after monkeys, not after you, so good-night."

Shaddy drew the sail over him as he stretched himself in the bottom of the roomy boat, and Rob crept in under the awning. The heavy breathing enabled him to make out exactly where his companions lay asleep, and settling himself down forward, he rested his head on his hand, convinced that sleep would be impossible, and preparing to listen to the faint rustling noise of the mooring rope on the gunwale of the boat, a sound which often suggested something coming on board.

Then he made sure what it was, and watched the faint glow thrown by the fire on the canvas till it seemed to grow dull—seemed, for the boatmen had arranged the wood so that from time to time it fell in, and hence it kept on burning up more brightly. But it looked dull to Rob and then black, for in spite of yells and screams and bellowings, the piping and fluting of frogs, the fiddling of crickets, and the drumming of some great toad, which apparently had a big tom-tom all to itself, Rob's eyes had closed, and fatigue made him sleep as soundly as if he had been at home.

The sun was up when he awoke with a start to find Joe having his wash in a freshly dipped bucket of clean water, and upon joining him and looking ashore, it was to see Brazier bringing his botanic treasures on board to hang up against the awning to dry; while Shaddy had taken the skin of the jaguar, pegs and all, rolling it up and throwing it forward. The boatmen kept the kettle boiling and some cake-bread baking in the hot ashes. At the same time a pleasant odour of frizzling bacon told that breakfast would not be long.

"You are going to stay here for a day or two?" said Rob to Mr Brazier as he rubbed his face dry in the warm sunshine.

"No. Naylor says we shall do better farther on, and keep on collecting as we go, beside getting a supply of ducks or other fowl for our wants. The farther we are from the big river the easier it will be to keep our wants supplied."

"Gun, sir!" said Shaddy just then; "big ducks coming up the river. Take it coolly, sir, and don't shoot till you can get two or three."

Brazier waited and waited, but the birds, which were feeding, came no farther.

"Hadn't Mr Rob better try too, sir?" whispered Shaddy; "he wants to learn to shoot."

Rob glanced at Brazier, who did not take his eyes from the ducks he was watching, and the boy hurriedly fetched his gun.

"What yer got in?" whispered Shaddy.

"Shot in one barrel, bullet in the other."

"Bah!" growled the guide. "You don't want bullet now. Yes, you do," he continued. "Look straight across the water in between the trees, and tell me if you see anything."

"No. Whereabouts?"

"Just opposite us. Now look again close to the water's edge, where there's that bit of an opening. Come, lad, where's your eyes?"

"I don't see anything but flowers and drooping boughs."

"And a deer just come down for a drink of fresh-water, ready to be shot and keep us in food for days."

"Yes, I can see it now," said Rob eagerly. "What a beautiful creature!"

"Yes, beautiful meat that we can cut up in strips and dry in the sun, so as to have a little supply in hand."

"But it seems—" began Rob.

"It's necessary, lad, and it's a chance. Sit down, rest your piece on the gunwale, and aim straight with your left barrel at the centre of its head. If you miss that you're sure to send the bullet through its shoulder and bring it down."

Feeling a great deal of compunction, Rob sank into the position advised, cocked his piece, and took careful aim.

"Make sure of him, my lad," whispered Shaddy. "It's a fine bit o' practice for you. Now then, hold the butt tight to your shoulder and pull the trigger gently; squeeze it more than pull. Covered him?"

"Yes."

"Then fire."

Bang! bang! Two shots in rapid succession, and the deer was gone, but a monkey unseen till then dropped head over heels into the water from one of the trees over the trembling deer, scared from its hold by the loud reports, and after a few moments' splashing succeeded in reaching a branch which dipped in the stream. In another moment or two it was in safety, chattering away fiercely as an ugly snout was protruded from the water where it fell.

"Got them this time!" said Brazier in a tone of satisfaction, as five ducks lay on the water waiting to be picked up. "You should have fired too, Rob. We want fresh provisions."

"What I told him, sir, but he took such a long aim that the deer said, 'Good-morning; come and be shot another time.'"

"Deer? What deer?"

"One t'other side, sir," said Shaddy, who had got out to unmoor the boat.

"I wish I had seen it; the meat would have been so valuable to-day."

"What I telled him, sir."

"And you didn't shoot!"

"I was just going to when you fired, and the deer darted away."

"Naturally," said Brazier, smiling; and by this time the boat was gliding down the river in the wake of the ducks. These were secured, all but one, which, being wounded, flapped and swam toward the shore, where it was suddenly sucked down by a reptile or fish. Those they secured dropped silvery little arrows, apparently, back into the water in the shape of the tiny voracious fish that had forced their way already between their feathers to reach the skin.

The birds secured, Rob sat gazing with delight at the fresh beauties of the river where it wound off to the right. Birds innumerable were flitting about, chirping and singing; noisy parrots were climbing and hanging head downwards as they hunted out a berry-like fruit from a tall tree; and toucans, with orange-and-scarlet breasts and huge bills, hopped about, uttering their discordant cries. Everything looked so beautiful and peaceful that for the moment he forgot the dangerous occupants of the river, and his eyes grew dim with the strange sense of joy that came over him that glorious morning. But the next moment he became aware of the fact that to all this beauty and brightness there was a terrible reverse side. For suddenly a great falcon dashed with swift wing high up along the course of the river, and cries of fear, warning, and alarm rang out from the small birds, the minute before happy and contentedly seeking their food.

The change was magical. At the first cry, all dropped down helter-skelter beneath the boughs and leaves, seeking shelter; and as the falcon gave a harsh scream it was over groves that had suddenly become deserted, not a tenant being visible, except some half-dozen humming-birds, whose safety lay in their tiny size and wonderful powers of flight. Three of these, instead of showing fear, became immediately aggressive, and, darting like great flies at the falcon, flashed about it in different directions, apparently acting in concert and pestering the great bird, so that it winged its way over the great wall of trees and was gone.

But almost at the same moment a vulture appeared, with its hideous naked head and neck outstretched, making the humming-birds ruffle up again and resume their attack till they literally drove the great intruder away.

"What daring little things they are!" said Rob, who was watching the tiny bird gems with keen delight, while Brazier's admiration was as much taken up by the clusters of blossoms hanging from a branch over the water.

"I shall be obliged to have those, Rob," he said, pointing to the orchids. "Do you think you could get out along that bough if the boat were run in to the bank?"

"Yes," said the boy; "but suppose I drop into the river! What then?"

"We would keep the boat under you."

"Can't be done," growled Shaddy, who had been trying to force the boat back to their little camp by paddling with one oar over the stern. "'Bliged to ask you, gentlemen, to take an oar apiece. Stream runs mighty fast here."

Rob seized an oar, and Brazier followed suit, at the same time glancing toward their last night's halting-place to see if their men were within reach to come and row and enable him to make an effort to obtain some of the green, bulbous-looking stems and flowers of the lovely parasite which had taken his attention. But they were as unobtainable as if they were a hundred miles away, for it would have taken them days to cut a way to opposite where the boat was now being held against the swift stream, and even when they had reached the spot it would have been impossible to force her in through the tangled growth to the shore.

"Now together, gentlemen!" growled Shaddy. "Keep stroke, please. Pull hard."

They were already tugging so hard that the perspiration was starting out upon Rob's brow, and in that short row, with Shaddy supplementing their efforts by paddling with all his might, they had a fair sample of the tremendous power of the stream.

"At last!" said Shaddy as they regained their old quarters, where Joe and the four men had stood watching them. "It will give my chaps a pretty good warming if we come back this way. Strikes me that we four had better practise pulling together, so as to be able to give them a rest now and then when the stream's very much againstus."

"By all means," said Brazier.

"You see, men ain't steam-engines, sir, and we might be where there was no place for landing. O' course we could always hitch on to the trees, but that makes poor mooring, and we should be better able to make our way. There's hardly a chance of getting into slack water in a river like this: it all goes along with a rush."

"But I must get that plant, Naylor," said Brazier. "If you'll believe me, sir," was the reply, "you needn't worry about that one. I'm going to take you where you'll find thousands."

"Like that?"

"Ay, and other sorts too. Seems to me, sir, we want to catch a monkey and teach him how to use a knife. He'd be the sort of chap to run up the trees." Rob laughed at the idea, and said it was not possible. "Well, sir," said Shaddy, "you may believe it or no, but an old friend of mine 'sured me that the Malay chaps do teach a big monkey they've got out there to slip up the cocoa-nut trees and twist the big nuts round and round till they drop off. He said it was a fact, and I don't see why not."

"We'll try and dispense with the monkey," said Brazier; and trusting to finding more easily accessible specimens of the orchid, he gave that up, and a couple of hours after they were gliding swiftly along the stream, rapt in contemplation of the wonders on either hand, Shaddy being called upon from time to time to seize hold of some overhanging bough and check the progress of the boat, so that its occupants might watch the gambols of the inquisitive monkeys which kept pace with them along the bank by bounding and swinging from branch to branch.

The birds, too, appeared to be infinite in variety; and Rob was never weary of watching the tiny humming-birds as they poised themselves before the trumpet blossoms of some of the pendent vines to probe their depths for honey, or capture tiny insects with their beaks.

Their journey was prolonged from their inability to find a suitable place for a halt, and it was easy work for the boatmen, who smiled with content as they found that only one was required to handle the oars, so as to keep the boat's head straight.

It was nearly night, when a narrow place was found where by the fall of a huge tree several others had been torn up by their roots, and lay with their water-worn branches in the river.

The place offered just room to run the boat between two of the trees, but it could be easily moored, and there was the clear sky overhead. Moreover, they had an ample supply of dead wood to make a fire, and by the time this was blazing merrily and lighting up the wall of trees and the river night had fallen intensely dark.

The lads were for leaping out directly and climbing about amongst the fallen trunks which nearly filled the opening, but Shaddy checked them.

"Wait a while, my lads, till the fire's been burning a bit. I don't quite like our quarters."

"But that fire will scare away any wild beasts that may be near," said Rob.

"Yes, but the place looks snaky, Mr Rob; and I daresay there's lots o' them big spiders about."

"What big spiders?"

"Them as bites so bad that you remember it for months. Why, there's one sort out in these parts as'll run after you and attack you—fierce."

"No, no, Shaddy, not spiders," said Rob, laughing.

"Look ye here, Mr Rob, sir," said Shaddy solemnly, "when I tell you a story of the good old traveller sort—I mean a bouncer—you'll see the corners of my lips screwed up. When I'm telling you what's true as true, you'll see I look solid as mahogany; and that's how I'm looking now."

"Yes, it's true, Rob," said Joe. "There are plenty of spiders out on the pampas—great fellows that will come at you and bite horribly."

"I should like to see one," said Rob.

"Wait a bit, my lad, and you shall," said Shaddy.—"Humph! don't like this place at all," he growled. "Look there!" he continued, pointing at where three big trees lay close together, with their branches worn sharp by the action of the water. "If there ain't 'gators under all them sharp snags my name ain't Shadrach Naylor! Water's quite still, too, there. I hope there ain't anything worse."

"Do you think we had better go on?" said Brazier.

"Nay, we'll risk it, sir. Let's wait till the fire burns up big and strong. We'll have a roarer to-night, and that'll scare away most of the trash. Worst of it is, I'm 'fraid it 'tracts the 'gators and fish."

Chapter Eleven.

An Eventful Night.

"I do like a good fire, Joe," said Rob, as he gazed at the ruddy flames rushing up.

"Why, you're not cold?"

"No, I'm hot, and this fire brings in a breeze and makes it cooler—on one side. But what I like in a fire of this kind is that you can burn as much wood as you like, and nobody can say it's waste, because it's doing good—clearing the ground for the trees around to grow. I say, look at the birds."

"After supper," said Joe, as he watched the actions of the principal boatman, who was head cook, busily preparing the ducks and two good-sized fish which they had caught by trailing a bait behind the boat as they came.

"Yes, I'm hungry," said Rob. "What's that?"

"It was Shaddy."

"What! tumbled in?" said Rob excitedly.

"No; he took hold of a thick piece of branch and threw it into the water. What did you do that for?"

"Scare them 'gators, my lad. There's a whole school of 'em out there, and I think they mean coming to supper. And fish too," he added, as there was another splash and then another.

By this time he was close alongside of the boat, under whose tent Mr Brazier was busy by the light of a lanthorn making notes and lists of the flowers and orchid bulbs which he had secured that day.

"Hadn't we better put out a line, Shaddy? If we caught a fish or two the men would be glad of them in the morning."

"No, Mr Rob, sir; I don't suppose they'd bite now, and even if they did, so sure as you hooked one a smiler would get hold of it, and you don't want another fight of that sort. I'm beginning to think that we'd best get our bit o' food, and then drop slowly down the river again."

"What's that?" said Brazier, looking up from his work. "That will not do, Naylor; we should miss no end of good plants."

"Well, sir, better do that than get into a row with any of the natives here," growled Shaddy.

"Why, you said there were no Indians near."

"Tchah! I mean the other natives—'sects and rept'les and what not. But there, if we put a rope to the end of that largest tree and anchor ourselves yonder I don't suppose we shall hurt. Eh? All right," he cried, in answer to a hint from the men; "supper's ready, gentlemen."

"And so are we," said Rob with alacrity; and he leaped off the gunwale on to the tree trunk by whose side it was moored.

To all appearance it was a solid-looking stem of tons in weight, but covered with mosses, creepers, and orchids, which pretty well hid its bark.

Rob's intention was to run along it to the root end, which stood up close to the fire; but, to his intense astonishment, he crashed through what was a mere outer shell of bark into so much dust and touchwood right up to the armpits, where he stuck, with a hedge of plants half-covering his face.

Joe burst out into a fit of laughing, in which Rob joined as soon as the first startled sensation was over.

"Who'd have thought of that?" he cried. "But, I say, I'm fast. Come and lend me a hand. I thought it was a great solid trunk, and all inside here you can see it looks as if it were on fire. Oh! oh! Ah! Help!"

"What's the matter?" cried Brazier excitedly, as Shaddy and he stepped cautiously to the boy's side, Joe having already mounted on the tree trunk. "Not on fire, are you?"

"No, no," gasped Rob in agonised tones; and, speaking in a frightened whisper, "There's something alive in here."

"Nippers o' some kind, eh?"

"No, no," cried Rob faintly; "I can feel it moving. Oh! help! It's a snake."

As he spoke there was a curious scuffling noise inside, as if something was struggling to extricate itself, and Shaddy lost no time. Bending down, he seized Rob by the chest under the armpits, stooped lower, gave one heave, and lifted him right out; when, following close upon his legs, the head of a great serpent was thrust up, to look threateningly round for a moment. The next, the creature was gliding down through the dense coating of parasitical growth, and before gun could be fetched from the cabin, or weapon raised, the rustling and movement on the side of the trunk had ceased, and Joe in turn gave a bound to one side.

"It's coming along by here," he cried, as, in full belief that he would the next moment be enveloped in the monster's coils, he made for the fire.

"Where is it now?" cried Shaddy, knife in hand.

"The grass is moving there," said Brazier, pointing a little to the right, where the tree trunks cast a deep shadow.

"Can't see—so plaguey dark," growled the guide; "and it's no good if I could. Yes, I can see the stuff moving now. He's making for the water. Now, sir, send a charge o' shot where the grass is waving."

But before Brazier could get a sight of the reptile it had glided into the river, down among the branches of the fallen tree, as if quite used to the intricate tangle of pointed wood beneath the bank, and accustomed to use it for a home of refuge, or lurking place from which to strike at prey.

"Did it seize you?" said Brazier excitedly.

"No, I only felt it strike against my leg and then press it to the side. I think I trod upon it."

"Made its home, I suppose, in the hollow tree. But you are sure you are not hurt, my boy—only frightened?"

"I couldn't help being frightened," said Rob, in rather an ill-used tone.

"Nobody says you could," said Brazier, laughing. "Master Giovanni seems to have been frightened too. Why, Rob, my lad, it would have almost frightened me into fits: I have such a horror of serpents. There, I believe after all these things are not so very dangerous."

"Don't know so much about that, sir," said Shaddy. "I've know'd 'em coil round and squeeze a deer to death, and then swallow it."

"Yes, a small deer perhaps; but the old travellers used to tell us about mighty boas and monstrous anacondas which could swallow buffaloes."

"Ah! they don't grow so big as that now, sir. I've seen some pretty big ones, too, in my time, specially on the side of the river and up the Amazons."

"Well, how big—how long have you ever seen one, Naylor?"

"Never see one a hundred foot long," said Shaddy drily.

"No, I suppose not. Come, what was the largest?"

"Largest I ever see, sir, was only the skin, as I telled Mr Rob about. Some half-caste chaps had got it pegged out, and I dessay skinning had stretched it a bit."

"Well, how long was that, Naylor?"

"That one was twenty-six foot long, sir, and nine foot across; and you may take my word for it as a thing like that, all muscles like iron—say six-and-twenty foot long and bigger round than a man—would be an awkward customer to tackle. Big enough for anything."

"Quite, Naylor."

"But how big was this one, do you think?" said Rob, who was getting over the perturbation caused by his adventure.

"Well, my lad, seeing what a bit of a squint I had of it, I should say it were thirteen or fourteen foot—p'raps fifteen."

"I thought it was nearer fifty," said Rob.

"Yes, you would then, my lad. But, never mind, it didn't seize you. I dessay you scared it as much as it did you."

"You will not be able to eat any supper, Rob, I suppose?" said Brazier rather maliciously.

Rob looked doubtful, but he smiled; and they went to the clearest place they could find, but not without sundry misgivings, for another tree sheltered them from the fire, which now sent forth a tremendous heat, and a cloud of golden sparks rose eddying and circling up to a dense cloud of smoke which glowed as if red-hot where it reflected the flames. This huge trunk, like the one through which Rob had slipped, was coated with parasitical growth, and though apparently solid, might, for all they knew, be hollow, and the nesting-place of half a dozen serpents larger than the one they had seen.

"Hadn't we better shift our quarters?" said Brazier.

"Yes, do," said Joe eagerly; "I hate snakes."

"Nobody's going to jump through that tree and 'sturb 'em, so I don't s'pose they'll 'sturb us. You see, they're a curious kind o' beast, which is all alive and twine for a day or two till they get a good meal, and then they go to sleep for a month before they're hungry again. It's wonderful how stupid and sleepy they are when they're like this. It takes some one to jump on 'em to rouse 'em up, like Mr Rob did."

"Well, we must chance it," said Brazier; and they seated themselves to their *al fresco* supper, over which Rob forgot his fright—his appetite returning, and the novelty of the position making everything delightful, in spite of the discomfort of their seat. For all around was so new, and there was a creepy kind of pleasure in sitting there by that crackling fire eating the delicious, hot, juicy birds, and all the while listening to the weird chorus of the forest, now in full swing.

Rob paused in the picking of a tasty leg, deliciously cooked, and sat in a very unpolished way listening to the curious cries, when, raising his eyes, they encountered Brazier's, who was similarly occupied.

"We've come to a wild enough place, Rob, my lad," he said; "but I don't think we wish to change."

"Oh! no," said Rob, in a whisper. "One can't help being a bit frightened sometimes, but it is grand even if we see nothing more."

Shaddy uttered a low, jerky sound, which was meant for a laugh.

"See nothing more, lad!" he cried. "Why, look here, you may go hundreds of miles to the south, the west and the north, and it's all savage land that man has hardly ever crossed. Don't you think there's something more to be seen there? Why, who knows but what we may come upon strange wild beasts such as nobody has ever set eyes on before, and— Why, what's the matter with our young skipper?"

Joe was opposite to him, staring wildly, his eyelids so drawn back that he showed a circle of white around the irises, and his lips were apart from his teeth.

"Why, what's the matter, lad? They haven't put any poison stuff in your victuals, have they?"

Joe made no reply, but sat staring wildly still, not at Shaddy, but in the direction of the river beyond.

"What's the matter, my lad?" said Brazier.

"I know!" cried Shaddy; "where's your guns? It's them 'gators coming up out of the water, and it's what I expected."

"No, no," whispered the boy excitedly: "look lower!"

All followed his pointing finger, but for the moment they could see nothing, one of the men having thrown some fresh fuel upon the fire, which was emitting more smoke than blaze.

"Hi! one of you!" cried Shaddy, "stir that fire."

One of the men seized the end of a burning limb, shook it about a little, and a roar of flame ascended skyward, lighting up the river and the trees beyond, but above all, striking just upon the rotten trunk through which Rob fell. There they saw a something glistening and horrible, as it swayed and undulated and rose and fell, with its neck all waves and its eyes sparkling in the golden blaze of the fire. Now it sank down till it was almost hidden among the parasitic plants; now it slowly rose, arching its neck, and apparently watching the party near the fire; while moment by moment its aspect was so menacing that Joe thought it would launch itself upon them and seize one to appease its rage.

"It's—it's come back!" he whispered faintly.

"Not it," growled Shaddy; "this one's twice as big as t'other. It's its father or mother, p'r'aps. Better have a shot at it, sir."

"Yes," said Brazier, slowly raising his gun, "but this light is so deceptive I am not at all sure that I can hit."

"Oh, you'll hit him full enough," said Shaddy. "You must hit it, sir. Why, if you missed, the beast would come down upon us as savage as a tiger. Take a good, quiet aim down low so as to hit his neck, if you don't his head. Are you cocked?"

"Tut! tut!" muttered Brazier, who in his excitement had forgotten this necessary preliminary, and making up for the omission.

"Come, Mr Rob, sir, don't miss your chance of having a shot at a 'conda. 'Tain't everybody who gets such a shot as that."

Rob mechanically picked up his piece, examined the breech, and then waited for Mr Brazier to fire, feeling sure the while that if it depended upon him the creature would go off scathless.

"Now's your time, sir!" whispered Shaddy. "He is put out, and means mischief. I'd let him have the small shot just beneath the jaws, if I could. Wait a moment, till he's quiet. Rather too much waving about him yet. Look out, sir! he's getting ready to make a dart at us, I do believe!"

But still Brazier did not fire, for the peculiar undulatory motion kept up by the serpent, as seen by the light of the fire, was singularly deceptive, and again and again the leader of the little expedition felt that if he fired it would be to miss.

Shaddy drew in a long breath, and gazed impatiently at Brazier, who was only moved by one idea—that of making a dead shot, to rid their little camp of a horrible-looking enemy.

Then the chance seemed to be gone, for by one quick movement of the lithe body and neck the head dropped down amongst the plants which clothed the tree trunk.

"Gone!" gasped Rob, with a sigh of satisfaction.

"Eyes right!" cried Shaddy; "he hasn't gone. He'll rise close in somewhere. Look out, gentlemen—look out!"

He was excited, and drew his knife, as if expecting danger. And it was not without cause, for almost directly after the keen steel blade had flashed in the light of the fire, the hideous head of the serpent rose up not ten feet away, with its eyes glittering, the scales burnished like bright, many-shaded bronze, and the quick, forked tongue darting in and out from its formidable jaws.

The head kept on rising till it was fully six feet above the growth, when it was rapidly drawn back, as if to be darted forward; but at that moment both Rob and Brazier fired together, and as the smoke cleared away another cloud of something seemed to be playing about on the ground, but a solid cloud, before which everything gave way, while some great flail-like object rapidly beat down plant and shrub.

All shrank away, and, as if moved by one impulse, took refuge behind the roaring fire, feeling, as they did, that their dangerous visitor would not attempt to pass that in making an attack upon those sheltered by so menacing an outwork.

There was something terribly appalling in the struggles of the silent monster, as it writhed and twisted itself into knots; then unfolded with the rapidity of lightning, and waving its tail in the air, again beat down the bushes and luxuriant growth around.

"AT THAT MOMENT ROB AND BRAZIER FIRED TOGETHER."

That it was fearfully wounded was evident, for after a few moments all could plainly see that it was actuated by a blind fury, and in its agony vented its rage upon everything around. And as it continued its struggles, moment by moment it approached nearer to the blazing fire, till all stood waiting in horror for the moment when one of its folds would touch the burning embers and the struggles come to a frightful end.

But all at once the writhings ceased, and the reptile lay undulating and heaving gently among the dense beaten-down growth.

"Stop!" said Brazier sharply, as the guide moved; "what are you going to do?"

"Put him out of his misery," replied Shaddy, quietly. "Hi! you there: give me the axe."

"No," said Brazier, firmly, "it is too risky a task; you shall not attempt it."

Shaddy uttered a low growl, like some thwarted animal, and said, in an ill-used tone,—

"Why, I could fetch his head off with one good chop, and—"

"Look, look!" cried Joe. "Mind! Take care!"

"Yes," shouted Rob; "it's coming round this way."

Neither could see the reptile; but the swaying herbage and the rustling, crackling sound showed that it was in rapid motion.

"Nay," growled Shaddy, "he ain't coming this way—only right-about-facing. It is his nature to; he's going to make for the water. That's what those things do: get down to the bottom and lie there, to be out o' danger. Look, Mr Rob, sir; you can see now what a length he is. One part's going one way, and the t'other part t'other way. Now he's turned the corner, and going straight for the river."

With Shaddy's words to guide them, they could easily make out what was taking place, as the reptile now made for the place of refuge already sought by its companion.

Just then Brazier cocked his piece—*click, click*—and took a few steps forward to try and get a sight of the creature before it reached the river bank.

"May as well save your shot, sir," said Shaddy gruffly. "He's going into the water bleeding pretty free, I know; and there's them waiting below as will be at him as soon as they smell blood."

"How horrible!" cried Rob.

"Ay, 'tis, sir, or seems so to us; but it's nature's way of clearing off all the sickly and wounded things from the face of the earth."

"But what will dare to attack such a terrible beast?"

Shaddy chuckled.

"Anything—everything, sir; little and big. Why, them little pirani fishes will be at him in thousands, and there's 'gators enough within fifty yards to make a supper of him as if he was spitchcocked eel. Ah! there he goes—part of him's in the water already; but I should have liked the master to have his skin."

Invisible though the serpent was, its course was evident by the rustling and movement of the growth, and some idea too was gained of the reptile's length.

"There! what did I say?" shouted Shaddy excitedly, as all at once there was the sound of splashing and agitation in the water down beneath the submerged trees; and directly after the serpent's tail rose above the trunk of one of those lying prone, and gleamed and glistened in the blaze as it undulated and bent and twined about. Then it fell with a splash, and beat the water, rose again quivering seven or eight feet in the air, while the water all around seemed terribly agitated. There was a snapping sound, too, horribly ominous in its nature, and the rushing and splashing went on as the tail of the serpent fell suddenly, rose once more as if the rest of the long lithe body were held below, and finally disappeared, while the splashing continued for a few minutes longer before all was silent.

Rob drew a long breath, and Joe shuddered.

"Well," said Shaddy quietly, "that's just how you take it, young gentlemen. Seems so horrible because it was a big serpent. If it had been a worm six inches long you wouldn't have thought anything of it. Look at my four chaps there: they don't take any notice—don't seem horrid to them. You'll get used to it."

"Impossible!" said Brazier.

"Oh! I don't know, sir," continued Shaddy. "You've come out where you wanted to, in the wildest wilds, where the beasts have it all their own way, and they do as they always do, go on eating one another up. Why, I've noticed that it isn't only the birds, beasts, and fishes, but even the trees out here in the forest do just the same."

"Nonsense!" cried Rob merrily. "Eat one another?"

"Yes, sir; that's it, rum as it sounds to you. I'll tell you how it is. A great ball full of nuts tumbles down from one of the top branches of a tree, when it's ripe, bang on to the hard ground, splits, and the nuts fly out all round, right amongst the plants and rotten leaves. After a bit the nuts begin to swell; then a shoot comes out, and another out of it. Then one shoot goes down into the ground to make roots, and the other goes up to make a tree. They're all doing the same thing, but one of 'em happens to have fallen in the place where there's the best soil, and he grows bigger and stronger than the others, and soon begins to smother them by pushing his branches and leaves over them. Then they get spindly and weak, and worse and worse, because the big one shoves his roots among them too; and at last they wither and droop, and die, and rot, and the big strong one regularly eats up with his roots all the stuff of which they were made; and in a few years, instead of there being thirty or forty young trees, there's only one, and it gets big."

"Why, Naylor, you are quite a philosopher!" said Brazier, smiling.

"Am I, sir? Didn't know it; but a man like me couldn't be out in the woods always without seeing that. Why, you'd think, with such thousands of trees always falling and rotting away, that the ground would be feet deep in leaf mould and decayed wood; but if you go right in the forest you'll find how the roots eat it up as fast as it's made."

"But what about these big trunks?" said Joe, pointing to the fallen trees.

"Them? Well, they're going into earth as fast as they can, and in a few years there'll be nothing of 'em left. Why, look at that one; it's as if it were burning away now," he continued, pointing to the hole through which Rob had fallen: "that's nature at work making the tree, now it's dead, turn into useful stuff for the others to feed on."

"Yes," said Brazier, as he broke out a piece of the luminous touchwood, which gleamed in the darkness when it was screened from the fire: "that's a kind of phosphoric fungus, boys."

"Looks as if it would burn one's fingers," said Joe, handling the beautiful piece of rotten, glowing wood.

"Yes; and so do other things out here," said Shaddy. "There's plenty of what I call cold fire; but you'll soon see enough of that."

Shaddy ceased speaking, for at that moment a strange, thrilling sound came from the depths of the forest, not more, apparently, than a hundred yards away.

Its effect was electrical.

The half-bred natives who formed Shaddy's crew of boatmen had watched the encounters with the two serpents in the most unconcerned way, while the weird chorus of sounds from the depths of the forest, with yells, howls, and cries of dangerous beasts, was so much a matter of course that they did not turn their heads even at the nearest roar, trusting, as they did, implicitly in the security afforded them by the fire. But now, as this strange sound rang out, silencing the chorus of cries, they leaped up as one man, and made for the boat, hauling on the rope and scrambling in as fast as possible.

Rob's first impulse was to follow suit, especially as Giovanni took a few hurried steps, and tripping over a little bush, fell headlong. But seeing that Shaddy stood fast, and that Brazier cocked his piece, he stopped where he was, though his heart throbbed heavily, and his breath came as if there were some strange oppression at his chest.

"What's that?" whispered Brazier, as the thrilling sound died away, leaving the impression behind that some huge creature must be approaching in a threatening manner, for a curious rustling followed the cry.

"Well, sir," said Shaddy, taking off his cap, and giving his head a rub as if to brighten his brain, "that's what I want to know."

"You don't know?"

"No, sir," said the man, coolly; "I know pretty well every noise as is to be heard out here but that one, and it downright puzzles me. First time I heard it I was sitting by my fire cooking my dinner—a fat, young turkey I'd shot—and I ups and runs as hard as ever I could, and did not stop till I could go no further. Ah! I rec'lect it now, how hungry and faint I was, for I dursen't go back, and I dessay whatever the beast was who made that row ate my turkey. Nex' time I heard it I didn't run. I was cooking ducks then, and I says to myself, 'I'll take the ducks,' and I did, and walked off as fast as I could to my boat."

"And you did not see it?"

"No, sir. P'r'aps we shall this time; I hope so, for I want to know. Third time never fails, so if you don't mind we'll all be ready with our guns and wait for him. May be something interesting to a nat'ral hist'ry gent like you, and we may get his head and skin for you to take home to the Bri'sh Museum. What do you say?"

"Well," said Brazier, drily, "self-preservation's the first law of nature. I do not want to show the white feather, but really I think we had better do as the men have done—get on board and wait for our enemy there. What do you say, lads!"

"Decidedly, yes," cried both eagerly.

"But we don't know as it is our enemy yet, sir," replied Shaddy, thoughtfully. "Hah! hark at that!"

They needed no telling, for all shivered slightly, as another cry, very different from the last, rang out from the forest—half roar, half howl, of a most appalling nature.

"Here, let's get on board," said Brazier.

"Not for that, sir," cried Shaddy, with one of his curiously harsh laughs. "Why, that's only one of them big howling monkeys who would go off among the branches twisting his tail, and scared 'most into fits, if you looked at him."

"A monkey!" cried Rob. "Are you sure?"

"Oh, yes, I'm sure enough 'bout that, gentlemen. It's the other thing that puzzles me."

They ceased speaking and stood watchfully waiting; but after a retrograde movement toward the boat, so as to be able to retreat at any moment. The cry was not repeated, though, and the feeling of awe began to die off, but only to return on Shaddy continuing,—

"There's a something there, or else that there howler wouldn't have hollered once and then gone off. The lions and tigers, too, have slinked away. That's a lion—puma you call him—ever so far off; and, I can hear a couple of tigers quite faint-like; but all the things near here have stopped calling, and that shows there's that thing prowling about."

"But the men?" whispered Rob. "They ran away as if they knew what it was."

"Tchah! They don't know. Their heads are full of bogies. Soon as they hear a noise, and can't tell what it is, they say it's an evil spirit or a goblin or ghost. Babies they are. Why, if I was to go near a lot of natives in the dark, hide myself, and let go with Scotch bagpipes, they'd run for miles and never come nigh that part of the forest again."

All at once the chorus in the forest was resumed, with so much force that it sounded as if the various creatures had been holding their noises back and were now trying hard to make up for the previous check.

That was Rob's opinion, and he gave it in a whisper to his companion.

"Then, it's gone," said Joe. "I say, didn't you feel scared?"

"Horribly."

"Then I'm not such a coward after all. I felt as if I must run."

"So you did when the serpent came."

"Well, isn't it enough to make one? You English fellows have the credit of being so brave that you will face anything without being frightened; but I believe you are frightened all the same."

"Of course we are," said Rob, "only Englishmen will never own they are frightened, even to themselves, and that's why they face anything."

"Then you are not an Englishman?" said Joe.

"No, only an English boy," said Rob, laughing. "I say, though, never mind about bragging. I'm precious glad, whatever it was, that it has gone."

"I remember, now, my father telling me about his hearing some horrible noise in the Grand Chaco one night when the schooner was at anchor close in shore. He said it gave him quite a chill; but I didn't take any more notice of it then. It must have been one of those things."

"No doubt," said Brazier, who had overheard his words; "but there, our adventure is over for this time, and it will be something to think about in the future."

"Perhaps we shall see it yet," said Rob.

"I hope not," cried Joe uneasily.

"Gone, Naylor?" continued Brazier.

"Yes, sir, I think so."

"Good job too. Why, Naylor, my man, I never thought you were going to bring us to such a savage, dangerous place as this."

"What? Come, sir, I like that! Says to me, you did, 'I want you to guide me to some part of the country where I can enter the prime forest.'"

"Primeval," said Brazier, correctively.

"That's right, sir. 'Where,' you says, 'the foot of man has never trod, and I may see Natur' just as she is, untouched, unaltered by any one. Do you know such a place?' Them was your very words, and Master Rob heered you."

"Quite true, my man."

"And I says to you, 'I knows the spot as'll just suit you. Trust to me,' I says, 'and I'll take you there, where you may see birds, beasts, and fishes, and as many o' them flowers'—orkards you called 'em—'as grows on trees, as you like;' and now here you are, sir, and you grumble."

"Not a bit, Naylor."

"But, begging your pardon, sir, you do; and I appeals to Master Rob whether I arn't done my dooty."

"No need to appeal to Rob, Naylor, for I do not grumble. You have done splendidly for me. Why, man, I am delighted; but you must not be surprised at my feeling startled when anacondas come to supper, and we are frightened out of our wits by cries that impress even you."

"Then you are satisfied, sir?"

"More than satisfied."

"And you don't want to go back?"

"Of course not. What do you say, Rob? Shall we return?"

"Oh no—not on any account; only let's keep more in the boat."

"Yes, I think we are safer there," said Brazier. "But our friend, or enemy, seems to have gone."

"Wait a bit, sir," replied Shaddy; "and glad I am that you're satisfied. Let me listen awhile."

They were silent, and stood listening as well, and watching the weird effects produced by the fire, as from time to time one of the pieces of wood which the men had planted round the blaze in the shape of a cone fell in, sending up a whirl of flame and glittering sparks high in air, lighting up the trees and making them seem to wave with the dancing flames. The wall of forest across the river, too, appeared to be peopled with strange shadows, and the effect was more strange as the fire approached nearer to the huge butt of the largest tree, throwing up its jagged roots against the dazzling light, so that it was as if so many gigantic stag-horns had been planted at a furnace mouth.

And all the while the fiddling, piping, strumming and hooting, with screech, yell and howl, went on in the curious chorus, for they were indeed deep now in one of Nature's fastnesses, where the teeming life had remained untouched by man.

"Well," said Brazier at last to the guide, whose figure, seen by the light of the fire, looked as wild as the surroundings, "had we not better get on board? You can hear nothing through that din."

"Oh yes, I can, sir," replied Shaddy. "I've got so used to it o' nights that I can pick out any sound I like from the rest. But we may as well turn in. The fire will burn till morning, and even if it wouldn't, those chaps of mine wouldn't go ashore again to-night; and I certainly don't feel disposed to go and mend the fire myself, for fear of getting something on my shoulder I don't understand."

"It has gone, though," said Brazier.

"Something moving there," whispered Rob, pointing to the gilded mass of foliage beyond and to the left of the fire.

"Eh! where?" cried Shaddy. "Nay, only the fire making it look as if the trees were waving. Nothing there, my lad. Whatever it is, it has slinked off into the forest again. The fire drew it this way, I suppose. There, we've heard the last of him for to-night. Sings well when he do oblige."

"I should have liked to hear the cry once more, though," said Brazier; and as the words left his lips the horrible noise rang out, apparently from behind the fire, and without hesitation the little party hurried on board the boat.

Chapter Twelve.

Shaddy's Remorse.

That last movement was not performed without difficulty, for at this fresh alarm, urged by a desire for self-preservation, the men had thrust the boat away from the bank, and were actually in the act of unfastening the mooring rope, when Rob shouted to Shaddy.

"What!" he roared, running to the other end where it was fast to a branch, and then yelling out such a furious tirade of words in their own tongue that the men shrank back, and the boat was drawn close in among the boughs that were worn sharp by the action of the stream.

"Lucky for them," growled Shaddy, as he held the boat's gunwale for the others to get on board, while the singular silence which had followed the first cry of the beast was again maintained. "I never did break a man's neck yet, Master Rob," he whispered, as they took their places on board, "and I never mean to if I can help it; but if those fellows had run off and left us in the lurch I'd have gone as far as I could without doing it quite."

"First catch your hare," whispered back Rob, who felt better now he was safe on board, with the boat gliding outward to the full length of the mooring line.

"Eh! what hare? No hares about here," said Shaddy.

"I mean, how would you have managed to punish the men if they had gone off and left us here?"

"I never thought of that," said Shaddy, shaking his head; and then they all sat in the boat listening, and thinking that it was a good thing they had had enough supper before the interruption.

There was no fresh alarm for awhile. The birds, insects, quadrupeds, and reptiles resumed their performances, the boatmen settled down to sleep, and at last, after watching the fire sinking, rising up as some piece of wood fell in, and then blazing brightly just beyond the great root, the hole from which this had been wrenched having been selected by the crew of the boat as an excellent place for cooking, Rob suddenly fell asleep, to dream of huge boa constrictors and anacondas twisting themselves up into knots which they could not untie.

It only seemed to be a few minutes since Rob had lain down, when he awoke with a start to gaze about him, wondering where he was and why the awning looked so light. Then coming to the conclusion that it was sunrise, and being still weary and drowsy, he was about to close his eyes again and follow the example of those about him, when he became conscious of a peculiar odour and a choking smell of burning.

This completely aroused him, and hurriedly creeping from beneath the awning without awakening his companions, he found that the boatmen and Shaddy were fast asleep and a line of fire was rapidly approaching them from the shore; not with any rush of flame, but in a curious sputtering, smouldering way, as the touchwood of which the huge trunk, to which they were tethered, was composed rapidly burned away.

It was all plain enough: the root had caught fire at last from the intense heat so near and gradually started the rest, so that as Rob gazed shoreward there was a dull incandescent trunk where the previous night there had been one long line of beautiful orchids and epiphytic plants.

But there was no time to waste. Waking Shaddy with a sharp slap on the shoulder, that worthy started up, saw the mischief pointed out, and shouting, "Only shut my eye because the fire made it ache," he took up a boat-hook, went right forward, trampling on the boatmen in his eagerness, and, hauling on the line, drew the boat close up to the glowing trunk, hitching on to one of the neighbouring branches.

It was only just in time, for the rope gave way, burned through as he got hold, and the smouldering end dropped into the water, giving a hiss like a serpent as the glowing end was quenched.

Brazier and Giovanni were aroused before this, and were fully alive to the peril which had been averted by Rob's opportune awakening.

"Why," cried Brazier, "we should have been drifting down the stream, and been carried miles, and in all probability capsized."

Shaddy made no reply for the moment, but busied himself in altering the position of the boat before letting go, and then hooking the bough of another of the trees, one which did not communicate with the fire, and to this he made fast before rising up in the boat, taking off his cap, and dashing it down.

"Yes," he said harshly, "right, sir. We should have been carried right down the stream— Be off, you brute!"

This was to an alligator which was approaching the boat with the protuberances above its eyes just visible, and as he uttered the adjuration he made a stroke with the hitcher harpoon fashion, struck the reptile full on its tough hide, and there was a swirl, a rush, and a tremendous splash of water full in Shaddy's face as the creature struck the surface with its tail and then disappeared.

"Thank ye," growled Shaddy, wiping his face; "but you got the worst of it, mate. As aforesaid, maybe, Mr Brazier, sir, we should ha' been carried right down the stream, and run on a sharp root or trunk as would ha' drove a hole through the boat or capsized us, and there'd ha' been the end."

"What could you have been thinking of, Naylor?" cried Brazier angrily; while Rob looked pityingly and feeling sorry for the staunch, brave man, who stood there abashed by his position.

"Warn't thinking at all, sir," he growled. "Only ought to ha' been. There, don't make it worse, sir, by bullying me. You trusted me, and

I thought I was fit to trust, but there's the vanity o' man's natur'. I arn't fit to trust, so I'd take it kindly if you'd knock me overboard; but you'd better knock my stoopid head off first to save pain."

This was all spoken with the most utter seriousness, and as Shaddy finished he slowly laid down the boat-hook and looked full in Brazier's eyes, with the result that Rob burst into a roar of laughter. Joe followed suit, and after an attempt to master himself and frown Brazier joined in, the mirth increasing as Shaddy said sternly,—

"Oh, it arn't nothing to laugh at! If Master Rob there hadn't woke up before morning, the 'gators and pirani, without counting the other critters, would have been having a treat. I tell you I'm ashamed of myself, and the sooner an end's made of me the better. Why, you ought to do it, sir, in self-defence."

"How near are we to morning?" said Brazier.

"'Tis morning now, sir. Sun'll be up in less an half an hour. No dawn here."

"Then we had better have breakfast at once, and start, for this is anything but a pleasant spot."

"Ain't you going to knock me overboard, sir?" said Shaddy.

"No."

"Well, ain't you going to knock me down?"

"No; I'm not going to knock you down either, my good fellow. You've made a mistake. Over-tired, I suppose, and you dropped asleep. It was terribly neglectful of you, but I hope and trust that such an error may not be made again."

"What?"

"Surely I need not repeat my words. You were overcome by fatigue and slept. I ask you for all our sakes to be more careful in the future."

"Here, I say, Master Rob," cried Shaddy huskily, and he gave his eyes a rub, "am I still asleep?"

"No, Shaddy, wide awake, and listening to Mr Brazier."

"Well, then, it's a rum 'un. But, I say, look here, sir; you're never going to trust me again?"

"I am going to treat you with full confidence, just as I trusted you before, Naylor," replied Brazier.

"Master Rob's asleep too," growled the man. "It can't be true. Here, I say, Mr Jovanny, give a look at me and tell me, am I awake or no?"

"Awake, of course," said Joe.

"Then all I can say is, Mr Brazier, sir," said the guide, "you've made me ten times more ashamed of myself than I was before, and that hurt I can't bear it like."

"Say no more about it, man," said Brazier. "There, it's all over now. Let's have breakfast, and then start for a long day's collecting."

"Not say no more about it?" cried Shaddy.

"Not a word. It is all past and forgotten."

"Can't be," growled Shaddy.

"It shall be," said Brazier, turning to get his gun from under the canvas cabin.

"One moment—look here, sir," said Shaddy; "do you mean to say that you forgive me?"

"Yes, of course."

"And I am not to say another word?"

"No."

"Then I'll think," said Shaddy, "and punish myself that way, Master Rob. I'll always think about it at night when I'm on the watch. It ain't likely that I shall ever go to sleep again on dooty with idees like that on my brain."

"No more talking; breakfast at once," cried Brazier, issuing from the cabin.

"Right, sir," said Shaddy, working the boat in close to the bank. "Quick, my lads, and get that fire well alight."

The men were set ashore just as the sun rose and flooded everything with light, while a quarter of an hour later, as Brazier was patiently watching one of the tunnel-like openings opposite in the hope of seeing a deer come down to drink and make them a good meal or two for a couple of days, Shaddy drew Rob's attention to the black-looking forms of several alligators floating about a few feet below.

"The brutes!" said the lad. "Just like efts in an aquarium at home."

"Only a little bigger, my lad. I say, there he is—one of 'em."

He pointed down through the clear water, illumined now by the sun so that the bottom was visible, and there coiled-up and apparently asleep lay either the anaconda of the previous night or one of its relatives, perfectly motionless and heedless of the boat, which floated like a black shadow over its head.

"Might kill it if we had what sailors call the grains to harpoon him with," said Shaddy; "but I don't know, he'd be an ugly customer to tackle. I say, look out, sir," he whispered, "yonder across the river."

Brazier glanced a little to his left, and directly after his piece rang out with a loud report and a deer fell dead—not having moved an inch, when the boat was with difficulty rowed across, and the welcome addition to their larder secured amidst the chattering of monkeys and the screaming of great macaws.

An hour later breakfast was at an end, the boat loosened from the moorings where the anaconda still lay asleep in ten feet of water, and they glided down the stream to commence another adventurous day, amidst scenery which grew more wondrously beautiful with every mile.

Chapter Thirteen.

The Lily Lagoon.

"Like it, gentlemen? That's right. On'y you are sure—quite sure?"

"Oh yes, we're sure enough!" replied Rob, as he watched the endless scenes of beautiful objects they passed. "It's glorious."

"Don't find it too hot, I s'pose, sir?"

"Oh, it's hot enough," interposed Giovanni; "but we don't mind, do we, Rob?"

"Not a bit. What fruit's that?"

"Which?" said Shaddy.

"That, on that tree, high up, swinging in the wind—the dark brown thing, like a great nut with a long stalk."

He pointed to the object which had taken his attention.

"G'long with yer," growled Shaddy. "I thought you was in arnest."

"So I am," cried Rob, looking at the man wonderingly. "I mean that one. It isn't a cocoa-nut, because the tree is different, and I know that cocoanuts grow on a kind of palm."

"And that kind o' nut don't, eh?" said Shaddy, puckering his face. "Why you are laughing at me."

"Nonsense! I am not!" cried Rob. "You don't see the fruit I mean. There, on that tallest tree with the great branch sticking out and hanging over the others. There now! can you see?"

"No," said Shaddy grimly; "it's gone."

"Yes; how curious that it should drop just at that moment. I saw it go down among the trees. You did see it?"

"Oh yes. I see it plain enough."

"And you don't know what fruit it was?"

"Warn't a fruit at all, sir."

"What then? some kind of nut?"

"No, sir; warn't nut at all. It was a nut-cracker."

Rob looked at him seriously.

"Who's joking now?" he said.

"Not me, sir," replied Shaddy. "That was a nut-cracker sure enough."

"Is that the native name?"

Joe burst into a roar of laughter, and Rob coloured, for there was a feeling of annoyance rising within him at being the butt of the others' mirth.

"Have I said something very stupid?" he asked.

"Why, couldn't you see?" cried Joe eagerly. "It was a monkey."

"I did not see any monkey," said Rob coldly. "I was talking about that great brown husky-looking fruit, like a cocoa-nut hanging by a long stalk in that tree. Look! there are two more lower down!" he cried eagerly, as the boat glided round a bend into a long reach, two of the men being at the oars backing water a little from time to time with a gentle dip, so as to keep the boat's head straight and check her to enable Brazier to scan the banks through the little binocular glass he carried, and be rowed close in when he wished to obtain specimens.

"Yes: there's two more lower down," said Shaddy, with his face puckered up like the shell of a walnut, and then Rob's mouth expanded into a grin as wide as that of Joe's, and he laughed heartily.

"Well," he cried, "that is comic, and no mistake. I really thought it was some kind of fruit. It *was* a monkey."

"You ain't the first as made that mistake, Mr Rob, sir," said Shaddy. "You see, they just take a turn with their tails round a branch, draws their legs up close, and cuddles them with their long arms round 'em, and then they looks just like the hucks of a cocoa-nut."

"Like the what?" cried Rob.

"Hucks of a cocoa-nut."

"Oh—husk."

"You may call it 'husk' if you like, sir: I calls it 'hucks.' Then they hangs head downwards, and goes to sleep like that, I believe. Wonderful thing a monkey's tail is. Why I've seen the young ones hold on to their mother by giving it a turn round the old girl's neck. They're all like that out here. Ring-tail monkeys we call 'em."

While they were talking the last two monkeys had swung themselves to and fro, and then lowered themselves down among the branches to get close to the river and watch the boat, like a couple of tiny savages stricken with wonder at the coming of the strange white men, and chattering away to each other their comments on all they saw.

The progress made was very slow, for the boat was constantly being anchored, so to speak, by the men rowing in and holding on by the hanging boughs of trees, while Brazier cut and hacked off bulb and blossom in what, with glowing face, he declared to be a perfect naturalist's paradise.

They had been floating down a few miles when, right ahead, the stream seemed to end, the way being blocked entirely by huge trees, and as they drew nearer there appeared to be a repetition of the entrance from the great river, where they passed along through the dark tunnel overhung by trees.

"Oh, it's all right, sir," said Shaddy, on being appealed to. "Dessay we shall find a way on."

"Of course," replied Brazier, who only had eyes for the plants he was collecting and hardly looked up; "this great body of water must go somewhere."

"Look sharp round to the left!" cried Rob, standing up in the boat as they glided round a bend where the stream nearly turned upon itself and then back again, forming a complete S; and as they moved round the second bend Rob uttered a shout of delight, for the banks receded on either hand, so that they appeared to have glided into a wide opening about a mile long, floored with dark green dotted with silver, through which in a sinuous manner the river wound. A minute later, though, the two lads saw that the river really expanded into a lake, the stream in its rapid course keeping a passage open, the rest of the water being densely covered with the huge, circular leaves of a gigantic water-lily, whose silvery blossoms peered up among the dark green leaves.

"Look at the jacanas!" cried Joe, pointing to a number of singular-looking birds like long-necked and legged moorhens, but provided with exaggerated toes, these being of such a length that they easily supported their owners as they walked about or ran on the floating leaves.

"Wouldn't be a bad place for a camp, sir," suggested Shaddy, when they were about half-way along the lake, and he pointed to a spot on their left where the trees stood back, leaving a grassy expanse not unlike the one at which they had first halted, only of far greater extent.

"Yes, excellent," replied Brazier; "but can we get there?"

"Oh yes, sir; I'll soon make a way through the leaves."

Shaddy seized a pole, said a few words to his men, and stepped right to the front of the boat, where he stood thrusting back the vegetation as it collected about the bows, while the men rowed hard forcing the boat onward, the huge leaves being sent to right and left and others passing right under the keel, but all floating back to their former positions, so that as Rob looked back the jacanas were again running over the vegetation which had re-covered the little channel the boat had made.

In all probability a vessel had never entered that lake before, and it caused so little alarm that great fish, which had been sheltering themselves beneath the dark green disk-like leaves, lazily issued from their lurking places to stare so stupidly, often even with their back fins out of water, that the boys had no difficulty in startling a few of them into a knowledge of their danger by gently placing a hand under and hoisting them suddenly into the boat, where they displayed their alarm by leaping vigorously and beating the fragile bottom with their tails.

"Better hold hard, young gentlemen!" cried Shaddy, as soon as half a dozen were caught; "them fish won't keep, and we can easily catch more. Ah! Why, Mr Joe, sir, I did think you knowed better."

This was to Joe, who had leaned over as far as he could to try and perform the same feat upon a long dark object floating half hidden by a leaf, but was met by a quick rush and a shower of water as the creature twisted itself round and dived down.

"It was only a little one, Shaddy," said Joe.

"Little dogs have sharp teeth, my lad; and them small 'gators can bite like fury. You take my advice, and don't do it again."

"Hah!" cried Brazier as he leaped ashore, "this is glorious. We can make quite a collection here. See that the boat is fast, Naylor."

This was soon done, and the men were about to light a fire, but Brazier checked them, preferring to make a little expedition for exploration purposes all about their new camping place, partly to see if there were noxious beasts at hand, partly to try and secure a few natural history specimens, especially birds, which abounded, before the noise and the fire should drive them away.

"Hand out the guns and cartridge bags," said Brazier; and this being done the men were left in charge of the boat, and the little party started, keeping close up to the trees on their left with the intention of going all round the opening and so returning by the right side to the boat.

The walking was hard, for the earth was tangled with dense growth so that they progressed very slowly, while the heat was intense; but that passed unnoticed in the excitement caused by the novel objects which met their eyes at every step—flowers, such as Rob had never before seen, looking up as if asking to be plucked; butterflies which flapped about so lazily that they could, he felt, easily be caught, only without net or appliances it seemed wanton destruction to capture and mutilate such gorgeously painted objects. There were others too, resembling the hawk-moths in shape, with thick body and long pointed wing, which were constantly being taken for humming-birds, so rapid was their darting flight. As for these latter, they flashed about them here, there, and everywhere, now glittering in the sunshine, now looking dull and plum-coloured as they hovered on hazy wings before the long trumpet blossoms of some convolvulus-like flower whose twiny stems trailed over or wrapped the lower growth.

Beetles, too, were abundant in every sun-scorched spot or on the bare trunks of the trees, though bare places were rare, for the trees were clothed densely with moss and orchid.

Rob's fingers itched as bird after bird flew up, and he longed to bring them down for specimens, whose brilliant colours he could gloat over. Now it was a huge scarlet-and-blue macaw, now one painted by Nature's hand scarlet, yellow, and green, which flew off with its long tail feathers spread, uttering discordant shrieks, and startling the smaller parrots from the trees which they were stripping of their fruit.

But Brazier had told him not to fire at the smaller birds, as it was a necessity to keep their larder supplied with substantial food, the four boatmen and Shaddy being pretty good trencher-men, and making the deer meat disappear even without the aid of trenchers.

"We ought to find a deer here surely," said Brazier, when they were about half-way round.

"Well, I don't know, sir," replied their guide; "deer ain't like human beings, ready to go walking in the hot sunshine in the middle of the day. They like to lie up in the shade all through the sunny time, and feed in the morning and evening."

"Then you think we shall not see a deer?"

"Can't say, sir; but if a turkey goes up I should make sure of him at once. So I should if we came upon a carpincho, for this is a likely place for one of them."

"But are they good eating?"

"Capital, sir. Now, look at that."

He faced round at a loud, fluttering sound, and guns were raised, but the great bird which had taken flight was far out of shot, and winging its way higher and higher, so as to fly over the tops of the trees and away into the forest.

"Fine great turkey that, sir," said Shaddy.

"Yes: can we follow it?"

Shaddy shook his head.

"Far more sensible for us to walk straight away, sir, through the open where that turkey got up: we might start another or two."

"But the going is so laborious," pleaded Brazier; "some of us would be having sunstroke. No, let's keep on, we may put up something yet."

"And try for the turkeys toward sundown, sir?"

"Yes. Come on," said Brazier; "we had better get slowly back now to the boat. It is too hot."

He stood wiping the perspiration from his forehead as he spoke, and then, with Shaddy by his side carrying a spare gun, went on along by the edge of the forest, Rob and Joe following some distance behind.

"I might as well have shot some of those beautiful toucans," said Rob; "I could have skinned them, and they would be delightful to bring out at home and show people, and remind one of this place in years to come."

"Yes, we shouldn't have scared away much game," replied Joe. "What's that they can see?"

For Shaddy was holding up his hand to stop them, and Brazier, who had forgotten all about being languid and weary in the hot sunshine, was hurrying forward bending down and making for one of several clumps of bushes about half-way between them and the river.

Rob noted that clump particularly, for it was scarlet with the blossoms of a magnificent passion-flower, whose steins trailed all over it, tangling it into a mass of flame colour, looking hot in the sunshine, which made the air quiver as if in motion.

The lads stopped at Shaddy's signal and looked intently, but they could see no sign of any game, and, rightly concluding that the object of Brazier's movement must be hidden from them at the edge of the forest, they crouched down and waited for fully five minutes.

"Here, I'm sick of this," whispered Rob at last; and he rose from his uncomfortable position.

"So am I," said Joe, straightening himself. "Hullo! Where's old Shaddy?"

"Lying down and having a nap, I expect," replied Rob. "I can't see him nor Mr Brazier neither. Shall we go on."

"No: let's wait a bit. They may be seeing a chance for something good at supper-time."

They waited another five minutes, ten minutes, and had at last determined to go on, when Brazier's piece was heard, the sharp report coming from about three hundred yards farther on toward the river.

"There's Shaddy running," cried Joe; and they saw now where he had been crawling, far beyond the scarlet passion-flower, from whose shelter Mr Brazier had evidently made a long stalk till he was close to the object of his search, a bird or animal, which had probably fallen, from the haste being made to reach the spot.

"Let's make haste," cried Joe, pushing forward.

"No, thank you; I'm too tired," said Rob. "I was not so fagged before, but after lying down there so long I'm as stiff as can be. Oh, bother! something stung me. It's one of those ants. Brush them off."

Joe performed the kindly duty, and they were on the way to join the others, when there was a rustling sound just in front, and the young Italian started back.

"A snake—a snake!" he panted, as he caught Rob's arm. "Shoot!"

"Well, you shoot too," said the latter rather sharply, for Joe seemed to have forgotten that he had a gun in his hand.

But Rob could not boast, for as the dry grass and scrubby growth in front moved he raised his piece, and drew first one trigger, then the other: there was no result—he had forgotten to cock.

Lowering the gun he rapidly performed this necessary operation, and was about to raise it again and wait, for in the hurry and excitement he had been about to obey his companion and deliver a chance shot almost at random amongst the moving grass—so great was the horror inspired by the very name of one of the reptiles which haunted the moist swamps near the riverside.

But, to the surprise of both, it was no huge anaconda which had been worming its way toward them; for at the sound of the lock—*click*, click—a beautiful warm-grey creature bounded lithely out almost to where they stood, and there paused, watching them and waving its long black tail.

"A lion," whispered Joe, who remained as if paralysed by the sudden bound of the cat-like creature, which stood as high as a mastiff dog, but beautifully soft-looking and rounded in its form, its ears erect, eyes dilated, and motionless, all but that long writhing tail.

In those few moments Rob's powers of observation seemed as if they were abnormally sharpened, and as he noted the soft hairs toward the end of the tail erected and then laid down, and again erected, making it look thick and soft, he noted too that the muzzle was furnished with long cat-like whiskers, and the head was round, soft, and anything but cruel and fierce of aspect.

"Shoot—shoot!" whispered Joe: "the ball—not the small shot."

But Rob did not stir; he merely stood with the muzzle of the gun presented toward the beast, and did not raise it to his shoulder. Not that he was stupefied by the peril of his position, but held back by the non-menacing aspect of the puma. Had there been a display of its fangs or an attempt to crouch for a spring, the gun would have been at his shoulder in a moment, and, hit or miss, he would have drawn the trigger.

"Why don't you shoot?" whispered Joe again.

"I can't," replied Rob. "It must be a tame one."

"Nonsense! You're mad. We're right away in the wilds."

"I don't care where we are," said Rob, who was growing cool and confident; "this must be a tame one. I shall go forward."

"No, no—don't! He'll claw you down."

"He'd better not. I've got my finger on the trigger. Here! Hallo, old chap! puss! puss! whose cat are you?"

"He's mad," whispered Joe as Rob advanced, and the puma stood firm watching him, till they were so close together that, in full confidence that they had met with a tame beast, the property of some settler or Indian, he laid his gun in the hollow of his left arm, and stretched out his right hand.

The puma winced slightly, and its eyes grew more dilate; but, as Rob stood still, the wild look passed slowly away, and it remained motionless.

"Don't! pray don't!" cried Joe in a hoarse whisper; "it will seize your hand in its jaws."

"Nonsense! It's as tame as an old tom-cat," said Rob coolly. "Poor old puss, then!" he continued, reaching out a little farther, so that he could just softly touch the animal's cheek, passing his fingers along toward its left ear.

"There, I told you so," he said, with a laugh, for the puma pressed its head against his hand, giving it a rub in regular cat fashion, while as, to Joe's horror, Rob continued his caress and began gently rubbing the animal's head, it emitted a soft, purring noise, rolled its head about, and ended by closing up and leaning against the lad's leg, passing itself along from nose to tail, turning and repeating the performance, and again on the other side.

"I am glad I didn't shoot," said Rob, bending down to stroke the animal's back. "I say, isn't he a beauty! Come and make friends. He's a bit afraid of us yet."

Joe stood fast, with the loaded gun presented, ready to fire and save his friend's life the moment the creature seized him, when, to his astonishment, the puma so thoroughly approved of the first human caress it had ever received that it lay down, rolled over, wriggling its spine when all four legs were in the air, rolled back again, scratching the ground, and finally crouched and looked up as much as to say, "Go on."

Rob answered the appeal he read in the puma's eyes, and going down on one knee, he patted and stroked it, when, quick as the movement of a serpent, it threw itself over on its back, seized the lad's hand between its bent paws, patted it from one to the other, and then held it tightly as it brought down its mouth as if to bite, but only began to lick the palm with its rough tongue.

"There!" said Rob; "what do you say now? Isn't it a tame one?"

"I—I don't know yet. Hadn't I better fire and kill it?"

"You'd better not," cried Rob. "That'll do, old chap; you'll have the skin off. I say, his tongue is rough. Why, what beautiful fur he has, and how soft and clean! I wonder whose he is."

In the most domestic cat-like fashion the puma now curled itself round, with its forepaws doubled under, and kept up its soft purr as it watched the lad by its side. But as he rose the animal sprang up too, butted its head affectionately against his leg, and then looked up as if to say,—

"What next?"

"Why don't you come and stroke it?" cried Rob. "Because I'm sure it's wild and fierce," was the reply. "Well, it isn't now."

"Ahoy!" came from a distance, and the puma looked sharply about, with ears erect and an intense look, as if it were listening.

"Ahoy!" shouted back Rob. "Let's go to them. Come along, puss."

He took a few steps forward, the puma staring at him and twisting its tail from side to side; but it did not stir. "There, I told you so. It is wild."

"Well, it may be, but it's quite ready to make friends, and it will not hurt us. Come along."

Joe did not possess his companion's faith, and keeping his face to the puma as much as he could, he advanced toward where they could see Brazier waving his hand to them to come on.

As they advanced Rob kept on stopping and looking back at the puma, calling it loudly; but the animal made no response. It stood there with its eyes dilating again, waving and twisting its tail, till they were thirty or forty yards distant, when, with a sudden movement, it half turned away, crouched, its hind legs seemed to act like a spring, and it was shot forward into the low growth and disappeared.

"Gone!" said Joe, with a sigh of relief.

"Why, you're actually afraid of a cat," said Rob mockingly.

"I am—of cats like that," replied his companion. "I've heard my father say that some of them are friendly. That must be a friendly one, but I'm sure they are not fit to be trusted. Let's make haste."

Rob did not feel so disposed, and he looked back from time to time as they forced their way through the grass and low growth, but there was no puma visible, and finally, taking it for granted that the animal was gone, but making up his mind to try and find it again if they stayed, he stepped out more quickly to catch up to Joe, who was pressing on toward where he could now see both of their companions and a hundred yards beyond the boatmen coming to meet them.

"Hi! What have you shot, Mr Brazier?" cried Rob as he drew nearer.

"Deer! Very fine one!" came back the reply.

"Venison for dinner, then, and not 'only fish,'" said Rob as he changed shoulders with his gun. "Shouldn't care to be always tied down to fresh-water fish, Joe. They're not like turbot and soles."

"I say, don't talk about eating," said the young Italian testily.

"Why not?"

"Makes me so hungry."

"Well, so much the better. Proves that you enjoy your meals. I say, I wish that great cat had followed us."

"Nonsense! What could you have done with it?"

"Kept it as a pet. Taught it to catch birds for us, and to fetch those we shot like a dog. Oh, what a beauty!"

This was on seeing the fine large fat deer which had fallen to Brazier's gun.

"Yes," said Brazier, with a satisfied smile; "it was a piece of good fortune, and it will relieve me of some anxiety about provisions."

"But it will not keep," said Rob.

"Yes; cut in strips and dried in the sun, it will last as long as we want it. You see, we have no means of making up waste in our stores, Rob, and the more we get our guns to help us the longer our expedition can be."

The boatmen and the two lads reached the deer just about the same time, and the latter stood looking on with rather an air of disgust upon their countenances as the crew set to work and deftly removed the animal's skin, which was carried off to the boat to be stretched over the awning to dry, while those left rapidly went to work cutting the flesh in strips and bearing it off to the boat.

"I say, Mr Brazier," said Rob after watching the proceedings for some time, "hadn't those strips of flesh better be dried on shore somewhere?"

"Why?"

"Because they'll smell dreadfully."

"I hope not," said Brazier, smiling.

"Not they, sir," put in Shaddy. "Sun soon coats 'em over and takes the juice out of them. They won't trouble your nose, Master Rob, sir, trust me; and as to drying 'em on shore, that would be a very good plan in every way but one."

"What do you mean?"

"Why, that it would be very convenient, sir, and the meat would dry nicely; but when we wanted it you may take my word it wouldn't be there."

"Would some one steal it?" cried Rob. "No; you told me there were no Indians about."

"So I did, sir; but there are hundreds of other things would take it."

"Hang it up in a tree, then."

"Ready for the vultures to come and carry it off? That wouldn't do, sir. No; there's no way of doing it but hanging it up in your boat. The animals can't get at it, nor the ants neither, and the birds are afraid to come."

"I did not think of that," said Rob apologetically.

"No, sir, s'pose not. I used to think as you did. I didn't want to have anything that might smell on my boat, and I did as you advised till I found out that it would not do. Don't take too much at a time," he growled to the man who was loading himself, "and mind and lay out all the pieces separate. Is the fire burning?"

The man replied in his own tongue, and went off.

"I'll get on now, sir," said Shaddy, "and see to the pieces frizzling for our dinner, if you'll stop and see that the men don't leave before they are done."

"How am I to speak to them? I don't know their tongue."

"No need to speak, sir. If they see you're watching them they won't neglect anything, but will do it properly. I was only afraid of their wanting to step off to the fireside to begin broiling bones."

Shaddy shouldered his gun, and went off after the man who was loaded with strips of flesh to make what is called biltong, and the two left worked on very diligently, with the boys wandering here and there in search of objects of interest and finding plenty—brilliant metallic-cased beetles, strange flowers which they wanted named, birds which it was a delight to watch as they busied themselves about the fruit and flowers of the trees at the forest edge.

"I shall be glad when they've done," said Joe at last, as they were walking back to where Brazier stood leaning upon the muzzle of his gun. "I am so hungry. Wonder whether these berries are good to eat!"

He turned aside into the bushes to begin picking some bright yellow fruit, and scaring away a little parrot from the feast.

"I want something better than those," said Rob contemptuously; and he went on, expecting that Joe was close behind.

All at once, when he was about twenty yards away from where Brazier was standing, Rob saw him start, raise his gun, and cock it as he glared wildly at his young companion.

"Anything the matter, sir?" cried Rob, hastening his steps.

"Yes!" cried Brazier hoarsely. "Stand aside, boy! Take care! Out of my line of fire! You're being stalked by a wild beast!"

Rob stared, looked round, and saw at a glance that the puma had evidently been hiding among the dead grass and thick growth, but had been following and watching him ever since he had seen it leap into the bushes. Then the truth dawned upon him that of course Mr Brazier could not know what had passed, and there he was with his gun raised to fire.

"Stand aside, boy!" was roared again; and, obeying the stronger will, Rob sprang aside, but only to leap back.

"Don't fire! don't fire!" he shrieked, but too late. The gun belched forth rapidly its two charges, and Rob fell and rolled over upon the earth.

Chapter Fourteen.

Frightened by False Fires.

"Naylor—Giovanni—help! help!" cried Brazier. "What have I done?"

As in a voice full of agony Brazier uttered these words, the dense smoke from the gun which had hidden Rob for the moment slowly rose and showed the lad lying motionless upon the earth. Shaddy rushed up, dropped upon one knee and raised the boy's head, while with his keen knife held across his mouth he looked sharply round for the South American lion, ready to meet its attack.

But the animal was not visible, and it was directly after forgotten in the excitement centred on Rob.

"Tear off his clothes! Where is he wounded? No doctor! Run to the boat for that little case of mine. Here, let me come."

These words were uttered by Brazier with frantic haste, and directly after he uttered a cry of horror and pointed to Rob's forehead close up amongst the hair, where a little thread of blood began to ooze forth.

"That ain't a shot wound," growled Shaddy. "Hi! One of you get some water."

One of the boatmen, who had hurried up, ran back toward the stream, and just then Rob opened his lips said peevishly,—

"Don't! Leave off! Will you be quiet? Eh! What's the matter?"

As he spoke he thrust Brazier's hand from his head, opened his eyes and looked round.

"What are you doing?" he cried wonderingly.

"Lower him down, Naylor," whispered Brazier hoarsely; and Shaddy was in the act of obeying, but Rob started up into a sitting position, and then sprang to his feet.

"What are you doing, Shaddy?" he cried angrily, as he clapped his hand to his brow, withdrew it, and looked at the stained fingers. "What's the matter with my head?"

He threw it back as he spoke, shook it, and then, as if the mist which troubled his brain had floated away like the smoke from Brazier's gun, he cried:

"I know; I remember. Oh! I say, Mr Brazier, you haven't shot that poor cat?"

"Rob, my boy, pray, pray, pray lie down till we have examined your injuries."

"Nonsense! I'm not hurt," cried the lad—"only knocked my head on a stump. I remember now: I caught my right foot in one of those canes, and pitched forward. Where's the cat?"

He looked round sharply.

"Never mind the wretched beast," cried Brazier. "Tell me, boy: you were not hit?"

"But I do mind," cried Rob. "I wouldn't have had that poor thing shot on any account."

"Are you hurt?" cried Brazier, almost angrily.

"Of course I am, sir. You can't pitch head first on to a stump without hurting yourself. I say, did you hit the cat?"

"Then you were not shot?" cried Brazier.

"Shot? No! Who said I was?"

"And not likely to miss," said Rob sadly. "But I should like its skin, Shaddy."

"And you shall have it, sir, if he's dead. If he isn't he has p'raps carried it miles away into the woods, and there's no following him there."

Rob gazed wistfully across the opening now beginning to look gloomy, and his eyes rested on the figures of the boatmen who were busily piling up great pieces of dead wood to keep up the fire for the night, the principal objects being to scare away animals, and have a supply of hot embers in the morning ready for cooking purposes. And as the fire glowed and the shadows of evening came on, the figures of the men stood out as if made of bronze, till they had done and came down to the boat.

An hour later the men were on board, the rope paid out so that they were a dozen yards from the shore, where a little grapnel had been dropped to hold the boat from drifting in, and once more Rob lay beneath the awning watching the glow of the fire as it lit up the canvas, which was light and dark in patches as it was free from burden or laden with the objects spread upon it to dry. From the forest and lake came the chorus to which he was growing accustomed; and as the lad looked out through the open end of the tent—an arrangement which seemed that night as if it did nothing but keep out the comparatively cool night air—he could see one great planet slowly rising and peering in. Then, all at once, there was dead silence. The nocturnal chorus, with all its weird shrieks and cries, ceased as if by magic, and the darkness was intense.

That is, to Rob: for the simple reason that he had dropped asleep.

Chapter Fifteen.

Foe or Friend?

It was still dark when Rob awoke, and lay listening to the heavy breathing of the other occupants of the boat. Then, turning over, he settled himself down for another hour's sleep.

But the attempt was vain. He had had his night's rest—all for which nature craved—and he now found that he might lie and twist and turn as long as he liked without any effect whatever.

Under these circumstances he crept softly out and looked at the cool, dark water lying beneath the huge leaves, some of which kept on moving in a silent, secretive manner, as if the occupants of the lake were trying to see what manner of thing the boat was, which lay so silent and dark on the surface.

It had been terribly hot and stuffy under the awning, and the water looked deliciously cool and tempting. There was a fascination about the great, black leaves floating there, which seemed to invite the lad to strip off the light flannels in which he had slept, to lower himself gently over the side, and lie in and on and amongst them, with the cool water bracing and invigorating him ready for the heat and toil of the coming day.

It would be good, thought Rob. Just one plunge and a few strokes, and then out and a brisk rub.

But there were the alligators and fish innumerable, nearly all of which had been provided by nature with the sharpest of teeth.

He shuddered at the thought of how, as soon as his white body was seen in the water, scores of voracious creatures might make a rush for him and drag him down among the lily stems for a feast.

"Won't do," he muttered; "but what a pity it does seem!"

He sat watching the surface, and, as he saw how calm and still it was, the longing for a bathe increased. It would, he felt, be so refreshing—so delicious after the hot night and the sensations of prickly heat. Surely he could get a quick plunge and back before anything could attack him; and as he thought this the longing increased tenfold, and plenty of arguments arose in favour of the attempt. There were numbers of great fish and alligators, he knew, but they were not obliged to be there now. Fish swam in shoals, and might be half a mile away one hour though swarming at another.

"I've a good mind to," he thought, and as that thought came he softly unfastened the collar of his flannel shirt.

But he went no farther, for common sense came to the front and pointed out the folly of such a proceeding, after the warnings he had had of the dangers of the river teeming as it did with fierce occupants.

"It will not do, I suppose," he muttered. "I should like to try it, though."

He glanced around, but no one was stirring. The men forward were silent beneath their blankets, and the occupants of the canvas cabin were all sleeping heavily, as their breathing told plainly enough, so there was no fear of interruption.

"I'll try it," said the lad, in an eager whisper.

"No. There is no one to help me if I wanted any. And yet is there likely to be any danger? Most likely the alligators would swim away if they saw me, and would be more frightened of me than I should be of them. While as to the fish— Bah! I'm a coward, and nothing else. Dare say the water's as cool as can be, while I'm as hot as any one could get without being in a fever."

He rolled up the sleeve of his shirt above the elbow, and, leaning over the side, thrust it down between the curves of two lily leaves which overlapped.

"It is delightfully cool," he said to himself, and he thrust his arm down farther, when his fingers came in contact with something rough, which started away, making the water swirl in a tremendous eddy, and caused the sudden abstraction of the lad's arm, but not so quickly that he did not feel a sharp pang, and a tiny fish dropped from the skin on to the bottom of the boat.

"The little wretch!" muttered Rob; and the lesson was sufficient. He did not feel the slightest desire to tempt the cool water more, but applied his lips to the little bite, which was bleeding freely, thinking the while that if one of those savage little fish could produce such an effect, what would be the result of an attack by a thousand.

Day was near at hand as Rob sat there, though it was still dark, and a cold mist hung over the water; but the nocturnal creatures had gone to rest, and here and there came a chirrup or long-drawn whistle to tell that the birds were beginning to stir, instinctively knowing that before long the sun would be up, sending light and heat to chase away the mists of night. Now and then, too, there was a splash or a wallowing sound, as of some great creature moving in the shallows, close up beneath where the trees overhung the water, and the boy turned his head from place to place, half in awe, half in eagerness to know what had made the sound.

But he could make out nothing that was more than twenty or thirty yards from where the boat swung to her moorings; and, turning his head more round, he sat thinking of the adventures of the previous day, and wondered where the puma might be.

"It was a stupid thing to do to run right before that gun," he said to himself; "but I hadn't time to think that Mr Brazier would fire, and I didn't want the poor beast to be killed."

Rob sat thinking of how gentle and tame the great cat-like creature seemed, and a curious sensation of sorrow came over him as he thought of it crawling away into some shelter to die in agony from the effects of the deadly wounds inflicted by Brazier's gun.

"And if I had not tumbled down," he said to himself, "it would have been me instead;" and now he shuddered, for the full truth of his narrow escape dawned upon him.

"It would have been horrid," he thought; "I never felt before how near it was."

He leaned back and looked around at the misty darkness and then up at the sky, where all at once a tiny patch began to glow and rapidly become warmer, till it was of a vivid orange.

"Morning," said Rob half aloud; and feeling quite light-hearted at the prospect of daylight and breakfast, he sat up and looked round him at the positions, now dimly seen, of his companions, and was just thinking of rousing up the men to see to the fire, when the latter took his attention, and he turned to see if it was still glowing.

For some minutes he could not make out the exact spot where it had been made. It was in a little natural clearing about twenty yards from the bank, but the early morning was still too dark for him to make out either bank or clearing, till all at once a faint puff of air swept over the lake, and as it passed the boat, going toward the forest, there was a faint glow, as of phosphorescence, trembling in one particular spot, and he knew that it must be caused by the fanning of the embers.

That faint light was only visible for a few moments, then all was dark again, but it was a transparent darkness, gradually growing clearer. Then a tree seemed to start up on the scene, and a clump of bushes nearer the fire. Soon after he could make out a great patch of feathery green, and this had hardly grown clear enough for him to be certain what it was, when something misty and undefined appeared to be moving along the bank close to the tree to which the boat was tethered. The next moment it melted away into the soft darkness.

"Fancy!" said Rob to himself. But directly after he knew it was not fancy, for he could hear a peculiar scratching, rending sound, which put him in mind of a cat tearing with its claws at the leg of a table.

And now as if by magic there was a soft warm glow diffused around, and, to his surprise and delight, he saw again the object he had before noticed, but no longer undefined. It was grey, and looked transparent, but it was a warm-grey, and grew moment by moment less transparent, gradually assuming the shape of his friend of the previous day, alive and to all appearances uninjured, as, with its soft, elastic, cat-like step and undulating body and tail, it walked slowly down to the edge of the bank, and stood staring at Rob as if waiting for him to speak.

For a few moments the lad was silent and motionless, as he strove hard to detect signs of injury upon the soft, coat of the puma, but nothing was visible, and the animal remained as motionless as he, save that the long tail writhed and curled about as a snake might if gently held by its head.

The next minute Rob had decided what to do.

Creeping silently astern, he unfastened and paid out a good deal of the line which held the boat to the grapnel. Then refastening it, he went silently forward, and began to haul upon the other line, which was secured to the tree ashore, thus bringing the boat's head close up to the bank and within half a dozen yards of the puma, which stood watching him till the boat touched the bank, when, without hesitation or fear of consequences, Rob stepped ashore.

"Fine chance for him if he does mean to eat me!" thought Rob, with a laugh. But the next moment he did feel startled, for the animal suddenly crouched, gathered its hind legs beneath it, and he could see them working as the agile creature prepared to spring.

Rob's heart beat heavily, and a cry rose to his lips, but was not uttered, for he felt paralysed, and he would have proved to be an unresisting victim had the puma's intentions been inimical. But the lad soon knew that they were friendly, for the great bound the creature gave landed it at his feet, where it immediately rolled over on to its side, then turned upon its back, and with touches soft as those of a kitten pulled at the boy's legs and feet, looking playfully up at him the while.

"Why, you are a tame one," said Rob, with a sigh of relief. "There's no danger in you whatever," and sinking on one knee, he patted and rubbed the great soft head which was gently moved about in his hand.

So satisfactory was this to the puma that it rolled itself about on the ground, pressed its head against Rob's knee, and finally turned over once more, couched, laid its head against him, and gazed up in his eyes as he placed his hand upon the soft browny-grey head.

"Well, there's no mistake about this," said Rob aloud; "you and I are good friends, and you must be a tame one. The thing is, where is your master?"

Rob had hardly uttered the word "tame" before the puma's eyes dilated, and it uttered a low, deep growl, staring fiercely the while at the boat.

Rob followed the direction of the animal's eyes, and saw that it was watching Brazier, who had just stepped out from the canvas cabin, holding a gun in his hand.

"Don't! don't do that!" cried Rob excitedly. "It's quite tame, Mr Brazier. Look!"

He was about to bend down and caress the puma again; but as he turned it was only to see its soft, tawny skin and outstretched tail as it made one bound into the thick, low growth of bush and feathery grass, and it was gone.

"Why, Rob," cried his leader, "how could you be so foolish as to go near that savage beast?"

"ROB FOLLOWED THE DIRECTION OF THE ANIMAL'S EYES."

"But it isn't savage," said the lad eagerly; "it's as tame as any cat. It must belong to some one near."

By this time Shaddy had heard the talking and risen, rather apologetic for sleeping so long, and as soon as he had called up his men and sent them ashore to see to the fire the case was laid before him.

"Nay, Master Rob," he said, "there's no one about here to tame lions. It's a wild one sure enough. Dessay he never saw a man or boy before, and he's a young one perhaps, and a bit kittenish. Wants to make friends."

"Friends with a dangerous beast like that, man?" cried Brazier. "Absurd!"

"Oh, they're not dangerous, sir; that is, not to man. I never heard of a lion touching a man unless the man had shot at and hurt him. Then they'll fight savagely for their lives. Dangerous to monkeys, or dogs, or deer; but I'm not surprised at its taking to Master Rob here, and don't see no call to fear."

"Well, of course your experience is greater than mine, Naylor," said Brazier; "but I should have thought that at any moment the beast might turn and rend him."

"No, sir; no, sir; no fear of that! I daresay the crittur would follow him anywhere and be as friendly as a cat. The Indians never take any notice of lions. It's the tigers they're a bit scared about. Lions hate tigers too; and I've known 'em fight till they were both dying."

"Ah well, we need not discuss the matter, for the puma has gone."

"Thought you were going to shoot at it again, sir," said Rob in rather an ill-used tone, for he was disappointed at the sudden interruption to his friendly intercourse with the beautiful beast.

By this time Giovanni was out of the boat, and stared rather at the account of the morning's adventure; but the announcement soon after that the coffee was boiling changed the conversation, and for the time being the puma was forgotten.

The great natural clearing at the edge of the lake and the opening out of the river itself gave so much opportunity for Brazier to prosecute his collecting that he at once decided upon staying in the neighbourhood—certainly for that day, if not for one or two more, and in consequence the fire was left smouldering, while the boat was forced along close in shore, which was no easy task, on account of the dense growth of lilies.

The heat was great, but forgotten in the excitement of collecting, and, with the help of his young companions, Brazier kept on making additions to his specimens, while Rob's great regret was that they were not seeking birds and insects as well.

"Seems such a pity," he confided to Joe. "The orchids are very beautiful when they are hanging down from the trees, with their petals looking like the wings of insects and their colour all of such lovely yellows and blues, but we shall only have the dried, bulb-like stems to take back with us, and how do we know that they will ever flower again?"

"If properly dried, a great many of them will," said Brazier at that moment.

Rob started.

"I didn't know you were listening, sir," he said.

"I was not listening, Rob, but you spoke so loudly, I could not help hearing your words. I can quite understand your preference for the brilliant-coloured and metallic-plumaged birds, and also for the lovely insects which we keep seeing, but specimens of most of these have been taken to Europe again and again, while I have already discovered at least four orchids which I am sure are new."

"But if they do not revive," said Rob, "we shall have had all our journey for nothing."

"But they will revive, my boy, you may depend upon that—at least, some of them; and to my mind we shall have done a far greater thing in carrying to England specimens of these gorgeous flowers to live and be perpetuated in our hothouses, than in taking the dried mummies of bird and insect, which, however beautiful, can never by any possibility live again."

"I didn't think of that," said Rob apologetically.

"I suppose not. But there, be content to help me in my collecting; you are getting plenty of adventure, and to my mind, even if we take back nothing, we shall carry with us recollections of natural wonders that will remain imprinted on our brains till the end of our days."

"He's quite right," thought Rob as he sat alone some time after; "but I wish he wouldn't speak to me as if he were delivering a lecture. Of course I shall help him and work hard, but I do get tired of the flowers. They're beautiful enough on the trees, but as soon as they are picked they begin to fade and wither away."

The conversation took place at the end of the lake, just where the river issued in a narrow stream, walled in on either side by the trees as before, and the intention was to cross this exit and go back by the other side, round to the wide clearing where they had passed the previous night.

Plans in unknown waters are more easily made than carried out.

They had halted for a short time at the foot of a majestic tree, one evidently of great age, and draped from where its lower boughs almost touched the water right to the crown with parasitic growth, much of which consisted of the particular family of flowers Brazier had made his expedition to collect.

Here several splendid specimens were cut from a huge drooping bough which was held down by the men while the collector operated with a handy little axe, bringing down as well insects innumerable, many of which were of a stinging nature, and, to the dismay of both boys, first one and then another brilliantly marked snake of some three feet long and exceedingly slender.

These active little tree-climbers set to at once to find a hiding-place, and at once it became the task of all the band to prevent this unsatisfactory proceeding, no one present looking forward with satisfaction to the prospect of having snakes as fellow-travellers, especially poisonous ones. But they were soon hunted out and thrown by means of a stick right away into the water, but not to drown, for they took to it, swimming as actively and well as an eel.

"Why, that last fellow will reach one of those boughs and get back into a tree again," cried Joe.

"If a fish does not treat him like a worm," said Rob; and he did not feel at all hopeful about the little reptile's fate.

But the next minute he had to think of his own.

One minute the boat was being propelled gently through the still waters amongst the great lily leaves; the next they were in sight of the exit, and something appeared to give the boat a sudden jerk.

"Alligator?" asked Rob excitedly.

"Stream!" growled Shaddy, seizing an oar and rowing with all his might just as they were being swept rapidly down the lower river, the trees gliding by them and the men appearing to have no power whatever to check the boat's way as it glided on faster and faster, leaving the open lake the next minute quite out of sight.

Chapter Sixteen.

In a Tropic Storm.

Rob and Joe looked at each other quite aghast as the boat was literally snatched away out of the boatmen's control and went tearing down the river. For, beside the alteration in their plans, there was the fire waiting, all glowing embers, that would cook to perfection; there were wild fruits which the two lads had noted from the boat; and there was the puma, whose society Rob felt a strong desire to cultivate.

Then, too, there was something startling in being suddenly robbed of all power to act and being swept at a headlong speed along a rapid, for aught they knew, toward some terrible waterfall, over which they would be hurled. So that it was with no little satisfaction that they saw Shaddy seize the boat-hook and, after urging the crew to do their best to pull the boat toward the trees, stand up in the bows and wait his turn.

The crew worked hard, and kept the boat's head up stream, and by degrees they contrived to get it closer to the side, while Shaddy made three attempts to catch hold of a branch. In each case the bough snapped off, but at the fourth try the bough bent and held, though so great was the shock that when the hook caught, the strong-armed man was nearly drawn over the bows into the river, and would have been but for one of the boatmen's help.

It was a sharp tussle for a few moments, and then two of the men caught hold of hanging branches as the boat swung within reach. The next minute a rope was passed round a branch, and the boat was safely moored.

"Mind looking to see whether I've got any arms, Mr Rob?" said Shaddy. "Feels as if they were both jerked out of their sockets."

"Are you hurt much?" asked the boys in a breath.

"Pootty tidy, young gents; but I ain't going to holler about it. There's no time. I don't mind going fast, you know, either in a boat or on horseback, but I do hate for the boat or the horse to take the bit in its teeth and bolt as this did just now."

"What do you propose doing, Naylor?" said Brazier. "It is impossible to get back, and yet I should have liked a few hours more at that clearing."

"And them you shall have, sir, somehow. I'm not the man to be beaten by a boat without making a bit of a fight for it first. Let's get my breath and my arms—ah! they're coming back now. I can begin to feel 'em a bit."

He sat rubbing his biceps, laughing at the boys, Brazier looking up and down-stream uneasily the while.

"Do you know exactly where this river runs, Naylor?" he said at last.

"Well, not exactly, sir. I know it goes right through the sort of country you want to see, and that was enough for me; but I've a notion that it goes up to the nor'-west, winding and twisting about till it runs in one spot pootty nigh to the big river we left, so that we can perhaps go up some side stream, drag the boat across a portage, and launch her for our back journey over the same ground or water as we came up."

"But we shall never get back to the lake," said Rob, as he glanced at the running stream which glided rapidly by, making the boat drag at its tethering rope as if at any moment it would snatch itself free.

"Never's a long time, Mr Rob. We'll see."

He turned to his men, gave them a few instructions in a low tone of voice, and three seated themselves on the port side, while Shaddy and the fourth, a herculean fellow with muscles which bulged out like huge ropes from his bronzed arms, stood in the bows, the latter with the boat-hook and Shaddy with the rope.

"Praps you young gentlemen wouldn't mind putting a hand to the branches when you get a chance," said Shaddy; "every pound of help gives us a pound of strength."

Then, renewing his orders, he seized the light rope, hauled upon it, the man beside him making good use of his hook, and between them they dragged the boat a few feet and made fast the rope, hauled again, cast off the rope, and made fast again—all helping wherever a bough could be caught.

And so they slowly fought their way back against the gigantic strength of the rapid stream, but not without risks. Rob was hauling away at a bough with all his might, when it suddenly snapped, and he would have gone overboard had not Joe thrown himself upon him and held on just as he was toppling down without power to recover his balance.

"That was near," said Rob as he gazed on the young Italian's ghastly face. "I say, don't look scared like that."

Joe shuddered and resumed his work, while Rob put a little less energy into his next movements for a few minutes, but forgot his escape directly after, and worked away with the rest.

It was toil which required constant effort, and they won their way upward very slowly. Twice over they lost ground by the giving way of the branch to which the rope had been attached, and once the boat-hook slipped from the Indian's hand and floated down-stream past the boat, the heavy iron end causing it to keep nearly upright. For a few moments it disappeared, but came gently to the surface again just as it was passing the stern, when the boys gave a ringing cheer, for, leaning out as far as he could, Brazier secured it and passed it back to the man.

Of minor troubles there were plenty. At one moment they would be covered with insects which were rudely shaken from the boughs; at another some branch beneath which they were passing would threaten to sweep the canvas cabin out of the boat; and once it was

Joe, whose flannel was caught by a snaggy end and hung there with the boat passing from under him till a chorus of cries made the stalwart boatman cease his efforts and look back at the mischief he was causing as he hauled.

But, in spite of all difficulties, the boat was slowly drawn over the ground lost in the wild race downward, till at last the lake was reached, and a few sturdy efforts sufficed to drag it once more into still water.

"Once is enough for a job like that, Master Rob," said Shaddy, as he wiped his dripping brow with the back of his hand.

"It was hard work," replied Rob.

"Ay, 'twas; and if you wouldn't mind saying you were so hungry you didn't know what to do, it would be doing us all a kindness, and make Mr Brazier think about meat instead of vegetables."

He gave his head a nod sidewise at Brazier's back, for as the men rested under the shade of a tree the naturalist was busy hauling down some lovely clusters of blossoms from overhead.

"You mean you want some dinner, Shaddy?"

"That's it, sir. This here engine will soon stop working if you don't put on more coal."

"I'll give him a hint," said Rob, laughing; and he did, the result being that Brazier gave the word for the men to row right across toward the clearing—a task they eagerly commenced in spite of the heat and the sturdy effort required to force a way through the dense covering of broad green leaves. They had the river to cross on their way, and as the clear stream was neared a long way above its exit from the lake the men, as if moved by one impulse, ceased rowing, and paused to take their breath before making a sturdy effort to cross it without losing ground.

It was a necessary precaution, for the moment the bows of the boat issued from among the dense growth the stem was pressed heavily downward, and the opposite side of the stream was reached after quite a sharp fight. Then the long, steady pull was commenced again, and, with the leaves brushing against the side, they forced their way onward till the clearing came in view.

The faint curl of bluish smoke encouraged the men to fresh efforts, all thinking of broiled deer meat and a fragrant cup of coffee, both of which afforded grateful refreshment soon after they touched the shore.

"Will it be safe to attempt to continue our journey down that part of the river?" Brazier asked as they were seated afterward in the shade.

"Oh yes, sir, safe enough," replied Shaddy.

"But suppose we have to come back the same way?"

"Well, sir, we can do it, only it will take time."

"You will not mind, Mr Brazier?" said Joe, smiling.

"Indeed I shall, for the work is terrible. Why did you say that?"

"Because you will have such a chance to collect, sir. I saw hundreds of beautiful blossoms which I thought you would like to get, and you could gather them while the men rested."

"Ay, to be sure, sir. Don't you mind about that river being swift! Only wants contriving, and for you to know what's coming, so as to be prepared. Now I know what to expect, I can manage. I shall just set two of the fellows to pull gently, and go down starn first, and always sit there ready with the boat-hook to hitch on to a tree if we are going too fast. You trust me, sir, spite of all that's gone before, and I'll do my best for you and the young gents till your journey's done, though I don't see any coming back this way."

"Of course I shall trust you," said Brazier. "What's the matter?"

"Trust me now then, sir," cried Shaddy, who had leaped up, and was looking sharply round. "Get aboard, all of you. Now, boys!" he roared to his men, and he pointed to the sky.

Shaddy's orders were obeyed, and though there seemed to be no reason for the preparations made, the guide was so confident of the coming of a heavy storm that the waterproof sheet brought for such an emergency was quickly drawn over the canvas roof of their little cabin and made fast; the boat was moored head and stern close up to the bank and beneath a huge, sheltering tree, the balers were laid ready for use in the fore-part and the stern; and when this was all done, and the greatest care taken to keep powder and bedding dry, Brazier turned and looked at Shaddy.

"Well," he said, "is not this a false alarm?"

"No, sir; there's a storm coming. We shall have it soon. Good job we'd got the cooking done."

"But I can't see a cloud," said Rob.

"Don't matter," replied Joe, who was also looking keenly round. "I've seen the heavy rain come streaming down when the sky has been quite clear, and the water has felt quite warm. Look at those fellows; they know the storm's coming, or they would not do that."

He pointed toward the boatmen, who were throwing a tarpaulin across the bows, ready for them to creep under as soon as the rain came.

"False alarm, boys!" said Brazier.

Shaddy overheard him, and wrinkled up his face in a curious grin as he looked hard at Rob. It was as much as to say, "All right! Just you wait a bit and see who's right and who's wrong."

"My word, how hot!" cried Rob the next minute, for the sun appeared to be shining down through a kind of transparent haze so dense that it acted like a burning glass.

"Yes, this is fierce," said Joe, drawing back into the shade afforded by the great tree.

"It would give one sunstroke, wouldn't it, if we stopped in the full blaze?"

"I suppose so. But I say, Shaddy's right. We are going to have a storm."

"How do you know?"

"By the sun gleaming out like that."

"Oh, I don't think that's anything," said Rob. "Here, let's get up into this tree and collect some orchids for Mr Brazier."

He looked up into the large forest monarch as he spoke—a tree which on three sides was wonderfully laden with great drooping boughs. Consequent upon its position at the western corner of the clearing where the boat was moored, the boughs formed a magnificent shelter for their boat down almost to the water, while on the side of the opening they pretty well touched the ground.

But Rob paid little heed to this, his attention being taken up by the fact that, though there was perfect silence, the tree was alive with birds and monkeys, which were huddled together in groups, as if their instinct had taught them that a terrible convulsion of nature was at hand. As a rule they would have taken flight or scampered about through the branches as soon as human beings had come to the tree, but now, as if aware of some great danger, they were content to share the shelter and run all risks.

"See them, Master Rob?" said Shaddy, with a grin. "No mistake this time! Look out; I daresay there'll be snakes dropping down there by-

and-by, but so long as you don't touch 'em I don't s'pose they'll touch us. Shouldn't wonder if we get something else."

Just then Brazier called him to draw his attention to some of the covering, and they heard him say,—

"Don't see as we can do any more, sir. Things are sure to get wet; you can't stop it. All we can do is to keep 'em from getting wetter than we can help."

The sun still shone brilliantly, streaming down, as it were, through the leaves of the great tree like a shower of silver rain, but the silence now was painful, and Rob strained his ears to catch the peculiar modulation of one of the cricket-like insects which were generally so common around. But not one made a sound, and at last, as if troubled by the silence, the boy cried half jeeringly, "All this trouble for nothing! I say, Joe, where's the storm?"

"Here!" was the reply in a whisper, as all at once out of the clear sky great drops of rain came pattering down, then great splashes; and directly after, with a hissing rush, there were sheets of rushing water streaming through the branches and splashing upon the tarpaulin coverings of the boat.

"I say, I never saw it rain like this before," cried Rob as he sheltered himself beneath the tarpaulin and canvas. "Will it thunder—"

He was going to say, "too," but the word remained unspoken, and he shrank back appalled by a blinding flash of vivid blue lightning, which seemed to dash through beneath their shelter and make every face look of a ghastly bluish-grey.

Almost simultaneously there was a deafening peal of thunder, and, as if by an instantaneous change—probably by some icy current of air on high—the moisture-laden atmosphere was darkened by dense mists whirling and looking like foam, clouds of slaty black shut out the sun, and the rain came down in a perfect deluge, streaming through the tree and pouring into the lake with one incessant roaring splash.

One moment beneath the awning it was black as night, the next it was all one dazzling glare, while in peal after peal the mighty thunder came, one clap succeeding another before it had had time to die away in its long metallic reverberations, that sounded as if the thunder rolled away through some vast iron tunnel.

No one attempted to speak, but all crowded together listening awe-stricken to the deafening elemental war, one thought dominating others in their minds, and it was this: "Suppose one of these terrible flashes of lightning strikes the tree!"

Reason and experience said, "Why shelter beneath a tree at a time like this?" but the instinct of self-preservation drove them there to escape the terrible battering of the rain and the rushing wind.

For they had ample knowledge of the state of the lake, though, save in momentary glances, it was invisible beneath the black pall of cloud and rain, for waves came surging in, making the boat rise and fall, while from time to time quite a billow rushed beneath the drooping boughs, which partially broke its force ere it struck against the side of the boat with a heavy slap and sent its crest over the covering and into the unprotected parts.

There was something confusing as well as appalling in the storm, which was gigantic as compared to anything Rob had seen at home, and as he crouched there listening in the brief intervals of the thunder-claps, the rain poured down on the tarpaulin roof with one continuous rush and roar as heavily as if the boat had been backed in beneath some waterfall.

All at once from out of the darkness a curious startling sound was heard, which puzzled both lads for some minutes, till they suddenly recollected that Shaddy had placed tin balers fore and aft, and any doubt as to their being the cause of the peculiar noise was set at rest by Shaddy, who suddenly thrust in his head at the end of a deafening roar and shouted,—

"How are you getting on, gentlemen? Water got in there yet?"

"No, no," was shouted back, "not yet."

"That's right. We're pumping it out here as quick as we can. Comes in fast enough to most sink us."

Shaddy then went on working away out in the pelting rain, and a minute later they made out that his chief man was hard at work forward.

And still the rain came down, and the lightning kept on flashing through the dark shelter; while, if there was any change at all in the thunder, it was louder, clearer, and more rapid in following the electric discharge.

"I say, Joe," whispered Rob at last, with his lips close to his companion's ear, "how do you feel?"

"Don't know: so curious—as if tiny pins and needles were running through me. What's that curious singing noise?"

"That's just what I want to know. I can feel it all through me, and my ears are as if I had caught a bad cold. Like bells ringing; singing you call it."

Just then Shaddy's voice was heard in an interval between two peals of thunder shouting to his men in a tone of voice which indicated that something was wrong, and Brazier thrust out his head from the opening at one end of the awning to ask what was the matter.

"Matter, sir? Why, if we don't get all hands at the pumps the ship'll sink."

"Is it so bad as that? We'll all come at once."

"Nay, nay. I've got a strong enough crew, only we must use buckets instead of balers."

"But—"

"Go inside, sir, please, out of the wet, and see to your things being kept dry. I was 'zaggerating, being a bit excited; that's all. I don't want you, and I daresay the storm's nearly over now."

The sound of dipping water and pouring it over the side went on merrily in the darkness and brilliant light alternately, for, in spite of the guide's words, there seemed to be no sign of the storm abating, and while the men were busy outside Brazier and the two boys set to work piling the various objects they wished to keep dry upon the barrels which had been utilised for their stores, for the water had invaded the covered-in part of the boat to a serious extent, and threatened more damage every moment.

A few minutes later, though, the efforts of the men began to show, and Shaddy appeared again for one moment, his face being visible in the glare of light, but was hidden the next.

"Getting the water down fast now, sir," he said. "Hope you haven't much mischief done."

"A great many things soaked."

"That don't matter, sir, so long as your stores are right. Sun'll dry everything in an hour or two."

"But when is it coming, Shaddy?"

"'Fore long, sir."

They did not see him go, but knew from the sound of his voice the next minute that he was in the fore-part of the boat, ordering his men to take up some of the boards.

Ten minutes later the rain ceased as suddenly as it had begun. There was a vivid flash of lightning, a long pause, and then a deep-toned roar, while all at once the interior of the little cabin became visible, and a little later the sun came out to shine brilliantly on what looked like a lake of thick mist.

"Will one of you young gents unfasten the stern rope?" cried Shaddy, "and we'll get out from under this dripping tree."

"All right!" cried Rob, and he turned to throw open the stern end of the awning, while Brazier and Joe went in the other direction to where the men were still baling, but scraping the bottom hard at every scoop of the tins they were using.

The stern end of the canvas was secured by a couple of straps, similar to those used in small tents, and these were so wet that it was not easy to get them out of the buckles, but with a little exertion this was done, and Rob parted the ends like the curtains of a bed, peered out at the dripping foliage, and shut them to again, startled by what he saw.

After a few moments' hesitation, he was roused to action by a shout from Shaddy.

"Can't you get it undone, sir?"

"Yes, I think so. Wait a moment," cried Rob huskily, and opening the canvas curtain once more, he stepped out boldly and faced that which had startled him before, this being nothing less than the puma. For it had either leaped from the shore into the boat or crept out along one of the great horizontal boughs of the tree and then dropped lightly down to take its place right in the stern, where it was sitting up licking its drenched coat as contentedly as some huge cat.

It looked so different in its soaked state that for the moment Rob was disposed to think it another of the occupants of the forest, but his doubts were immediately set aside by the animal ceasing its occupation and giving its head a rub against him as, hardly knowing what to do, the boy unfastened the rope in obedience to orders, set the boat free, and then wished he had not done so till the puma had been driven ashore.

"All right, sir?" shouted Shaddy, who was hidden, like the rest, by the intervening cabin-like structure.

"Yes," cried Rob, as the puma set up its ears and looked angrily in the direction from which the voices came, while the boat began to glide out through the dripping boughs, and the next minute was steaming in the hot sunshine.

"What shall I do?" thought Rob, who was now in an agony of perplexity, longing to call to his companions and yet in his confusion dreading to utter a word, for the fear was upon him that the moment the puma caught sight of Brazier it would fly at him. And again he mentally asked the question, "What shall I do?"

Meanwhile the puma had continued contentedly enough to lick its coat, sitting up on the narrow thwart at the end once more exactly like a cat, and in such a position that Rob felt how easy it would be to give the creature a sharp thrust and send it overboard, when it would be sure to swim ashore and relieve him of his perplexity.

While he was hesitating, the word "Oh!" was uttered close behind him, and looking sharply round, there was the wondering face of Joe thrust out between the canvas hangings, which he held tightly round his neck, being evidently too much startled to speak or move.

"It came on board, Joe, during the storm," whispered Rob; "whatever shall we do?"

The lad made no answer for a few moments, and then in a hurried whisper—

"Call Mr Brazier to shoot it."

This roused Rob.

"What for?" he said angrily; "the poor thing's as tame as can be. Look!"

He took a step toward the great cat-like creature, and it ceased licking itself and leaned sideways as if to be caressed.

At that moment Joe popped back his head, and Brazier's voice was heard:—

"They want the grapnel lowered, Rob, my lad. Can you— Why, whatever is this?"

The aspect of the puma changed in an instant. Its ears went down nearly flat upon its head, and it started upon all-fours, tossing its tail about and uttering a menacing growl.

Brazier started back, and Rob knew for what.

"No, no, Mr Brazier," he cried; "don't do that. The poor thing came on board during the storm. It's quite tame. Look here, sir, look."

As he spoke in quite a fit of desperation, he began patting and soothing the animal, and when Brazier peered out again, in company with a loaded gun, the puma was responding to Rob's caresses in the most friendly way.

"Anything the matter, sir?" said Shaddy from beyond the cabin. "Can't you get the grapnel overboard?"

"Come and look here," whispered Brazier; and their guide crept into the cabin and peered out behind, his face puckering up into a grin.

"What is to be done?" whispered Brazier; "I can't fire without hitting the boy."

"Then I wouldn't fire, sir," replied Shaddy. "'Sides, there ain't no need. The thing's quite a cub, I think, and tame enough. I don't suppose it'll show fight if we let it alone."

"Stop, man! What are you going to do?"

"Go to 'em," replied Shaddy coolly.

"But it will spring at you. It turned threateningly on me just now."

"Don't seem to on Master Rob, sir, and I don't think it will. What do you say to going first, Mr Jovanni?"

"No," said the lad shortly. "I don't like animals."

"Well, then, here goes," said Shaddy coolly. "Don't shoot, sir, unless the crittur turns very savage, and then not till I say, 'Now!'"

He thrust the two canvas curtains apart quietly and stepped into the little open space astern, when once more the puma's aspect changed and it turned upon the new-comer menacingly.

"Pat him again, Master Rob," said Shaddy quietly. "I want to make friends too. Here, old chap," he continued, sitting down, as Rob hurriedly patted and stroked the animal's head, "let's have a look at you. Come, may I pat you too?"

He stretched out his hand, but the puma drew back suspiciously, and, with the others watching the scene, he remained quiet while Rob redoubled his caresses, and the puma began to utter its low, rumbling, purring sound.

"Only wants time, Mr Brazier, sir," said Shaddy quietly. "I don't think the brute's a bit savage. Only thinks we mean mischief and is ready to fight for himself. I could be friends with him in an hour or two. What's best to be done—get him ashore?"

"Yes, as soon as possible."

"All right, sir; you go and tell the men to back the boat in to where we landed before."

The canvas hangings dropped to, and Shaddy sat perfectly still, watching the actions of their strange visitor and talking in a low voice to Rob, while a low creaking began as two of the men forward thrust out their oars and backed water.

Slight as the sound was, that and the motion of the boat startled the animal, which began to look about uneasily, but a touch or two from Rob calmed it directly, and after responding to his caresses it turned to look curiously at Shaddy, taking a step forward and then stopping.

"Well, what do you think of me, puss, eh?" said Shaddy quietly. "I say, Mr Rob, you and I had better keep him and set up as lion-tamers."

The rough voice had its effect upon the animal, which ceased its purring sound and backed away close to Rob, against whom it stood, and began watching the bank toward which the boat was being thrust.

"How are we to get it ashore?" said Rob at last.

"You want it to go, then?"

"No," replied Rob, "I don't. It is so very tame, I should like to keep it, but it does not care for anybody else."

"Don't mind me seemingly," said Shaddy. "Well, the best thing will be for you to jump ashore as soon as we're close in, and then it strikes me he'll come after you, and if you kept on petting him he'd follow you anywhere."

"You think so, Shaddy?"

"Feel sure of it, sir, but it ain't like a dog. You can't make a companion of a scratching thing like that."

"Why not? A dog's a biting thing," said Rob shortly.

"Well, yes, sir, but here we are. Better get him ashore. There ain't room for him aboard here. There might be a row, for he ain't ready to make friends with everybody."

Rob stepped on to the gunwale rather unwillingly, for, in a misty way, he was beginning to wonder whether it was possible for him to retain the puma as a companion, though all the time he could see the difficulties in the way.

He leaped ashore, and, as Shaddy had suggested, the puma immediately made a light effortless bound and landed beside him, pressing close up to the lad's side and rubbing one ear against his hand, while the occupants of the boat looked wonderingly on.

"What am I to do next?" asked Rob. "If I jump back on board, he'll come too."

"Safe," said Shaddy; "and there's no more room for passengers. Here, stop a moment; I have it."

"What are you going to do?" said Brazier, who was watching the movements of the puma with anxiety on Rob's behalf, but with keen interest all the same, as he saw the active creature suddenly throw itself down by the boy's feet and, playful as a kitten, begin to pat at first one boot and then the other, ending by rubbing its head upon them, watching their owner all the time.

"I'm going to get Mr Rob aboard without that great cat, sir, and this seems best way."

He drew his knife, raised the tarpaulin, and cut off a good-sized piece of the deer meat; then, bidding the men to take their oars and be ready to row at the first command, he turned to Rob.

"Look here, sir," he said, "I'll pitch you the piece of dried meat. You catch it and then carry it a few yards, and let the lion smell it. Give it him behind one of those bushes, and as soon as he is busy eating it dodge round the bush and come aboard. We'll soon have the boat too far for him to jump."

He threw the piece of dry meat to the boy, who caught it and walked as directed, the puma following him eagerly and sniffing at the food.

The next minute those in the boat saw Rob disappear behind a clump of low growth, and directly after he reappeared running toward them just as, uneasy at his being out of sight with the fierce creature, Brazier had called upon Giovanni to bring his gun and accompany him ashore.

But Rob's reappearance of course stopped this, and the next minute he was on board and being rowed away from the shore.

"It seems too bad," cried Rob, "just as if one was cheating the poor thing. Look, there it is."

For just then the puma stalked out from behind the bushes and stood tossing its tail and looking round as if in search of Rob, ending by walking quickly down to the edge of the lake and standing there gazing after the boat, which was now being rowed slowly down once more toward the scene of their adventure with the swift current, Brazier having decided to stay one more day at the lower part of the lake before descending the river farther; and the object now in view was the discovery of a fresh halting-place for the night.

Chapter Seventeen.

An International Quarrel.

"What's the matter, Rob?" said Brazier, as he turned suddenly from where he had been laying various articles of clothing out in the warm sunshine to dry and found the two lads seated together in silence, Rob with his elbows on the side of the boat and his chin in his, hands, gazing back ashore.

"I can't get a word out of him, sir," said Joe. "I think it's because the lion was left behind."

"Nonsense! Rob is not so childish as to fret after a toy he cannot have. Come, my lad, there is plenty to do. We must make use of the evening sun to get everything possible dry. Come and help. Wet clothes and wet sleeping-places may mean fever."

Rob looked reproachfully at Joe, and began to hurry himself directly, his movement bringing him in contact with Shaddy, who was dividing his time between keeping a sharp look-out along the shore for a good halting-place suitable for making a fire, giving instructions to his men, and using a sponge with which to sop up every trace of moisture he could find within the boat.

"There, Mr Rob, sir," he said as he gave the sponge a final squeeze over the side, "I think that'll about do. It's an ill wind that blows nobody any good. That storm has done one thing—given the boat a good wash-out—and if we make a big fire to-night and dry everything that got wet, we shall be all the better for it. Don't see storms like that in England, eh?"

"No," said Rob shortly, and he took down and began rubbing the moisture from his gun.

"Ah, that's right, my lad; always come down sharp on the rust, and stop it from going any further. Why, hullo! not going to be ill, are you?"

Rob shook his head.

"You look as dumps as dumps, Mr Rob, sir. I know you're put out about that great cat being left behind."

Rob was silent.

"That's it. Why, never mind that, my lad. You can get plenty of things to tame and pet, if you want 'em, though I say as we eight folks is quite enough in one boat without turning it into a wild beast show."

Rob went on rubbing the barrel of his gun.

"What do you say to a nice young pet snake, sir?" said Shaddy, with his eyes twinkling, till Rob darted an angry glance at him, when he changed his tone and manner.

"Tell you what, sir, I'll get one of my boys to climb a tree first time I see an old one with some good holes in. He shall get you a nice young parrot to bring up. You'll like them; they're full of tricks, and as tame as can be. Why, one of them would live on the top of the cabin, and climb about in a way as would amoose you for hours."

Rob darted another angry look at him.

"And do you think I want a parrot to amuse me for hours?" he said bitterly.

"Have a monkey," said Joe, who had heard the last words. "Shaddy will get you a young one, and you can pet that and teach it to play tricks without any risk to anybody, if you must have a plaything."

He accompanied this with so taunting a look that it fired Rob's temper, just at a time when he was bitterly disappointed at the result of his adventure. Joe's words, too, conveyed the boy's feeling, which was something akin to jealousy of the new object which took so much of the young Englishman's thoughts.

Stung then by his companion's words and look, Rob turned upon him and said sarcastically,—

"Thank you: one monkey's enough on board at a time."

The young Italian's eyes flashed, as, quick as lightning, he took the allusion to mean himself, and he turned sharply away without a word, and went right aft to sit gazing back over the water.

"Well, you've been and done it now, Mr Rob, and no mistake," whispered Shaddy. "You've made Master Jovanni's pot boil over on to the fire, and it ain't water, but oil."

"Oh, I am sorry, Shaddy," said Rob in a low tone, for all his own anger had evaporated the moment he saw the effect of his words on the hot-blooded young Southerner.

"Sorry, lad? I should think you are. Why, if I said such a thing as that to an Italian man, I should think the best thing I could do would be to go and live in old England again, where there would be plenty of policemen to take care of me."

"But I was not serious."

"Ay, but you were, my lad, and that's the worst of it. You said it in a passion on purpose to sting him, and he's as thin-skinned as a silkworm. He has gone yonder thinking you despise him and consider he's no better than a monkey, and if you'd set to for six hundred years trying to think out the nastiest thing you could invent to hurt his feelings you couldn't have hit on a worse."

"But it was a mere nothing—the thought of the moment, Shaddy," whispered Rob.

"O' course it was, dear lad, but, you see, that thought of the moment, as you call it, has put his back up. For long enough now English folk have said nasty things to Italians, comparing 'em to monkeys, because of some of 'em going over to England playing organs and showing a monkey at the end of a string. You see, they're so proud and easily affronted that such a word feels like a wapps's sting and worries 'em for days."

"I'll go and beg his pardon. I am sorry."

"Won't be no good now, sir. Better wait till he has cooled down."

"I wish I hadn't said it, Shaddy."

"Ay, that's what lots of us feels, sir, sometimes in our lives. I hit a man on the nose aboard a river schooner once, and knocked him through the gangway afterwards into the water, and as soon as I'd done it I wished I hadn't, but that didn't make him dry."

"I wish he had turned round sharply and hit me," said Rob.

"Ah, it's a pity he didn't, isn't it?" said Shaddy drily. "You wouldn't have hit him again, of course. You're just the sort o' young chap to let a lad hit you, and put your fists in your pockets to keep 'em quiet, and say, 'Thanky,' ain't you?"

"What do you mean—that I should have hit him again?"

"Why, of course I do, and the next moment you two would have been punching and wrestling and knocking one another all over the boat, till Mr Brazier had got hold of one and I'd got hold of the other, and bumped you both down and sat upon you. I don't know much, but I do know what boys is when they've got their monkeys up."

"Don't talk about monkeys," whispered Rob hotly; "I wish there wasn't a monkey on the face of the earth."

"Wish again, Mr Rob, sir, as hard as ever you can, and it won't do a bit o' good."

"Don't talk nonsense, Shaddy," said Rob angrily.

"That's right, sir; pitch into me now. Call me something; it'll do you good. Call me a rhinoceros, if you like. It won't hurt me. I've got a skin just as thick as one of them lovely animals. Go it."

"I do wish you would talk sense," cried Rob, in a low, earnest whisper. "You know I've no one to go and talk to about anything when I want advice."

"No, I don't," said Shaddy gruffly. "There's Muster Brazier."

"Just as if he would want to be bothered when his head's full of his specimens and he's thinking about nothing else but classifying and numbering and labelling! He'd laugh, and call it a silly trifle, and tell us to shake hands."

"Good advice, too, my lad, but not now. Wait a bit."

"I can't wait, knowing I've upset poor old Joe like that. I want to be friends at once."

"That's good talk, my lad, only it won't work at present."

"Ah, now you're talking sensibly and like a friend," said Rob. "But why will it not do now?"

"'Cause Mr Jovanni ain't English. He's nursing that all up, and it isn't his natur' to shake hands yet. Give the fire time to burn out, and then try him, my lad; he'll be a different sort then to deal with."

Rob was silent for a few minutes.

"That's good advice, Mr Rob, sir, and so I tell you; but I mustn't stop here talking. It'll soon be sundown, and then, you know, it's dark directly, and 'fore then we must be landed and the lads making a good fire. I wish Mr Brazier would come and give more orders about our halting-place to-night."

"He's too busy with his plants, Shaddy; and I ought to be helping him."

"Then why don't you go, my lad?"

"How can I, with Joe sitting there looking as if I had offended him for life? I'll go and shake hands at once."

"No, you won't, lad."

"But I will."

"He won't let you."

"Won't he?" said Rob firmly. "I'm in the wrong, and I'll tell him so frankly, and ask him to forgive me."

"And then he won't; and, what's worse, he'll think you're afraid of him, because it is his natur' to."

"We'll see," said Rob; and going round outside the canvas awning by holding on to the iron stretchers and ropes, he reached the spot where Joe sat staring fixedly astern, perfectly conscious of Rob's presence, but frowning and determined upon a feud.

Rob glanced back, and could see Brazier through the opening in the canvas busily examining his specimens, so as to see if any had grown damp through the rain. Then, feeling that, if he whispered, their conversation would not be heard, Rob began.

"Joe!"

There was no reply.

“Joe, old chap, I’m so sorry.” Still the young Italian gazed over the lake. “I say, Joe, it’s like being alone almost, you here and I out there. We can’t afford to quarrel. Shake hands, old fellow.”

Joe frowned more deeply.

“Oh, come, you shall,” whispered Rob. “I say, here, give me your hand like a man. I was put out about losing the puma, because I was sure I could tame it; and it would have made such a jolly pet to go travelling with. It could have lived on the shore and only been on board when we were going down the river. It put me out, and I said that stupid thing about the monkey.”

Joe started round with his eyes flashing.

“Do you want me to strike you a blow?” he hissed angrily.

“No; I want you to put your fist in mine and to say we’re good friends again. I apologise. I’m very sorry.”

“Keep your apologies. You are a mean coward to call me a name like that. If we were ashore instead of on a boat, I should strike you.”

“No, you wouldn’t,” said Rob sturdily.

“What! you think I am afraid?”

“No; but you would be a coward if you did, because I tell you that I should not hit you again.”

“Because you dare not,” said the young Italian, with a sneer.

Rob flushed up angrily, and his words belied his feelings, which prompted him, to use his own expression, to punch the Italian’s head, for he said,—

"Perhaps I am afraid, but never mind if I am. You and I are not going to quarrel about such a trifle as all this."

"A trifle? To insult me as you did?"

"Don't be so touchy, Joe," cried Rob. "Come, shake hands."

But the lad folded his arms across his breast, and at that moment there was the sharp report of Brazier's gun and a heavy splashing in the water among the lily leaves close up to the drooping trees which hid the cause of the turmoil.

There was a little excitement among the men as the boat was rowed close in under the trees, and there, half in the water, lay one of the curious animals known as a water-pig, or carpincho.

A rope was immediately made fast to tow the dead animal to the halting-place to cut up for the evening meal, but before they had rowed far Shaddy shouted to the men to stop.

"That won't do," he cried.

"What's the matter, Shaddy?"

"Matter?" growled the guide; "why, can't you see, sir? There won't be a bit left by the time we've gone a mile. Look at 'em tearing away at it. Well, I never shall have any sense in my head. To think of me not knowing any better than that!"

He unfastened the rope hanging astern, and hauled the dead animal along the side to the bows of the boat, with fish large and small dashing at it and tugging away by hundreds, making the water boil, as it were, with, their rapid movement.

"Tchah! I'm growing stoopid, I think," growled Shaddy as he hauled the water-pig in over the bows, the fish hanging on and leaping up at it till it was out of reach; and then their journey was continued till a suitable halting-place was reached, where by a roaring fire objects that required drying were spread out, while the meat was cooked and the coffee made, so that by the time they lay down to rest in the boat there was not much cause for fear of fever.

Chapter Eighteen.

A Catastrophe.

The next morning the sun was drinking up the mists at a wonderful rate when Rob opened his eyes, saw Joe close by him fast asleep, and raised his hand to give him a friendly slap, but he checked himself.

"We're not friends yet," he said to himself, with a curious, regretful feeling troubling him; and as he went forward to get one of the men to fill him a bucket of water for his morning bath, for the first time since leaving England he felt dismal and low-spirited.

"Morning, sir!" said Shaddy. "Mr Joe not wakened yet?"

"No."

"Did you two make friends 'fore you went to sleep?"

"No, Shaddy."

"Then I lay tuppence it wasn't your fault. What a pity it was you let your tongue say that about the monkey!"

"Yes, Shaddy," said Rob as he plunged his head into the pail and had a good cool sluice. "I wish I hadn't now. It was a great pity."

"True, sir, it was. You see, there ain't no room in a boat for quarrelling, and if it came to a fight you'd both go overboard together and be eaten by the fish afore you knew where you were. And that would not be pleasant, would it?"

"Don't talk nonsense, Shaddy," said Rob shortly as he plunged his head into the bucket again.

"Certinly not, sir," replied the man seriously. "You see, I know how it would be as well as can be. 'Talian lads don't fight like English lads. They can't hit out straight and honest, but clings and cuddles and wrastles. Soon as ever you began he'd fly at you, and tie his arms and legs about you in knots, and hamper you so that you couldn't keep your balance, and as there's no room in the boat, you'd be ketching your toe somewhere, and over you'd go. If I were you, Mr Rob, sir, I wouldn't fight him."

"Will you leave off talking all that stupid nonsense, Shaddy?" cried Rob angrily as he began now polishing his head and face with the towel. "Who is going to fight? I suppose you think it's very clever to keep on with this banter, but I can see through you plainly enough."

Shaddy chuckled.

"All right, sir; I won't say no more. Give him time, and don't notice him, and then I daresay he'll soon come round."

"I shall go on just as if nothing had happened," said Rob quietly. "I apologised and said I was sorry, and when his annoyance has passed off he'll be friends again. What a glorious morning after the storm!"

"Glorious ain't nothing to it, sir. Everything's washed clean, and the air shines with it. Even looks as if the sun had got his face washed, too. See how he flashes."

"I can feel, Shaddy," said Rob, with a laugh.

"That's nothing to what's coming, my lad. Strikes me, too, that we shall find a little more water in the stream, if Mr Brazier says we're to go down the river to-day. Hear the birds?"

"Hear them?" cried Rob. "Why, they are ten times as lively to-day."

"That they are, sir. They're having a regular feast on the things washed out of their holes by the rain. As for the flowers, Mr Brazier will have no end of beauties to pick. They'll come out like magic after this rain. He won't want to go on to-day."

"Yes, I shall, Naylor," said Brazier, stepping out from under the awning. "We may as well go on, beautiful as all this is. Ah," he continued as he gazed round and took a long, deep breath, "what gloriously elastic air! What a paradise! Rob, my lad, there can be nothing fairer on earth."

"Don't you be in a hurry, sir!" growled Shaddy. "I'm going to show you places as beat this hollow."

"Impossible, my man!" said Brazier.

"Well, sir, you wait and see. Bit o' breakfast before we start?"

"Yes," said Brazier, and the men just then stirred the fire together, and called from the shore that the water was boiling and the cakes in the embers baked.

The sensation of delicious comparative coolness after the storm as they sat under the trees, and the fragrance borne from myriads of flowering plants was so delightful to the senses that Rob looked with dismay at the idea of leaving the place for the present. The thirsty ground had drunk up the rain, and only a little moisture remained where the sun could not penetrate, while the sky was of a vivid blue, without a speck of cloud to be seen.

But, though Brazier did not notice it, there was a jarring element in the concord of that glorious morning, for the young Italian was heavy and gloomy, and hardly spoke during the *alfresco* meal.

"What's that?" said Rob suddenly as there was a slight rustling among the boughs and undergrowth a short distance away.

"Might be anything, sir," said Shaddy. "Some little animal—monkey praps. It won't hurt us. Maybe it's a snake."

In spite of an effort to seem unconcerned, Rob could not resist the desire to glance at his comrade at the mention of the monkey, and, as he fully expected, even though he could not check it, there was Joe glaring at him fiercely.

Rob dropped his eyes, feeling that Joe fully believed he was doing it to annoy him, and that Shaddy had the same intention.

Meanwhile the sound had ceased, and was forgotten by the time they were all on board once more, the rope which had moored them to a tree being cast off.

"Now, my lads, away with you!" growled Shaddy, and the oars dropped among the lily leaves with a splash, startling quite a shoal of fish on one side and a large reptile on the other, which raised quite a wave as it dashed off with a few powerful strokes of its tail for deeper water.

They were about fifty yards from the shore, when Shaddy suddenly laid his hand upon Rob's shoulder and pointed back to the place they had just left.

"See that, my lad?"

"No. What?" cried Rob hastily. "Bird? lizard?"

"Nay; look again."

Rob swept the shore eagerly, and the next moment his eyes lit upon something tawny standing in a shady spot, half hidden by the leaves.

"The puma!" he cried excitedly, and as the words left his lips the animal made one bound into the undergrowth near the trees, and was gone.

"Or another, one, Rob," said Brazier. "It is hardly likely to be the same. There are plenty about, I suppose, Naylor?"

"Oh yes, sir. Can't say as they swarm, but they're pootty plentiful, and as much like each other as peas in a pod."

"But I feel sure that is the same one," cried Rob excitedly. "It is following us down the lake."

"Maybe," grumbled Shaddy, "but you couldn't tell at this distance."

Rob was going to speak again, but he caught sight of Joe's face, with a peculiar smile thereon, and he held his peace.

An hour later they were drawing close to the mouth of the river, where it quitted the lake, and Shaddy pointed to the shores on either side.

"Look at that," he said in a low tone. "I 'spected as much."

"Look at what?" said Rob.

"The trees. Water's two foot up the trunks, and the river over its banks, lad. We shall go down pootty fast it I don't look out."

But he did "look out," to use his own words, and getting the boat round, he set the four men to back stern foremost into the stream, keeping a long oar over the side to steer by and giving orders to the men to pull gently or hard as he gave instructions, for the river ran like a mill-race. It was swift enough before, but now, thanks to the tremendous amount of water poured into it through the previous night's storm, its speed seemed to be doubled.

Rob stood close by the steersman, while Joe was beside Mr Brazier, who, after the first minute or two of startled interest in their rapid descent, became absorbed in the beauty of the overhanging plants, and had no eyes for anything else.

"We're going along at a tidy rate, Master Rob," said Shaddy.

"Yes; the trees glide by very quickly."

"Ay, they do, sir," said the man, who did not take his eyes from the surface of the river before them. "I did mean to make the boys pull so that we could go down gently, but it wouldn't be much good, and only toil 'em for nothing."

"There's no danger, I suppose, Shaddy?"

"No, sir, no, not much, unless we run on a sharp snag or trunk of a tree, or get swept into a corner and capsized."

"What?" cried Rob.

"Capsized, sir. That would make an end of our expedition. Now, lads," he shouted to the men, "pull your best."

He gave his own oar a peculiar twist as the men obeyed, and Rob caught sight of the danger ahead for the first time. It was a huge tree which had been undermined by the water during the past few hours and fallen right out into the stream, its top being over a hundred feet from the shore and showing quite a dense tangle of branches level with the water, to have entered which must have meant wreck.

But Shaddy was too much on the *qui vive,* and his timely order and careful steering enabled him to float the craft gently by the outermost boughs.

They were going onward again at increased speed, when Brazier shouted,—

"Stop! I must have some of those plants."

Shaddy did not stir.

"Do you hear, man? Stop! I want to collect some of those epiphytic plants."

By this time they were nearly a hundred yards past, and Shaddy looked at the enthusiastic collector with a comical expression on his face.

"Always glad to obey orders, sir," he said drily; "but how can I stop the boat now? Look at the water."

"But you should have caught hold of one of the boughs, man."

"When we were fifty yards away, sir?"

"Then pull back to the tree."

Shaddy smiled again.

"It ain't to be done, sir, no, not if I'd eight oars going instead of four. There's no making head against the river now it's running like this."

"Then we've made a mistake in coming to-day," cried Brazier anxiously.

"Well, no, sir, because before night we shall have made a big run right into the country you want to see, without tiring my lads, and I want to save them up. But there's no stopping to-day for collecting."

"But shall we be able to land somewhere?"

"Hope so, sir. If we can't we shall have to go on. But you leave it to me, sir, and I'll do my best. Don't talk to me now, because I've got to steer and look out against an upset, and, as you know, bathing ain't pleasant in these waters."

Brazier looked uneasy, and went and sat down in the stern, to become absorbed soon after in the beauty of the scene as they raced down the silvery flashing river, while Joe, who was near him, appeared to be looking at the birds and wondrous butterflies which flapped across from shore to shore, but really seeing nothing but one of a company of monkeys, which, after the fashion of their kind, were trying to keep pace with the boat by bounding and swinging themselves from tree to tree along the shore.

That seemed to the young Italian's disordered imagination, blurred, as it were, by rankling anger, like the monkey to which his companion had compared him, and his annoyance grew hotter, not only against Rob, but against himself for refusing to shake hands and once more be friends.

Meanwhile Rob stayed in the fore-part of the boat talking to Shaddy, who stood on one of the thwarts, so as to get a better view of the river ahead over the cabin roof, and kept on making an observation to the boy from time to time.

"Easy travelling this, my lad, only a bit too fast."

"Oh, I don't know; it's very delightful," said Rob.

"Glad you like it, my lad; but I wish Mr Jovanni wouldn't sit on the starn like that. He ought to know better. Least touch, and over he'd go."

"Look: what's that, Shaddy?" cried Rob, pointing to a black-looking animal standing knee-deep in water staring at them as they passed.

Shaddy screwed his eye round for a moment, but did not turn his head.

"Don't you get taking my 'tention off my work!" he growled. "That's a—that's a—well, I shall forget my own name directly!—a what-you-may-call-it—name like a candle."

"Tapir," cried Rob.

"That's him, my lad. Any one would think you had been born on 'Merican rivers. Rum pig-like crittur, with a snout like a little elephant's trunk, to ketch hold of grass and branches and nick 'em into his mouth. I say—"

"Well, what, Shaddy?" said Rob. The man had stopped to bear hard upon his oar.

"Pull, my lads," he growled to his men. "Hold tight, every one. I didn't see it soon enough. Tree trunk!"

Rob seized one of the supports of the cabin roofing and gazed over it at what seemed like a piece of bark just before them, and the next moment there was a smart shock, a tremendous swirl in the water, and a shower of spray poured over them like drops of silver in the bright sunshine, as something black, which Rob took for a denuded branch, waved in the air, and Joe plumped down into the bottom of the boat.

Shaddy chuckled and wiped the water out of his eye.

"I'm thinking so much about trees washed from the bank that I can't see anything else."

"But it was only a small tree, Shaddy, and did us no harm."

"Warn't a tree at all, lad, only a 'gator fast asleep on the top of the water going west and warming his back in the sun same time."

"An alligator?"

"Yes, my lad. Didn't you see what a flap he gave with his tail! But now just look there at Mr Jovanni. I call it rank obstinit. Just as if there was no other place where he could sit but right on the starn! There, you're friends, and he'll take it better from you. Go through the cabin and ask him to get off. I don't want him to go overboard."

"Neither do I, Shaddy, but we are not friends, and if I ask him he will stop there all the more."

"Then I must," said Shaddy. "Hi, Mr Jovanni, sir! Don't sit there; it ain't safe."

"Oh yes, I'm quite safe," cried the boy sharply. "Never mind me."

"Hark at him! Don't mind him! What'll his father say to me if I go back without him? Pull, lads, pull!"

Shaddy's order was necessary, for a huge tree—unmistakably a tree this time—lay right across their way just where the river made a sudden bend round to their left.

The better way would have been to have gone to the right, where there was more room, but, the curve of the river being of course on that side greater, there would not have been time to get round before the boat was swept in amongst the branches, so perforce their steersman made for the left.

This took them close in to where the bank should have been, but which was now submerged, and the boat floated close in to the great wall of trees marking the edge of the stream, and so little room was there that, to avoid the floating tree-top, the boat was forced close in shore, where the stream at the bend ran furiously.

"Look out!" roared Shaddy. "Heads down!" and Rob, who had been watching the obstacle in their way, only just had time to duck down as, with a tremendous rushing and crackling sound, they passed right through a mass of pendent boughs which threatened to sweep the boat clear of cabin and crew as well, as the stream urged it on.

The trouble only lasted a few seconds, though, and then they were through and floating swiftly round the inner curve toward an open patch of the shore which rose all clear of water and tree.

"Anybody hurt?" cried Brazier from inside the cabin; "I thought the place was going to be swept away after I had dived in here."

"No, sir; we're all right," cried Rob. "I nearly lost my cap, though, and— Oh! where's Joe?"

"Eh?" cried Shaddy, looking forward. "Why, he was— gone!"

All faced round to look back just in time to catch an indistinct glimpse of their companion apparently clinging to a bough overhanging the stream; but the next moment the intervening branches hid him from their sight, and a look of horror filled every face.

"Did—did you see him, Shaddy?" panted Rob.

"Thought I did, sir, but couldn't be sure," growled Shaddy, and then furiously to his men, "Row—row with all your might!"

The men obeyed, making their oars bend as they tugged away with such effect that they advanced a few yards. But that was all. The current was too sharp, and they lost ground again. Then, in spite of all their efforts, the most they could do was to hold their own for a minute before having to give way, pull in shore, and seize the overhanging boughs to which Shaddy and Brazier now clung to keep the boat from drifting.

"Better land, sir," cried Shaddy. "We can't reach him this way."

"Reach him?" cried Rob piteously, and then to himself, "Oh! Joe, Joe, why didn't you shake hands?"

Chapter Nineteen.

A Fresh Peril.

Shaddy's advice was easier to give than to execute. For though by holding on to the boughs they were able to anchor the boat, it proved to be a difficult task to force it in among the submerged stems to the spot where the clear space of elevated ground offered a satisfactory landing-place.

Thanks to the skill of the boatmen, however, a landing was at last achieved, and as soon as Brazier leaped ashore he was followed by Rob and Shaddy, the latter giving his men a few sharp orders before joining the others, who were trying to force their way back along the bank toward where they had last seen their companion.

This was difficult, but possible for a short distance, and they pressed on hopefully, for, consequent upon the sudden turn of the river here forming a loop, they had only to cross this sharp bend on foot, not a quarter of the distance it would have been to row round.

But before they had gone fifty yards the high-and-dry land ended, and Rob, who was, thanks to his activity, first, was about to wade in and continue his way among the submerged roots.

But Shaddy roared at him,—

"No, no, my lad; don't make matters worse! You mustn't do that. The things have moved out of the river in here to be away from the rush and to get food. We don't want you pulled under."

"But we must go on, Naylor," cried Brazier in agony.

"It ain't the way to help him, getting ourselves killed, sir," retorted Shaddy. "Let's get more in. Water don't go far."

He was quite right, for after about ten minutes' struggle along the edge they found themselves as nearly as they could guess about opposite to the spot where their unfortunate companion had been swept out of the boat, but about a hundred yards inland and separated from the regular bed of the stream by a dense growth of trees, whose boughs interlaced and stopped all vision in every direction, more especially toward the river.

"You see, we must wade," cried Rob; and he stepped into the water with a plash, but Shaddy's strong hand gripped him by the shoulder and drew him back.

"I tell you it's madness, boy. If he's alive still you couldn't reach him that way."

"If he's alive!" groaned Rob.

"If he's alive," said Shaddy, repeating his words. "Steady a moment! He may be up in one of the boughs, for he's as active as a monkey in rigging and trees."

Then, putting his hands to his mouth, he shouted in stentorian tones,—

"Ahoy! ahoy!"

But there was no response, and Rob and Brazier exchanged glances, their faces full of despair.

"Ahoy!" shouted Shaddy once more.

Still no reply, and a cold chill ran through Rob and his eyes grew dim as he thought of the bright, handsome, dark-eyed lad who had been his companion so long, and with whom he had been such friends till the miserable little misunderstanding had thrust them apart.

“It must be farther on,” said Brazier at last, when shout after shout had been sent up without avail.

“Think so, sir?” said Shaddy gloomily. “I thought it was about here, but p’r’aps you’re right. Come on. River made a big twist there, and it’s hard to tell distance shut up half in the dark among the trees. I did hope,” he continued, as he forced his way in among the trees and held boughs aside for them to follow, “that the poor lad had swung himself up and would have made his way like a squirrel from branch to branch till he reached dry land, but it don’t seem to be so. There, sir, we must be ’bout opposite where we saw him. Can’t be no farther. Ahoy! ahoy! ahoy!”

They all listened intently after this, but there was no sound of human voice, only the shrieking of parrots and chattering of monkeys.

Shaddy shouted again, with the result that he startled a flock of birds which were about to settle, but rose again noisily.

They all shouted together then, but there was no response, and feeling that their efforts were useless, they went on a short distance, and tried once more without result.

“He’d have answered if he had been anywhere near, sir,” said Shaddy gloomily. “I’ll go on if you like, but take my word for it he ain’t here.”

Rob looked at both despairingly, but he was obliged to take the guide’s words for those of truth, and, feeling utterly crushed, he slowly followed the others as they began to return, feeling the while that if it had not been for the edge of the water by which they walked it would have been impossible to find their way back through the dense wilderness.

Their guide returned by their outward steps as accurately as he could, but it was not always possible, for in coming out the bushes had been forced on in the same direction and then sprung back together, after the fashion of the withes in a fish-trap, and presenting their points, thorns, and broken stems in a perfect *chevaux de frise*.

In these cases Shaddy had to select a different path, the exigencies of the way forcing him more inland, and at last, in spite of his experience, he stopped short, looked about him and then upwards, seeking to make out the sky, but it was completely shut off, and they stood in a twilight gloom.

"What's the matter, Shaddy?" said Rob at last, after looking at the man's actions wonderingly; but there was no reply.

"For goodness sake, man, don't say that you have lost your way," cried Brazier excitedly.

Shaddy still remained silent, and took off his hat to scratch his head.

"Do you hear me, man? Have you lost your way?"

"Don't see as there's any way to lose," growled Shaddy. "I ain't seen no path. But I have gone a bit wrong."

"Here, let me—" began Brazier, but Shaddy interrupted him.

"Steady, sir, please! Don't wherrit me. I shall hit it off directly. You two gents stand just as you are, and don't move. Don't even turn round, or else you'll throw me wrong worse than I am. You see, the place is all alike, and nothing to guide you. One can't tell which way to turn."

"But tell me," said Brazier, "what are you going to do?"

"There's only one thing to do, sir: find the river, and I'm going to make casts for it. You both stand fast and answer my whistles; then I shall know where you are and can come back and start again. If we don't act sensible we shall lose ourselves altogether and never get out of it."

"And then?" said Brazier.

"Oh, never mind about *then*, sir. I've lost my way a bit, and I'm going to find it somehow, only give me time."

"Which way do you think the river lies?" said Rob gloomily.

"I'm going to try out yonder, sir. You see we've turned and doubled so that I can't tell where we are."

"But it's out that way, I'm sure," said Rob, pointing in the opposite direction.

"Why are you sure, sir?"

Rob shook his head.

"Ah, to be sure, dear lad!" said the guide; "you only think it's out that way, and I daresay Mr Brazier here thinks it's out another way."

"Well, I must confess," said Brazier, "that I thought the river lay behind us."

"Yes, sir, that's it. I've been lost before with half a dozen, sir, and every one thought different. One wanted to go one way; one wanted to go another. Fact is, gentlemen, we neither of us know the way. It's all guesswork. Once lost, there's nothing to guide you. I can't recollect this tree or that tree, because they're all so much alike, and it's as puzzling as being in the dark. There's only one way out of it, and that is to do as I say; you stand fast, and I'll cast about like a dog does after losing the scent till I find the right track. Only mind this: if I don't have you to guide me back with whistle and shout I shall be lost more and more."

"You are right, Naylor," said Brazier; "we leave ourselves in your hands. Go on."

"Cheer up, Mr Rob, sir; don't be down-hearted. I shall find the way out of it yet."

"I was not thinking about myself, Shaddy," said Rob in a choking voice. "I was thinking about poor Joe."

"Ah!" said Shaddy in a suppressed voice. Then sharply, "I shall whistle at first, and one of you keep answering. By-and-by I shall shout like this."

He uttered a peculiarly shrill cry, and they all started, for it was answered from a distance.

"Why, that's Joe," cried Rob joyfully. "Ahoy! ahoy!" he cried, and paused to listen.

"Nay, sir, that wasn't Mr Jovanni, but one of the wild beasts. Sounded to me like one of them little lions. Stop a bit, though; let's try a shout or two to see if the boys in the boat can hear us now."

He hailed half a dozen times at intervals, but there was no reply.

"Thought not," he said. "Only waste of breath. We've wandered away farther than I thought, and the trees shuts in sound. Stand fast, gentlemen, till I come back."

He paused for a few moments, and then forced his way in amongst the trees in a direction which Rob felt to be entirely wrong, but in his despondent state he was too low in spirit to make any opposition, and after marking the spot where Shaddy had disappeared, he turned round suddenly, placed his arm across a huge tree trunk, rested his brow against it, and hid the workings of his face.

"Come, come, Rob, be a man!" cried Brazier, laying his hand upon the lad's shoulder. "Never despair, my boy, never despair!"

"Joe! Joe!" groaned Rob; "it is so horrible!"

"Not yet. We don't know that he is lost."

"He must be, sir, he must be, or he would have answered our hails."

At that moment there was a shout from out of the forest, and Rob started round as if thinking it might be their young companion, but the cry was not repeated; a shrill whistle came instead.

Brazier answered it with a whistle attached to his knife.

"It was only Shaddy," groaned Rob. "Mr Brazier, you don't know," he continued. "We two had quarrelled, and had not made friends, and now, poor fellow, he is gone."

"No, I will not believe it yet," cried Brazier; "for aught we know, he may have escaped. He is too clever and quick a lad not to make a desperate effort to escape. We shall run up against him yet, so cheer up. Ahoy!" he cried in answer to a hail, and followed it up with a whistle.

"Naylor said he should whistle for a time and then hail," said Brazier, trying to speak cheerfully. "Come, lad, make a brave fight of it. You are getting faint with hunger, and that makes things look at their worst, so rouse up. Now then, answer Naylor's signal."

"I can't, not yet," said Rob huskily. "I am trying, Mr Brazier, and I will master it all soon."

Just then the peculiar cry they had first heard rang out again from a distance.

"Was that Joe?" whispered Rob, with a ghastly look. "He must be in peril."

"No, no; it was a jaguar, I think. There goes Naylor again! Whistle! whistle!"

Rob only gazed at him piteously, and Brazier responded to the signal himself.

"Come, come, Rob," he whispered, "be a man!"

The lad made a tremendous effort to conquer his weakness, and turned away from the tree with his lips compressed, his eyes half closed, and forehead wrinkled.

"That's right," cried Brazier, clapping him on the shoulder. "Who says our English boys are not full of pluck?"

He whistled again in response to a signal from Shaddy, and then they listened and answered in turn for quite half an hour, during which the guide's whistles and cries came from further and further away, but sounded as if he were at last keeping about the same distance, and working round so as to come back in another direction.

Then for a time all signals ceased, and they heard the cry of the wild beast, followed by quite a chorus of shrieks and chatterings, which ceased as suddenly as they had begun.

"He has gone too far, Mr Brazier," cried Rob suddenly, a complete change having come over him, for he was once more full of excitement and energy.

"I hope not."

"But he is not signalling."

"I'll try again."

Brazier raised the little metal whistle to his lips and gave out a shrill, keen, penetrating note.

Then they listened, but there was no answer.

Brazier's brow wrinkled, and he refrained from looking at Rob as he once more raised the whistle to his lips, to obtain for answer the unmistakable cry of some savage, cat-like creature—jaguar or puma, he could not tell which.

"No guns! no guns!" he muttered; and moving away from Rob, he opened the long, sharp blade of his spring knife, one intended for hunting purposes, and thrust it up his sleeve.

Just then Rob whistled as loudly as he could, and they both listened, when, to their intense relief, there came a reply far to their left.

"Hurrah!" cried the boy excitedly, and then, "Oh, Mr Brazier, what a relief!"

Brazier drew a long, deep breath.

"Whistle again, boy," he said; but before Rob could obey there was another distant whistle, and on this being answered the signals went on from one to the other for quite half an hour, and at last there was a breaking and crashing noise, and Shaddy came within speaking distance.

"Hear that lion prowling about?" he shouted.

"Yes, several times."

"Ah, I began to feel as if a gun would be handy. He came too close to be pleasant."

"What have you found—the river?" cried Brazier.

"No, sir, not yet. I went far enough to be sure it ain't that way."

A few minutes later he forced his way to their side, looking hot and exhausted.

"Why didn't you answer me when I whistled and shouted?" he cried.

"We did, Shaddy, every time we heard you."

"Nay, my lad, didn't seem to me as if you did. S'pose the trees kep' it off at times. But all right, gentlemen, I shall soon hit it off, and we'll get to the boat, have a good feed, and go to work again. Don't look down, Mr Rob, sir! How do we know as Mr Jovanni isn't there already waiting for us?"

Rob shook his head.

"Ah, you don't know, sir. Seems queer, don't it, to get so lost! but it ain't the fust time. I've known men go into the forest only a score of yards or so and be completely gone, every step they took carrying 'em farther away and making 'em lose their heads till their mates found 'em."

"Stop! Which way are you going now?"

"This way," said Shaddy.

"But that's back—the way we came."

Shaddy laughed, and without another word forced his way again in among the trees.

"I give up," said Brazier in despair. "It is too confusing for ordinary brains. I could have taken an oath that he was wrong."

He answered a whistle, and they stood waiting till the crackling and rustling made by their guide's passage ceased.

"I couldn't have believed that we came so far," said Rob, breaking the silence.

"I don't think we did come very far, Rob," replied Brazier; "it is only that the place is so hopelessly puzzling and intricate. Time is getting on, too. We must not be overtaken by the night."

Rob could hardly repress a shudder, and, to make the dismal look of the narrow space, darkened by close-clustering trees, more impressive, the peculiar exaggerated cat-like call of the beast they had heard or another of its kind rang out hollowly apparently not very far-away.

Almost simultaneously, though, came Shaddy's whistle, and this was answered and repeated steadily at some little distance, but at last growing quite faint.

As they were waiting for the next call there was a rustling sound overhead, which took their attention, but for some time nothing but moving leaves could be made out in the subdued light, till all at once Brazier pointed to a spot some fifty feet above them, and at last Rob caught sight of the object which had taken his companion's attention.

"Looking down and watching us," he said quickly, as he gazed at the peculiar little dark, old-looking face which was suddenly withdrawn, thrust out again, and finally disappeared.

"There is quite a party of monkeys up there, Rob," said Brazier; "and the tree-tops are thoroughly alive with birds, but they are silent because we are here. Ahoy!" he shouted as Shaddy now hailed from somewhere nearer, and after a few shouts to and fro they heard him say,—

"Found it!"

A thrill of joy ran through Rob, but it passed away and he felt despondent again as they started to rejoin their guide, for the thoughts of poor Joe were uppermost, and he began thinking of the day when they should go back and join the schooner to announce the terrible accident that had befallen the captain's son.

But he had to toil hard to get through the trees, and this work took away the power of thinking much of anything but the task in hand. Shaddy, too, had stopped short, waiting for them to come to him, and they had to squeeze themselves between trees, climb over half-rotten trunks, and again and again start aside and try another way as they found themselves disturbing some animal, often enough a serpent.

"'Bliged to stop here, gen'lemen, and mark the direction," rang on their ears all at once. "You see, one can't travel in a straight line, and I was afraid of losing my way again."

"How far is the river away?"

"Not quarter of a mile if you could go straight, my lad, but it'll be half a mile way we have to twist about. But come along. Once we get to the water's edge, we'll soon make the boat."

He turned, and led on slowly and laboriously, the difficulties increasing at every step, and more than once Rob was about to break down. The last time he took hold of a tree to support himself, and was about to say, "I can go no further," when, looking up, there was Shaddy pointing down at the water, which had flooded over right in among the trunks.

Rob dropped upon his knees directly, bent down, placed his lips to the water, and drank with avidity, Brazier following his example.

The discovery of a guide which must lead them to the spot where they had left the boat, and the refreshment the river afforded, gave Rob the strength to follow Shaddy manfully along the margin of the flood over twice the ground they had traversed in the morning—for their wanderings had taken them very much further astray than they had believed—and the result was that just at sundown, after being startled several times by the cries of the jaguar or puma close on their left apparently, Shaddy suddenly gave a hoarse cheer, for he had emerged upon the clearing at whose edge the boat was moored.

Chapter Twenty.

A Terrible Surprise.

Shaddy looked sharply round as they crossed the clearing, all three breathing more freely at being once more in the open and without the oppression of being completely shut in by trees on all sides, while the dense foliage overhead completely hid the sky. This was now one glorious suffusion of amber and gold, for the sun was below the horizon, and night close at hand, though, after the gloom of the primeval forest, it seemed to Rob and his companions as if they had just stepped out into the beginning of a glorious day.

"Don't see no fire," growled Shaddy. "We're all horribly down about losing poor Mr Jovanni. But we must have rest and food, or we can't work. Here, my lads, where are you?" he shouted in the dialect the men best understood.

They were about half-way across the opening in the forest as he shouted to the men, and the river was running like a stream of molten gold; but the boat had been probably moored somewhere among the trees, so as to be safer than in the swift current, for it was not visible.

"D'ye hear, you?" roared Shaddy fiercely, for he was out of temper from weariness with his exertions during the day. "Are you all asleep? There's going to be about the hottest row over this, Mr Brazier, as ever them lazy half-breed dogs got into. You pay them well to work, and instead of there being a good fire, and cooked meat and fish, and hot cake, and boiling water, they're all fast asleep in that boat."

He stopped short and looked about him; then, placing both hands to his mouth to make a trumpet, he uttered a stentorian roar, which echoed from the tall bank of trees on the opposite side of the river.

The only answer was the shriek of a macaw from across the water, where a pair of the long-tailed birds rose from a tall tree and winged their way over the tops. Directly after there was a sharp yell, evidently the call of some cat-like beast.

"I'll go over yonder and look among the trees, Mr Brazier, sir," said Shaddy, after waiting for some more satisfactory reply, "and I'll take it kindly if you and Mr Rob will have a look among them standing in the water that side. I dessay the boat's run up close as they can get it one side or the other."

Brazier nodded, and went to one side of the clearing, while Shaddy forced his way through the low growth toward the other, Rob following close upon his leader's steps till they reached the submerged trees and worked along their edge, peering in amongst them as rapidly as they could, for there was no time to be lost. Night was coming on with tropical swiftness, and already the glorious amber tint was paling in the sky, and the water beneath the trees looking black.

"See anything of them, Rob?" cried Brazier again and again; but the answer was always the same: a low despondent "No."

All at once there was a loud shout, and they looked back to see Shaddy waving his cap and beckoning to them.

"Found them?" cried Rob as he ran to meet their guide.

"No, my lad; they're not here. Might have known it by there being no fire. Hi, Mr Brazier, sir!"

The latter came panting up, for it required no little exertion to get through the dense bushes and thick grass.

"What is it? Where are they?"

"That's what I want to know, sir. But look here, I'm so fagged out that my head won't go properly. I mean I can't think straight."

"What do you mean, man?"

"This, sir: look round, both of you, 'fore it gets darker. I'm all doubty, and I've got thinking that we've come to the wrong place."

"What?" cried Rob excitedly.

"I say I've got a fancy that this ain't the right place, for there's no one here, and no boat, and there ain't been no fire."

"How do you know, Shaddy?"

"'Cause, if the boys had made a fire, they would nat'rally have put it there under that patch of bushes near the trees."

"Why there, and not anywhere else?"

"'Cause that's the place any one used to making fires on the rivers would pick at once. It's shaded from the wind, handy to the trees, so as to get plenty of dead wood, and nigh the river to fetch water."

"But the other side would have done as well," said Rob excitedly.

"No, it wouldn't, sir, for the wind ketches there, and the sparks and smoke would be blowing all over the place. I say, is this the place where we left the boat this morning?"

"I—I dare not say, Naylor," replied Brazier, after a little hesitation. "I am so faint and worn-out that I too cannot be certain."

"I'm sure it is," said Rob quickly.

"There's some one who can think, then," cried Shaddy. "Stop a moment, though, Mr Rob, sir. Tell me how is it you are sure?"

"Because I noticed that big tree on the other side of the water—that one out of which those two big birds flew. There, you can see it plainly against the sky."

"Bah! nonsense, my lad! There are thousands of those great trees about."

"But not like that, Shaddy," said Rob eagerly. "Look there against the light. It's just like a man's face, a giant's, as if he were lying on his back, and you can see the forehead, nose, and chin, and a big beard quite plainly."

"Well, it do look like it, cert'nly," growled Shaddy.

"Then, too, I remember the shape of the bank, and look how the river bends round and comes in a curve. Of course this is the place; I'm quite sure it is."

"Right, my lad! so was I, quite sure," cried Shaddy dismally; "but I was hoping and praying that I might be wrong, because if you are right, sir— No, I won't say it."

"Yes, you will, Naylor," cried Brazier sternly. "Speak out."

"What! if it's very bad, sir?"

"Yes, my man; this is no time for trifling. Tell me the worst."

"There's Mr Rob here, sir," said the guide, in a tone full of protest.

"I want to know the worst, too, Shaddy," said Rob resignedly.

"Then I'll tell you, gentlemen, only don't blame me for making your hearts as sore as mine is now."

"Tell us everything, my man. For bad or good, in this journey we must work together for our mutual help and protection, not merely as master and paid servant, but as Englishmen in a strange country, as brothers in a foreign land."

"And that's how I'm trying to work for you, Mr Brazier, sir," said Shaddy huskily, "and it goes hard with me to tell you what I'm 'fraid on."

"And that is?" said Brazier, while Rob bent forward listening with throbbing heart.

"Either those lads of mine have met with a bad accident, or they have gone off with the boat and left us to starve and die."

"Taken—the boat—the stores—the guns?" faltered Rob.

"My collection and the means of prosecuting my researches?" cried Brazier.

"Yes, sir; that's it, I'm afraid, but I hope I'm wrong."

The two collectors stood silent for a few moments, for the announcement was appalling, and it took time to grasp all the horrors of their position. For to all intents and purposes they were as much cut off from help as if they had been upon some tiny islet in mid-ocean, the river being useless without a boat, and three days' experience alone sufficient to show them the madness of attempting to travel through the forest. In addition they were without food and wanting in the means of obtaining a meal, let alone subsistence from day to day.

Silence then, and with it darkness, fell upon the startled group, till Rob said sturdily,—

"We're all too tired to do anything or think anything till we have rested and had some food. I'm ready to drop."

"Them's wise words," said Shaddy. "No one could have said better. This way, gen'lemen, please!"

He turned sharply round and led them toward the side of the opening in the forest which had been the scene of his search.

"What are you going to do, Naylor?" asked Brazier.

"What every man does first, sir, when night comes on in the wilds: light a fire to keep off the wild beasts."

A thrill of dread passed through Rob at this, for he had been too intent upon the discovery they had made to think anything of their danger. But now he glanced uneasily round, and saw the eyes of wild beasts glaring at them from the dense forest in all directions, till he was ready to laugh at his folly, for the gleaming eyes were fire-flies.

Meanwhile Shaddy led them straight to the spot he had notified as being the one likely to be selected by a halting party for their fire, and here, with the help of the others, sufficient dead wood was collected to start a very small blaze, by whose light they proceeded to collect more and more from the edge of the forest beyond where the river had risen. But it was slow and arduous work for weary people, and they were constantly finding wood that was too small or else that which was too heavy to stir. Still they persevered, and at last so good a fire was burning that there was no fear of an attack by any prowling beast, and as its flames rose higher their task grew less difficult, and by joining hands a good pile of dead limbs was laid ready for keeping up the blaze.

"Something cheery 'bout a fire!" said Shaddy when it was decided that they had enough wood to last the night. "Next thing ought to be supper, gentlemen."

"And we have nothing," said Rob despairingly.

"On'y water," said Shaddy, "plenty of that."

"*Qui dort dine,* Rob," said Brazier quietly.

"Speak to me, sir?" said Shaddy.

“No, but I will, my man,” replied Brazier. “The French say that he who sleeps dines.”

“That’s true, sir,” said Shaddy, “on’y it’s disappointing when you wake. I’ve lain down to go to sleep lots of times like this, tired out and hungry, and dropped asleep directly; and as soon as I’ve been asleep I’ve begun to dream about eating all kinds of good things. It’s very nice in the dreaming, but it don’t keep up your courage.”

“There is nothing that we could possibly get to eat, is there, Shaddy,” said Rob,—“no berries nor fruit?”

“Couldn’t find ’em to-night, sir. In the morning I daresay I can get some berries; might manage a fish, too, to roast at daybreak.”

“But the ground! it is so damp,” said Rob.

“A few boughs will keep off the damp, Mr Rob, sir; so I say, let’s all sleep.”

“But oughtn’t we to keep watch in turns, Naylor?” said Brazier.

“In an ordinary way, sir, yes, one would say it’s a duty—what a man should do,” replied the guide gravely; “and I don’t deny there’s dangers about. But we’ve done all we can do, as men without weapons, by lighting that fire. I shall wake up now and then to throw on some branches and then lie down again. We can do no good more than we have done, and at a time like this I always think it is a man’s duty to say, ‘Can I do anything else?’ and, if he feels he can’t, just say his bit of prayer and leave it to One above to watch over him through the dark hours of the night.”

“Amen,” said Brazier solemnly, and half an hour after, a pile of freshly broken-off boughs had been laid near the fire, and all lay down in perfect faith and trust to sleep and wait for the next day.

Shaddy dropped off at once, while Brazier lay talking in a low tone to Rob, trying to instil some hopefulness.

"Please God," he said at last, "day will bring us help and counsel, my lad, and perhaps give prospects of finding poor Joe."

He ceased speaking, and directly after Rob knew by his regular breathing that he too was asleep. But that greatest blessing would not come to the boy, and he lay gazing now at the dancing flames, now trying to pierce the darkness beyond, and ever and again seeing dangers in the apparently moving shadows cast by the fire.

There were the noises, too, in the forest and along the river bank, sounding more appalling than ever, and as he listened and tried to picture the various creatures that howled, shrieked, and uttered those curious cries, he fully expected to hear that peculiar terror-inspiring sound which had puzzled even Shaddy, the old traveller and sojourner in the forest wilds.

The horrible cry did not come, but as Rob lay there, too weary to sleep, too much agitated by the events of the day to grow calm and fit for rest, that sound always seemed to the lad as if it were about to break out close to where he lay, and the fancy made his breath come short and thick, till the remembrance of his boy-comrade once more filled his mind, and he lay trying to think out some way by which it was possible that Joe had escaped that day. These thoughts stayed in his mind as the fire died out from before his heavy eyes, and at last, in spite of all, he too slept heavily, and dreamed of the young Italian coming to him holding out his hand frankly and then in foreign fashion leaning toward him and kissing him on the cheek.

At the touch Rob leaped back into wakefulness, rose to his elbow, and looked sharply round, perfectly convinced that his cheek had been touched, and that, though in his sleep, he had felt warm breath across his face.

But there was nothing to see save the blazing fire, whose snapping and crackling mingled with the croaking, hissing, and strange cries from the forest. Fire-flies glided here and there, and scintillated about the bushes; Brazier and Shaddy both slept hard; and the peculiar cry of a jaguar or other cat-like animal came softly from somewhere at a distance.

"Fancy!" said Rob softly as he sank down, thinking of Shaddy's last words that night. The troubles of the day died away, and he dropped off fast asleep again, to begin once more dreaming of Joe, and that they were together in the cabin of the boat side by side.

And it all seemed so real, that dream; he could feel the warmth from the young Italian's body in the narrow space, and it appeared to him that Joe moved uneasily when there was a louder cry than usual in the forest and crept closer to him for protection, even going so far as to lay an arm across his chest, inconveniencing him and feeling hot and heavy, but he refrained from stirring, for fear of waking him up.

Then the dream passed away, and he was awake, wondering whether he really was in the cabin again, with Joe beside him. No; he was lying on the boughs beside the fire, but so real had that dream seemed that the fancy was on him still that he could feel the warmth of Joe's body and the boy's arm across his chest.

"And it was all a dream," thought Rob, with the bitter tears rising to his eyes, as he gazed upward at the trees, "a dream—a dream!"

No, it was no dream. He was awake now, and there was a heavy arm across his chest and a head by his side.

"Joe! Oh, Joe!" cried Rob aloud; and he grasped at the arm, touched it, felt its pressure for an instant, and then it was gone, while at his cry both Shaddy and Brazier sprang up.

"What is it?"

"I—I—think I must have been dreaming," said Rob excitedly. "I woke with a start, fancying Joe had come back, and that he was lying down beside me."

"A dream, Rob, my lad!" said Brazier, with a sigh. "Lie down again, boy; your brain is over-excited. Try once more to sleep."

Rob obeyed, feeling weak and hysterical; but after a few minutes sleep came once more, and it was morning when he reopened his eyes.

Chapter Twenty One.

"Where there's a Will there's a Way."

A glorious, a delicious morning, with the mists passing away in wisps of vapour before the bright sunshine, the leaves dripping with dew, and bird and insect life in full activity.

But it was everything for the eye and nothing for the inner man. Waking from a most restful sleep meant also the awakening to a sensation of ravenous hunger, and directly after to the terrible depression caused by the loss sustained on the previous day and their position—alone, and without the means of obtaining food.

When Rob started up he found Brazier in earnest conversation with Shaddy, and in a few minutes the boy learned that their guide had been about from the moment he could see to make up the fire, and then he had been searching in all directions for traces of their companions.

"And you feel sure that they have gone?" Brazier was saying when Rob joined them.

"Certain sure, sir."

"But I still cling to the belief that we have blundered into the wrong place in our weariness and the darkness last night. Why, Naylor, there must be hundreds of similar spots to this along the banks of the river."

"Might say thousands, sir; but you needn't cling no more to no hopes, for this is the right spot, sure enough."

"How do you know?" cried Rob.

"'Cause there's the mark where the boat's head touched ground, where we landed, and our footmarks in the mud."

"And those of the men?" cried Brazier hastily.

"No, sir; they none of them landed. There's your footmarks, Mr Rob's, and mine as plain as can be, and the water has shrunk a bit away since we made 'em yesterday. No, sir, there's no hope that way."

"Then what ever are we to do, man?" cried Brazier.

"Like me to tell you the worst, sir?"

"Yes, speak out; we may as well know."

Shaddy was silent for a few moments, and then said,—

"Well, gen'lemen, those fellows have gone off with the boat and all in it. The guns and things was too much for 'em, and they've gone to feast for a bit and then die off like flies. They'll never work enough by themselves to row that boat back to Paraguay river, for one won't obey the other. They'll be like a watch without a key."

"Then they have gone down the river?" said Rob.

"Yes, sir, wherever it takes them, and they'll shoot a bit and fish a bit till they've used all the powder and lost their lines. So much for them. Let's talk about ourselves. Well, gentlemen, we might make a sort of raft thing of wood and bundles of rushes,—can't make a boat for want of an axe,—and we might float down the stream, but I'm afraid it would only be to drown ourselves, or be pulled off by the critters in the water."

"But the land, Shaddy!" cried Rob. "Can't we really walk along the bank back to where we started?"

"You saw yesterday, sir," said Shaddy grimly.

"But couldn't we find a way across the forest to some point on the great river, Naylor?" said Brazier.

"No, sir, and we've got to face what's before us. No man can get through that great forest without chopping his way with an axe, and he'd want two or three lifetimes to do it in, if he could find food as he went. I'm talking as one who has tried all this sort o' thing for many years, and I'm telling you the simple truth when I say that, situated as we are, we've either got to stop here till help comes, or go down the river on some kind of raft."

"Then why not do that and risk the dangers?" cried Rob.

"Yes," said Brazier. "Why not do that? No help can possibly come here unless Indians pass by in a canoe."

"Which they won't, sir, and if they did they'd kill us as they would wild beasts. I don't believe there's an Indian for a hundred miles."

"Then what do you propose doing first?" asked Brazier.

"Trying to kill the wolf, sir."

"What! hunger?"

"Yes, sir. He's a-gnawing away at me awful. Let's see what berries and fruit we can find, and then try whether we can't get hold of a fish."

"But we are forgetting all about poor Joe," said Rob in agonised tones.

"That we ain't, sir. I know you're not, and if you'll show me what I can do more than I did last evening and afternoon to find the poor boy, here's Shadrach Naylor ready to risk his life any way to save him. But set me to do it, for I can't see no way myself. Can you?"

Rob was silent, and Brazier shook his head.

"You see, it's like this, sir," continued Shaddy: "people as have never been in these woods can't understand what it means, when it's just this: Shut your eyes and go a dozen yards, turn round, and you're lost. There's nothing to guide you but your own footsteps, and you can't see them. You may live for a few days by chewing leaves, and then it's lie down and die, wishing you were a monkey or a bird. That's the truth, gentlemen."

"Then you give up in despair, Naylor?" said Brazier angrily.

"Not I, sir—not the sort o' man. What I say is, we can't do no good by wasting our strength in looking for Mr Joe. We've got to try and save our own lives by stopping where we are."

"And what shall we do first?"

"Use our brains, sir, and find something to eat, as I said afore. There's fruit to find, fish, birds, and monkeys to catch. Snakes ain't bad eating. There's plenty of water, and— Oh, we're not going to die yet. Two big men and a small one, and all got knives; so come along, and let's see what we can do."

Shaddy turned to the fire, taking out his knife and trying the edge.

"First thing I want, Mr Rob, is a bit of hard half-burnt wood—forked bit, out of which I can make a big fish-hook, a long shank and a short one. It must be hard and tough, and— Why, hullo! I didn't see these here before."

"What?" asked Rob and Brazier in a breath, and their companion pointed down at the earth.

"Fresh footmarks, gen'lemen," said Shaddy.

"Joe's?" cried Rob.

"Nay, my lad; it's a lion's, and he has been prowling round about our fire in the night."

Rob started, and thought of his realistic dream, but he was faint, confused in intellect, and could not fit the puzzle together then.

"Well, he hasn't eaten either of us," said Shaddy, with a grim smile, "and he'd better mind what he's about, or we'll eat him. Ah, here we are!" he exclaimed, pouncing upon a piece of burning wood. "Now you take your cap, Mr Rob, and hunt all round for any fruit you can find. Don't be wasteful and pick any that ain't ripe. Leave that for another day. We shall want it. And don't go in the forest. There's more to be found at the edge than inside, because you can't get to the tops of the trees; and don't eat a thing till I've seen it, because there's plenty poisonous as can be."

"All right!" said Rob, and he turned to go.

"And cheer up, both of you," said their companion. "We won't starve while there's traps to be made, and bows and arrows, and fishing tackle. Now, Mr Brazier, please, you'll sit down on that dead tree, take off that silk handkercher from your neck, and pull out threads from it one by one, tie 'em together, and wind 'em up round a bit of stick. Soon as I've made this big rough wooden hook, I'll lay the silk up into a line."

"But you've no bait," said Brazier, who was already taking off his necktie.

"No bait, sir? Mr Rob's going to find some wild oranges or sour sops, or something, and if he don't I still mean to have a fish. Why, if I can't find nothing else I'll have a bait if I come down to cutting off one of my toes—perhaps one o' Mr Rob's would be tenderer or more tempting—or my tongue p'r'aps, for I do talk too much. Work, both of you; I'll soon have a bait, for I want my breakfast like mad."

Rob hurried off, but did not reach the great trees which surrounded the open spot, for at the third clump of bushes he came upon an orange-coloured fruit growing upon a vine-like plant in abundance. It seemed to be some kind of passion-flower, and, in spite of

Shaddy's warning, he tasted one, to find it of a pleasant, sweetish, acid flavour.

Gathering a capful, he returned at once to where his companions in misfortune were hard at work.

"Hullo!" growled Shaddy. "Soon back! What have you got, my lad? Kind o' granadillas, eh? Well, they're good to eat, but not much to make a breakfast of. Better wait till I've done a bit o' conjuring and turned some of 'em into a fish. There, what do you say to that for a hook?"

He held up his piece of wood carving, which was about four inches long and two across, something in this shape:—

"Not much of a hook, Mr Rob, sir, but tough enough to hold a fish if we can coax him to swallow it by covering it with the fruit. We can get three of them juicy things on the shank and point. So now for the line! How are you getting on, Mr Brazier, sir?"

"Very slowly, Naylor," said Brazier, with a sigh.

"All the more surer, sir. You help, Mr Rob, sir, and I'll lay up some of my cotton handkercher for the snood. No; second thoughts is best. I'll make a loose hank of it, so that the fish's teeth may go through if he tries to bite the line, which of course he will."

The result was that in an hour or so a silk line of about twenty yards in length was twisted up and attached to the loose cotton bottom secured to the hook. This was baited, and, after selecting a suitable spot, Shaddy climbed out upon a half-fallen tree whose trunk projected over the river, and dropped his line into a deep eddying pool, where the water ran round and round in a way which made Rob feel giddy.

There was a steep slope just here, so that the bank was not flooded, and hence the angler was able to drop his line at once into deep water, where the action of the whirling current sufficed to suck the bait right down, while Brazier and Rob looked on with the interest of those who depended upon success to give them the food from the want of which they were suffering keenly.

"Now then," said Shaddy cheerfully, "if the bait don't come off, if a fish takes it, if there are any here, if the hook don't break and the line give way, I may catch our breakfast. Plenty of ifs, Mr Rob, sir! Remember the big doradoes we caught up yonder?"

"Oh, if you could catch one now!" replied the lad.

"Ah, if I could, sir! Perhaps I shall, but I don't want a big one. Now for it!"

A quarter of an hour passed away, during which time Shaddy pulled up and examined his bait twice, to see if it was safe, but there was no sign of fish there, though out in mid-stream and toward the farther shore there was evidently abundance, the water being disturbed and some big fellow springing out every now and then, to come down with a mighty splash, scattering the sparkling drops in all directions.

"I shall have to come down to a toe, Mr Rob, sir," said Shaddy grimly. "The fish don't seem to care for fruit so early in the morning. It's all very well for dessert, but they like a substantial meal first. Now then, get your knife ready. Whose is it to be? Shall we pull straws for the lot?"

"Try a little farther this way, Shaddy," said Rob, ignoring the remark.

"Right, sir! I will," said Shaddy, shifting the position of his bait, "but it strikes me we've got into a 'gator hole, and consequently there's no fish."

"Do you think they can see you?"

"No, sir. Water's too thick. Look yonder."

"What at?"

"Monkeys in that tree watching us. Now if you'd got a bow and arrows you might bring one or two down."

"What for?"

"What for, my lad?" cried the guide in astonishment. "And he asks what for, when we're all starving. Why, to eat, of course."

"Ugh! I'm not so hungry as that!" cried Rob, with a shudder.

"You ain't? Well, my lad, I am, and so I tell you. They're capital eating. Why, I remember once when I was up the river with a party we all had— A fish! a fish!" he cried as upon raising his line, to see if the bait were all right, he suddenly felt a fierce tug; and the next minute the pool began to be agitated in a peculiar way.

"Here, Mr Rob, I'm going to hand you the line, and you've got to run him out at once upon the bank. If I try to play him he's sure to go. There, I'll ease him down, and he'll think it's all right and be quiet. Then you draw in gently, and as soon as he feels the hook run him right out, and you, Mr Brazier, sir, stand ready at the water's edge to mind he don't get back. Mind, I don't say it ain't a small 'gator all the same."

He passed the end of the line to Rob as the captive, whatever it was, now lay quiet, but as soon as the lad began to draw the line ashore there was another heavy tug.

"Run him out, sir, not hand over hand; run and turn your back," shouted Shaddy, and as fast as he could get over the tangled growth amongst the trees Rob obeyed, with the result that he drew a large golden-scaled fish right out of the river and up the bank a couple of yards, when something parted, and Shaddy uttered a yell as he saw the captive flapping back toward the pool.

"Gone! gone!" cried Rob in dismay. "I knew—"

He said no more for the moment, and then uttered a shout of delight as he saw the efficacy of their guide's arrangements, for before the fish reached the edge Brazier had thrown himself upon it, and paying no heed to slime, spines, or sharp teeth, he thrust his hands beneath, and flung it far up toward where Rob in turn carried on the attack.

The next minute Shaddy was beside them, knife in hand, with which he rapidly killed, cleaned, and scaled the fish, finding the tough hook broken in two before chopping off a couple of great palm-like leaves, in which he wrapped his prize as he trotted toward the fire. Then with a half-burned branch, he raked a hole in the glowing embers, laid down the fish, raked the embers over again, and said,—

"Not to be touched for half an hour. Who'll come and try for more solid fruit?"

If Rob's spirits had not been so low he would have been amused by the boyish manner of their companion as he led them here and there. At the edge of the forest he mounted and climbed about a tree till he was well out on a great branch, from which he shook down a shower of great fruit that looked like cricket-balls, but which on examination proved to be the hard husks of some kind of nut.

"What are these?" cried Rob.

"Don't you know 'em?" said Shaddy as soon as he had descended.

"No."

"Yes, you do, my lad. You've seen 'em in London lots of times," and hammering a couple together, he broke open one and showed the contents: to wit, so many Brazil nuts packed together in a round form like the carpels of an orange.

"I never knew they grew like that," cried Rob eagerly.

"And I must confess my ignorance, too," said Brazier.

"Ah, there's lots to learn in this world, gen'lemen," said Shaddy quietly. "Not a very good kind o' nut, but better than nothing. Bit too oily for me, but they'll serve as bread for our fish if we get a couple of big stones for nutcrackers. They're precious hard."

"Then we shan't starve yet," cried Rob as he loaded himself with the cannon-ball-like fruit—pockets, cap, and as many as he could hold in his arms.

"Starve? I should think not," cried Shaddy, "and these here outsides'll have to serve for teacups."

"Without tea, Shaddy?"

"Who says so, my lad? You wait, and we'll find cocoa and mate, and who knows but what we may hit upon coffee and chocolate? Why, I won't swear as we don't find sugar-cane. 'T all events, we're going to try."

"Well, Naylor, you are putting a different complexion on our prospects," said Brazier, who had joined them.

"Yes, sir, white one instead of a black one. Next thing is to get a roof over our heads ready for the heavy rains, and then we've got to save all the feathers of the birds we catch or shoot for feather beds. We shall have a splendid place before we've done, and you can mark out as big an estate as you like. But come along; I'm thinking that fish must be done."

Upon Shaddy sweeping its envelope clean of the embers, he found it was quite done, and soon served it out brown and juicy upon a great banana-like leaf.

"Now, gentlemen, grace! and fall to," said their cook merrily. "Nuts afterwards when I've found two big stones."

There was not much of the delicious fish left when a quarter of an hour had passed, and then Rob uttered a grumble.

It was very good, he said, only they had no salt.

"If you'd only spoken a bit sooner, Master Rob, I could have got you some pepper," said Shaddy, "but salt? Ah, there you beat me altogether. It's too far to send down to the sea."

Chapter Twenty Two.

Brave Efforts.

That same afternoon after a quiet discussion of their position, the result of which was to convince Brazier and Rob of the utter hopelessness of any attempt to escape, they joined with Shaddy in the most sensible thing they could do, namely, an attempt to forget their sorrow and misery in hard work.

"If we want to be healthy," Shadrach had said, "we must first thing get a shelter over our heads where we can sleep at nights, clear of the heavy dews, and which we can have ready next time it comes on to rain."

A suitable position was soon found high up where no flood was likely to reach, and presenting several attractions.

First, it was at the head of the clearing exactly facing the river, so that a passing boat could be seen. Secondly, it was between two great trees, apparently twins, whose smooth columnar trunks ran up some twenty feet without a branch; after that they were one mass of dense foliage, which drooped down nearly to the ground and looked thick enough to throw off, as the leafage lay bough above bough, any fall of rain short of a waterspout.

The trees were about twelve feet apart, and from a distance the boughs had so intermingled that they looked like one.

"That's the spot, sir!" Shaddy exclaimed. "Now then, the first thing is to find a branch that will do for a ridge pole."

That first thing proved to be the most difficult they could have undertaken, for a long search showed nothing portable at all likely to answer the purpose; and though palm after palm was found, all were too substantial to be attacked by pocket-knives. They were getting in despair, when Rob hit upon one close down to the river, which the united strength of all three, after Rob had climbed it and by his weight dragged the top down within reach, sufficed to lever out of the saturated ground.

As soon as the young palm was down, Shaddy set Brazier and Rob to cut off the roots and leaves, which latter they were told to stack ready for use, from where they hung six or eight feet long, while he—Shaddy—knife in hand, busied himself in cutting long lianas and canes to act as ropes.

An hour later they had the young palm bound tightly to the trees about six feet from the ground, after which branches were cut and carried, so that they could be laid with the thick ends against the ridge pole and the leaves resting upon the ground from end to end.

This done, others were laid on in the same way, the leaves and twigs fitting in so accurately that after a busy two hours they had a strong shed of branches ready for stopping up at one end with thorns and more boughs, while Rob had to climb up the slope and thatch the place with the palm leaves, forming a roof impervious to any ordinary rain.

"That will do for sleeping, eh, gen'lemen?" said Shaddy. "We'll finish it another time. We can rest in shelter. Now then for getting our wages—I mean a decent supper."

Rob had been conscious for some time past of sundry faint sensations; now he knew that they meant hunger, and as they left the hut they had made he did not look forward with any great feelings of appetite to a meal of nuts.

But it soon became evident that Shaddy had other ideas, for he went to the fire again to obtain a hardened piece of wood for fashioning into a hook, when an idea struck Rob, and he turned to their guide eagerly.

"Did you ever sniggle eels?" he said.

"Did I ever what, sir?"

"Sniggle eels."

Shaddy shook his head.

"No. I've bobbed for 'em, and set night lines, and caught 'em in baskets and eel traps after storms. Is either of them sniggling?"

"No," cried Rob eagerly, "and you might catch fish perhaps that way. I'll show you; I mean, I'll tell you. You take a big needle, and tie a piece of strong thin silk to it right in the middle."

"Ay, I see," said Shaddy.

"Then you push the needle right into a big worm, and stick the point of the needle into a long thin pole, and push the worm into a hole in a bank where eels are."

"Yes, I see."

"Then one of the eels swallows the worm, and you pull the line."

"And the worm comes out."

"No, it does not," said Rob. "As it's tied in the middle, it is pulled right across the eel's throat, and you can catch it without being obliged to use a hook."

"That's noo and good," said Shaddy eagerly. "I could fish for doradoes that way, but I've got no needle."

"Wouldn't this do, Shaddy?" said the lad, and he took a steel needle-like toothpick out of the handle of his pocket-knife.

"The very thing!" cried Shaddy, slapping his leg, and, after tying his newly made line to the little steel implement in the way described, he bound over it with a silken thread a portion of the refuse of the fish they had previously caught. Going to his former place, he cast in his line, and in five minutes it was fast to a good-sized fish, which after a struggle was landed safely, while before long another was caught as well.

"Man never knows what he can do till he tries," cried Shaddy merrily. "Why, we can live like princes, gentlemen. No fear of starving! Fish as often as we like to catch 'em, and then there's birds and other things to come. You don't feel dumpy now, Mr Rob, do you?"

"I don't know, Shaddy. I'm very hungry and tired."

"Wait till we've had supper, my lad, and then we'll see what we can do about making a bow and arrows."

As he spoke he rapidly cleaned the fish, treated them as before, and placed them in the embers, which were glowing still.

While the fish cooked Shaddy busied himself in crushing some of the nuts by using one stone as a hammer, another as an anvil, and some of them he set to roast by way of a change.

By the time the fish were ready the sun was rapidly going down, and when the meal was at an end—a meal so delicious, in spite of the surroundings, that it was eaten with the greatest of enjoyment—it was too dark to see about bows and arrows, and the disposition of all three was for sleep.

So the boughs collected on the previous night were carried in beneath the shelter and made into beds, upon which, after well making up the fire, all stretched themselves, and, utterly wearied out by the arduous toil of the day, fell asleep at once, in spite of the chorus of nocturnal creatures around, among which a couple of cicadas settled in their rudely made roof and kept up a harsh chirping loud enough to have kept awake any one who had not gone through as much work as two ordinary men.

"But it can't be morning," thought Rob as he was awakened by Shaddy touching him on the shoulder, and then he uttered his thought aloud.

"Well, if it ain't, my lad, the sun's made a mistake, for he'll be up directly. Coming out?"

"Yes; wait till I wake Mr Brazier."

"Nay; let him be till we've got breakfast ready, my lad. He looked regularly done up last night. He can't bear it all like young chaps such as we."

Rob laughed, and then a cloud came over him as he stepped out into the soft grey morning, for he had caught sight of the hurrying river, and this brought up the boat and the loss of his companion and friend.

"Look here, Mr Rob," said Shaddy, changing the current of the boy's thoughts directly, "I've been thinking out that bow and arrow business."

"Yes, Shaddy."

"And I've found out some splendid tackle for making arrows."

"What! this morning? Then you have been out and about!"

"Yes, soon as I could see my way. I found a bed of reeds which will make capital arrows with a point of hard wood a bit burned, and there's no end of 'em, so there's our shot all straight as— well, as arrows. Now you and I are going to get a fish and put him to cook, and after that we'll try and find a bit of wood good enough for a bow."

"And where's your string, Shaddy?"

"Round your neck, sir. You don't think you're going to indulge in such luxuries as silk han'kerchers at a time like this, do you? Because, if you do, I don't; so you'll have to pull out all the threads and wind 'em up, like Mr Brazier did. His han'kercher will do for fishing-lines. Yours shall be bow-strings. Why, who knows but what we may get a deer? Anyhow we may get one of them carpinchos, and not bad eating, either."

The fish was soon caught in the swift clear water, but all attempts to take another failed. It was, however, ample for their meal, and after it had been placed in the fire, which had never been allowed to go out since first lit, Rob's companion pointed out more footprints of a puma, and soon after those of a deer, both animals having evidently been in the opening within the last few hours, from the freshness of the prints.

The reeds for the arrows were cut, and proved to be firm, strong, and light, but the selection of a branch for the bow proved to be more of a task. One was, however, decided upon at last, roughly trimmed, and thrown on the fire for a few minutes to harden, and it was while the pair were busy over this task, watching the tough wood carefully, that Brazier found them, apologising for his so-called idleness and eagerly asking what he should do to help.

"Nothing, sir, at present, but have your breakfast. Would you mind picking a few plates and a dish, Mr Rob? Let's have the green pattern again."

Rob smiled as he went to the arum-like plant which had supplied him before, and returned to the fire just as Shaddy was apologising seriously for its being fish again for breakfast and promising a change before night.

The apology was uncalled for, the freshly caught, newly roasted fish proving to be delicious; and roasted nuts, though they were not chestnuts and were often flavoured with burned oil, were anything but a bad substitute for bread.

"There, gen'lemen," said Shaddy as they finished, "next thing seems to be to go down to the waterside and have a good drink of nature's own tea and coffee. Worse things than water, I can tell you. I always think to myself when I've nothing else that what was good enough for Adam and Eve ought to be good enough for me."

"Water's delicious," cried Rob as they reached a convenient place and lay down to scoop up the cool clear fluid with their hands and drink heartily.

"So it is, Mr Rob, sir, 'llcious," said Shaddy; "but wait a bit, and you shall have something to put in the water, if it's only fruit juice to flavour it. But what I want to find is some of those leaves they make into South American tea."

Just then Shaddy smiled and rose to his knees, watching Brazier, who had moved off thirty or forty yards away.

"What are you laughing at?" asked Rob.

"Mr Brazier's want of good manners, sir. Don't seem the thing for a gen'leman like him to go washing his face and hands in his tea and coffee-cup; now do it?"

"Plenty of room, Shaddy!" said Rob. "I'm going to follow his example."

He stretched out over the water from the bank, reached down his hands, and began to bathe his face, the water feeling deliciously cool to his brow and eyes as he scooped up handsful, and he was just revelling in an extra good quantity, when he uttered an ejaculation of alarm, for he felt himself seized by the collar as if he were about to be hurled into the river, but it proved only to be Shaddy snatching him away.

"Why did you do that?" cried Rob angrily, as he pressed the water out of his eyes and darted a resentful look at the big rough fellow, who stood looking at him coolly.

"'Cause we wanted you to be useful, my lad, and because you didn't want to go below yonder and feed the fishes," replied Shaddy, laughing. "Didn't you see that 'gator?"

"No. Where? Was it near me?"

"Pretty near, sir. I happened to look, and saw him coming slowly nearer and nearer, ready for making a dash at you, and as I'd neither gun nor spear to tackle him, I had to pull you out of the way."

"Was it big?" said Rob, with a shudder.

"No, sir, only a little one, about six foot long, but quite strong enough to have hung on and overbalanced you into the water, where there would have been plenty more to help him. Now I tell you what, sir, Mr Brazier had better be told to be careful," continued Shaddy. "Ah, he sees danger; so it's all right."

For Brazier suddenly shrank away from the edge of the river, rose, and called to them.

"Take care, Rob!" he shouted; "the water here swarms with alligators. One little wretch was coming at me just now."

"Yes, sir, better mind!" cried Shaddy. "We've just had one here." Then turning to Rob,—

"Now, Master Rob, sir, what do you say to our spending the day making bows and arrows?"

"I'm ready."

"And perhaps, Mr Brazier, sir, you wouldn't mind trying for another fish for dinner, in case we don't get our shooting tackle ready."

Brazier nodded, and soon after prepared to fish, but even in their peculiar strait he could not refrain from looking longingly at plant, insect, and bird, especially at a great bunch of orchids which were pendent from a bough.

He did not seem likely to have much success in the pool or eddy where the other fish had been caught, and soon after moved off to another place, but meanwhile Rob and Shaddy were busy in the extreme, the latter making some half-charred pieces of wood from the fire into little hardened points ready for Rob to fix into the cleft he split in the end of each reed and then binding them tightly in, making a notch for the bow-string at the other end, and laying them down one by one finished for the sheaf he had set himself to prepare.

These done, Rob began upon the silken bow-string, pulling out the threads from his neckerchief and tying them together till he had wound up what promised to be enough, afterwards doubling and twisting them tightly, while Shaddy was whistling softly and using his pocket-knife as if it were a spoke-shave to fine down the thick end of the piece of wood intended for the bow.

"Strikes me, Mr Rob," he said, "that we shall have to use this very gingerly, or it will soon break. I know what I wish I had."

"What?" asked Rob.

"Rib of an old buffalo or a dead horse."

"What for?"

"To make a bow, my lad. It would only be a short one, but wonderfully strong. You'd have to use short arrows, and it would be hard to pull, but with a bow like that you could send an arrow through a deer. But as we haven't got one, nor any chance of finding one, we must do the best with this."

Rob watched with the greatest of interest the progress of the bow, busying himself the while with the string, which was finished first; and as it displayed a disposition to unwind and grow slack, it was thoroughly wetted and stretched between two boughs to dry.

“Shall you succeed in getting a bow made?” said Brazier, coming up.

“Oh yes, sir, I think so,” said the guide; “better bow than archer, I’m thinking, without Mr Rob here surprises us all by proving himself a clever shot.”

“Don’t depend upon me,” said Rob mournfully, for his thoughts were upon Joe and his sad end, and when by an effort he got rid of these depressing ideas, his mind filled with those of the Indians turning against them in so cowardly a way, leaving them to live or die, just as it might happen, while they escaped with the plunder in the boat.

“What are you thinking about, Rob?” said Brazier, after speaking to him twice without eliciting an answer.

“Of the men stealing our boat. It was so cruel.”

“Don’t you fret about it, Mr Rob! They’ll soon get their doo of punishment for it. Worst day’s work they ever did in their lives. You’d think that chaps like they would have known better, but they’re just like children. They see something pretty, and they’ll do anything to get hold of it, and when they’ve got it they find it’s of no use to ’em and are tired of it in an hour. I’ll be bound to say they’re wishing they hadn’t gone and were back along of us.”

“Then they may repent and come?” said Brazier.

Shaddy uttered a low chuckling sound.

“And I shall save my collection after all.”

“Don’t you think it, sir!” said Shaddy seriously. “They couldn’t get back, as I said; and if they could they daren’t, on account of you and me. They’ve got a wholesome kind of respect for an Englishman, and no more dare face us now than fly.”

Brazier sighed.

"Oh, never mind, sir!" said Shaddy cheerily. "Things might be worse than they are. We're alive, and can find means to live. We don't know but what we may get away all right after all. If I might give you my advice—"

"Give it, by all means," said Brazier.

"Well then, sir, seeing that you came out to collect your flowers and plants, I should say, 'Go on collecting just as you did before, and wait in hopes of a boat coming along.'"

"But it might be years first."

"Very well, sir; wait years for it. You'd have made a fine collection by that time."

Brazier smiled sadly as he thought of his dried-up specimens.

"Me and Mr Rob here will find plenty of some sort or another for the kitchen, so as you needn't trouble about that. What do you say?"

"That you teach good philosophy, and I'll take your advice. Not much virtue in it, Rob," he said, smiling, "for we cannot help ourselves. There, I will do as you suggest as soon as we have made a few more arrangements for our stay."

"You leave them to us, sir," said Shaddy. "Mr Rob and I are quite strong enough crew for the job, and I saw some wonderful fine plants right at the edge of the forest yonder. I'd go and try for 'em now, sir."

"Shaddy's afraid that some one will come along and pick them first," cried Rob, laughing.

"No fear, sir, unless it's some big, saucy monkey doing it out of imitation and mischief. What do you say?"

"I say yes," replied Brazier. "It would be wrong to despair and foolish to neglect my chance now that I am thrown by accident among the natural history objects I came so many thousand miles to find."

As he spoke he moved off in the direction pointed out by their guide, while Shaddy chuckled directly they were alone.

"That's the way, Mr Rob," he said; "give him something to think about and make him busy. 'A merry heart goes all the day; a sad one tires in a mile,' so the old song says. Mind, I don't mean he's merry, but he'll be busy, and that's next door to it. Now then, I'm ready. Let's get the string on and bend our bow."

Chapter Twenty Three.

A Sudden Alarm.

The silken string Rob had twisted was found to be quite dry, and pretty well kept its shape as it was formed into a loop and passed over the end of the bow nicked for its reception, and after bending secured with a couple of hitches over the other.

"Now, Mr Rob, sir, try it, and send one of your arrows as far as you can. Never mind losing it; we can soon make plenty more. That's the way! Steady! Easy and well, sir! Now then, off it goes!"

Twang! went the bow-string, and away flew the arrow high up toward the river, describing its curve and falling at last without the slightest splash into the water.

"Well done!" cried Shaddy, who had watched the flight of the arrow, shading his eyes with his hand. "That's good enough for anything. A little practice, and you'll hit famously."

"Oh, I don't know, Shaddy."

"Well, but I do, sir. If Indians can kill birds, beasts, and fish with their bows and arrows, surely a young Englishman can."

"I shall try, Shaddy."

"Of course you will, and try means win, and win means making ourselves comfortable till we are taken off."

"Then you think we shall be some day?"

"Please God, my lad!" said Shaddy calmly. "Look! Yonder goes Mr Brazier. He's forgetting his troubles in work, and that's what we've got to do, eh?"

Rob shook his head.

"Ah, you're thinking about poor young Jovanni, sir," said Shaddy sadly, "and you mustn't. It won't do him no good, nor you neither. Bring that bow and arrows along with us. I'm going to try and get a bamboo to make a spear thing, with a bit of hard wood for a point, and it may be useful by-and-by."

Rob took up the bow and arrows, but laid the larger part of his sheaf down again, contenting himself with half a dozen, and following Shaddy along the edge of the forest to what looked like a clump of reeds, but which proved to be a fringe of bamboos fully fourteen feet high.

Shaddy soon selected a couple of these suitable for his purpose, and had before long trimmed them down to spear shafts nine feet in length.

"There, sir," he said, "we'll get a couple of heads fitted into these to-night. First thing is to get something else to eat, so let's try for fruit or a bird. Now, if we could only come upon a deer!"

"Not likely, as we want one," responded Rob, who was looking round in search of Mr Brazier, and now caught sight of him right at the far end of the clearing, evidently engaged in cutting down some of his favourite plants.

"Mr Brazier is busy," said Rob; "but isn't it a pity to let him waste time in getting what can never be wanted?"

"How do we know that?" replied Shaddy. "Even if they're not, I did it for the best."

"But is it safe to leave him alone?"

"Safe as it is for us to go out here alone into the forest."

"Are we going into the forest?"

"Must, my lad—a little way."

"But are there likely to be any Indians about?"

"I should say not, Mr Rob, so come along."

Shaddy led the way to where the clearing ceased and the dense growth of the primeval forest began, and after hesitating a little and making a few observations as to the position of the sun—observations absolutely necessary if a traveller wished to find his way back—the guide plunged in amongst the dense growth, threading his way in through the trees, which grew more and more thickly for a short distance and then opened out a little, whereupon Shaddy halted and began to reconnoitre carefully, holding up his band to enforce silence and at the end of a few minutes saying eagerly to Rob,—

"Here you are, my lad! Now's our chance. There's nearly a dozen in that big tree to the right yonder, playing about among the branches, good big ones, too. Now you steal forward a bit, keeping under cover, then lay all your arrows down but one, take a good long aim, and let it go. Bring one down if you can."

"What birds are they?" whispered Rob.

"Who said anything about birds?" replied Shaddy sourly; "I said monkeys."

"No."

"Well, I meant to, my lad. There: on you go."

"Monkey—a little man," said Rob, shaking his head. "No, I couldn't shoot one of them."

"Here, give us hold of the bow and arrow, then, my lad," cried the old sailor. "'Tisn't a time for being nice. Better shoot a monkey and eat it than for me and Mr Brazier to have to kill and eat you."

Rob handed the newly made weapons, and Shaddy took them grumblingly.

“Not the sort of tackle I’m used to,” he said. “Bound to say I could do far better with a gun.”

He fitted the notch of the arrow to the string and drew the bow a little as if to try it; then moving off a few yards under cover of the trees, Rob was about to follow him, but he turned back directly.

“Don’t you come,” he said; “better let me try alone. Two of us might scare ’em.”

But Shaddy did not have any occasion to go further, for all at once, as if in obedience to a signal, the party of monkeys in the forest a short distance before them came leaping from tree to tree till they were in the one beneath which the two travellers were waiting, stopped short, and began to stare down wonderingly at them, one largish fellow holding back the bough above his head in a singularly human way, while his face looked puzzled as well as annoyed.

“Like a young savage Indian more than an animal,” said Shaddy softly, as he prepared to shoot. “Now I wonder whether I can bring him down.”

“Don’t shoot at it, Shaddy!” said Rob, laying his hand upon his guide’s arm.

“Must, my lad. Can’t afford to be particular. There, don’t you look if you don’t like it! Now then!”

He raised the bow, and, after the fashion off our forefathers, drew the arrow right to the head, and was about to let it fly after a long and careful aim; but being, as he had intimated, not used to that sort of tackle, he kept his forefinger over the reed arrow till he had drawn it to the head, when, just as he had taken aim and was about to launch it at the unfortunate monkey, the reed bent and snapped in two.

Probably it was the sharp snap made by the arrow which took the monkey's attention, for it suddenly set up a peculiarly loud chattering, which acted as a lead to its companions, for the most part hidden among the boughs, and it required very little stretch of the imagination to believe it to be a burst of derisive laughter at the contemptible nature of the weapons raised against their leader's life.

"Oh, that's the way you take it, is it, my fine fellow?" cried Shaddy, shaking the bow at the monkey. "Here, give us another arrow, Mr Rob, sir; I'll teach him to laugh better than that. I feel as if I can hit him now."

Rob made no attempt to hand the arrow, but Shaddy took one from him, fitted it to the string, raised it to the required height, and was about to draw the reed to its full length, but eased it back directly and left go to rub his head.

"See him now, Mr Rob, sir?"

"No," said Rob, looking carefully upward among the branches; and, to his great satisfaction, not one of the curious little four-handed animals was visible.

"Right!" said Shaddy. "He has saved his skin this time. Here, take the bow again. It may be a bird we see next."

"Hadn't we better go back to the river?" said Rob. "Perhaps I should be able to shoot a duck if I saw one swimming about."

"Daresay you would, my lad," said the old sailor drily, "send the arrow right through one; but what I say is, if the 'gators want a duck killed they'd better kill it themselves."

"I don't understand you," said Rob.

"Understand, my lad? Why, suppose you shoot a duck, it will be on the water, won't it?"

"Of course!"

"Then how are you going to get it off?"

"I forgot that," said Rob. "Impossible, of course."

"Come on, then, and don't let's waste time. We'll keep along here and get some fruit, perhaps, and find birds at the same time."

Their journey through the forest was very short before they were startled by a sudden rush and bound through the undergrowth. So sudden was it that both stopped short listening, but the sound ceased in a few moments.

"What's that?" whispered Rob.

"Deer, I thought at first, my lad; but it could not have been, because a deer would have gone on racing through the forest, and one would have heard the sounds dying away, not end suddenly like those did. You see, there was a sudden rustle, and then it stopped, as if whatever it was had been started up by our coming and then settled down again to hide and watch us."

"Indian?" whispered Rob uneasily.

"Nay, more like some great cat. Strikes me it was one of the spotted tigers, and a hardened arrow's not much good against one of those beasts. I say, let's strike off in the other direction, and try if we can find something there. Cats are awkward beasts to deal with even when they're small. When it comes to one as strong as a horse, the best way to fight 'em is to get out of their way."

Shaddy took a few steps forward so as to be able to peer up through a green shaft among the trees to the sunshine and satisfy himself as to their position, and then led off again.

"Can't be too particular, Mr Rob, sir," he said; "stitch in time saves nine. Bit of observation now may save us hours of walking and fighting our way through the tangle."

Rob noted his companion's careful management, and that whenever they had to pass round a tree which stood right in their way Shaddy was very exact about starting afresh exactly straight, and after a time in making off again to their left, so as to hit the river near the clearing. But for some time they found nothing to take their attention.

"And that's the way of it," said Shaddy in reply to an observation of Rob's. "You generally find what you are not looking for. Now, if we wanted plenty of fine hardwood timber, here it is, and worth fortunes in London town, and worth nothing here. I'd give the lot, Mr Rob, for one of our fine old Devonshire apple-trees, well loaded down with yellow-faced, red-cheeked pippins, though even then we've no flour to make a dumpling."

"And no saucepan to cook it in."

"Oh, we could do without that, my lad. Worse things than baked dumplings."

"Are we going right, Shaddy?" said Rob suddenly.

The old sailor took an observation, as he called it, before he answered, so as to make sure.

"Yes," he said thoughtfully, "and if we keep straight on we shall hit the clearing. Strikes me that if we go pretty straight we shall come upon Mr Brazier loaded down to sinking point with plants, and glad of a bit of help to carry 'em. Don't you be down-hearted, sir! This is a bit of experience; and here we are! something at last."

As he spoke he pointed to a tree where the sun penetrated a little, and they could see that it was swarming with small birds evidently busy over the fruit it bore. Shaddy was pressing forward, but Rob caught his arm.

"What is it, lad?"

"Look!" whispered Rob. "What's that?"

"Eh? Where? See a tiger?"

"No, that horrible-looking thing walking along the branch. It has gone now."

"Ugly monkey?"

"Oh no," whispered Rob, "a curious creature. Alligators don't climb trees, do they?"

"Never saw one," said Shaddy. "Might if they were taught, but it wouldn't be a pleasant job to teach one. Well, where is it?"

"Gone," whispered Rob. "No; there it is on that branch where it is so dark."

"I see him," said Shaddy in a subdued tone. "Ought to have known. Now then, your bow and arrows! That's a skinful of good meat for us. You won't mind shooting that?"

"No," said Rob, quickly fitting an arrow to the string, "I don't mind shooting that. But not to eat, thank you."

"You will not be so particular soon. That's iguana, and as good as chicken. Ready?"

Rob nodded.

"Keep behind the trees, then, and creep slowly forward till you are pretty close—I daresay you'll be able to—and then aim at his shoulder, and send the arrow right through."

"I will," said Rob drily, "if I can."

"Make up your mind to it, my lad. We want that sort of food."

"You may," thought Rob as he began to stalk the curious old-world, dragon-like beast, which was running about the boughs of a great tree in complete ignorance of the neighbourhood of human beings, probably even of their existence.

The lad's heart beat heavily as he crept from tree to tree in full want of faith as to his ability to draw a bow-string with effect; for his experience only extended to watching ladies shooting at targets in an archery meeting; and as he drew nearer, stepping very softly from shelter to shelter and then peering out to watch the reptile, he had an admirable opportunity for noting its shape and peculiarities, none of which created an appetite for trying its chicken-like flesh. He gazed at a formidable-looking animal with wide mouth, a hideous pouch beneath its jaw, and a ridge of sharp-looking, teeth-like spines along its back ending in a long, fine, bony tail. These, with its fierce eye and scaly skin, and a habit of inflating itself, made it appear an object which might turn and attack an aggressor.

This struck Rob very strongly as he stopped at last peering round the bole of a huge tree. He was about thirty yards from the lizard now, and in a position which commanded its side as it stood gazing straight before it at some object, bird or insect, in front.

It was just the position for resting the bow-arm against the tree for steadiness of aim, and feeling that he could do no better, but doubtful of his skill and quite as doubtful of the likelihood of the wooden arrow-head piercing the glistening skin of the iguana, Rob took a careful aim, as he drew his arrow to his ear in good old archer style, and let his missile fly.

Roughly made, unfeathered, and sent by a tyro, it was no wonder that it flew far wide of the mark, striking a bough away to the left and then dropping from twig to twig till it reached the undergrowth below.

Where it struck was some distance from the lizard, and the sound and the falling of the reed gave it the idea that the danger point was there, so that it directed its attention in that quarter, stood very erect, and swelled itself out fiercely.

This gave Rob ample time to fit another arrow to his string, correct his aim, and loosen the shaft after drawing it to the head. This one whizzed by the iguana, making it flinch slightly; but treating it as if it had been a bird which had suddenly flashed by, the lizard fixed its eyes on the spot where this second arrow struck.

"I shall never hit the thing," thought Rob as he fitted another arrow and corrected his aim still more, but this time too much, for the arrow flew off to the lizard's right.

"Three arrows gone!" muttered the lad as he prepared for another try, took a long aim, and, to his great delight, saw the missile strike the bough just below where the iguana stood, but only for it to make a rush forward out of his sight.

"But I should have hit it if I had only aimed a little higher," he thought.

The lizard being invisible, he was about to return to Shaddy, thinking of his companion's disappointment, when, to his surprise, he suddenly saw the reptile reappear upon a lower branch, where it stood watchful and eager, and once more presenting a splendid opportunity for a skilled archer.

"It's of no good," thought Rob. "I must practise every day at a mark," and once more taking aim without exercising much care, but more with an idea of satisfying his companion if he were watching his actions than of hitting his mark, he drew the arrow quickly to the head, gave one glance along the slight reed at the iguana, the bow-string twanged, and the next moment the reptile was gone.

"That settles it," said Rob as he listened to the rustling of the leaves and twigs; "but I must have gone pretty near for it to have leaped off the bough in such a hurry. I'll be bound to say poor old Joe would have made a better shot. Italian! Genoese archers!" he continued thoughtfully. "No, they were cross-bow-men. Poor old Joe, though! Oh, how shocking it does seem for a bright handsome lad like he was to—"

"Here! hi! T'other way, my lad! He dropped down like a stone."

"No, no; leaped like a deer off the branch. I saw him."

"Well, so did I," cried Shaddy, hurrying up. "The arrow went clean through him."

"Nonsense!"

"Nonsense, sir? What do you mean?"

"I did not go near him."

"What? Why, you shot him right through the shoulder. I haven't got much to boast about except my eye, and I'll back that against some people's spy-glasses. That iguana's lying down there at the bottom of the tree dead as a last year's butterfly, and I can put my foot right on the place. Come along."

Rob smiled, raised his eyebrows a little, and followed.

"Better let him convince himself," he thought; and as Shaddy forced back the low boughs and held them apart for his companion to follow, he went on talking.

"I knew you could do it by the way you handled your bow and arrow. Your eyes are as straight as mine is, and I watched you as you sent an arrow first one side and then another till you got the exact range, and then it was like kissing your hand: just a pull of the string, off goes the arrow, and down drops the lizard, and a fine one, too. Round that trunk, my lad! There you are, and there he lies, just down in that tuft of grass."

"Where?" said Rob banteringly. "Why, Shaddy, I thought your eye was better than spy-glasses."

Shaddy made a dash at the tuft of thick growth beneath the bough where the iguana had stood, searched about, and then rose and took off his cap to give his head a scratch.

"Well, I never!" he said in a tone full of disappointment; "I was as sure as sure that you hit that thing right through."

He looked round about, and then all at once made a rush at a spot whence came a faint rustling; and the next minute he returned dragging the iguana by the tail, with the half of the arrow through its shoulder.

"Now then," he cried, "was I right, or was I wrong? He made a big scramble to get away, and hid himself in that bush all but his tail. My word, Mr Rob, sir, what a shot you will make!"

"Nonsense, Shaddy!" said the lad, looking down with a mingling of compunction and pride at his prize.

"Ah, you may call it nonsense, Mr Rob. I calls it skill."

"Why, it was a mere accident."

"Hark at him!" cried Shaddy, looking round at the trees as if to call their attention to the lad's words. "Says it was an accident when I told him to aim straight at the thing's shoulder, and there's the arrow right through it from one side to the other, and the poor brute dead as dead."

"But I hardly aimed at it, Shaddy," protested Rob.

"Of course you didn't. A good shot just makes up his mind to hit a thing, and he hits it same as you did that lizard. Well, sir, that's one trouble off my mind; and I can say thankfully we shan't starve. There'll be times when the river's so flooded that we can't fish, and then we might have come worst off; but you can shoot us birds and beasts. Then we can find eggs, and lay traps, and search for fruit. Why, Mr Rob, sir, we're going to have our bread buttered on both sides, and we can keep Mr Brazier going while he collects. It looked very black indeed time back, but the sun's shining in on us now. We shall be a bit like prisoners, but where are you going to find a more beautiful prison for people who want to study natural history? Hooray I look here, too—mushrooms."

"What, those great funguses?"

"To be sure: they're good eating. I know 'em, sir. Found 'em before, and learnt to eat 'em off the Indians. Here, wait a moment; let's take enough of 'em for supper, and then get back to the kitchen and have a turn at cooking. That's enough," he continued, picking up from the mouldering stump of a huge decaying tree a great cluster of fungi; "those others'll do for another time."

"I hope you will not be disappointed in my shooting next time," said Rob, taking the cluster of mushroom growth and thrusting an arrow through it like a skewer. "I have very little faith in it myself, Shaddy."

"More likely to do good, and I believe in you all the more, Mr Rob," said the man, seizing the lizard, tying its legs together with a band of twisted twigs, thrusting his bamboos through, and swinging the prize over his shoulder. "If you went puffing and blowing about and saying you was going to shoot this, and hit that, I should begin to wonder how ever we were to get our next dinner. Never you mind about feeling afraid for yourself. 'Modesty's the best policy,' as the old saying goes, or something like it. Now then, best foot foremost! Tread in my steps, and I think I can lead you straight for the head of the clearing, pretty close to home, sweet home. D'yer mind what I say?" he continued, with a queer smile. "Think. I ain't quite sure, my lad, but I'll try."

Shaddy took a fresh observation, and then gave a satisfied nod of the head.

"Forrard!" he said; and he made off as if full of confidence, while Rob followed behind, taking care of his mushrooms and watching the nodding head of the iguana low down at Shaddy's back in a curiously grim fashion, and thinking that it looked anything but attractive as an object for the cook's art.

They had been walking nearly an hour, very slowly—for it was difficult work to avoid the tangled growth which hemmed them in—when Shaddy, who had been chatting away pleasantly about the trees and their ill-luck in not finding more fruit out in the forest, warning his companion, too, every now and then about ant-hills and thorns, suddenly exclaimed, "Wonder what luck Mr Brazier's had?" and almost directly after as they entered an open place where orchids were growing, some of which had suggested the man's last speech, he cried, "Why, hullo! Look here, Mr Rob; look here," and as he pointed down at the dead leaves beneath their feet, Rob started back with a shudder of horror, and looked wildly round for the cause of that which he saw.

Chapter Twenty Four.

A Gap in the Ranks.

That which Shaddy pointed out was startling enough to cause Rob a shudder; for, plainly seen upon a broad leaf, trampled-down amongst others that were dead and dry, were a few spots of blood.

But after the momentary feeling of dread caused by the discovery there came a reaction, and Rob exclaimed eagerly, "Some wild beasts have been fighting;" and then as his companion shook his head, the boy uttered a forced laugh, and, to carry off the excitement, said:

"I know what it is, Shaddy: two monkeys coming home from school have had a fight, and one made the other's nose bleed."

"Wish I could laugh and joke about it like you do, squire," said Shaddy sadly, as he peered about. "It's serious, my lad. Something very wrong, I'm afraid."

"Don't say that, Shaddy," cried Rob huskily. "I only tried to turn it off because I felt afraid and didn't want to show it. Do you really think there's something very serious?"

"I do, my lad."

"Not that Mr Brazier has been here?"

"That's just what I do think, my lad; and I feel as if it was my fault for sending him hunting and collecting by himself, instead of us waiting on him and watching him."

"Shaddy, don't say anything has happened to him!" cried Rob in horror.

"I don't say as there is," said Shaddy; "I don't say as there ain't, my lad: but you see that," he said, pointing down, "and you know that

Mr Brazier's a fine brave English gentleman, but, like all the natural history people I ever see, so full of what he's doing that he forgets all about himself and runs into all kinds of danger."

"But what kind of danger could he have run into here?"

"Don't know, my lad—don't know. All I do know is that he has been here and got into trouble."

"But you don't know that he has been here," cried Rob passionately.

"What's this, then?" said Shaddy, holding out a piece of string, which he had picked up unnoticed by his companion. "Mr Brazier had got one of his pockets stuffed full of bits o' spun yarn and band, like that as we used to tie up his plants with, and it looks to me as if he'd dropped this."

"But couldn't— Oh no, of course not—it's impossible," cried Rob; "no one else could have been here?"

"No, sir; no one else could have been here."

"Yes, they could," cried Rob excitedly: "enemies!"

Shaddy shook his head as he peered about, stooping and examining the trampled-down growth.

"Wish I could track like an Indian does, Mr Rob, sir. He has been here sure enough, but I can't make out which way he has gone. There's our footmarks pressing down the twigs and moss and stuff; and there's his, I fancy."

"And Indians?"

"Can't see none, sir; but that means nothing: they tread so softly with their bare feet that a dozen may have been here and gone, and we not know it."

"Then you do think he has been attacked by Indians, Shaddy?" cried Rob reproachfully.

"Well, sir, I do, and I don't. There's no sign."

"Then what could it have been, — a jaguar?"

"Maybe, Mr Rob."

"Or a puma!"

"Maybe that, sir; or he may have come suddenly upon a deer as gave him a dig with its horns. Here, let's get on back to camp as quickly as we can."

"But he may not be there," cried Rob excitedly, as he looked round among the densely packed trees. "Let's try and find some track by which he has gone."

"That's what I've been trying to do, and couldn't find one, sir. If he's been wounded, somehow he'd nat'rally make back for the hut, so as to find us and get help. Come along."

"Oh, Shaddy, we oughtn't to have left him. We ought to have kept together."

"No good to tell me that, Mr Rob, sir; I feel it now, but I did it all for the best. There, sir, it's of no use to stay here no longer. Come on, and we may hit upon his backward trail."

Rob gave another wild look round, and then joined Shaddy, who was carefully studying the position of the sun, where a gleam came through the dense foliage high above their heads, and lightened the deep green twilight.

"That's about the course," he muttered, as he gave the iguana a hitch over to his right shoulder. "Now then, Mr Rob, sir, let's make a swift passage if we can, and hope for the best. Pah! Look at the flies already after the meat. No keeping anything long here."

The remark struck Rob as being out of place at such a time, but he was fain to recall how he had made speeches quite as incongruous, so he followed his companion in silence, trusting to him implicitly, and wondering at the confidence with which he pressed on in one direction, with apparently nothing to guide him. In fact, all looked so strange and undisturbed that Rob at last could not contain himself.

"Mr Brazier cannot have been anywhere here, Shaddy," he cried excitedly. "Two wild beasts must have been fighting."

"For that there bit o' string, sir?" said the man, drily. "What do you call that, then, and that?"

He pointed up to a bough about nine feet above him, where a cluster of orchids grew, for the most part of a sickly, pallid hue, save in one spot, where a shaft of sunlight came through the dense leafy canopy and dyed the strangely-formed petals of one bunch with orange, purple and gold, while the huge mossy tree trunk, half covered with parasitic creepers, whose stems knotted it with their huge cordage, showed traces of some one having climbed to reach the great horizontal bough.

"That looks like Mr Brazier, his mark, sir, eh?"

"Yes, yes," cried Rob eagerly.

"Come on then, sir: we're right."

"But did he make those marks coming or returning?"

"Can't say, sir," said Shaddy, gruffly; and then, to himself, "That ain't true, for he made 'em coming, or I'm a Dutchman."

He made another careful calculation of their position, and was about to start again, when he caught sight of something about Rob, or rather its absence, and exclaimed,—

"Why, where's them mushrooms?"

"Mushrooms, Shaddy! I—I don't know."

"But, Master Rob!"

"Oh, who's to think about eating at a time like this? Go on, pray; I shall not feel happy till I see Mr Brazier again."

Shaddy uttered a low grunt, gazed up at the shaft of light which shone upon the cluster of flowers, and then shifted the iguana again, and tramped on sturdily for about an hour, till there was a broad glare of light before them, and he suddenly stepped out from the greenish twilight into sunshine and day.

"Not so bad, Mr Rob, sir, without a compass!" he said, with a smile of triumph.

But Rob, as he stepped out, was already looking round for their fellow-prisoner in the forest, but looking in vain. There was no sign of human being in the solitude; and a chilly feeling of despair ran through the lad as he forgot his weariness and made a move for the hut, about a hundred yards away.

It was hard work to get through the low tangled growth out there in the sunlight; and before he was half-way there he stumbled and nearly fell, but gathered himself up with a faint cry of fear, for there was a low growl and a rush, as something bounded out, and he just caught a glimpse of the long lithe tawny body of a puma as it sprang into a fresh tangle of bush and reed, while Rob stood fast, and then turned to look at Shaddy.

The man's face was wrinkled up, and for the moment he evidently shared the boy's thoughts. Stepping close to him, he began to peer about amongst the thick growth from which the animal had sprung, while Rob felt sick as his imagination figured in the puma's lair the torn and bleeding body of his friend; and as Shaddy suddenly exclaimed, "Here's the place, sir!" he dared not look, but stood with averted eyes, till the man exclaimed:

"Had his nest here, sir, and he was asleep. Bah! I ought to have known. I never heard of a puma meddling with a man."

"Then Mr Brazier is not there?" said Rob faintly.

"Why, of course he ain't," replied the man sourly. "Come along, sir, and let's see if he's in the hut."

They rushed to their newly thatched-in shelter, and Rob seized the side and peered in, where all was black darkness to him, coming as he did from the brilliant sunshine.

"Mr Brazier," he cried huskily; but there was no reply. "Mr Brazier," he shouted, "why don't you answer?"

"'Cause he ain't there, my lad," said Shaddy gruffly. "Here, wait till I've doctored this iguana thing and hung it up. No, I'll cover it with grass here in the cool, and then we must make back tracks and find Mr Brazier before night."

"Oh, Shaddy!" cried Rob in an anguished tone, "then he has been horribly hurt—perhaps killed!"

The man made no reply, but hurriedly cut open and cleaned the lizard at some distance from the hut, then buried it beneath quite a pile of grass, dead leaves and twigs, before stepping back to his companion in misfortune.

"Oh, why did you stop to do that," cried Rob, "when Mr Brazier may be lying dying somewhere in the forest?"

"Because when we find him, we must have food to eat, lad, and something for him too. That thing may save all our lives. Don't you think I don't want to get to him, because I do. Now then, sir, we've got to go straight back the way we came, and find him."

"You'll go right back to where the spots—I mean, where we found the piece of string?" whispered Rob, whose feeling of weariness seemed to disappear at once.

"Yes, sir, straight back as an arrow, and it's of no use to hide facts; you must take your place as a man now, and act like one, having the hard with the soft, so I shall speak plainly."

"You need not, Shaddy," said Rob sadly. "You are afraid he has been badly hurt and carried off by Indians—perhaps killed."

"Nay, my lad; that's making worse of it than I thought. My ideas was bad enough, but not so bad as yours, and I think mine's right."

"Then what do you think?" said Rob, as after a sharp glance round they made for the spot where they had re-entered the clearing from the forest.

"Tell you what I *don't* think first, my lad," replied Shaddy: "I don't think it's Indians, because I haven't seen a sign of 'em, and if I had I fancy they'd be peaceable, stupid sort of folk. No: he's got into trouble with some beast or another."

"Killed?"

"Nay, nay; that's the very worst of all. There's hundreds of ways in which he might be hurt; and what I think is, that he has started to come back, and turned faint and laid down, and perhaps gone to sleep, so that we passed him; or perhaps he has lost his way."

"Lost his way?" cried Rob, with a shiver of dread.

"Yes, my lad. It's of no use to hide facts now."

"Then we shall never find him again, and he will wander about till he lies down and dies."

"Ah! now you're making the worst of it again, sir. He might find the way out again by himself, but we've got to help him. Maybe we shall be able to follow his tracks; you and me has got to try that: an Indian or a dog would do it easily. Well, you and me ought to have more stuff in us than Indians or dogs, and if we make up our minds to do it, why, we shall. So, come along, and let's see if we can't muster up plenty of British pluck, say a bit of a prayer like men, and with God's help we'll find him before we've done."

He held out his hand to Rob, who made a snatch at it and caught it between his, to cling to it tightly as he gazed in the rough, sun-blackened face before him, too much oppressed by emotions to utter a word.

But words were not needed in the solemn silence of that grand forest. Their prayer for help rose in the midst of Nature's grandest cathedral, with its arching roof of boughs, through which in one spot came a ray of brilliant light, that seemed to penetrate to Rob's heart and lighten him with hope; and then once more they swung round and plunged into the forest depths.

Chapter Twenty Five.

The Woodland Foes.

They took the same path without much difficulty, Shaddy tracing it carefully step by step; and for a time Rob eagerly joined in the tracing, every now and then pointing out a place where they had broken a twig or displaced a bough; but after a time the gloom of the forest began to oppress him, and a strange sensation of shrinking from penetrating farther forced him to make a call upon himself and think of the words uttered before they recommenced their search.

For there was always the feeling upon him that at any moment danger might be lurking thus in their way, and that the next moment they might be face to face with death.

"But that's all selfishness," he forced himself to think. "We have to find Mr Brazier."

This fresh loss to a certain extent obliterated the other trouble, and there were times when poor Giovanni was completely forgotten, though at others Rob found himself muttering,—

"Poor Joe! and now poor Mr Brazier! Whose turn will it be next? And those at home will never know of our fate."

But it generally happened that at these most depressing times something happened to make a fresh call upon his energies. Now it would be a fault in the tracking, their way seeming to be quite obliterated. Now Shaddy would point out marks certainly not made by them; for flowers of the dull colourless kind, which flourished so sickly here in these shades, had been broken-off, as if they had been examined, and then been thrown aside: convincing proofs that Brazier had been botanising there, collecting, and casting away objects unworthy of his care.

At one spot, unnoticed on their return, quite a bunch of curious growths lay at the foot of a huge buttressed tree, where there were indications of some one having lain down for a time as if to rest. Farther on, at the side of a tree, also unnoticed before, a great liana had been torn away from a tree trunk, so that it looked as if it had been done by one who climbed; and Shaddy said, with a satisfied smile,—

"He's been along here, Mr Rob, sure enough. Keep a good heart, sir; we're getting cleverer at tracking."

On they went in silence, forcing their way between the trees, with the forest appearing darker than ever, save here and there, where, so sure as a little light penetrated, with it came sound. Now it was the hum of insect life in the sunshine far above their heads; now it was the shrieking or twittering of birds busy feasting on fruit, and twice over an angry chattering told them that they had monkeys for their companions high overhead; but insect, bird, and the strangely agile creatures which leaped and swung among the boughs, were for the most part invisible, and they toiled on.

All at once Rob raised the bow he carried, and touched Shaddy sharply on the shoulder.

"Eh? what's the matter, my lad?" cried the man, turning quickly.

"Look! Don't you see?" whispered Rob. "There, by that patch of green light? Some one must have climbed up that green liana which hangs from the bough. It is swinging still. Do you think a monkey has just been up it, or is it some kind of wild cat?"

Shaddy uttered his low chuckling laugh as he stood still leaning upon his bamboo staves.

"If it had been a cat we should have seen a desperate fight, my lad," he replied. "If it was a monkey I'm sorry for him. He must have gone up outside and come down in. Why, can't you see what it is?"

"A great liana, one of those tough creeper things. Look how curiously it moves still! Some one's dragging at the end. No, it isn't. Oh, Shaddy, it's a great serpent hanging from the bough!"

"That's more like it, my lad. Look! You can see its head now."

In effect the long, hideous-looking creature raised its head from where it had been hidden by the growth below, twisted and undulated about for a few moments, and then lifted it more and more till it could reach the lower part of the bough from which it hung, and then, gradually contracting its body into curves and loops, gathered itself together till it hung in a mass from the branch.

"Not nice-looking things, Mr Rob, sir. Puts me in mind of those we saw down by the water, but this looks like a different kind to them."

"Will—will it attack us?" said Rob in a hoarse whisper.

"Nay, not it. More likely to hurry away and hide, unless it is very hungry or can't get out of the road. Then it might."

"But we can't pass under that."

"Well, no, Mr Rob, sir; it don't look like a sensible sort of thing to do, though it seems cowardly to sneak away from a big land-eel sort of a thing. What do you say? Shall we risk it and let go at my gentleman with our sticks if he takes any notice of us, or go round like cowards?"

"Go round like cowards," said Rob decisively.

"Right!" said Shaddy, who carefully took his bearings again, and, in order to have something at which he could gaze back so as to start again in the direction by which they had come, he broke a bough short off with a loud crack.

The effect was instantaneous on the serpent.

The moment before the whole body had hung in heavy loops from the bough, but at the first snap every part of it appeared to be in motion, and, as dimly seen, one fold glided slowly over another, with a curious rustling sound.

Rob made a start as if to dash off, but checked himself, and glanced at Shaddy, who was watching him; and the boy felt the colour flush into his cheeks, and a curious sense of annoyance came over him at the thought that his companion was looking upon him as a coward.

"It's all right, my lad," said the guide quietly; "you needn't mind me. You're a bit scared, and nat'rally. Who wouldn't be if he wasn't used to these things? I was horribly afraid of the one I first saw, and, for the matter of that, so I was about the next; but I've seen so many big snakes that, so long as I can keep at a little distance, they don't trouble me much. You see, they're not very dangerous to man, and always get out of his way if they have a chance. There's been a lot said about their 'tacking folk; and if you were to rouse that gentleman I daresay he'd seize you, and, if he got a hold for his tail, twist round and squeeze you to death; but you leave him alone and give him anything of a chance, he'll show you the tip of his tail much sooner than he'll show you his head. Look here!"

Shaddy looked round and picked up a short piece of a branch, which he was about to throw, but the boy caught his arm.

"Don't make it angry," he said in a whisper. "The horrible thing may come at us."

"I'm not going to make it angry," said Shaddy; "I'm going to make it afraid," and he hurled the piece of mouldering wood with so good an aim that it struck the branch near where the serpent was coiling itself more closely and flew to pieces.

The serpent threw itself down with a crashing sound amongst the dense undergrowth beneath, and disappeared from their sight.

"There," said Shaddy, "that's the way, you see. Gone?"

"No, no. Look out, Shaddy; it's coming this way," cried Rob excitedly, as a rustling was heard, and directly after there was a low hiss; and the movement among the twigs and dried leaves told that the creature was coming toward them.

Whether it was coming straight for where they stood neither of them stopped to see, but hurried off onward in the direction of the spot where they had seen the marks upon the leaf, and in a very short time the forest was silent again.

"Was not that a very narrow escape, Shaddy?" said Rob at last.

"No, my lad, I think not. Some people would say it was, and be ready to tell no end of cock-and-bull stories about what that serpent was going to do; but I've never known them play any games except once, and then the creature only acted according to its nature. It was in a sort of lake place, half pool, half river, and pretty close to the sea. It was near a gentleman's plantation, and the black folk used to go down every day to bathe. This they did pretty regularly till one day while they were romping about in the shallow water, which only came up to their middles, one of them shouted for help, saying that a 'gator had got hold of her, and then laughed. The others took no notice, because it was a 'sterical sort of laugh, as they call it, and thought she was playing tricks; but all at once they saw that she was struggling hard and being drawn backwards. That was enough. They all made a rush and caught hold of her arms just as she was being slowly drawn down lower, and when they dragged her nearer the shore, whatever it was that held her yielded a little, though it still hung on to the poor girl; while as they got her nearer a shriek rose, and every one nearly let go, for the head of a big snake was drawn right out of the water, but at the next snatch it loosed its hold and dropped back with a splash."

They were by this time approaching the spot where they had seen the marks, and Shaddy advanced more cautiously, scanning every leaf and twig before he stepped forward for signs of him they sought. Here and there he was able to point out marks such as Mr Brazier might have made—marks that had been passed over during their journey in the other direction. For there were places where he had evidently torn down leaves, mosses, and curious shade-loving growths, some of which he had carelessly tossed aside, and in one case the fragment thrown down was about half of the bulb of an orchid, whose home had been upon the mossy limb of a great tree overhead.

"He has been by here, sure enough, Mr Rob," said Shaddy in a subdued voice; "and, between ourselves, it was quite a bit of madness for him to come right out here alone. Now then, sir, keep a sharp look-out, and let's see if we can't find the spots straight off. They were pretty nigh, I think."

"Just there, I think," said Rob, looking excitedly round and pointing to a darker patch of the great forest where they were.

"Nay, it wasn't dark like that, my lad," replied Shaddy. "It was more hereabouts."

"Are you sure, Shaddy?"

"Pretty tidy, sir. No, I'm not. Seems to me that you are right, and yet it was this side of that great tree. I remember it now, the one with the great branch hanging right to the ground."

"I don't remember it, Shaddy," said Rob. "But I do, sir. It had a bunch of those greeny-white, sickly-looking plants growing underneath it, and we shall know it by them."

"Then it isn't the right one, Shaddy; we must try again."

"But it is the right one, my lad. It's bad enough work to find a tree in this great dark place. Don't say it isn't right when I've found it. Come now, look. Ain't I right?"

"Yes, Shaddy, right," said Rob as he looked up and saw the faded orchids hanging beneath the branch. "Then the place is close here somewhere."

"You're almost standing upon it, Mr Rob," said Shaddy. "You see, I have hit the spot," he continued, with a look of triumph. "There, I will not be proud of it, for it comes very easy to find your way like this after a bit of practice. There you are, you see; so now where to go next?"

"I don't know," cried Rob despondently. "Can't you see any fresh traces for us to follow?"

Shaddy set off, with his face as near to the ground as he could manage, and searched all round the spot where the stained leaf lay, but without effect; and after a few moments' examination he started off again, making a wider circle, but with no better result.

"Can't have been anything to do with a wild beast, my lad," he said in a low, awe-stricken voice, "or some signs must have been left. It's a puzzler. He was here—there's no doubt about that—and we've got to find him. I'll make a bigger cast round, and see what that will do."

"Can you find your way back here?" asked Rob anxiously.

"I must," replied Shaddy, with quiet confidence in his tones. "It won't do to lose you as well."

He started again, walking straight on for a couple of hundred yards through the trees and then striking off to his left to form a fresh circle right outside the first, and at the end of five minutes Rob, who stood by the great tree listening for every sound and wondering whether his companion would find his way back, and if he did not what he would do, heard a cry.

For the moment he thought it was for help, but it was repeated, and realising that it was an animal's, he started forward in the direction of the sound, though only to halt the moment after in alarm and look back. At the end of a few seconds he set it down to fancy and went on again, but only to stop once more, for there was a rustling sound behind him; and he awoke at once to the fact that the noise could only have been made by some wild beast stealing softly after him, stalking him, in fact, and preparing to make a spring and bring him down.

Rob felt the perspiration ooze out of every pore as he stood looking back in the direction of the sound, which ceased as soon as he halted. He would have given anything to have held a gun in his hands and been able to discharge it amongst the low growth where the animal was hidden, but he was as good as helpless with only the bow and an arrow or two; and he stood waiting till he started, for he heard Shaddy's cry again, and in a fit of desperation he shouted aloud in answer, and sprang forward to try and reach his side.

But as he made his way onward there again was the soft stealing along of his pursuer, whatever it was, for though he tried hard to pierce the low growth, the gloom was so deep that he never once obtained a glimpse of the animal.

Again Shaddy shouted, and he answered, the cry sounding not a hundred yards away; and in the hope that their voices might have the power of scaring the enemy, he shouted again, and was answered loudly and far nearer, making him give a rush forward in his desperation, and following it up with a gasp of agony, for there was a fierce roar through the forest on his left.

It seemed as if the animal, in dread of losing him by his forming a junction with his friend, had bounded on to get between them and crouch ready to spring upon him; but Rob could not hold back now, and pressed forward.

"Shaddy," he shouted—"Shaddy, there is some wild beast close here."

"Wait a bit, my lad," was shouted back; and the crushing and rustling of boughs told of Shaddy's coming, while Rob faced round now, staring wildly at a dark part among the trees where he thought he saw the undergrowth move but not daring to stir, from the feeling that if he did turn his back the beast would spring upon him and bring him down.

Thought after thought flashed like lightning through his brain, and in imagination he saw himself seized and bleeding, just as Mr Brazier must have been, for he felt sure now that this had been his fate.

It was a nightmare-like sensation which paralysed him, so that, though he heard Shaddy approaching and then calling to him, he could neither move nor answer, only stand crouching there by a huge tree, with the bow held before him and an arrow fitted ready to fly, fascinated by the danger in front.

He could not see it, but there was no doubt of its presence, and that it was hiding, crouched, ready to bound out, every movement suggesting that it was some huge cat-like creature, in all probability a jaguar, nearly as fierce and strong as a tiger. For at every rustle and crash through the wood made by Shaddy there was a low muttering growl and a sound as if the creature's legs were scratching and being gathered together for a spring.

Rob felt this, and stood motionless, thinking that his only chance of safety lay in gazing straight at the creature's hiding-place and believing that as long as he remained motionless the animal would not spring.

"Hi! where are you, my lad?" said Shaddy, from close at hand; but Rob's lips uttered no sound. He felt a slight exhilaration at the proximity of his companion, but he could not say, "Here!" and the next minute Shaddy spoke again, depressing the lad's spirits now, for the voice came from farther away. Again he shouted, "Hi! why don't you answer? Where are you, lad?" but Rob heard the earth being torn up by the fierce animal's claws, and now even heard its breathing, and his voice died away again as a choking sensation attacked his throat.

And there he crouched, hearing the help for which he had called come close to him, pass him, and go right away till Shaddy's anxious cries died out in the solemn distance of the forest, leaving him alone to face death in one of its most terrible forms.

He knew he could launch the arrow at the beast, and that at such close quarters he ought to, and probably would hit it, but a frail reed arrow was not likely to do more than spur the creature into fierce anger.

He could see it all in advance. A jaguar was only a huge cat, and he would be like a rat in its claws, quite as helpless; and he shuddered and felt faint for a few moments. But now that he was entirely alone, far from help, and self-dependent, a change came over him. He knew that he must fight for life; he felt as if he could defend himself; and, with his nerve returning, his lips parted to utter a shout.

But he did not cry, for he knew that Shaddy was too far off to hear him, and with a feeling of desperation now as he recalled that he had his keen knife in his pocket, he loosened his hold of his arrow and thrust in his hand to withdraw the weapon, seized the blade in his teeth, and dragged it open.

"He shall not kill me for nothing," he thought, and he stood on his guard, for his movements excited the animal to action, and with a roar and a rush it sprang right out from the undergrowth to within three yards of him, but, instead of crouching and springing again, it stood up before him, with its back slightly arched, lashing its sides gently with its long tail.

It was no spotted jaguar, with teeth bared, but, as dimly seen there in the semi-darkness of the forest, a noble-looking specimen of the puma family, and, to Rob's astonishment, it made no sign of menace, but remained in the spot to which it had sprung, watching him.

And here for quite a minute they stood face to face, till, with a faint cry of wonder, the lad exclaimed,—

"Why, it must be my puma! And it has followed us all along by the banks to here."

Then came thought after thought, suggesting that it must have been the footprints of this beast which they had seen over and over again by the side of their fire; that it was this animal which had crept to him when he was asleep; that it kept in hiding when he was with his companions, but that it had been tracking him till he was alone, and that after all he had nothing to fear.

But still he was afraid and uncertain, so that some time elapsed during which the puma stood writhing its tail, watching him before he could summon up courage enough to take a step forward.

He made that step at last, knowing that if he were mistaken the animal would at once draw back and make for a spring; but, instead of moving, the puma raised its tail erect, making the three or four inches at the end twine a little, and the next minute Rob was talking to it softly, with his hand upon its head, when the animal began to give forth a curious sound somewhat resembling a purr and pressed up against him.

"Poor old chap, then!" cried Rob; "and I was frightened of you, when all you wanted to do was to make friends. Why, you are a fine fellow, then."

His words were accompanied by caresses, and these were evidently approved of, the puma crouching down and finally lying on its side, while Rob knelt beside it and found that he might make free with it to any extent.

Then, suddenly recollecting how Shaddy was hunting for him and their object, he sprang to his feet, and placing his hands to his mouth, sent forth as loud a shout as he could give.

As he sprang up the puma also leaped to its feet, watching him in a startled way.

Rob shouted again, and as a reply came from not far distant a low growl arose from the animal by his side.

But he shouted again, and an answer came from much nearer, when with one bound the animal sprang out of sight amongst the trees, and though Rob called to it again and again in the intervals of answering Shaddy's cries, there was not a sound to suggest the creature's presence.

"It's afraid of Shaddy," Rob concluded, and feeling bound to continue his signals, he kept on till his companion joined him.

"Why, my lad," cried the latter, "I thought I'd lost you too," and as soon as Rob had explained the reason for his silence, "Enough to make you, lad. But that's right enough. He's took a fancy to you. Only hope he won't show fight at me, because if he does I shall have to hit hard for the sake of Shadrach Naylor; but if he's for giving the friendly hand, why so am I. But come along; we mustn't be belated here. I've found fresh signs of Mr Brazier while I was hunting you."

"You have?" cried Rob joyfully.

"Yes, my lad, not much; but I came upon a spot where he had been breaking down green-stuff."

"Since he—met with that accident?" said Rob hesitatingly.

"Ah, that's what I can't say, Mr Rob, sir. Let's get to it, and try and follow up his trail. No; we can't do it to-day. We must get back to the hut to-night, and all we can do is to take the spot I came to on the way. We shall only get there before dark as it is."

"Oh, but we can't leave him alone in the forest—perhaps wounded and unable to find his way out."

"But we must, my lad," said the guide firmly. "We can do him no more good by sleeping here than by sleeping there under cover."

"Who can think of sleeping, Shaddy, at a time like this?"

"Natur' says we must sleep, Mr Rob, and eat too, or we shall soon break down. Come along, my lad; there's always the hope that we may find him back at camp after all."

"But he must be wanting our help, Shaddy," said Rob sadly.

"Yes, my lad, and if he can, camp's the place where he'll go to look for it, isn't it?"

"Yes, of course."

"Then we ought to be there to-night in case he comes to it. So now then let's start at once. Sun goes down pretty soon, and I've got to take you by a round to where he broke down those flowers. Ready?"

"Yes," said Rob sadly; and they made a fresh start.

Chapter Twenty Six.

In Painful Quest.

At the end of a few minutes Shaddy turned his head and spoke over his shoulder.

"Hear anything of your puss, Mr Rob?"

"I have fancied I heard him twice."

"Then he's after us, safe—depend upon it. These sort of things go along on velvet, and can get under the trees and branches for hours without your knowing anything about their being so near. Let's be friends with him, my lad. We're lonely enough out here, and he'll get his own living, you may depend upon that."

Shaddy pressed on as rapidly as he could, for the evening was drawing nigh, and, as he said, it would be black night in there directly the sun went down; but it was a long way, and Rob was growing weary of seeing his companion keep on halting in doubt, before, with a look of triumph, he stopped short and pointed to a broken-down creeper, a kind of passion-flower, which had been dragged at till a mass of leafage and flower had been drawn down from high up in the tree it climbed, to lie in a heap.

"There you are, Mr Rob, sir."

"No, no, Shaddy; that might have been dragged down by a puma or jaguar," said Rob sadly.

"Then he must have carried a good sharp knife in his pocket, my lad," replied the old hunter. "Look at this."

He held up the end of the stem, for Rob to see that it had been divided by one clean chop with a big knife.

"Yes, of course. He must have been here," cried Rob joyfully. "Now then, we must find his trail and follow it on."

"We must make straight for camp, Mr Rob, sir," replied Shaddy, "hoping to find him there, for in less than an hour's time we shall have to feel our way."

"Oh, Shaddy!"

"Must, sir, and you know it. We must try all we know to get back, and I tell you it's as much as I can do to find the way there. I'm sure I can't follow Mr Brazier's trail."

Rob looked at him sternly.

"Fact, sir. You know I'm doing my best."

"Yes," said Rob, reproach sounding in his tones; but he could not help feeling that he was a little unjust, as he tramped steadily on behind his companion, who was very silent for some time, working hard to make his way as near as possible along the track by which they had come.

Rob was just thinking that from the tone of the gloom around him the sun must be very low, when Shaddy turned his head for a moment.

"Don't think you could find your way, do you, Mr Rob?"

"I'm sure I couldn't," was the reply.

"So am I, my lad."

"But you have it all right?"

"Sometimes, my lad; and sometimes I keep on losing it, and have to make a bit of a cast about to pick it up again. We're going right, my lad, so don't be down-hearted. Let's hope Mr Brazier is precious anxious and hungry, waiting for us to come to him."

"I hope so, Shaddy."

"But you don't think so, my lad."

Rob shook his head.

"Heard your cat, sir?"

"No."

"More have I. Scared of me, I suppose. Rec'lects first meeting."

They went on again in silence, with the gloom deepening; but the forest was a little more open, and all at once Shaddy stopped short, and holding one hand behind him signed to Rob to come close up.

"Look!" he whispered: "just over my shoulder, lad. I'd say try your bow and arrow, only we've got plenty of food in camp, and had better leave it for next time."

"What is it, Shaddy? I can't see. Yes, I can. Why it's a deer. Watching us too."

The graceful little creature was evidently startled at the sight of human beings, and stood gazing ready to spring away at the slightest motion on their part. The next instant there was a sudden movement just before them, as a shadow seemed to dart out from their right; and as the deer made a frantic bound it was struck down, for a puma had alighted upon its back, and the two animals lay before them motionless, the puma's teeth fast in the deer's neck, and the former animal so flattened down that it looked as if it were one with the unfortunate creature it had made its prey, and whose death appeared to have been almost instantaneous.

"Why, it must be my puma!" cried Rob.

"That's so, my lad, for sartain," replied Shaddy. "Now, if we could get part, say the hind-quarter of that deer, for our share, it would be worth having. What do you say?"

Rob said nothing, and Shaddy approached; but a low, ominous growling arose, and the great cat's tail writhed and twined about in the air.

"He'll be at me if I go any nearer," said Shaddy. "What do you say to trying, Mr Rob, sir?"

"I don't think I would," said the lad; and he stepped forward, with the result that the puma's tone changed to a peculiar whining, remonstrant growl, as it shifted itself off the dead deer, but kept its teeth buried in its neck, and began to back away, dragging the body toward the spot from which it had made its bound.

"Let it be, Mr Rob, sir. The thing's sure to be savage if you meddle with its food. We can do without it, and there's no time to spare. Come along."

There was a fierce growl as Shaddy went on, and Rob followed him; but on looking back he saw that the puma was following, dragging the little deer, and after a few steps it took a fresh hold, flung it over its back, followed them for a few minutes, and then disappeared.

They had enough to do to find their way now, for darkness was coming on fast, and before long Shaddy stopped short.

"It's of no use, my lad," he said. "I'm very sorry, but we've drove it too late. The more we try the farther we shall get in the wood."

"What do you mean to do, then?" said Rob, wearily.

"Light a fire, and get some boughs together for a bed."

"Oh, Shaddy, don't you think we might reach camp if we went on?" cried Rob, despairingly.

"Well, we'll try, Mr Rob, sir; but I'm afraid not. Now, if your friend there would be a good comrade and bring in our supper, we could roast it, and be all right here, but he won't, so we'll try to get along. We shall be no worse off farther on, only we may be cutting ourselves out more work when it's day. Shall we try?"

"Yes, try," said Rob; and he now took the lead, on the chance of finding the way. A quarter of an hour later, just as he was about to turn and give up, ready for lighting a fire to cook nothing, but only too glad of the chance of throwing himself down to rest, Shaddy uttered a cheery cry.

"Well done, Mr Rob, sir!" he said. "You're right. Camp's just ahead."

"What! How do you know?"

"By that big, flop-branched tree, with the great supports like stays. I remember it as well as can be. Off to the right, sir, and in a quarter of an hour we shall be in the clearing."

"Unless that's one of thousands of trees that grow like it," said Rob sadly, as he pressed on.

"Nay, sir, I could swear to that one, sir, dark as it is. Now, you look up in five minutes, and see if you can't make out stars."

Rob said nothing, but tramped on, forcing his way among trees which he only avoided now by extending his bow and striking to right and left.

Five minutes or so afterwards he cast up his eyes, but without expecting to see anything, when a flash of hope ran through him, and he shouted joyfully,—

"Stars, Shaddy, stars!" and as a grunt of satisfaction came from behind, he raised his voice to the highest pitch he could command, and roared out, "Mr Brazier I Mr Brazier! Ahoy!"

Shaddy took up the cry in stentorian tones—

"Ahoy! Ahoy! Ahoy!" and the shout was answered.

"There he is!" cried Rob, joyfully. "Hurrah!"

Shaddy was silent.

"Didn't you hear, Shaddy? Mr Brazier answered. You are right: he did get back, after all."

Still Shaddy remained silent, only increasing his pace in the darkness, lightened now by the stars which overarched them, so as to keep up with Rob's eager strides.

"Why don't you speak, man? Let's shout again: Mr Brazier! Ahoy!"

"Mr Brazier! Ahoy!" came back faintly.

"I don't like to damp you, Mr Rob, sir," said Shaddy, sadly, "but you don't see as we're out in the clearing again. That's only the echo from the trees across the river. He isn't here."

"No," said Rob, with a groan; "he isn't here."

Just then there was a rustling sound behind them, and a low growl, followed by a strange sound which Rob understood at once.

Chapter Twenty Seven.

The Four-Footed Friend.

The lad said nothing, so great was the change from hope to despondency; and he hardly noticed the sound close beside him, as Shaddy said gruffly—

“Well, if any one had told me that, I wouldn’t have believed it!”

“Is it any use to shout again, Shaddy?” said Rob, as he looked down at the indistinctly-seen shape of the dull tawny-coated puma, which had carried its captive after them to the clearing, and had now quietly lain down to its feast.

“No, Mr Rob, sir; if he’s here, it’s in the shelter-place we made, utterly done up with tramping. Let’s go and see.”

It was no easy task to get even there in the darkness, but they soon after stood at the end, and Rob convinced himself in a few moments that they were alone.

“Oh, Shaddy!” he cried piteously, “he hasn’t come back. What can we do to find him?”

“I’ll show you, sir,” said the man, quietly. “First thing is to make up the fire.”

“For him to see? Yes; that’s right.”

“Man couldn’t see the fire many yards away in the wood, Mr Rob, sir. I meant for us, so as to roast a bit of that deer, if the lion’ll let us have it.”

“I must do something to help Mr Brazier!” said Rob, angrily.

"That's helping him, my lad—having a good meal to make us strong. After that we'll have a good sleep to make us rested."

"Oh, no! no!" cried Rob, angrily.

"But I say yes, yes, yes, sir!" said Shaddy, firmly. "I know what you feel, my lad, and it's quite nat'ral; but just hark ye here a moment. Can we do anything to find him in that black darkness to-night?"

"No," said Rob, in despair; "it is, I know, impossible."

"Quite right, my lad. Then as soon as it's daylight oughtn't we to be ready to go and help him?"

"Of course, Shaddy."

"Then how can we do most good,—as half-starved, worn-out fellows, without an ounce of pluck between us, or well-fed, strong, and refreshed, ready to tramp any number of hours, and able to carry him if it came to the worst? Answer me that."

"Come and light the fire, Shaddy," said Rob, quietly.

"Ah!" ejaculated the old sailor, and he led the way to where the embers lay, warm still, and with plenty of dry wood about. Five minutes after the fire was blazing merrily and illumining the scene.

"Now," cried Shaddy, "if your Tom would play fair, and let us have the hind-quarters of that deer, we might have it instead of the lizard. He'll only eat the neck, I daresay. Shall we try him? I don't think he'd show fight at you, sir."

"Let's try," said Rob, quietly. "I don't think I'm afraid of him now."

"Not you, Mr Rob, sir," said Shaddy; and they went together to where they had left the puma feasting upon the deer, but, to the surprise of both, there lay the carcass partly eaten about the throat and breast, and the puma had gone.

"He can't have had enough yet," growled Shaddy, dropping upon his knees, knife in hand; and, seizing hold of the deer, he drove his blade in just across the loins, separating the vertebrae at the first thrust, but started back directly, as a low and fierce growl came from the edge of the forest, where they could see a pair of fiery eyes lit up by the blaze they had left behind.

"I know," cried Shaddy; "he was scared off by our fire, but he don't want to lose his supper. What shall we do, Mr Rob? Two more cuts, and I could draw the hind-quarters away. I'll try it."

The puma was silent, and Shaddy slowly approached his hand, thrust in his knife, and made one bold cut which swept through the deer's flank; but another growl arose, and there was a bound made by the puma—which, however, turned and crept slowly back to cover, where it stood watching them, with the fire again reflected in its eyes.

"He don't mean mischief, Mr Rob, sir," said Shaddy. "I'll have another try. I may get through it this time."

"No, no, don't try; it's dangerous."

"But you don't fancy that lizard thing, my lad; and I want you strong to-morrow. Now, look here: I'll get close again, and risk it; and if, just as I say 'Now,' you'd speak to the beast quiet like, as you would to a dog, it might take his attention, and so we'd get the hind part clear off."

"Yes," said Rob, quietly. "Shall I walk to it?"

"No, I wouldn't do that, but go a little way off sidewise, just keeping your distance, talking all the while, and he'd follow you with his eyes."

Rob nodded, and turned off, as Shaddy crept close once more and stretched out his hand.

"Now!" he said; and Rob began to call the beast, fervently hoping that it would not come, but to his horror it did; and he could just dimly make out its shape, looking misty and dim in the firelight, with its eyes glowing and its tail writhing, as it slowly approached, while Rob walked farther away from his companion still.

All at once the puma stopped short, swung itself round, and, to Rob's horror, crouched, bounded back toward where the carcass lay, leaping right to it, and burying its jaws in the deer's neck with a savage snarl.

"Run, Shaddy," shouted Rob.

"It's all right, my lad," came from a little distance: "I did. I've got our half, and he's got his. Speak to him gently, and leave him to his supper. We won't be very long before we have ours."

"Got it?" cried Rob, eagerly, as he hurried after his companion.

"Yes, my lad—all right;" and a few minutes later pieces of the tender, succulent flesh, quite free from marks of the puma's claws, were frizzling over the clear embers and emitting an appetising odour, which taught the boy how hungry he was; and as they were cooking, Shaddy talked of how tame he had known pumas to be, and of how they seemed to take to man.

"I wouldn't trust a tiger the length of his tail," he said, as they raked hot coals nearer to the roasting meat; "but I should never feel skeart of a lion, so long as I didn't get fighting him. Strikes me that after a fashion you might get that chap kind of tame. Shouldn't wonder if, when he's done, he comes and lies down here for a warm."

Rob thought of his former night's experience, when something came and nestled near him; and the next minute he was doing the same as the puma—partaking of the nourishing meat, every mouthful seeming to give him fresh strength.

It was a rough, but enjoyable meal, nature making certain demands which had to be satisfied; and for the moment, as he fell to after his long fast, Rob forgot his boyish companion and the second loss he had sustained. But as soon as he had finished, the depression came back, and he felt ashamed of himself for having enjoyed his food instead of dwelling upon some means of finding out where Mr Brazier had strayed.

His attention was taken off, though, directly by Shaddy, who said slowly:

"That's better. Nothing like a good honest meal for setting a man going again and making him ready to think and work. I say, look yonder at your tom-cat."

The fire had just fallen together, and was blazing up so as to spread a circle of light for some distance round; and upon looking in the direction of the puma Rob could see it lying down feasting away upon its share of the deer, apparently quite confident that it was in the neighbourhood of friends, and not likely to be saluted with a shot.

It struck Rob that the animal must be pretty well satisfied now with food, and in consequence less likely to be vicious, so he rose.

"Where are you going, Mr Rob, sir?" said Shaddy.

"Over to the puma."

"I wouldn't. Oh, I don't know. Best time to make friends—after dinner. I'd be careful, though, my lad."

"Yes; I'll take care," said Rob, who felt a strong desire to find another friend out there in the wilderness, now that his companions were dropping away; and thinking that the time might come when he would be quite alone, he walked slowly toward where the puma was crunching up some of the tender bones of the deer.

Rob kept a little to one side, so that his shadow should not fall upon the animal, which paid no heed to his approach for a few moments; then uttered a low fierce snarl and laid down its ears, making the boy stop short and feel ready to retreat, as the animal suddenly sprang up and stood lashing its tail and licking its lips. But it made no further menacing sign, and walked quietly toward him and then stood waiting.

Rob hesitated. Nature suggested flight, but Rob wanted to tame the beast, and mastering his dread he advanced, and in spite of a warning admonition from Shaddy, took another step or two and stopped by the puma, which stared at him intently for a few moments. It then set all doubts as to its feelings at rest by suddenly butting its head against Rob's leg, and as the lad bent down and patted it, threw itself on one side, and with the playful action of a kitten curved its paws, made dabs with them at the lad's foot, and ended by holding it and rubbing its head against his boot.

"Well done, beast tamer!" cried Shaddy; and the puma threw up its head directly and stared in the direction of the sound; but a touch from Rob's hand quieted it, and it stretched itself out and lay with its eyes half closed, apparently thoroughly enjoying the caresses of its human friend.

"Better get to the shelter, Mr Rob, sir," said Shaddy suddenly; and after a final pat and stroke, the boy turned away from the puma and walked back to the fire, finding that the animal had sprung up and followed him directly for about half the distance, but only to stop short and stand there, handsome and lithe, watching them and the fire, while its tail played about and the fine hairs glistened.

"He don't know what to make of me, Mr Rob, sir; and as we've no dog I may as well be friends too. Try and bring him up. He won't be a bad companion, 'specially if he hunts deer for us like he did to-night. He'll be good as a gun."

"He doesn't seem to like you, Shaddy."

"No, sir. I'm old and tough; you're young and tender," said the guide grimly. "He's cunning, as all cats are; and some day, when he's hungry and is enjoying you, he'll say to himself—'This is a deal better than that tough old sailor, who'd taste strong of tar and bilge.' Here, what are you going to do?"

"Try and fetch him here," said Rob, smiling as he went close up to the puma, which crouched again at his approach; and full of confidence now, the lad went down on one knee, patting and stroking the beast for a minute, talking softly the while.

The result was that as he rose the puma leaped up, bounded round him, and then followed close up to the fire, but met all Shaddy's advances with a low growl and a laying down of its ears flat upon its head.

"All right," said Shaddy, "I don't want to be friends if you don't, puss; only let's have a—what-you-may-call-it?"

"Truce," suggested Rob.

"That's it, sir. I won't show fight if he won't. Now then, sir, let's make up the fire; and then—bed."

Shaddy quickly piled up a quantity of wood on the embers, beating and smothering it down, so that they might have it as a protection against enemies and as a ready friend in the morning. Then, shouldering the portion left of the deer, he led the way to the rough hut, hung the meat high up in a tree and crept in, Rob following and wondering whether the puma would stop near them.

But the animal hung back as Rob followed his companion into the dark triangular-shaped space, where, after a short time devoted to meditation, he threw himself upon his bed of leaves to lie and think of his two lost companions.

At least, that was his intention, but the moment Rob rose in the darkness from his knees and lay down with a restful sigh, he dropped into a deep dreamless sleep, from which he half awoke once to stretch out his hand and feel it rest upon something furry and warm, which he dimly made out to be the curled-up body of the puma. Then he slept again till broad daylight showed in through the end of the bough, but half shut away by the figure of the guide, who said roughly:

"Now you two: time to get up."

At that moment Rob's hand rested upon a round, soft head, which began to move, and commenced a vibratory movement as a deep humming purr filled the place.

Chapter Twenty Eight.

The End of the Quest.

It was hard work to be dull and low-spirited in the midst of the beautiful scene which greeted Rob as he stepped out and followed Shaddy down to the fire. The clearing was one mass of glorious colour, the sky gorgeous with the sunrise tints, and the river flushed with orange, blue and gold. Birds sang, piped, and shrieked loudly, butterflies were beginning to flutter about, and a loud chattering from the nearest tree roused Rob to the fact that the puma had been following him, for it suddenly made three or four leaps in the direction of the sounds, and then crouched down to gaze at a party of monkeys, which were leaping about, scolding, shrieking and chattering angrily at the enemy watching their movements. Directly after, though, the puma returned to Rob's side, uttering a sound strongly suggestive of the domestic cat.

"Going to have a dip, Mr Rob, sir?" said Shaddy. And then—"I'd be very careful, sir; you know how full of biting varmin the river is. Look sharp; breakfast's ready, and as soon as we've done we'll go and find Mr Brazier."

"Try to," cried the boy sadly.

"Find him, Mr Rob, sir. Bah! who's going to say die on a lovely morning in a lovely place like this?"

Rob thought of his companion's words as he turned down to the edge of the water and bathed, with the puma sitting near watching him, apparently with wonder. Then, refreshed and invigorated, he hastened back to where there was the appetising odour of roasting meat, while the puma returned to the remains of its last night's feast.

Half an hour after, armed with rough spear, bow and arrows, and a big package of roasted meat, consisting of deer legs, and the best parts of the iguana which Shaddy had taken out and begun cooking while Rob still slept, they were threading their way amongst the trees once more, with the puma somewhere behind them, for they could hear it utter a curious cry from time to time, though they never once caught sight of it in the dense growth.

"Feel as if I was right, don't you, my lad?" said Shaddy, as they tramped on. "Couldn't have got through the trees like this without rest and food."

"You were quite right," replied Rob. "Where are you making for?"

"The place I showed you last night. I think we'll start from there."

It was a long time before they reached the spot, and examined it carefully, to find more traces of Mr Brazier having been there and stopping. So they shouted and whistled again and again, but there was no response, and trying to pick up the trail they started again—now utterly baffled and ready to return, now gathering fresh hope on suddenly coming upon a scrap of orchid or a bunch of woodland flowers, which had been carefully gathered and thrown down, apparently by some one wearied out. Then Rob uttered a cry of excitement, for he stumbled suddenly upon a spot which was comparatively open, so that the sunshine penetrated. It was no doubt the work of a hurricane, for great trees lay prostrate, decaying fast, and fresh flowery growths had sprung up. Birds and insects were plentiful, and the spot looked lovely after the gloom of the forest shades. Here was the crushed-down growth where he they sought had lain down to sleep, unless it was the resting-place of an Indian.

Rob suggested it and Shaddy replied angrily:

"Look here, youngster, if ever you want a nickname call yourself Wet Blanket. What a fellow you are for making the worst of everything! Some one lay down to rest here, didn't he?"

"Yes, I think so."

"And I'm sure. Now look at the places where the flowers have been snapped off. I know what you're saying to yourself: 'wild beast or Indian!' Now, I ask you, sir, as a young English gent who has been to school and can read and write, do wild beasts and Indians go about picking flowers or collecting anything that isn't good to eat?"

"Ah, Shaddy," said Rob sadly, "you beat me at arguing. I'm afraid to hope that we shall find him alive, but you're quite right, and I will try and believe."

"Bravo, Mr Rob, sir! Three cheers for that! Never fear, we'll find him alive yet; weak and done up, but keeping himself going. He has found bits of fruit and nuts, and when he couldn't find them there's something in the tops of tender grasses. Cheer up, sir! Now then, let's give a big shout here."

Shaddy set the example, and at the tremendous yell he sent forth there was a rush of wings from one of the trees a short distance away, where all had been perfectly still the moment before; and as a flock of birds hidden by the leaves dashed off, quite a little shower of fruit was dropped by them among the leaves.

"There, sir—that was food," cried Shaddy; "and a gentleman who knows all about such things, as Mr Brazier does, would find them and keep himself going. Now it's your turn. Shout, sir."

Rob uttered as loud a cry as he could, and then twice over imitated the Australian "cooee," following it up with a shrill piercing note from a little silver whistle; but the only response was the cry of an *ara,* one of the great scarlet and blue long-tailed macaws, whose harsh shriek came softened from the distance.

"Not right yet, Mr Rob, sir," said Shaddy, quietly; "but we're not going to despair, boy. I aren't a religious man your way, but after my fashion I trust in God and take the rough with the smooth. What is to be will be, so don't let's kick against it. We've got our duty to do, my lad, and that's to keep on trying. Now then, what do you say to a bit of a snack?"

"No, no—not yet, Shaddy; let's go on."

"Right, my lad."

They started again, and pressed on through the breathless heat of the woods, but without finding further sign of any one having passed that way; and at last Shaddy stopped short on the banks of a running stream, which impeded farther progress, and whose waters offered refreshing draughts to those who were getting in sore need.

"We're off his track, Mr Rob. He's not likely to have crossed a river like this; but welcome it is, for it shows us the way back just when I was getting a bit muddled."

"How does it?" said Rob, wonderingly.

"Because it must flow into the big river somewhere below our camp."

"Then you have seen no traces of him lately?"

"Nothing, my lad, since we left that open patch where the birds flew out of the trees."

"Then we must go back at once, Shaddy."

"Not until we've trimmed the lamps again, my lad. Sit down on that old trunk— No, don't; I daresay it's full of stinging ants and things, and perhaps there's a snake or two. We'll sit on this root and have a good feed, and then take up our track again."

Rob seated himself sadly down, while the guide unpacked his store of meat wrapped in green leaves; and the boy felt annoyed with himself for his want of forethought on seeing how carefully his companion put back and bound up some of the best, nodding, as he caught Rob's eyes fixed upon him.

"For Mr Brazier," he said. "He'll be glad enough of a bit o' meat when we find him."

They began eating directly, washing down the savoury roast with handfuls of clear water scooped up from the stream which bubbled and foamed by in its rocky bed.

"Well, now look at that!" cried Shaddy the next minute, as with one tremendous bound the puma alighted just before them, and stood looking at Rob and lashing its tail. "Why, he must have come after us all the time. Trust an animal for smelling meat."

Rob shared his portion with the great cat, which also crunched up the bones. Then once more they began their search, taking up their own trail backward, and with no little difficulty following it to the opening, from whence they kept on making casts, till night was once more approaching. They tramped back to the hut just in time to save their fire; but they had nothing to cook, the remains of the iguana being too far gone, and their meal consisted of nuts and water; though the puma feasted well.

The next morning they were off again soon after daylight, after breakfasting off fish secured by Shaddy as soon as it was light, while a couple more were roasted and taken with them.

This time they tried a fresh direction, trusting more to chance; and as they toiled on Shaddy grew more and more serious while forcing his way through the trees, and his manner was softer and gentler to his companion, who rarely spoke now save to the puma, which grew hourly more confident, and kept close at Rob's heels, giving his leg a rub whenever he stopped short to glance about him through the solemn shadows of the forest.

For this was the third day of their search, and it was impossible to help feeling that it was the very last upon which they could cling to hope.

It passed as the others had done—in one weary tramp and struggle, but without a single sign of the lost one to give them encouragement to proceed; and at last, when they were bound to return if they intended to sleep again in camp, Shaddy said suddenly:

"God help him, my lad: we've done all we can. Let's get back now. I may think out something fresh by to-morrow morning. I can't do anything to-night, for my head's like my legs—dead beat out."

Rob answered with a sigh, for his heart was very heavy now; and as his companion stood calculating for a few minutes which way they should go, he waited, and then followed behind him without a word.

They were a little earlier this time, but the sun had gone down before they got out of the forest at the extreme corner on the right of their hut; and as they trudged back the puma made two dashes at prey unseen by the travellers, but without success, returning after each cautious crawl and final bound to walk quietly along behind Rob, who, in a dull, heavy, unthinking way, reached back to touch the beast, which responded with a friendly pressure and rub of its head against the extended hand.

And as they crept slowly on, with the trees crowding round them as if to hinder their progress, and the darkness of the umbrageous foliage seeming to press down upon their heads, their journey was made with greater difficulty than ever; for the spirit or energy had gone out of Shaddy, who tramped on as if he were asleep.

It struck Rob once that this was the case, and he increased his own rate so as to try and get ahead of his companion, but as soon as he drew close up his comrade stopped.

"Like to go first, my lad?"

"No, no," said Rob hurriedly. "Are you sure of the road?"

"No, my lad, because there isn't one. I'm only pretty sure that we are in the right direction."

It proved that he was correct when in due time they stood out in the clearing, with the darkness falling fast; and then Shaddy said suddenly, and as if with an effort:

"Come, Mr Rob, sir, we mustn't give up. Let's have some food, or we shall be done. No deer meat to-night, no iguana. Get the fire going while I go and try for a fish; there'll just be time."

Rob tramped heavily to the fire, and the guide went to the tree where he had hung the line, baited it from the remains of the food, and strode down to his favourite spot for fishing; while Rob busied himself raking the fire together with a half-burned branch, and then, as it began to smoke, piled on it the partly-burned brands, and upon them the pieces industriously heaped together.

The blaze began to creep up and lick the twigs and branches as the blue smoke rose. Then the fire increased to a ruddy glow; and feeling chilly after the heat to which he had been exposed, Rob sat listlessly down gazing at the increasing flames, which lit up his sun-browned face as he thought and thought of his boyish comrade, then of Mr Brazier, and at last of himself.

They were sad thoughts, for he felt that he should never see home again, that he would be the next to be struck down by some savage beast, bitten by a poisonous snake, or lost in the forest, where he would be too weak to find his way back. And as he thought he wondered what Shaddy would do when he was gone—whether he would be picked up by some passing boat, or live on in a kind of Robinson Crusoe life to a good old age.

Rob started involuntarily as he reached this point, for something touched him; and turning sharply, he found that the puma was rubbing its head against his shoulder, the beautiful creature uttering its peculiar purring sound as Rob threw an arm round its neck and began to caress it, ready as he was out there to cling to anything in his weariness and desolation.

He was thus occupied when the puma started away, for there was a step behind him.

"Tired, my lad? Only got one, but he's a fine fellow," said Shaddy, who rapidly chopped off the head and a good-sized piece of the tail of a fine dorado.

"Not so very; only low-spirited."

"Not you, my lad: hungry's the word. That's what's the matter with me. Here, I say, squire, if you're anything of a cat you'll like fish," he continued, as he threw the head, tail, and other portions of the fish toward the puma, which hesitated for a few moments and then secured and bore them off.

Meanwhile, to help his companion more than from any desire for food, Rob had risen and cut some big palm leaves, laid them down, and then raked a hole in the heap of embers ready for the fish.

"That's better," said Shaddy, as he lifted the great parcel he had made of the fish; and depositing his load in the embers, he took the rough branch they used for a rake and poker in one, and covered the packet deeply.

"There, Mr Rob, sir; that's the best thing for our low spirits. We shall be better after that physic."

"Hush!" cried Rob excitedly.

"Eh! What? Did you hear something?"

"Yes: a faint cry."

"No!"

"But I did. And look at the puma: he heard it too. Didn't you see it start and leave the fish?"

"Yes, but I thought I startled it. He's very suspicious of me, and I don't suppose we shall ever be good friends."

"No, it was not that," whispered Rob, whose voice trembled as if he were alarmed.

"Then it was some beast in the forest. There they are, any number of them. Frog perhaps, or an owl: they make very queer sounds."

Rob shook his head.

"I say, don't look so scared, my lad, just as if you were going to be ill. I tell you what it was: one of those howling spider monkeys at a distance."

"There again!" cried Rob, starting up,—an example followed by the guide, who was impressed by the peculiar faint cry; and as Rob seized his companion's arm, the latter said, with a slight suggestion of nervousness in his tone:

"Now, what beast could that be? But there, one never gets used to all the cries in the forest. Here, what's the matter? Where are you going, my lad?"

"To see—to see," gasped Rob.

"Not alone, Mr Rob, sir. I don't think it is, but it may be some dangerous creature, and I don't want you to come to trouble. Got enough without. Hah! there it goes again."

For there was the same peculiar smothered cry, apparently from the edge of the forest, close to where they had raised their hut.

"Come along quickly," whispered Rob, in a faint, panting voice.

"Yes, but steady, my lad. Let's try and see, our way. We don't want to be taken by surprise. Get ready an arrow, and I may as well have my knife."

"THE PAIR SPRANG FORWARD TOGETHER."

"No: come on; don't you know what it was? It was close here somewhere. Can't you tell?"

"No, my lad, nor you neither. I've been a little longer in the woods than you."

"How can you be so dull?" cried Rob. "Now, quick: it must have been somewhere here. I heard 'Help' as plainly as could be."

"What?"

Just then the cry arose again, not fifty yards away; and unmistakably that word was uttered in a faint, piteous tone:

"Help!"—and again, "Help!"

The pair sprang forward together, crashing recklessly among the branches in the direction of the sound; but as they reached the place from whence it seemed to have come all was still, and there was no response to their cries.

"All a mistake, my lad," said Shaddy. "We're done up, and fancied it."

"Fancied? No, it was Mr Brazier," cried Rob excitedly. "I'm sure of it; and— Yes, yes, quick; this way. Here he lies!"

Chapter Twenty Nine.

Friend and Patient.

They had sought in vain for the lost man; and when in utter despair they had been on the point of giving up the search, he had struggled back to them, his last steps guided by the fire when he had felt that he must lie down utterly exhausted, to die.

"Mr Brazier! At last!" cried Rob; and he went down upon his knee and grasped his leader's hand, but there was no response, and the fingers he held were cold as ice.

"Here, lend a hand, Mr Rob, sir," cried Shaddy roughly, "and help me to get him on my back."

"Let me help carry him."

"No, sir; my way's easiest—quickest, and will hurt him least. He's half dead of starvation, and cold as cold. Quick, sir! let's get him down by the fire. It will be too dark in the hovel to do anything."

Rob helped to raise the wanderer, Shaddy swung him on his back lightly and easily, and stepping quickly toward the fire, soon had the poor fellow lying with his feet exposed to the blaze, while water was given to him a little at a time, and soon after a few morsels of the tender fish, which he swallowed with difficulty.

They had no rest that night, but, with the strange cries and noises of the forest around them, mingled with the splashings and danger-threatening sounds of the river, they tended and cared for the insensible man, giving him food and water from time to time, but in quantities suggestive of homoeopathic treatment. Still they felt no fatigue for the great joy in both their hearts, for neither of them had the faintest hope of ever seeing their leader again.

Once or twice during the night Mr Brazier had seemed so cold and rigid that Rob had glanced wildly at the guide, who replied by feeling the insensible man's feet.

"Only sleep, my lad!" he said softly. "I daresay he will not come to for a couple of days. A man can't pass through the horror of being lost without going off his head more or less."

"Do you think he'll be delirious, then?"

"Off his head, my lad? Yes. It will be almost like a fever, I should say, and we shall have to nurse him a long time till he comes round."

The guide was quite right. The strong man was utterly brought down by the terrible struggle of the past three days, and as they looked at his hollow eyes and sunken cheeks it was plain to see what he had suffered bodily from hunger, while his wanderings told of how great the shock must have been to his brain.

The mystery of the blood was explained simply enough by his roughly bandaged left arm, on which as they examined it, while he lay perfectly weak and insensible, they found a severe wound cleanly cut by a knife.

"He must have been attacked, then," cried Rob as he looked at the wound in horror, while in a quiet, methodical way Shaddy proceeded to sew it together by the simple process of thrusting a couple of pins through the skin and then winding a thread of silk round them in turn from head to point, after which he firmly bandaged the wound before making a reply to Rob's words.

"Yes, my lad," he said; "right arm attacked his left. He must have been making a chop at some of the plants on a branch, and the tool slipped. You take out his knife and open it, and see if it ain't marked."

Shaddy was quite right, for there on the handle were some dried-up traces of how the wound must have bled.

It was a week before the patient began to show tokens of amendment, during which time Rob and Shaddy had been hard pressed for ways to supply his wants. There were endless things necessary for the invalid which they could not supply, but, from old forest lore and knowledge picked up during his adventurous life, the guide was able to find the leaves of a shrub, which leaves he beat into a pulp between two pebbles, put the bruised stems into the cup of a water flask, added water, and gave it to the patient to drink.

"It is of no use to ask me what it is, Mr Rob, sir," said the guide; "all I know is that the Indians use it, and that there isn't anything better to keep down fever and get up strength."

"Then it must be quinine," said Rob.

"No, my lad; it isn't that, but it's very good. These wild sort of people seem to have picked up the knack of doctoring themselves and of finding out poisons to put on their arrows somehow or another, and there's no nonsense about them."

The prisoners in the vast forest—for they were as much prisoners as if shut up in some huge building—had to scheme hard to obtain their supplies so as to make them suitable to their patient. Fish they caught, as a rule, abundantly enough; birds they trapped and shot with arrows; and fruit was to be had after much searching; but their great want was some kind of vessel in which to cook, till after several failures Rob built up a very rough pot of clay from the river bed by making long thin rolls and laying one upon the other and rubbing them together. This pot he built up on a piece of thin shaley stone, dried it in the sun, and ended by baking it in the embers—covering it over with the hot ashes, and leaving it all one night.

Shaddy watched him with a grim smile, and kept on giving him words of encouragement, as he worked, tending Mr Brazier the while, brushing the flies away and arranging green boughs over him to keep him in the shade, declaring that he would be better out there in the open than in the forest.

"Well done, my lad!" said the old sailor as Rob held up the finished pot before placing it in the fire; "'tis a rough 'un, but I daresay there has been worse ones made. What I'm scared about is the firing. Strikes me it will crack all to shivers."

To Rob's great delight, the pot came out of the wood ashes perfectly sound, and their next experiment was the careful stewing down of an iguana and the production of a quantity of broth, which Shaddy pronounced to be finer than any chicken soup ever made; Rob, after trying hard to conquer his repugnance to food prepared from such a hideous-looking creature, said it was not bad; and their patient drank with avidity.

"There," said Shaddy, "we shall go on swimmingly in the kitchen now; and as we can have hot water I don't see why we shouldn't have some tea."

"You'd better go to the grocer's, then, for a pound," said Rob, with a laugh.

"Oh no, I shan't," said Shaddy; "here's plenty of leaves to dry in the sun such as people out here use, and you'll say it ain't such bad tea, neither; but strikes me, Mr Rob, that the sooner you make another pot the better."

Rob set to at once, and failed in the baking, but succeeded admirably with his next attempt, the new pot being better baked than the old, and that night he partook of some of Shad's infusion of leaves, which was confessed to be only wanting in sugar and cream to be very palatable.

That day they found a deer lying among the bushes, with the neck and breast eaten, evidently the puma's work, and, after what Shaddy called a fair division, the legs and loins were carried off to roast and stew, giving the party, with the fruit and fish, a delightful change.

The next day was one to be marked with a red letter, for towards evening Mr Brazier's eyes had in them the look of returned consciousness.

Rob saw it first as he knelt down beside his friend, who smiled at him faintly, and spoke in quite a whisper.

From that hour he began to amend fast, and a week after he related how, in his ardour to secure new plants, he had lost his bearings, and gone on wandering here and there in the most helpless way, sustaining life on such berries and other fruits as he could find, till the horror of his situation was more than his brain could bear. Face to face with the fact that he might go on wandering there till forced by weakness to lie down and die, he said the horror mastered him all at once, and the rest was like some terrible dream of going on and on, with intervals that were full of delight, and in which he seemed to be amongst glorious flowers, which he was always collecting, till the heaps crushed him down, and all was horror, agony, and wild imagination. Then he awoke lying beneath the bower of leaves, shaded from the sunshine, listening to the birds, the rushing sound of the river, and, best of all, the voices of his two companions.

Chapter Thirty.

An Unexpected Enemy.

Mr Brazier's recovery took a month from the day of his regaining the balance of his reason, and even then he was weak; but he was about again, and, though easily fatigued, took his part in the many little duties they had to fulfil to sustain life in their forest prison. All thought of escape by their own efforts had been given up, and they had all taken the good course, roughly put by Shaddy as "making the best of things."

In fact, the horror and shock of their position had grown fainter, the loss of poor Giovanni a softened memory, and the cowardly desertion of the Indians with the boat a matter over which it was useless to murmur. For the human mind is very plastic, and, if fully employed, soon finds satisfaction in its tasks.

It was so here. Every day brought its work, for the most part in glorious sunshine, and scarcely a night arrived without one of the three having something to announce in the way of discovery or invention for the amelioration of their lot.

"There is always the possibility of our being sought out and escaping," Mr Brazier said; "and in that hope I shall go on collecting, for the plants here are wonderful; and if I can get specimens home to England some day there will be nothing to regret."

In this spirit he went on as he grew stronger; and as for some distance inland in the triangle of miles, two of whose sides were the greater river and its tributary, they had formed so many faint trails in their hunting and fruit-seeking expeditions, the chances of being "bushed," as the Australians call it, grew fewer, plenty of collecting expeditions were made, at first in company with Shaddy and Rob, afterwards alone.

One evening a tremendous storm of wind and rain, with the accompaniments of thunder and lightning of the most awe-inspiring nature, gave them a lesson in the weakness of their shelter-place, for the water swept through in a deluge, and after a terrible night they gazed in dismay at the river, which was running swiftly nearly up to the place where they kept their fire going. That the flood was increasing they had not the slightest doubt, and it promised before long to be right over where they stood, fortunately now in the brilliant sunshine, which rapidly dried their clothes and gave them hope as well.

"We shall have to go inland and seek higher ground," Mr Brazier said at last.

"And where are you going to find it, sir?" said Shaddy rather gruffly. "There's high land away back on the far side of the river, but we can't get there, and all out as far as I've been on this is one dead level. Look yonder; there's a lesson for us what to do if it gets much worse," he continued, pointing toward a great tree at the edge of the forest.

"Yes," said Rob as he watched a little flock of green-and-scarlet parrots circling round and perching in the upper branches, "but we have no wings, Shaddy."

"No, my lad, and never will have; but I didn't mean that. Look a bit lower."

"Oh, you mean in that next tree. Ugh! how horrible!" cried Rob, with a shudder. "Has that been driven here by the water?"

"I don't know what you're talking about, sir. I mean that tree I pointed to. Look there in the fork."

"Yes; I can see it, Rob," said Mr Brazier. "It's comfortably asleep. We must do as it does. Not the first time an animal has given men a lesson."

Rob stared from one to the other as if wondering why they did not see with his eyes.

"Can't you see it, Rob—your puma?"

"Eh? Oh yes, I see him now, but I meant in the other tree. Look! the great brute is all in motion. Why, it's a perfect monster!"

"Phew!" whistled Shad; "I didn't see it. Look, Mr Brazier, sir. That is something like a snake."

He pointed now to where a huge serpent was worming its way about the boughs of one of the trees in a slow, sluggish way, as if trying to find a spot where it could curl up and be at rest till the water, which had driven it from its customary haunts, had subsided.

"What shall we do, Shaddy?" whispered Rob. "Why, that must be nearly sixty feet long."

"It's nearer two foot long, Mr Rob, sir. My word! how people's eyes do magnify when they're a bit scared."

"But it is a monstrously huge serpent," said Brazier, shading his eyes, as he watched the reptile.

"Yes, sir, and as nigh as one can judge, going round his loops and rings, a good five-and-twenty foot, and as big round as my thigh."

"We can't stay here, then!" cried Rob excitedly.

"Don't see why not, sir. He hasn't come after us, only to take care of himself; and I'm beginning to think it's a bad sign."

"That it does mean to attack us?" said Brazier.

"Not it, sir. I mean a bad sign about the flood, for somehow, stupid as animals seem, they have a sort of idea of when danger's coming, and try to get out of its way. I should say that before long the waters will be all up over where we are, and that it's our duty to get up a bit, too, and take enough food to last till the flood's gone down."

"And how long will that be?" Rob asked.

"Ah! that's what I can't say, sir. Let's get together all we can, and I'm sorry to say it ain't very much, for we punished the provisions terribly last night."

"Yes, we are low," said Brazier thoughtfully.

"There's some nuts on that tree where the lion is, so we'll take to that," said the old sailor thoughtfully. "He'll have to turn out and take to another, or behave himself. Now what's to be done beside? We can't get any fire if the flood rises much, and for certain we can't catch any fish with the river like this. What do you say to trying to shoot the big boa with your bow and arrows?"

"What?" cried Rob, with a look of disgust.

"Oh! he's not bad eating, my lad. The Indians feast on 'em sometimes, cutting them up into good stout lumps, and it isn't so much unlike eel."

"What, have you tasted it?"

"Oh yes, sir; there's precious few things used for food when men are hungry that I haven't had a taste of in my time."

Just then Mr Brazier pointed to the place where they kept their fire, and over which the water was now lapping and bearing off the soft grey ashes, which began to eddy and swim round the little whirlpools formed by the swift current, before the light deposit from the fire was swept right away.

By this time, as Rob kept his eyes upon it, the great serpent had gradually settled itself down upon one of the far-spreading horizontal boughs of the huge monarch, which, growing upon the edge of the forest, found ample space for its spreading branches, instead of being kept back on all sides by fellow-trees, and so directing all its efforts in the way of growth upward toward the sun.

Brazier noticed Rob's looks, and laid his hand upon the lad's shoulder.

"I don't think we need fear any attack from that, Rob," he said, "for the water, if it goes on rising like this, will soon be between us, and I don't suppose the serpent will leave one tree to get up into another."

"Not it, sir," interposed Shaddy; "and, excuse me, let's be sharp, for the water's coming down from miles away on the high ground, and it will be over here before long. Look at that!"

They were already looking at a great wave sweeping down the furious river, which was covered with boughs and trees, the latter rolling over and over in the swift current, now showing their rugged earth and stone-filled roots, now their boughs, from which the foliage and twigs were rapidly being stripped.

"Why, it's right over our kitchen now."

"And will carry away my pots!" cried Rob, running away to save the treasures which had caused him so much trouble to make.

"Look sharp, sir!" cried Shaddy; "here's quite a torrent coming. We'll make for the tree at once, or we shall be lost once more."

"All right!" cried Rob, as he ran to the far edge of their fireplace, where the boughs and pieces of wood collected for fuel were beginning to sail away, and he had just time to seize one great rough pot as it began to float, when a wave curled over toward the other and covered the lad's feet.

But he snatched up the vessel and hurried toward the tree in which the puma was curled up, Brazier and Shaddy following, with the little food they had left, and none too soon. They handed Rob's two pieces of earthenware up to him, and then joined him in the fork of the tree.

The water was by now lapping softly about its foot, but from time to time a wave came sweeping down the river as if sudden influxes of water kept on rushing in higher up to increase the flood, and in consequence ring after ring or curve of water swept over the land, gliding now up amongst the trees of the forest, penetrating farther and farther each time, and threatening that the whole of the country through which the river passed would be flooded for miles.

The puma snarled and looked fierce as the two men followed Rob, but it contented itself with a fresh position, higher up in a secondary fork of the tree, where it crouched, glaring down at those below, but hardly noticed, for, after recovering their belongings, the attention of those on the fork was divided between the rising of the water and the uneasy movements of the great occupant of the next tree.

"I suppose we may confess to being afraid of a reptile like that," said Brazier, measuring the distance between the trees with his eyes and looking up to see if the branches of either approached near enough to enable the reptile to make its way across.

"No fear, sir!" said Shaddy, with a smile, as he read his companion's thoughts. "We've only the water to trouble us now."

"But it will never get up so high as this?" cried Rob in alarm, as he thought of the trees which he had seen swept down the river, forest chiefs, some of them, which had been washed out by floods.

"I hope not, sir; but we have to be ready for everything in this country, as you've found out already."

This set Rob thinking as he watched the waves coming down the river, each sweeping before it a mass of verdure, pieces at times taking the form of floating islands, with the low growth upon them keeping its position just as the patches had broken away from undermined banks.

"Don't you wonder where it all goes, Mr Rob?" said Shaddy suddenly.

"Yes; does it get swept out to sea?"

"Not it, sir. Gets dammed up together in bends and corners of the river, and makes it cut itself a fresh bed to right or left. This country gets flooded sometimes for hundreds upon hundreds of miles, so that you can row about among the trees just where you like. Ah! it would be a fine time for Mr Brazier when the flood's at its height, for we could row about just where we liked—if we had a boat," he added after a pause.

Just then the puma gave a savage growl.

"Here, what's the matter with you?" cried the guide sharply.

The puma snarled again and showed its teeth, but they saw that it was staring away from the tree.

"He can see the serpent," said Rob eagerly; and they now saw the reason, for, evidently aware of their proximity, and from a desire to escape, the great reptile was all in motion, its fore-part beginning slowly to descend the tree, the head and neck clinging wonderfully to the inequalities of the bark for a part of the way, and then the creature fitted itself in the deep groove between two of the buttress-like portions, which ran down right away from the main trunk.

They all watched the reptile with curiosity, for its actions were singular, and it was exciting to see the way in which the whole length of the animal was in action as the head, neck, and part of the body glided down in a deliberate way, with the tongue darting out and flickering about the hard, metallic-looking mouth, while the eyes glistened in the sunshine, which threw up the rich colours and pattern of the scaly coat.

"He don't like it, and is going to swim off," said Shaddy suddenly, as the head of the serpent was now approaching the surface of the water. "I never saw one of this kind take to the water before. Say, Mr Rob!"

Rob turned to him.

"You had better get your cat down here, in case he means coming across to this tree.—No: there won't be any need. I don't think he could swim against this current: it might sweep him away."

Rob drew a breath full of relief as he glanced at Brazier, whose face, pallid with his late illness, certainly looked paler, and his eyes were contracted by his feeling of horror. But their companion's last words relieved him from his dread, and he sat there upon the huge branch that was his resting-place watching the actions of the serpent, which still glided on, and moved with its head close to the groove in the trunk till it was close to the water slowly rising to meet it, and a length of quite twelve feet reached down from the fork, like the stem of some mighty climbing fig which held the tree in its embrace.

"Yes, he's going to swim for it," said Shaddy eagerly. "Fancy meeting a thing like that on the river! I thought it was only the anacondas which took to the water, and— Well, look at that!"

The man's exclamation was caused by the action of the serpent, for just as its head reached the surface of the flood one of the waves came rushing inland from the river, leaped up the tree three or four feet, deluging the head and neck of the serpent and sinking down again almost as quickly as it had risen. The reptile contracted itself as rapidly, drawing back, and, evidently satisfied with the result of its efforts to escape, began to climb again, holding on by its ring-like scales as it crept up and up till its head was back in the great fork of the tree, and the anterior part of the body hung down in a huge loop, which was gradually lessened as the great creature resumed its place.

There was nothing to fear from the serpent, to the great relief of those who watched; but it had begun to be questionable how long their present position would be safe, for the water was rising now with wonderful rapidity, great waves tearing down the river from time to time, bearing enormous masses of tangled tree and bush and sending out masses of foam, sweeping over the clearing with an angry rush, which changed into a fierce hiss as of thousands of serpents when the wave reached the edge of the forest and ran an among the trees with a curious wail till it died away in the distance.

When the waves struck the tree amongst whose branches the party were ensconced, the puma growled at the heavy vibrations, and began to tear at the bark with its claws. As one, however, worse than usual struck the trunk, it gathered itself together, uttered a harsh growl, and was about to spring off and swim, as if it feared being crushed down by the branches of the washed-out tree; but a few words from Rob pacified it, and it settled down once more, half hanging, as it were, across the fork, where it was swinging its tail to and fro and gazing down at the human companion it had chosen.

Chapter Thirty One.

A Forest Feud.

The little party sat there waiting patiently for the next event, their eyes being mostly directed across the waste of water toward the well-marked course of the stream, with its rush, swirl and eddy; and before long there was another heaving up, as if a liquid bank descended the river, spread across the opening, and directly after struck the tree with a blow which made it quiver from root to summit.

"Will it hold fast, Naylor?" said Brazier, rather excitedly.

"Hope so, sir. I think it's safe, but it's growing in such soft soil, all river mud, sand, and rotten wood, that the roots are loose, and it feels as if it would give way at last. I daresay this was a bend of the river once."

"But if it does give way, what are we to do?" cried Rob excitedly.

"Swim for the next tree, sir."

"But that has a great snake in it."

"Can't help that, Mr Rob. Rather have a snake for a mate than be drowned. He's too much frightened to meddle with us. Look out, every one, and try to keep clear of the boughs, so as not to be beaten under."

This was consequent upon the rushing up in succession of three great waves, which struck the tree at intervals of a few seconds, the last sending the water splashing up to where they sat, and at the same time deluging the serpent in the next tree, making it begin to climb higher, and exciting the puma so that Rob could hardly keep it from leaping off.

"The roots must be undermined," cried Brazier. "Look—look!"

He pointed at the effect of the waves on the forest, for from where they sat the whole side was a ridge of foam, while the tree-tops were waving to and fro and undulating like a verdant sea as the water rushed on among their trunks.

"Can't get much worse than this, I think," said Shaddy, when the water calmed down again to its steady swift flow; "only it's spoiling our estate, which will be a bed of mud when the flood goes down."

"But will it go down?" asked Rob excitedly.

"Some time, certain," replied Shaddy. "The rivers have a way in this country of wetting it all over, and I daresay it does good. At all events, it makes the trees grow."

"Yes, but will it sweep them away?" said Rob, looking round nervously.

"It does some, Mr Rob, sir, as you've seen to-day, but I think we're all right here."

Rob glanced at Brazier, whose face was very stern and pale; and, consequent upon his weakness, he looked ghastly as another wave came down the river, and swept over the deeply inundated clearing, washing right up to the fork of the tree, and hissing onward through the closely-packed forest.

Another followed, and then another, each apparently caused by the bursting of some dam of trees and *débris* of the shores; but they were less than those which had preceded them, and an hour later the water was perfectly calm and motionless, save in the course of the river, where it rushed onward at a rapid rate.

"We've passed the worst," said Shaddy; and after glancing at him quickly, to see if he meant it or was only speaking to give him encouragement, Rob sat looking round at the watery waste, for as far as his eyes could penetrate there was no sight of dry land. Everywhere the trees stood deep in water, that was still as the surface of a lake through which a swift river ran, with its course tracked by rapid and eddy, and dotted still with the vegetation torn out from the banks.

As the boy turned to the great tree beside him he could not keep back a shudder, for the monstrous serpent was in restless motion, seeking for some means of escape; and though there was no probability of its reaching their resting-place, the idea would come that if the writhing creature did drop from the tree, overbalancing itself in its efforts to escape, it might make a frantic struggle and reach theirs.

As he thought this he caught sight of the guide watching him.

"What is it, my lad?" he whispered; and the lad, after a little hesitation, confided in the old sailor, who chuckled softly. "You needn't be alarmed about that," he said. "If such a thing did happen your lion would be upon his head in a moment, and in a few minutes there'd be no lion and no snake, only the mud stirred up in the water to show which way they'd gone."

"The water is sinking, Naylor," cried Brazier just then, in an excited tone.

"Yes, sir, but very slowly."

"How long will it take to go down?"

"Days, sir. This place will not be dry for a week."

"Then what about food and a place to rest?"

"We've got enough to last us two days with great care," said the man slowly, "and we shan't want for water nor shelter from the sun. Rest we must get as we can up here, and thankfully too, sir, for our lives are safe. As to what's to come after two days I don't know. There is, I say, no knowing what may happen out here in two days."

"No," said Brazier sadly. "In one hour we lost our young companion and my first collection; in one minute I was hopelessly lost; and now this morning all my second collection has been swept away. As you say, Naylor, we do not know what a couple of days may bring forth."

"No, sir," replied the old sailor; "and there's plenty of time yet. Every day brings its own trouble."

"Yes," said Brazier solemnly; "and every morning brings with it fresh hope."

"Hope!" thought Rob; "hope, shut up here in the middle of this waste of water—in this tree, with a little food, a wild beast, and that horrible serpent looking as if it is waiting to snatch us all away one by one. How can a fellow hope?"

It was a time to think about home and the chances of ever getting back in safety, and Rob found it impossible to help wishing himself on board the great river boat as the evening drew near. At last, after standing up to talk to the puma, which accepted his caresses as if they were comforting in such a time of peril, the question arose as to how they would settle themselves for the night.

"I needn't say one of us must keep watch," said Brazier sadly, "for I suppose that no one will wish to sleep."

"Couldn't if we wanted to," said Rob, in rather an ill-used tone; and Shaddy chuckled.

"Oh, I don't know, Mr Rob, sir. Nice elevated sort o' bedroom, with a good view. Plenty o' room for swinging hammocks if we'd got any to swing. There, cheer up, my lad,—there's worse disasters at sea; and our worst troubles have come right at last."

Rob looked at him reproachfully, for he was thinking of Giovanni being snatched away from them, and then of the loss of the boat.

Brazier read his face, and held out his hand, which Rob eagerly grasped.

"Cheer up, my lad," said Shaddy, following suit. "One never knows what's going to happen; so let's look at the best side of things. There, gen'lemen, it's going to be a fine warm time, and we know it might have been a drowning storm like it was last night; so that's better for us. It will be very tiring, but we must change our position now and then, and spend the night listening to the calls in the forest and trying to make out what they are."

So as not to be left longer than they could help without food, they partook of a very small portion that night, and then settled themselves down; the puma became more watchful as the darkness approached, and whined and snuffled and grew uneasy. Now it was making its way from one bough to another, and staring hard at the tops of the trees away from the river; now its attention was fixed upon the great coiled-up serpent, which lay with fold heaped over fold and its head invisible, perfectly still, and apparently sleeping till the flood had subsided.

But Rob thought with horror of the darkness, and the possibility of the great reptile rousing up and making an effort to reach them, though he was fain to confess that unless the creature swam it was impossible.

Then the stars began to appear and the noises of the forest commenced; and, as far as Rob could make out, they were as loud as ever.

"One would have thought that nearly everything had been drowned," he said in an awe-stricken whisper to his companions.

Brazier was silent, so after waiting for a few moments Shaddy replied:

"We're used to floods out here, Mr Rob, sir; and the things which make noises live in the water as well as in the trees. I don't suppose many of 'em get drowned in a flood like this. Deer and things of that sort make for higher ground when there's a chance of the water rising; the cats get on the trees, and the monkeys are already there, with the insects and birds sheltered under the big leaves; and the snakes crawl up too, so that there isn't much left to drown, is there?"

Rob made no reply, but changed his position, for he was stiff and weary from sitting so long.

"Take care, Mr Rob, sir, or you may slip down. No fear of your being swept away, but it's as well not to get a wetting. Warm as it is, you might feel cold, and that would bring on fever."

"I'll take care," said Rob quietly; and in spite of hunger only half appeased, weariness, and doubt as to their future and the length of their imprisonment, he could not help enjoying the beauty of the scene. For the water around was now one smooth mirror-like lake, save where the river rushed along with a peculiar hissing, rushing sound, augmented by a crash as some tree was dashed down and struck against those at the edge of the forest which rose above the water. In the smooth surface the stars were reflected, forming a second hemisphere; but every now and then the lad saw something which raised his hopes, and he was after a silence about to speak, when Brazier began.

"What is it keeps making little splashes in the water, Naylor?"

His voice sounded strange in the midst of the croaking, chirping, and crying going on, but it started conversation directly.

"I was just going to speak about it, sir, to Mr Rob here. Fish—that's what it is. They're come up out of the deep holes and eddies where they lie when the river's in flood, and spread all about to feed on the worms and insects which have been driven out by the water. If we only had the fishing-line there'd be no fear of getting a meal. Oh, there is no fear of that. We shall be all right till the water goes down, and be able to provide for the cupboard somehow."

"Hush! what's that?" whispered Rob, as a terrible and mournful cry rang out from somewhere among the trees—a cry which made the puma move uneasily.

"Monkey," said Shaddy. "One of those long spider-like howlers. I daresay it was very pleasant to its friends—yes, hark: there's another answering him."

"And another, and another," whispered Rob, as cries came from a distance. "But it does not sound so horrible, now that you know what it is."

Then came the peculiar trumpet-like cry of a kind of crane, dominating the chirping, whistling, and croaking, while the shrieking sounds over the open lake-like flood and beneath the trees grew more frequent.

There was plenty to take their attention and help to counteract the tedium of the night; but it was a terribly weary time, and not passed without startling episodes. Once there was the loud snorting of some animal swimming from the river over the clearing toward the forest. It was too dark to make it out, but Shaddy pronounced it to be a hog-like tapir. At another time their attention was drawn to something else swimming, by the peculiar sound made by the puma, which suddenly grew uneasy; but the creature, whatever it was, passed on toward the trees.

Several times over Rob listened to and spoke of the splashings and heavy plunges about the surface.

"'Gators," said Shaddy, without waiting to be questioned. "Fish ain't allowed to have it all their own way. They came over the flooded land to feed, and the 'gators came after them."

It was with a wonderful feeling of relief that Rob heard Brazier say, "Morning can't be far distant," and the guide's reply:

"Daylight in less than an hour, sir. Croakers and squeakers are all going to sleep fast till darkness comes again."

"Hist! listen!" whispered Rob excitedly.

"Yes, I hear it, sir. Something moving towards us."

"What is it?"

"Don't know, sir. May be a deer. If it is, so much the better for us, even if it has to be eaten raw. But it's more likely some kind of cat making for the trees. Hark at your lion there; he's getting uneasy. Mate coming to keep him company, perhaps."

They could see the reflections of the stars blurred by the movements of the swimming animal, and that it was going on past them; but it was too dark for them to distinguish the creature, which apparently was making for the forest, but altered its course and began to swim for the tree where the party had taken refuge.

"Oh, come: that will not do," cried Shaddy; "we're full here. That's right: drive him away."

This last was to the puma, which suddenly sprang up with an angry snarl, and stood, dimly seen against the stars, with its back arched, tail curved, and teeth bared, uttering fiercely savage sounds at the swimming creature approaching.

"Some kind of cat," said Shaddy in a low voice. "Can't be a mate, or it would be more friendly. Hi! look out," he said sharply, his voice full of the excitement he felt. "It's a tiger as sure as I'm here. Out with your knives: we mustn't let him get into the tree. No, no, Mr Brazier; you're too weak yet. I'll tackle him. There's plenty of room in the other trees. We can't have the savage brute here."

As the man spoke, he whipped out and opened his keen-bladed Spanish knife, and, getting flat down on his chest to have his arms at liberty, he reached out the point of his knife like a bayonet.

"Take care, Shaddy," cried Rob hoarsely, as, knife in hand and holding on by the nearest bough, he peered forward too.

"Trust me, sir. Perhaps if I can get first dig at him before he claws me, he may sheer off. Ah, mind, sir! you'll have me off. Oh! it's you, is it?"

The first was a fierce shout of warning, but the second was in a tone of satisfaction.

"I thought it was you come down on my back," growled Shaddy; "but this is as it should be. You never know who's going to help you at a pinch."

For without warning the puma had silently made one bound from its perch, and alighted upon the flattish surface presented by the old sailor's back. Then planting itself with outstretched paws firmly on his shoulders, and lowering its head, it opened its jaws and uttered a savage yell, which was answered from the golden-spangled water where the new-comer was swimming.

"It is a tiger, and no mistake," said Shaddy in a low voice; "and we'd better let our lion do the fighting, so long as they don't claw me. Mind, old fellow! That's right. I've got fast hold now."

As he was speaking he took a firm grip of a bough by his side, and with breathless suspense Rob and Brazier waited for the next phase in the exciting episode, for they were in momentary expectation of the jaguar, if such it was, reaching the tree, climbing up, and a fierce battle between the two savage creatures ensuing, with a result fatal to their companion, unless in the darkness, while they were engaged in a deadly struggle, he could contrive to direct a fatal blow at the bigger and fiercer beast.

They could now dimly make out its shape as it swam to and fro, hesitating about coming up; for the puma, generally so quiet, gentle and docile, had now suddenly become a furious snarling and hissing creature, with its ears flat to its head and paw raised ready to strike.

"I don't know what's going to happen next," said Shaddy in a low voice, "for this is something new to me. I did think I'd gone through pretty well everything; but being made into a platform for a lion and a tiger to fight out a battle's quite fresh. Suppose you gentlemen get your knives out over my head, so as to try and guard it a bit. Never mind the lion; he won't touch you while that thing's in front of him. He can't think of anything else. I can't do anything but hold on. That's right, messmate," he cried, as the puma made a stroke downward with one paw. "You'll do the business better than I shall."

"It will be light soon," whispered Brazier, as he leaned forward as far as he could, knife in hand.

"Look out, gentlemen; he's going to land now!"

For the jaguar made a dash forward, after drawing back a bit, and came close up, so that they could see the gleaming of its eyes in its flattened, cruel-looking head.

The puma struck at it again with a savage yell, but it was beyond the reach of its powerful paw, and the jaguar swam to and fro again in front of their defender, evidently feeling itself at a disadvantage and warily waiting for an opportunity to climb up the tree.

This, however, it could not find, and it continued its tactics, swimming as easily and well as an eastern tiger of the Straits, while the puma shifted its position from time to time on Shaddy's back, making that gentleman grunt softly:

"That's right: never mind me, messmate. Glad you've got so much confidence in me. Keep him off, and give him one of those licks on the side of the head if he does come within reach. You'll be too much for him, of course. Steady!"

By this time Rob had shifted his position, and was crawling down on the other side of the puma, ready to make a thrust with his knife.

Still the jaguar did not come on, but swam warily to and fro, as a faint light began to dawn upon the strange scene; and the change came rapidly, till there before them was the fierce creature, which paused at last and seemed to float out slowly, raising its paws, while its long tail waved softly behind it on the surface of the water like a snake.

"Now," cried Rob, "he's going to spring."

He was quite right, for the jaguar gathered itself together, and made a dash which shot it forward; but there was water beneath its powerful hindquarters instead of solid earth, and instead of its alighting from its bound right upon the puma it only forced itself within reach of the tawny animal's claws, which struck at it right and left with the rapidity of lightning on either side of its neck, and drove it under water.

It rose to the surface to utter a deafening roar, which was answered with savage defiance by the puma from its post of vantage upon Shaddy; but the jaguar was satisfied of its powerless position, and turned and slowly swam toward the huge tree upon their left.

"Why, it's going to climb up there by the serpent!" cried Rob, in a voice husky with excitement.

At that moment the puma leaped from Shaddy's back up one of the great branches nearest to the next tree, whence he poured down a fierce torrent of feline defiance upon his more powerful enemy; while Shaddy rose and shook himself just as the rising sun sent a glow of light in the heavens, and illuminated the savage drama commencing in the neighbouring tree.

Chapter Thirty Two.

"Out of the Frying-Pan into the Fire."

For all at once, as the jaguar reached the huge trunk, and rapidly clawed its way to the fork, bleeding from both sides of its head, the serpent awoke to the presence of the intruder; its scaly folds glistened and flashed in the morning light, as it quivered in every nerve and coiled itself fold over fold, and the head rose up, the neck assumed a graceful, swan-like bend, and the jaws were distended, displaying its menacing sets of teeth, ready to be launched forward and fixed with deadly tenacity in an enemy's throat.

"I'm thinking that we're going to get rid of an unpleasant neighbour," said Shaddy slowly, as the jaguar, reaching the fork of the trunk, seemed for a moment to be about to spring upon its fellow-prisoner in the tree, and then bounded to a great bough and ran up three or four yards. Here it was right above the serpent, with the large bough between them, round which it peered down at its enemy, as it crouched so closely to the rugged bark that it looked like some huge excrescence.

The serpent shrank back a little, lowering its head, but keeping it playing about menacingly, as its eyes glittered in the sunlight.

Then there was a pause, during which the puma crouched down above Rob's head, uttering from time to time a low growl, as it watched the jaguar, which began passing its paws alternately over its wounded head and licking them, exactly as a cat would have done on a rug before the fire.

"Doesn't look like a fight now," whispered Rob.

"Not just now, sir; he has hauled off to repair damages, and he wants all his strength and lissomeness to tackle a great worm like that. Wait a bit, and you'll see."

As he waited, Rob climbed up to where he could reach the puma, hesitating a little before he attempted to touch it, for the animal's fur was erect, and it was growling and lashing its tail angrily.

But at the sound of the boy's voice it responded by giving a low whimpering cry, turned to him, and gave its head a roll, as if in answer to a friendly rub.

"That's right," said Rob gently; "you're good friends with me, aren't you?" and he patted and rubbed the beautiful creature's head, while it let it lie on the branch, and blinked and purred.

All of a sudden, though, it raised its head excitedly, and Rob could feel the nerves and muscles quivering beneath its soft, loose skin.

Just at the same moment, too, Brazier and Shaddy uttered warning cries to the lad to look out, for the war had recommenced in the next tree, the jaguar having ceased to pass its paws over its head, and assumed a crouching position, with its powerful hind legs drawn beneath it and its sinewy loins contracted, as if preparing to make a spring.

The serpent had noticed the movement, and it too had prepared itself for the fray by assuming as safe a position for defence and menace as the limited space would allow.

Then came another pause, with the jaguar crouching, its spine all in a quiver, and a peculiar fidgeting, scratching movement visible about its hind claws, while the serpent watched it with glittering eyes, its drawn-back head rising and falling slightly with the motion of its undulating form.

"Do you think the jaguar will attack it, Naylor?" whispered Brazier.

"Yes, sir; they're nasty spiteful creatures, and can't bear to see anything enjoying itself. There's room in the tree for both of them, and you'd think that with the flood underneath they'd be content to wait there in peace till it was gone. But if the snake would the tiger won't let him: he's waiting for a chance to take him unawares, and so not get caught in his coils, but I don't think he'll get that this time. My word! Look!"

For as he was speaking the jaguar seemed to be shot from the bough, to strike the serpent on the side of the head, which it seized just at the thinnest part of the neck, and held on, tearing the while so fiercely with its hind claws that the reptile's throat was in a few moments all in ribbons, which streamed with blood. The weight of the jaguar, too, bore down the serpent, in spite of its enormous strength, and it appeared as if victory was certain for the quadruped; but even as Rob thought this, and rejoiced at the destruction of so repellent a monster, the serpent's folds moved rapidly, as if it were writhing its last in agony, and the next instant those who watched the struggle saw that the jaguar, in spite of its activity, was enveloped in the terrible embrace. There was a strange crushing sound, a yell that made Rob's fingers go toward his ears, and then a rapid movement, and the water was splashed over where they sat.

For the tree was vacant, and beneath it the flood was being churned up in a curious way, which indicated that the struggle was going on beneath the surface. Then a fold of the serpent rose for a moment or two, disappeared, and was followed by the creature's tail. This latter darted out for an instant, quivered in the air, and then was snatched back, making the water hiss.

During the next five minutes the little party in the tree sat watching the water where they had last seen it disturbed; but it had gradually settled down again, and, for aught they could tell to the contrary, their two enemies had died in each other's embrace.

But this was not so; for all at once Shaddy uttered an ejaculation, and pointed along the edge of the submerged trees, to where something was moving about in the bright morning's light.

It was right where the beams of the freshly risen sun gilded the rippling water, sending forth such flashes of light that it was hard to distinguish what it was. But directly after, there, before them, swimming slowly and laboriously, in undulatory motion, was the serpent, which they watched till it passed in among the branches of the submerged trees and disappeared.

"Then the tiger was killed?" cried Rob, excitedly.

"Yes, sir; I thought it was all over with him when the snake made those half hitches about his corpus and I heard his bones crack. Ah! it's wonderful what power those long sarpentiny creatures have. Why, I've known an eel at home, when I was a boy, twist itself up in a regular knot that was as hard and close as could be, and that strong it was astonishing."

"But surely that serpent can't live?" said Brazier.

"It's sartain, sir, that the tiger can't," replied the old sailor. "You see, beside his having that nip, he was kept underneath long enough to drown him and all his relations. As to the sarpent—oh yes, he may live. It's wonderful what a good doctor Nature is. I've seen animals so torn about that you'd think they must die, get well by giving themselves a good lick now and then, and twisting up and going to sleep. Savages, too, after being badly wounded, get well at a wonderful rate out here without a doctor. But now let's see what the river's doing."

He bent down and examined the trunk of the tree, and came to the conclusion that the flood was about stationary; and as all danger of its rising seemed to be at an end, Shaddy set to work with his knife, lopping off branches, and cutting boughs to act as poles to lay across and across in the fork of the tree, upon which he laid an abundance of the smaller stuff, and by degrees formed a fairly level platform, upon which he persuaded Brazier and Rob to lie down.

"THE WEIGHT OF THE JAGUAR BORE DOWN THE SERPENT."

"I'll keep watch," he said, "and as soon as you are rested I'll have my spell below."

They were so utterly wearied out that they gladly fell in with the old sailor's plan, and dropped off almost as soon as they had stretched themselves upon the boughs.

Chapter Thirty Three.

Reality or a Dream?

It was evening when Rob awoke, and found the guide waiting as he had left him when he lay down.

"Only gone down about an inch, Mr Rob, sir," he said. "Feel as if you could do your spell at the watch now?"

"Of course. But, Shaddy, I'm terribly hungry."

"So am I, sir. To-morrow morning we must see if we can't do something to catch some fish."

"Why not to-night?"

Shaddy shook his head, lay down, and in a moment or two was breathing heavily in a deep sleep.

"I can't watch all night without food," thought Rob, as he looked round at the waste and wondered how soon the flood would go down. He knew what food there was, and how it would have to be served, and longed for his share; but felt that unless the others were present he could not take his portion, though how he would be able to wait till morning was more than he felt able to tell.

He looked up at the puma, to see that it had carefully lodged itself on the upper fork, and was asleep. So was Mr Brazier. Only he was awake and hungry. Yes, Brazier was, too, for he woke about then with a start, to question Rob about the advance of time, and their position; ending, as he heard that the flood had hardly sunk at all, by saying that they would be compelled to watch fasting that night, so as to make the provisions last longer.

Rob gave him an agonised look, and, plucking a twig, began to pick off the leaves to chew them.

"I don't feel as if I could wait till to-morrow," he said faintly.

"It is a case of *must,*" said Brazier. "Come, try a little fortitude, my lad."

"But a little fortitude will not do," said Rob drily. "It seems to me that we shall want so much of it."

"You know our position, Rob. There, lad; let's be trustful, and try and hope. We may not have to wait longer than to-morrow for the subsiding of the flood."

How that night passed neither of them knew, but at last the sun rose to show that the waters, which had seemed to be alive with preying creatures, had sunk so that they could not be above four feet in depth; and just as they had concluded that this was the case Shaddy sprang up, and sat staring at them.

"Why!—what?—Have I slept all night?" he cried. "Oh, Mr Rob!"

"We both felt that you must have rest, Naylor," said Brazier quietly.

"That's very good of you, sir; but you should have been fairer to yourselves. Did you—?"

He stopped short.

"Hear anything in the night?" asked Rob.

"Well, no, sir, I was going to say something else, only I was 'most ashamed."

"Never mind: say it," said Brazier.

"I was going to ask if you had left me a little scrap of the prog."

Rob looked at him sharply and then at Brazier, who did the same, but neither of them replied; and the old sailor put his own interpretation upon their silence.

"All right, gentlemen," he said; "you must have both been terrible hungry. Don't say anything about it. Now, how could I manage to catch a fish?"

"After breakfast, Shaddy, please," said Rob merrily. "Mr Brazier thought we ought to wait for you."

"What! You don't mean to say you haven't had any?"

"When three people are situated as we are, Naylor, a fair division of the food is necessary. Get it at once."

"Well!" ejaculated the old sailor, as he took down the packet from where he had secured it in the upper branches; and again, as he placed it on the loose platform, "Well!" Then—"There, gentlemen, I can't tell you how thankful I am to you for being such true comrades. But there, let's eat now. The famine's over, and I mean to have some more food soon."

"How, Shaddy?" said Rob, with his mouth full; "you can't wade because of the reptiles, and the piranas would attack you."

"No, sir, I can't wade unless I could make stilts, and I can't do that. It will be a climb for fruit, like the monkeys, for luncheon if the water doesn't go down."

To the despair of all, the day passed on till it was getting late in the afternoon, and still the water spread around them right into the forest; but it was literally alive with fish which they could not see their way to catch.

Rob and Shaddy set to work making a fishing-line. A piece of the toughest wood they could find was fashioned into a tiny skewer sharpened at both ends and thrust into a piece of fruit taken from high up the tree, where Rob climbed, but soon had to come back on account of the puma following him.

Then they angled, with plenty of shoals swimming about the tree, as they could see from the movement of the muddy water; but so sure as a fish took the bait there was a short struggle, and either the line broke or the apology for a hook gave way, till first one and then the other gave up in sheer despair, and sat looking disconsolate, till Shaddy's countenance expanded into a broad grin.

"I don't see anything to laugh at," said Rob. "Here we have only a few scraps to save for to-morrow, and you treat it all as if it were a matter of no consequence."

"Warn't laughing at that, Mr Rob. I was only thinking of the fox and the grapes, for I had just said to myself the fish ain't worth ketching, just as the fox said the grapes were sour."

"But unless the waters go down ours is a very serious position," said Brazier.

"Very, sir. And as to that bit of food, strikes me that it will be good for nothing soon; so I say let's wait till last thing to-night, and then finish it."

"And what about to-morrow?" said Rob gloomily.

"Let to-morrow take care of itself, sir. Plenty of things may happen to-morrow. May be quite dry. If not, we must kill the puma and eat it."

"What!" cried Rob in horror.

"Better than killing one of ourselves, sir," said the man grimly. "We must have something to eat, and we can't live on wood and water."

The result was that they finished the last scrap of food after Shaddy had spent the evening vainly looking out for the carcass of some drowned animal. Then night came once more, and all lay down to sleep, but only to have a disturbed night through the uneasy wanderings of the hungry puma, which kept climbing from branch to branch uttering a low, muttering cry. Sometimes it curled up beside Rob and seemed to sleep, but it soon rose again and crawled down the most pendent branch till it could thrust its muzzle close to the surface of the water and quench its thirst.

"We shall have to shove it off to swim ashore," said Shaddy the next morning.

"Why?" cried Rob. "The fish and alligators would attack it."

"Can't help it, sir," replied the old sailor. "Better eat him than he should eat us."

"Why, you don't think—" began Rob.

"Yes, I do, sir. Wild beasts of his kind eat enough at one meal to last 'em a long time; but when they get hungry they grow very savage, and he may turn upon us at any time now."

Rob looked at the puma anxiously, and approached it later on in the day, to find the animal more gentle than ever; though it snarled and ruffled up the hair of its back and neck whenever there was the slightest advance made by either of the others.

That day passed slowly by—hot, dreamy, and with the water keeping exactly to the same depth, so that they were hopelessly prisoned still on their tree. They tried again to capture a fish, but in vain; and once more the night fell, with the sounds made by bird, insect, and reptile more weird and strange to them than ever.

Rob dropped asleep from time to time, to dream of rich banquets and delicious fruits, but woke to hear the croaking and whistling of the different creatures of the forest, and sit up on the pile of boughs listening to the splash of the various creatures in the water, till day broke, to find them all gaunt, wild-eyed, and despairing.

"We must try and wade to shore, and chance the creatures in the water," said Brazier hoarsely, for, on account of his weakness, he seemed to suffer more than the others. "Where's shore, sir?" said Shaddy gruffly. "Well, the nearest point, then."

"There ain't no nearest point, sir," said the man. "Even if we could escape the things swarming in the muddy water, we could not wade through the forest. It's bad enough when it's hard; now it's all water no man could get through the trees. Besides, the land may be a hundred miles away."

"What can we do, then?" cried Rob in desperation. "Only one thing, sir: wait till the water goes down."

"But we may be dead before then—dead of this terrible torture of hunger."

"Please God not, sir," said the old sailor piously: and they sat or lay now in their terrible and yet beautiful prison.

From time to time Shaddy reached out from a convenient branch, and dipped one of Rob's vessels full of the thick water, and when it had been allowed to settle they quenched their burning thirst; but the pangs of hunger only increased and a deadly weakness began to attack their limbs, making the least movement painful.

For the most part those hours of their imprisonment grew dreamy and strange to Rob, who slept a good deal; but he was roused up by one incident. The puma had grown more and more uneasy, walking about the tree wherever it could get the boughs to bear it, till all at once, after lying as if asleep, it suddenly rose up, leaped from bough to bough, till it was by the forest, where they saw it gather itself up and spring away, evidently trying to reach the extreme boughs of the next tree; but it fell with a tremendous splash into the water, and the growth between prevented them from seeing what followed.

Rob uttered a sigh, for it was as if they had been forsaken by a friend; and Shaddy muttered something about "ought not to have let it go."

They seemed to be very near the end. Then there was a strange, misty, dreamy time, from which Rob was awakened by Shaddy shaking his shoulder. "Rouse up, my lad," he said huskily. "No, no: let me sleep," sighed Rob. "Don't—don't!"

"Rouse up, boy, I tell ye," cried the old sailor fiercely. "Here's help coming, or I'm dreaming and off my head. Now; sit up and listen. What's that?"

Rob struggled feebly into a sitting position, and fancied he could hear a sound. There was moonshine on the smooth water, and the trees cast a thick shade; but he closed his eyes again, and began to lower himself down to drop into the sleep from which there would be no waking here on earth.

"Ask—Mr Brazier—to look," he muttered feebly, and closed his heavy eyes.

"No, no: you," cried Shaddy, who was kneeling beside him. "He's asleep, like. He can't move. Rouse up, lad, for the sake of home and all you love. I'm nearly beat out, but your young ears can listen yet, and your eyes see. There's help coming, I tell you."

"Help?" cried Rob, making a snatch at his companion's arm.

"Yes, or else I'm dreaming it, boy. I'm off my head, and it's all 'mazed and thick. That's right, listen. Hold up by me. Now, then, what's that black speck away yonder, like a bit o' cloud? and what's that noise?"

"Oars," said Rob huskily, as he gave a kind of gasp.

"What?"

"Oars—and—a boat," cried the boy, his words coming with a strange catching of the breath.

"Hurray! It is—it is," cried Shaddy; and collecting all his remaining strength, he uttered a hoarse hail, which was supplemented by a faint harsh cry from Rob, as he fell back senseless in their rough nest of boughs in the fork of that prison tree.

Chapter Thirty Four.

All for the Best.

Shaddy had preceded him, and neither of them heard the regular beat of oars and the faint splashing of water as four rowers, urged on by one in the stern, forced their way toward the spot from whence the hail had come, till the boat went crashing among the drooping boughs, was secured to the huge trunk, and after water and a little sopped bread had been administered, the three sufferers were carefully lowered down and laid under the shed-like awning.

Three weary days of delirium ensued before the first of the sufferers unclosed his eyes, illumined by the light of reason, and had the bright semicircle of light facing him eclipsed for the moment by a slight figure which crept in beneath the awning to give him food.

And then two more days elapsed before Rob could say feebly,—

"Tell me, Joe, have I been asleep and dreaming?"

"I hope so," said the young Italian, pressing his hand.

"Then you are not dead?"

"Do I look like it? No; but I thought you were. Why, Rob, old chap, we only got back to you just in time."

"But I thought—we thought that—"

Rob ceased speaking, and Giovanni, who looked brown, strong, and well, finished his companion's sentence after turning to where the two famine-pinched feeble men lay listening for an explanation of the events of the past.

"You thought I had been drowned, and that the men had carried off the boat while you were all looking for me?"

Rob's eyes said, "Yes," as plainly as eyes could speak. "Of course you would," said Joe, laughing merrily. "You couldn't help thinking so; but I wasn't drowned, and the men didn't steal the boat. What say, Shaddy?"

For there was a husky whisper from where the old sailor lay—a ghost of his former self.

"Say?" whispered the guide sourly,—"that we can see all that."

"Tell us how it was," said Rob, holding out his hand, which Joe grasped and held, but he did not speak for a few minutes on account of a choking sensation in his breast as the sun glanced in through the ends of the awning, after streaming down like a silver shower through the leaves of the huge tree beneath which the boat was moored, while the swift river, once more back within its bounds, rippled and sang, and played against the sides.

"The men told me," said Joe at last, with a slight Italian accent in the words, now that he was moved by his emotion—"they told me all about what horror and agony you showed as you all went off to rescue me, while there I was perched up in the branches of the great tree, expecting every moment that it would be rolled over by the river, unless I could creep up to the next bough and the next, all wet and muddy as they were, and I knew that I could not keep on long at that. But all at once, to my horror, we began to glide down—oh, so swiftly, but even then I felt hopeful, for the tree did not turn, and I was far above the water as we went on swifter and swifter, till all at once I caught sight of the boat, moored some distance onward, with the four men in it sitting with their backs to me. I made up my mind to leap into the water and swim to them, but the next minute I knew that it would be impossible, and that the branches would stop me, entangle me, and that I should be drowned. Then the tree began to go faster and drift out toward the middle, but it was caught by an eddy and swept in again toward the shore, so that I felt I should be carried near to the boat, and I shouted to them then to throw me a rope."

"No good to try and throw a rope," growled Shaddy faintly.

"Go on, my lad," whispered Brazier, for Joe had stopped.

"They saw me for the first time, and gave a shout, but they all stood up directly, horrified, for the fierce stream now bore me swiftly on right down upon them, and before we could all realise it the boughs were under and over the boat, and it was carried away from where it was moored. And there it was just beneath me, with the boughs going more and more over and under it, and our speed increasing till I began to wonder whether we should roll right over and force it down, or the lower boughs lift and raise it right up. Then there was another thing to consider—whether I ought to try and drop down into the boat, or they ought to climb up to me."

"Ah!" ejaculated Rob, heaving a long sigh and then breathing hard.

"And all this time," continued Joe, "we were being swept down the stream at a tremendous rate, too frightened to do anything, making up our mind one way one minute, altering it the next; while, to my great delight, the tree kept in just the same position, which, I have since supposed, must have been because the roots were so laden with earth and stones that it served as a balance to the boughs.

"We went on down like this for hours, expecting every minute would be our last, for so sure as the tree touched bottom or side it must have been rolled over by the swift current, but the water was so deep that we kept on, and, at last gaining courage, I lowered myself a little and got upon another bough, which was very near to the boat, and there I stood upright.

"'Shall I jump?' I said, and they stood up ready to catch me, but I hesitated for a few moments before making a spring, which would take me through some thin twigs between us.

"In my hurry and excitement, I jumped with all my force, but caught one foot against a little branch, and was jerked forward so violently into the boat that in their efforts to save me they made her give a great lurch, and she began to rock violently, and nearly sent two of them overboard. The next minute we saw that she had been driven clear of the boughs which held her and was floating away, but at the same moment the branches above us began to descend slowly, for the tree was rolling over, the buoyancy of the boat wedged in among the branches having kept it stationary so long.

"Our position was now terribly dangerous, for the size and force of the boughs were sufficient, with the impetus they now had from being in motion, to drive us right under, an accident which meant death if we could not escape, but in their desperation the men seized the oars, and by pushing against the tree thrust the boat so far toward the clear water that we were only brushed by the outer twigs and thinnest parts as we were caught by the swift stream and went on down at a tremendous rate.

"It was not until night was drawing near that we thought of making fast to a tree at the side where we could rest for the time and then start back in the morning to reach you again as soon as we possibly could, for I knew you would be fancying still that I was dead, and that the men had forsaken you. So we had a meal, and I set the watches, meaning to see to the men taking their turn. Then, feeling tired out, I lay down for a few minutes to rest, but—I dropped asleep."

"'Course you did," said Shaddy sourly.

"And when I awoke in a fright the sun was shining, the men were all asleep at the bottom of the boat, and we were spinning down the river as hard as we could go."

"Sarved you all right if you'd been upset," growled Shaddy. "That would have woke some of you up."

"Don't scold me, Shaddy," said the lad humbly. "I know I ought not to have gone to sleep, but I thought I could trust the men."

"Thought you could trust them?" cried the old sailor. "Why, you couldn't even trust yourself!"

"No," said Joe humbly.

"Why, Mr Brazier, the pains I've took to make a seaman of that young chap, no one knows. I only wonder as they weren't all wrecked and drowned," protested Shaddy.

"Let him go on, Naylor."

"Ay, go on, Mr Jovanni. If there's anything more you ought to be ashamed on, speak it out and get it over. You'll be better after."

"Isn't he hard upon me, Rob?" said Joe, smiling.

"Yes, but it all turned out for the best," said his companion.

"I didn't think so then," continued Joe, "when I began to find that we must have been gliding down the river fast all that night, and what I had begun to find out then I knew more and more as we tried to work our way back. We couldn't pole because the water was too deep, and we had to work our way along by the trees, sometimes getting a little way up the river and then making a slip and being swept down again for far enough, till I gave it up in despair. The men worked till they could work no longer. And all the time you were left alone without the guns and fishing tackle and food, and it used to make me mad to have to use any of the stores; so I made them fish all I could, and I did a little shooting, so that we didn't use much."

"Oh, come," said Shaddy in a more agreeable tone, "that's the best thing we've heard you say yet, Mr Jovanni. That's where my teaching comes out, but don't you never say a word to me again about your seamanship!"

"But you are keeping him from telling us how he came and saved us just as he did in the nick of time, Shaddy," said Rob.

"All right, sir, all right! won't say another word," cried the old sailor querulously, "only don't let him get bragging no more about his seamanship and management of a crew."

"I never will, Shaddy, and I hope I shall never be placed in such a predicament again."

"How did you manage to get up the river?" asked Rob.

"Oh, that was easy enough as soon as the flood came; we should never have got to you without; but as soon as the land was all flooded, I found that we could get right away from the swift stream and keep along at a distance, poling generally. Then we were able to take short cuts across the bends. We did get caught now and then and swept back a bit, but every day we made a good many miles, and at last as we were rowing steadily on over the flooded land, which is a good deal more open below, we neared the opening, and thought it was a good deal altered; but the men said I was wrong. I felt sure that I was right, and had just come to the conclusion that you must all have been swept away and drowned, when I heard the hail, and you are all safe once more."

Chapter Thirty Five.

Peace in the Forest.

The three sufferers had no illness to fight against, and began to regain their normal strength very rapidly, while nature was hiding the destruction wrought upon the face of the land at a rapid rate. Tropical showers washed the mud left by the flood from leaf and twig, and the lower boughs, which had been stripped of leaves by the rushing waters, put forth new ones, so that in a very few days' time not many traces of the flood were visible, save where banks had crumbled in and great gaps of broken earth stood out.

Fully equipped once more, Brazier, as he regained his strength, went on adding to his collection of choice plants, which had come back to him intact; and as they dropped on and on down the river, finding clearings at pretty frequent intervals, greater and greater grew the natural stores of botanical treasures, so that the collector was more than satisfied with Shaddy's guiding.

"But what I want to know is how we are to get back," Rob said over and over again. "We shall never be able to pull the boat up again."

Shaddy chuckled.

"Might have another big storm and a flood, Mr Rob," he said, "and get back as Mr Jovanni did."

"But you don't mean to go back that way?"

"Right, sir! I don't. But you go on with your fishing and shooting, and let Mr Brazier do his vegetables up in his baskets. Leave the rest to me."

The task was left to him, and they went on down the river day after day till one evening they rounded a bend, and, in obedience to their leader's orders, the boat was rowed into a narrow stream which joined that which they had left, the junction being plainly marked by the distinct colour of the waters.

"Going up this, Naylor?" asked Brazier wonderingly.

"Yes, sir. It's the place I've been making for, and I'm thinking you'll find something quite fresh along here, for it leads up into higher ground on and on into the mountains, where the trees and flowers are quite different."

"Of course—yes," said Brazier eagerly. "Let's go up it."

"But there's one thing to be said, sir."

"What's that?"

"We shall have to be careful."

"Is the river dangerous?"

"Tidy, sir; but we can get over that. It's the Indians."

"Indians?"

"Yes, sir; some of them may be along the side, but if we are on the watch and take care, being well armed and a fairly strong party, I think they are not likely to interfere with us much."

Rob pricked up his ears at this as they began gliding up the stream, noting the difference directly, for it was far less powerful, the men having no difficulty at all in forcing the boat along, save here and there where they encountered a rapid, up which they thrust the boat with poles.

"Did you hear what old Shaddy said?" Rob whispered to his companion.

"Yes. We shall have to look out then and have our guns ready."

“But have the Indians guns?”

“No, spears and blowpipes, through which they send poisoned arrows.”

“Ugh!” ejaculated Rob uneasily.

“Horrid things! Shaddy has often told me about them,” said Joe.

“What has he often told you about, my lad?”

The boys started, for the old sailor had approached them unheard.

“Indians’ blowpipes,” said Joe.

“Ah, yes; they’re not nice things, my lads. Can’t say as I would like to be killed by one of their arrows.”

“Why?” said Rob. “What are they like?”

“Stop a moment, my lad, and I’ll tell you.”

He left them to give some instructions to the men as to the use of their poles, but returned directly.

“Know what we’re doing now?” he said, with one of his dry quaint smiles on his weather-beaten face.

“Yes, going up this river.”

“Right, my lad! But we’re going upstairs like. You’ll see we shall keep on rowing along smooth stretches where the water seems easy; then we shall come to rapids and have to pole on against a swift rush of water, and every time we get to the top of the rapid into smooth water we shall have gone up one of my water steps, and so by degrees get right up into the mountains.”

"Why are we going up into the mountains? Is it to get back to the main river?" said Rob.

"Wait a bit, my lad, and you'll see. Besides, Mr Brazier'll get plants up here such as he never saw before. But you were talking about the Indians and their blowpipes. I don't mind the blowpipes; it's the arrows."

"Poisonous?"

"Horrid, my lad. They're only little bits of things with a tuff of cotton at one end and the wood at the other sharpened into a point, but they dip it into poison, and just before they shoot it out of the blowpipe they hold it nipped between the jaws of one of those little sharp-toothed piranis, then give it a bit of a twirl with their fingers, and the teeth saw it nearly through."

"What's the use of that?" asked Rob.

"Makes it so that the arrow breaks off and leaves the point in the wound. Anything don't live very long with one of those points left in its skin."

"Think we shall meet any Indians, Shaddy?" said Joe.

"Maybe yes, my lad; maybe no. You never know. They come and go like wild beasts—tigers, lions, and such-like."

"Do you think my lion will follow us, Shaddy?" said Rob eagerly.

"No, my lad; I don't. He had a long swim before him to get to shore; and it's my belief that he would be 'tacked and pulled under before he had gone very far."

"How horrible!"

"Yes, my lad; seems horrid, but I don't know. Natur's very curious. If he was pulled under to be eaten it was only to stop him from pulling other creatures down and eating them. That's the way matters go on out in these forests where life swarms, and from top to bottom one thing's killing and eating another. It's even so with the trees, as I've told you: the biggest and strongest kill the weak 'uns, and live upon 'em. It's all nature's way, my lads, and a good one."

"Well, we don't want the Indians to kill us, Shaddy," said Rob merrily.

"And they shan't, my lad, if I can help it. Perhaps we mayn't see any of them, and one side of the river's safe, so we shall keep that side; but if they come any of their nonsense with us they must be taught to keep to themselves with a charge or two of small shot. If that don't teach them to leave respectable people alone they must taste larger shot. I don't want to come to bullets 'cept as a last resource."

"I should have liked to have found the puma again," said Rob after a time.

"Perhaps it's as well not, my lad," said their guide. "It was all very well, and he liked you, but some day he'd have grown older, and he'd have turned rusty, and there would have been a fight, and before he was killed you might have been badly clawed. Wild beasts don't tame very well. You can trust dogs and cats, which are never so happy as when they are with human folk; but I never knew any one who did very well with other things. Ah, here's another of my steps!"

He went to his men again, for they were rowing along a smooth-gliding reach, at the end of which rough water appeared, and all hands were called into requisition to help the boat up the long stretch of rapids, at the end of which, as they glided into smooth water again, Shaddy declared that they had mounted a good twenty feet.

Day after day was spent in this steady journeying onward. The weather was glorious, and the forest on either side looked as if it had never been trod by man. So full of wonders, too, was it for Brazier, that again and again as night closed in, and they moored on their right to some tree for the men to land and light their fire and cook, he thanked their guide for bringing him, as the first botanist, to a region where every hour he collected treasures.

"And some folk would sneer at the pretty things, and turn away because they weren't gold, or silver, or precious stones," muttered Shaddy.

All this time almost imperceptibly they were rising and climbing Shaddy's water steps, as he had called them. They fished and had success enough to keep their larder well stocked. Birds were shot such as were excellent eating, and twice over Shaddy brought down iguanas, which, though looked upon with distrust by the travellers, were welcomed by the boatmen, who were loud in their praise.

It was a dream-like existence, and wonderfully restful to the lads who had passed through so many troubles, while the boat presented an appearance, with its load of drying specimens, strongly suggestive of there being very little room for more.

Chapter Thirty Six.

War.

They had literally climbed a long rapid one morning, and entered a broad reach of the river which resembled a lake in its extent. The water here was smooth, and had a current that was barely perceptible, hence their progress was swift, and as they were rowing round a bend the question arose where they should halt for the midday rest, when suddenly an ejaculation escaped from their guide's lips, and the men ceased pulling, leaving the boat to drift slowly on over the glowing mirror-like surface, which was as if of polished steel.

"What is it, Shaddy?" cried Rob quickly. "Are we going wrong?" But as he spoke he caught sight of the reason for the sudden stoppage, for there right in front, ashore and in canoes, were about twenty Indians, standing up and apparently watching them in speechless astonishment.

"Indians!" cried Rob.

"Yes, my lad, and we've done pretty well to come all these hundreds of miles without hitting upon them before. Don't hurry, Mr Brazier, sir, and don't let them think that we mind 'em, but lay the guns ready, and the ammunition, so that we can give them as good as they send, and mind, if it comes to fighting, every one's to lie down in the boat and keep under cover."

"Perhaps there will be no trouble," said Brazier quietly. "They seem to be peaceable enough."

"Yes, sir, seem to be; but you can't trust 'em."

Just then the Indians ceased staring at the party in the boat, and went on with the pursuit in which they were engaged as the boat swept round the bend. This was shooting at some object in the water, apparently for practice, but in a peculiar way, for the lads saw the men take aim high up in the air, so that their arrows turned far on high and fell with lightning-like rapidity upon certain shiny spots just flush with the surface of the water; and while Rob was wondering the guide whispered,—

"Shooting turtles! They're wonderful clever at it. If they fired straight, the arrows would start off. This way they come down, go through the rough hide, and kill the turtle."

Of this they had proof again and again as they rowed slowly on, their course taking them close to one canoe whose owner had gone off from near the shore to recover a turtle that he had shot.

This Shaddy tried to obtain, offering something by way of barter, but the man bent down to his paddle with a face full of mistrust, and forced his light vessel toward where his companions had gathered to watch the strangers.

"I don't like that," muttered Shaddy in Rob's hearing, and at the same moment Joe whispered,—

"They don't mean to be friends, and we shall have to look out."

As he spoke he stretched out his hand for his gun, and began to examine it carefully, a proceeding that was imitated by the others, but in a quiet unostentatious way, so as not to take the attention of the Indians.

A few moments' counsel ended in a determination not to try again to make advances, by no means to halt for the midday rest, but to keep steadily on without paying any heed to the Indians, who followed slowly as the oars were plied, and at a respectful distance.

"How far does this smooth water go, Naylor?" asked Brazier.

"Six or seven miles, sir."

"And is there a long rapid at the end?"

"Yes, sir, as long as any we have passed."

"Where they could take us at a disadvantage?"

"Yes, sir," said Shaddy, grimly indeed. "If it's to come to a fight, we had better have it out here in the open, where we can shelter ourselves in the boat."

"Then you think it will come to an encounter?"

"I'm afraid so, sir, if you must have the truth."

"What about your men?"

"Oh, they'll fight for their lives if they're driven to it, sir; but the worst of it is, these sort of fellows fight in a cowardly way, either with poisoned arrows or by shooting their arrows up straight in the air so that they come down upon you when you least expect it and can't shelter against them."

"A false alarm!" cried Rob joyously, for the Indians had all ceased paddling, and after a minute or two, as if by one consent, turned the heads of their canoes to the shore and went straight away, disappearing at last amongst the trees which overhung the river bank.

Shaddy made no reply to the speaker, but, the way being clear, bade his men to row steadily on for another half-hour, when a halt was called, and refreshments served round in the boat, but with orders for them to be hastily eaten.

After this the rowing was resumed till the afternoon was far advanced, and the end of the lake-like reach was still apparently far-away. The broad expanse had for a long time past been entirely free from all signs of the Indians, and Rob was congratulating himself upon their escape, when Joe pointed straight back along the broad river-lake to where a canoe suddenly shot round a corner; then another came into view, and another, and another, till there were between thirty and forty visible, each bearing four or five men, and a chill of horror shot through Rob as he felt that this must mean war, and that they would be helpless in the extreme if so large a body of men made a determined attack.

"I was afraid of that," said Shaddy quietly, "Strange as they can't leave us alone."

"What do you propose doing, Naylor?" said Mr Brazier eagerly.

"There ain't no proposing, sir. It's all driving to do what is for the best. We must face 'em."

"Why not land and try and find shelter in the woods?"

"Because, sir, they'd destroy our boat and follow us and shoot us down like so many wild beasts. Our only hope is to keep on as long as we can, and if the chance comes take to the rapid and get on it. They mightn't care about venturing in their light boats. But we shall see."

There was a very stern look in Brazier's countenance, a look that seemed to have been reflected from that of the old sailor, as weapons were once more examined.

"I don't like fighting, boys," he said, "but if we are driven to it, we must defend our lives."

Then turning to Shaddy, "Can't you depend upon your men to help us, Naylor?" he said.

"I'm going to depend upon 'em to row, sir," said the old sailor sternly. "We can kill quite enough people without their help. They're the engines, sir, to take us out of danger, while we keep the enemy at a distance."

Meanwhile the boat was being steadily propelled toward the end of the lake-like enlargement of the river, where a few low hills rose, showing where the rapids would be which they had to surmount; but it soon became evident that the light canoes would be alongside before the exit from the lake could be reached, and Rob said so.

"Yes, sir, you're quite right, unless we can scare them off," said the guide, who had been busy making a rough barricade in the stern by piling boxes and barrels one upon another, leaving openings through which they could fire, saying, "It isn't strength we want so much as shelter to baulk their aim, for they're terribly clever with their bows and arrows, Mr Rob, sir."

But very little was said in those anxious minutes, with the little party, after their many struggles with nature, now called upon to prepare to face man in his savage form.

"Feel frightened, Joe?" whispered Rob as the two boys lay together by a couple of loopholes, well sheltered beneath the awning.

"Shall you laugh at me if I say yes?"

"Not likely, when I own to it too. I say, I wish they'd leave us alone."

"Look here, Mr Brazier, sir," said the old sailor just then, after admonishing his men to pull their best, "I'm going to ask you to let me manage this."

"No," said Brazier sternly; "I wish to avoid all the bloodshed possible."

"So do I, sir—specially ours," said Shaddy drily; "and mine would be the way."

"Quick, then: explain," said Brazier, as the boys listened eagerly. "Make haste, for the enemy are very near."

"Soon done," said Shaddy, "only what I proposed, sir: you folk keep me supplied with guns, and I'll try 'em with gentle measures first, and rough ones after. I'm a tidy shot, eh, Mr Jovanni?"

"Yes, excellent," said the lad.

"Very well, then, you shall try to stop them," replied Brazier, "but I warn you that if I am not satisfied I shall take the lead myself."

"All right, sir, but don't you make the mistake of giving up and trusting these people! That means death for all of us. *They must be beaten off.*"

There was something very startling in Shaddy's tones as he uttered these words, and Brazier looked at him wonderingly.

"We shall have to come back this way, so why not retreat at once with the stream?"

"Because we don't come back this way, sir; that's all. Didn't the lads tell you? I'm going to take you into the big river another way."

"I say, look out!" cried Rob excitedly, as he saw the water flashing behind at the rapid dip of the Indians' paddles and noticed the stolid look in the heavy round faces of the men astern, who sat ready with their bows and arrows, the spears of the paddlers projecting from the front.

Almost directly after the intentions of the Indians were shown not to be peaceful, for a straggling flight of arrows came whistling through the air, several of the missiles falling just astern, some in front, but for the most part striking the boat and sticking in the awning and the shelter made astern.

"Any one hurt?" shouted Shaddy sternly, and receiving an answer in the negative, he muttered as he thrust the double gun he held through an opening,—

"That's because they're on the move and we're on the move. If we'd been standing still, and them too, every shot would have told. Look out; they're going to fire again. My turn first. Pull, my lads; don't you mind me."

As the words left his lips he fired at intervals of about a quarter of a minute both barrels of the fowling-piece; and at the flash of fire, followed by smoke curling up slowly and hiding the boat, the Indians stopped paddling and sat watching.

"That has beaten them off," cried Rob eagerly. "Was it blank cartridge, Shaddy?"

"Yes, my lad. Next's going to be number six if they come on after us."

The men pulled hard and increased the distance between them and the canoes rapidly, while the travellers' hopes grew high. But all of a sudden there was a yell, paddles splashed again, and satisfied of the harmlessness of the fire and smoke, the Indians took up the pursuit again.

"Oh, very well, if you will be hurt," said Shaddy, "it's your fault, not mine," and he thrust the barrels once more through the opening in the barrier of boxes.

"How long will it take us to reach the next rapid, Naylor?" asked Brazier excitedly.

"Half 'hour, sir, but we must beat 'em off before we can land, or they'll stick us so full of arrows, we shall look like hedgehogs. Hi! sit and lie close, every one. Look out! Arrows!"

But the flight was not discharged until the Indians had gained a good deal more ground. Then the whistling was heard, accompanied or followed by sharp raps, but again, in answer to Shaddy's inquiry, there came a cheery "No!"

"Now then," he said, "let's see what they say to us, sir, and how far the charge will scatter and carry."

As he spoke he took careful aim a little to his right and fired quite low, changed the position of his piece, and fired again a little to his left.

The smoke hung so heavily for a minute or two that there was quite a screen between them, beyond which shouts, savage yells, and cries of pain could be heard, while upon rowing beyond the smoke and into full view of the fleet of canoes the fugitives could see that the paddling had again ceased, and men were standing up gesticulating, while others were evidently in great pain from the stinging shots.

"Now you know that we can bite as well as bark," growled Shaddy, "and if you'll all take my advice you'll go back home and leave us alone, because if you don't I shall use buckshot, and some of you mayn't be able to handle a paddle again."

The babble of voices sounded strange as the oars dipped fast, and for a time they were allowed to pursue their way in peace, but at last it was seen that the wounded had all been transferred to certain of the canoes, and with a fierce yell the Indians came on again, with paddles beating, and the water splashing; while another flight of arrows whistled about the travellers, fortunately without hurting a soul.

"I shall have to give them a stronger dose this time," said Shaddy. "I'll try swan shot first," and inserting a couple of cartridges loaded with heavy pellets, he took careful aim, and fired twice.

This time there were loud shrieks mingled with the fierce, defiant cries, and as the smoke was left behind it was plain to see that there was consternation in the little fleet, and for some time they did not pursue.

"What are you two about?" said Shaddy suddenly as he caught sight of Rob and Joe making some preparation.

"Wait a minute, and you'll see," said Rob, and he went on with his task, which was the preparation of something in the fashion of a torpedo, for about a pound of powder had been transferred from their keg to a small tin canister, in whose lid they drove a hole, and passed through it a slow match, made by rubbing a strip of rag with moistened gunpowder, which dried up at once in the hot evening sunshine. At the bottom of the canister a charge of shot had been placed, and upon trying it in a bucket the tin floated with about an inch of its top out of water.

"Now," said Rob when he had finished, Brazier nodding his head in approval—"it's quite calm, and when the enemy comes on again I'm going to stick a wax match in the hole with the end touching the slow match, set light to it, and let it float down towards the Indians. The wax match will burn nearly a minute, and I want them to paddle up round it to see what the floating light means, and then if we're in luck it will go off bang and give them a startler."

"And suppose it goes off while you are lighting it, and gives you a startler, and sends us all to the bottom, how then?"

"Oh, we must risk that," said Rob coolly.

"I'm willing, if Mr Brazier is," said the old sailor quietly.

"Rob will be careful," said Brazier, and they waited with the contrivance ready, but all hoping that Shaddy's last shots had produced the desired effect.

It was a vain hope, for once more the canoes tore on to make up for lost ground, and at last, when Brazier and Shaddy made ready to fire at the enemy, Rob gave the word for the men to cease rowing, and as the boat steadied he told Joe to light a match and lowered the canister into the water.

"Be careful, Rob," cried Mr Brazier. "See that there is no powder loose."

"Be quick, my lad, or they'll be on to us."

Crack! went the match, and as it blazed up it was applied to one stuck upright in the top of the canister. This blazed in turn, and the flame flickered a little and threatened to go out as the nearly submerged tin glided away with the stream; but directly after the flame burned up steadily, and as Rob gave the word to row once more the dangerous contrivance was left behind. A minute later they had the satisfaction of seeing the canoes gather round the tiny light and their occupants cease rowing as they sat evidently wondering what was the meaning of the fire burning in the midst of the water—a perfect novelty to them.

"No go!" said Shaddy suddenly. "Match has gone out."

"Burned out," said Brazier.

"All the same, sir, and hasn't started the touch-rag. Wish it had answered, because it was clever and would have given the beggars a good lesson not to meddle with respectable people. Here, we shall have to fire, sir. They're coming on again."

But they were not, for the whole fleet was gathered about the canister, which, unseen by the occupants of the boat, was emitting a sputtering little fire as the touch-rag burned slowly; and the wonder of this going on from a round, silvery-looking object just above the surface of the water kept the ignorant enemy at a respectable distance.

"Pull, my lads," shouted Shaddy. "We may get into a better place if we reach the next rapid."

As he spoke there was a deafening roar, a column of water rose in the air, and a dull concussion struck the boat, while a cloud of smoke hung over the group of canoes, and, lifting, showed half of them to be swamped, and dozens of the Indians swimming about trying to reach the boats which floated still.

As far as the little party could make out, no one had been hurt, but the consternation was terrible. No further efforts were made in pursuit, and for the next half-hour the boat was rowed on and reached the rapid before the enemy was seen again.

"Now then," said Brazier, as the rough, swift water of the river was once more reached, "shall we wait to give them another lesson or go on?"

"Go on," said Shaddy firmly. "They may not follow us up now. Mind, I only hope that; but we shall see."

Chapter Thirty Seven.

The Last Days.

Food was served out, the men drank eagerly of the water passed to them, and poling, wading, and tracking with a rope, the boat began to ascend the rapid, while the long lake-like reach was left behind, a turn or two completely hiding the enemy from sight; and though twice over they heard their shouts and yells, the scare created by the explosion had been sufficient to make them give the party what Shaddy called "a wide berth."

"How far have we to go up this river?" asked Brazier as the men toiled on, wading and tracking in a part that was one furious torrent, which threatened to swamp the boat.

"Ah, that's what I can't tell you, sir," answered the old sailor. "I've only got notions, you see."

"Notions, man?"

"Yes, sir: that if we go right up to the head of this stream we can make a portage somewhere, and strike another, which will lead us down east, and so hit the Paraguay again."

Rob laughed, and the man gave him an inquiring look.

"Make a portage," he said, "and strike this stream and hit that? Not very plain English, Shaddy."

"Then I don't know what is," growled the old sailor, who held up his hand and listened for a few moments. "Thought I heard 'em coming up after us," he said. "Strikes me, Mr Rob, that you'd better have another of them powder tins ready, so that we could contrive to let it off and startle 'em, if they come nigh. We've plenty of powder, and it's better than shooting the poor wretches, who don't know any better. They're used to seeing one thing kill another, and I suppose they think they ought to do the same, and we can't teach 'em any better."

It was rapidly getting dark now, but they reached the top of the torrent, passing again into comparatively smooth water, along which the boat was rowed for some distance before a suitable spot was found for the night's shelter—a night full of anxiety, during which careful watch was kept.

But day broke without there being any sign of the enemy, and as soon as a hurried meal had been despatched, at which they had to dispense with freshly made bread and tea, the men, too, with their maté, a new start was made, and another rapid ascended, after which for many miles the river wound, with plenty of deep water, through valley after valley.

All this time they were on the alert for pursuing Indians, but by degrees they were able to feel confidently that they had journeyed beyond the territory occupied by the inimical people, and Brazier began his collecting once more, and the boys their fishing and shooting.

"It's absurd, Rob," said Brazier one evening, when the crisp cool air told that they must during the past week have attained to far above the dense forest regions. "I could have filled this boat a dozen times over."

"Yes," said Rob, peering hard at the stacks of dried and half-dried plants around them; "but you have got a great many."

"A mere nothing, boy, as compared to what there is about us! Why, up here we are surrounded by quite a different growth of flowers and plants."

"And the birds are different, too, and the insects, and fish, specially the latter," said Rob drily.

"Indeed? I did not notice anything about the fish."

"Good reason why," said Rob, laughing merrily: "there haven't been any to notice."

Two days after, when they were in quite a desolate region, where the trees and shrubs were thin and poor, Shaddy came to Mr Brazier to announce that he and two of the men were going to leave them camped for a few hours, while they sought out the most likely course for their portage.

"But surely it will be impossible to work the boat along overland," said Brazier. "We shall have to go back."

"To meet the Indians, sir? No, that wouldn't do. Perhaps I'm wrong, but we're up here now where several streams begin, and if we can only find one, no matter how small, that flows to the east, we're all right."

The men set off the next morning as soon as it was light, and the party in camp shot, collected, kept up the fire, and waited impatiently for the return of the little expedition, but waited in vain; and at last in alarm Rob and Joe set off in search of them, tramping till midday and stopping to rest by a fount which bubbled out of the earth and flowed away. After resting a while they started again to tramp here and there for hours in the beautiful region near the camp, to which they returned without having seen a sign of those they sought.

It must have been toward morning that Rob, who was keeping watch, heard distant voices, and hailing, to his great delight heard an answer.

Ten minutes later the guide and his two companions staggered up to the fire utterly exhausted, for they had finished their supply of food, and were worn-out with their exhausting tramp.

"Well," said Mr Brazier, after the men had taken a good long rest, "have you found the river to which we are to take the boat?"

"No, sir. I'm all wrong, and we shall have to go back. There isn't a stream runs toward the east anywhere near here."

"That there is," cried Joe, "for we found one yesterday."

"Eh? What? Where?" cried Shaddy, springing up, utterly forgetful of his weariness; and following the two lads, who warned him that the water was of no use for a boat, the fount was reached, and, after a very brief examination, Shaddy cried,—

"There, I'm growing old and worn-out. You two lads found directly what we three men, used to the country, couldn't see."

"But this place is of no use!" cried Rob.

"What?"

"There are only a few inches of water."

"Well, they'll help carry the boat, won't they? and the water flows our way."

"But you can't get the boat along."

"Eh? Eight of us, and not get that boat half a mile downhill? Wait a bit, my lad, and you'll see."

The lads did see, for after three or four days' arduous labour expended in getting the boat up a long slope, she was guided into a great groove in the mountain side pieces of wood placed beneath her, and from that hour it was not a question of dragging, but of holding back the vessel, till the stream was struck far below its source.

Here there was no smooth water to float her, but still, as Shaddy said, enough to help lift her over the shallows, with here and there a good stretch of deep channel, along which they floated merrily before there was any need for fresh toil.

At the end of a couple of days several tiny streams had increased the body of water, and soon after they had rapids to descend, while at the end of another day so many had been the additions that the little river had grown to be of respectable size.

It was all steady descent now till a lake was reached, across which an outlet was found leading exactly in the right direction, Shaddy declared. The river proved to be fairly smooth and deep, so that the work grew very light, and the only one on board who bemoaned their fate was Brazier, who had to pass endless specimens which he could not have for want of room.

"If I'm right in my calculations, Mr Rob, sir," said the old sailor one morning, after many days' journey, "we shall hit the big river before to-night, and not very far from the falls."

"What falls?" asked Rob.

"The great cat'ract which comes down a big gorge, which hasn't been explored yet, and which we might as well try if Mr Brazier thinks good, for I should say there's a deal to be seen in a land like that, where no man has been as I've ever heered on."

"I'll ask Mr Brazier, and hear what he says," said Rob. But the naturalist thought they had done enough for one trip.

The guide was right, for as evening drew near a peculiar dull, heavy roar came to them on the wind, and this increased till it was felt to be prudent to moor the boat for the night. The next morning the roar which had been in their ears all night increased, and long before noon they had glided imperceptibly into the great river, which here rushed along so impetuously that much care was necessary in the navigation of their overladen craft.

But the weather was calm, and the guide's knowledge of the management of a boat as near perfection as could be, so that in due course, after three or four more halts, they rowed one day close up among the shipping lying off the city from which they had started, and here, while waiting for an opportunity to take passage, with the great packages of plants they had prepared, they found time to make short expeditions up the river, one of which was to the mouth of the swift stream which swept off west through the great veil of trees, and from which they had struck out north and made quite a circuit through an unknown land.

A month later Brazier and Rob were once more on board Captain Ossolo's great orange schooner, which, deeply laden as it was, found room for the specimens collected amidst so much peril and care.

The hours and days flew swiftly now amid rest and ease, use making them pay little heed to the constant ether-like odour of the orange cargo. Then, after checks on sandbanks and hindrances from pamperos, Buenos Ayres was touched at, then Monte Video, with its busy port.

Here there was a long halt before a passage could be taken east, and Rob and Brazier had plenty of opportunity for studying the slaughter of cattle, salting of hides, and to visit the home of the biscacho, that troublesome burrower of the pampas and layer of traps for unwary horsemen.

At last the vessel by which they were to return was loaded up, and good-bye said to the worthy Italians, father and son, the former being warm in his thanks for the care taken of his boy.

"What," cried old Shaddy as he stood on the deck of the great vessel the day they were to sail, "good-bye? Not a bit of it, Mr Rob, sir! All being well, if you and Mr Brazier don't run out to try and find a way up the gorge where the great falls rush down, I'm coming over to the old country to see you. But there, you'll be out our way again soon."

"What did Naylor say?" asked Brazier that evening.

"That he could take us to fresh places where you would find plants more worthy of your notice than those you found."

"Ah! Yes," said Brazier thoughtfully as he watched the fading shore. "I should like to go again in spite of all we suffered. As for you, Rob, I suppose you would not care to go again?"

"Not care to go again!" cried Rob; and his eyes grew dim as he half closed them and recalled to memory the great rivers, the glorious trees, and the many wonders of those untrodden lands. "I could go back now," he said, "and face all the fight again;" but even as the words left his lips other memories came floating through his brain, and from that hour his thoughts were directed eastward to his kindred and his native land.

The End.